ROOK

Also by Sharon Cameron

THE DARK UNWINDING

A SPARK UNSEEN

ROOK

SHARON CAMERON

Scholastic Press
New York

Library of Congress Cataloging-in-Publication Data

Cameron, Sharon, author.
    Rook / Sharon Cameron.—First edition.
        pages cm
    Summary: In the Sunken City that was once Paris the guillotine rules again, while
Sophia Bellamy from the Commonwealth across the Channel Sea tries to rescue as many
of the revolution's victims as she can smuggle out, and some prisoners disappear from
their cells, with a red-tipped rook feather left in their place—but who is the mysterious
Red Rook and where does Sophia's wealthy fiance, Rene Hasard, fit in?
    ISBN 978-0-545-67599-4 (jacketed hardcover) 1. Adventure stories. 2. Rescues—
Juvenile fiction. 3. Secrecy—Juvenile fiction. 4. Paris (France)—Juvenile fiction.
[1. Adventure and adventurers—Fiction. 2. Rescues—Fiction. 3. Secrets—Fiction.
4. Paris (France)—Fiction. 5. France—Fiction.] I. Title.
    PZ7.C1438Ro 2015
    [Fic]—dc23

                                                                2014038853

10 9 8 7 6 5 4 3 2 1   15 16 17 18 19

Printed in the U.S.A.   23
First edition, May 2015
Book design by Sharismar Rodriguez

For the lovers of story

The heavy blade hung high above the prisoners, glinting against the stars, and then the Razor came down, a wedge of falling darkness cutting through the torchlight. One solid thump, and four more heads had been shaved from their bodies. The mob around the scaffold roared, a sudden deluge of cheers and mockery that broke like a wave against the viewing box, where the officials of the Sunken City watched from velvet chairs. The noise gushed on, over the coffins, around bare and booted feet crowding thick across the flagstones, pouring down the drains and into the deep tunnels beneath the prison yard like filth overflowing the street gutters. The city was bloodthirsty tonight.

Sophia dropped her gaze from the prison yard drains, where the din of the mob cascaded from high above her head, and squinted into the gloom of the subterranean passage. The tunnel was one of dozens like it, long and narrow, a mausoleum of rough rock and stink and rows of heavy, locked doors. It was why they called it the Tombs. Sophia pulled the door to prison hole number 1139 shut behind her, letting the iron lock clank quietly back into place.

She had planned for five prisoners to be in hole 1139, not thirteen, and there were not enough coffins to smuggle them out. Not all of them. She needed a new plan. She needed to think. She turned her head toward the echoing creak of hinges. A point of yellow light had entered the far end of the tunnel, descending step by step from the higher levels of the Tombs. Sophia looked down at the child that was standing on her boot top, clinging hard to her right leg. The little girl stared back up at her with solemn eyes.

"Quiet," she hissed in Parisian, "and hold tight! Do you understand?" The child nodded, and Sophia dropped the long, dark robes of a holy man she was wearing over the blond head. The child disappeared beneath the voluminous black cloth. The little girl was tiny but still miraculously strong, her small hands digging into the back of Sophia's thigh. She'd gone rigid and still, like a rabbit in the shadow of a hawk.

"Good girl," Sophia whispered.

A woman was begging in the prison yard above them, screaming for her life before the Razor sliced the sound away. The scorn of the mob fell like rain. Sophia narrowed her eyes at the yellow light swinging down the tunnel, the Sunken City blue of the gendarmes' uniforms now clearly visible. One of them was whistling. She stepped back into the shadows, the little girl beneath her robes, and drew up the black hood of the holy man, darkening her face.

Gerard followed the lantern light, whistling as he picked his way through the tunnel muck of the Tombs. Three more gendarmes of the Sunken City marched with him, blue uniforms making black shadows on the rough-hewn stone. One had his sword propped on a shoulder, fraying cloth at the point of his elbow just on the verge of becoming a hole. The sight made Gerard shake his head. He felt almost sorry for these men. They were not like him; they were not going to impress LeBlanc. He tugged on his jacket, brushing a hand over the space where his commandant's badge would be sewn. It was a fine night for an execution, and an even finer night for a promotion.

The ropes of the Razor were straining in the prison yard above them, pulleys creaking as the finishing team hauled the gigantic blade back to its full height. The chanting of the mob matched them pull by pull, demanding more heads. Demanding the head of Ministre Bonnard. Gerard picked up the pace. It had taken weeks to have Ministre Bonnard denounced as a traitor, and then more weeks after that, scouring the countryside where the family had scattered, hiding their children like rats will hoard scraps. But LeBlanc had ferreted them out. LeBlanc had found them; Gerard had held them; and now they would die. The last of the ministres of the old Sunken City. A triumph of the new. A triumph of Gerard. LeBlanc would make him a commandant before the sun rose.

Gerard stopped, the gendarmes around him only just avoiding a collision. Prison hole number 1139. He straightened his back, put his key to the lock, and then stepped to one side as the holy man materialized from the murk of the narrow passage. Gerard tipped his hat. The holy man bowed slightly. There was something wrong with his leg tonight, Gerard saw. He was limping as he shuffled past, face half-hidden in an overlarge hood, the blue and white of the Allemande government pinned across the black robes. The holy man had been in the Tombs three nights this week. But if the condemned wanted to buy their final blessings from a priest who had replaced his vows to the saints with an oath to Allemande, then why should he, Gerard, be deprived of the bribes for letting the young man in? LeBlanc didn't need to know everything.

A hint of a smile showed from beneath the holy man's hood, the heavy robes just brushing Gerard's knees before melting slowly back into the dark maze of the Tombs. Gerard waited until his gendarmes had brought their swords into position. Then he turned the key and thrust open the door of the prison hole.

"Family Bonnard! You have refused the oath of Premier Allemande and have been found guilty of treason against the Sunken City. You are sentenced to . . . you . . . you are . . ."

The well-practiced words caught in his throat like bones. Gerard snatched the lantern from the gendarme behind him and ran inside the fetid hole, turning a full circle before bringing a sleeve up to his nose. The cell was empty. Thirteen prisoners, including LeBlanc's prize, all of them gone.

He kicked through the thin layer of rotting straw, as if some of the smaller ones might be hiding beneath it, strands of human hair sticking to his boot. And then he froze. The men who had come to cut the hair, to bare the necks for the blade. Gerard spun around.

"Go!" he bellowed. The three gendarmes in the doorway wore matching stares. "Seal the doors, you fools! Quick!"

They ran. The Razor thumped and the mob in the prison yard chanted again for the Bonnards. Fear seeped into Gerard's chest, like the blood traveling down the scaffold, pooling in the cracks of the paving stones. There would be no promotion, and LeBlanc was not going to be impressed. LeBlanc was going to have his job. Or an ear. Or maybe his head.

Gerard took three steps to run for the messengers, to have the tunnels and the muddy streets of the Lower City searched, the gates blocked, and the roads watched. But his boot brushed a bit of color, something alien in a world of stench and rot and stone. He bent down. A single black feather lay in the straw, its tip a brilliant red.

And then there was an explosion in the prison yard.

Sophia hunched down in the seat of the haularound, the holy man's hood obscuring her face, and handed a stack of papers to the gendarme in charge of the gates. The horses' sides were heaving, their flanks dark with sweat. She held the reins loose in her hands. Behind her was the steep, zigzagged road cut into a leaning cliff face, the only way up and out of the chasm that was the center of the Sunken City. Behind the gendarme rose the gates, part of the miles of barrier fence running along the edge of the cliff tops, encircling the enormous hole, keeping the tall, stone-carved buildings of the Upper City safely away from the mud and shanties of the Lower City far below them. There were explosions somewhere down there, beneath the reek and fog, bright flashes of color and short, sharp pops—like the bedtime myths mothers told of guns. Sophia took no notice of them, and neither did the gendarme in charge of the gates. He was drunk. He tossed back the papers with barely a glance.

"This delivery will be searched," he slurred, beckoning to the other guards.

Sophia glanced behind her, putting a hand on the small lump that had squirmed once beneath the robes. Thirteen large sacks, bulky and tied with string, lay in the open bed of the haularound.

"Is it necessary?" she asked in Parisian. She made her voice raspy, full of stones. "I need to be on my way before nethermoon."

But two gendarmes were already climbing over the wooden rails and into the haularound, swords glinting in the light of a bonfire. Before Sophia could protest further, one of them raised his arms above his head and thrust his sword straight down into the nearest sack, piercing the thing inside it with an audible *snick*.

Sophia turned away, smoothing the voluminous black robes while the gendarme grunted, twisting, trying to pull the blade back out again. The other guard stabbed sacks with abandon, ripping at the coarse cloth. When they had finished their search thirteen sacks lay in shreds, and the bed of the haularound had become a sea of rolling potatoes.

The more sober guards were at the cliff's edge now, pointing down into the fuming hole, the people of the Upper City doing the same from their balconies, dark figures many stories high, calling to one another across the air bridges. The iron gates swung open. Down in the chasm, a fire bell tolled.

"Long may you rise above the city," Sophia said in the voice of the holy man, smiling at the swaying gendarme as the haularound rattled through the gates.

LeBlanc leaned back in his chair, a slow smile curling the corners of his mouth. Gerard had not screamed. LeBlanc was impressed.

He gave the man a moment, in case he should retch, but Gerard merely panted, leaning over the puddle of blood on the table. The end of Gerard's forefinger now lay several inches from the rest of his hand. Two of the gendarmes released their tight grip on his arms while the third, a man with a wispy brown mustache, thrust a bloody knife back into his belt. LeBlanc twirled a black-red feather between a finger and thumb, his voice soft, almost pleasant.

"Do you know rooks, Gerard? Survivors of the Time Before, a symbol of those who have lived and overcome. The divine spirit who took the form of a rook during the Great Death, leading the sick and dying to the safety of the hidden catacombs beneath the city. The rook that became a streak of light, flying across the night sky to light their way. Surely you were told that story as a child? We all were. But do you know the true story, Gerard? That the light was only what was called a satellite, a machine of the Ancients, burning and falling to its ruin near the entrance of the catacombs, the emblem of a bird still visible on the metal of the wreckage. Fate struck down the satellite, Gerard, so that what would be would be, to show her strength as a Goddess, and in so doing she showed her mastery over the weakness of technology. Those with wits enough to use the Luck that Fate sent found their way to the underground and survived. That is how the world works. But the people now, Gerard, they think only of the myth. Of the benevolent, saintly rook leading them from death into life."

LeBlanc tsked, his eyes on the red-tipped feather. "Forty-eight we have lost to this thief, this 'Red Rook.' Forty-eight prisoners who rejected our revolution, refused the oath of Allemande, and are subverting his justice. And now the Red Rook makes fools of us again, this time with fire and noise. The people in the streets are talking of magic, and the divine power of the saint. But revolution replaced the holy man as well as the government, Gerard. Allemande is in charge now. The Goddess Fate has decreed it."

LeBlanc discarded the feather and stood, sighing as he went to stand before a tall stone window. The nethermoon lit the odd streak of gray running pale through his hair, and beamed light down every story of the white stone building, all the way to the cliff edge, through its fencing, and straight across the flat expanse of fog stretching over the massive chasm that was the Lower City. The spreading fog looked almost like the land that must have once been there, when the city was Paris and on one level, before the streets collapsed and sank into the tunnels and quarried caverns beneath it. Now lamps and candles twinkled yellow from Upper City buildings on the encircling cliffs, some too distant to be seen, while beneath the cloud bank one place pulsed with intermittent splashes of lurid green. The Red Rook's fire, still exploding in the Lower City. It mirrored the green of the north lights, swirling in multicolored swaths around the stars and moon. LeBlanc turned on his heel.

"Fate is our true Goddess, Gerard, and Luck is her handmaiden. Luck has been with the Red Rook tonight and not with you. The next time you allow traitors to walk out of the Tombs, you shall be unlucky indeed. One piece of you for each prisoner that is lost, one inch at a time. Do you believe that I will do this?"

Gerard nodded, his eyes closed, round face beaded with sweat. His hand lay exactly where it had been, bleeding onto the polished wood.

"Then we have an understanding."

Gerard nodded more vigorously, breath hissing from between his teeth.

"Good. That is good. You will begin at dawn, with the cells that are the closest. One of them will have seen. And if they do not tell me what they have seen, I will make them beg for the blade. They will run up the steps of the scaffold."

LeBlanc moved smoothly across the room to the door. "You should see to that wound, Gerard, so you do not lose the hand. Heat would be best, I think." He paused before a gilded mirror, amending a slight deficiency in his neckwear. "And do clean up the desk," he added.

When LeBlanc shut the door of his office he found Renaud, his secretary, emerging from the far end of the corridor.

"They will be in boats, Renaud," he said. "Have the gendarmes ready and send a courier to our ships on the coast. He has taken too many this time. They will be difficult to disguise."

The words had been muted, but Renaud had good ears. He bowed and slid away as LeBlanc tilted his head toward the office door, waiting. When the sizzle of hot metal on wounded flesh finally reached his ears, he smiled. This time Gerard had not held back his scream. And it had been impressive.

Sophia ran the horses down a dirt road through the land the Parisians called The Désolation. The haularound rattled and bumped beneath her, the fading nethermoon a passing glimpse of white through entwining limbs, the north lights twisting like green and purple smoke in the sky. Finally she turned onto a grassy track, loose potatoes rolling from side to side, until the forest opened into a small clearing that was almost perfectly square. It was probably a ruin, this clearing, like most of them, a thick layer of concrete or asphalt close enough to the surface to discourage the trees. The haularound rolled to a stop, and behind the sudden silence ebbed a distant rush and boom. The sea.

Sophia lifted the edge of the holy man's robes and found the little girl, soft blond hair shorn ragged about the ears, still clinging to her leg. She'd fallen asleep. Sophia disentangled the child's limbs, ignoring her protests as she slung her over a shoulder and climbed down from the seat.

She hurried to the back of the haularound. A latch clicked, a long board went clattering to the ground, and a jumble of two dozen feet was revealed in the narrow, hidden space beneath. Moans fell from mouths like the potatoes to the ground. She'd had the space made for weapons and supplies, not people.

"Out!" Sophia commanded, voice gruff and in Parisian, one arm full of a child who was done with being still. Marie Bonnard scooted out from the space, wearing a dress possibly held together by its own dirt, tugging out her two older children before stumbling over to snatch up her little girl. When the haularound had emptied there were thirteen faces turned to the holy man, all showing differing levels of desperation, hope, and inquiry. And then, like puppets on the same string, every head jerked to look back down the grassy track. Another rhythm had joined the remote sound of surf, a thunder that resolved into the harsh tattoo of hoofbeats, coming fast and closing in on the clearing.

Panic moved through the group like contagion. Ministre Bonnard's hollow eyes darted to the woods and back, chest heaving beneath a once-fine vest, then five gendarmes burst from the trees, sword hilts winking in the moonlight. Ministre Bonnard let out a yell like an animal. He went for the holy man's throat with surprising speed, crying out as an even quicker hand shot from beneath the black robes, catching the man's wrist and twisting. The ministre gasped, clutching his wrist to his chest.

"Friends," Sophia whispered. "They are friends."

Ministre Bonnard gaped incoherently while his wife sank to her knees, trying to bounce and shush their little girl. The gendarmes dismounted and without a word began putting the former prisoners of hole 1139 in the saddles. One of them, tall, blond, and with broad shoulders only just stuffed into the short, tight coat of an officer, tossed his reins around a limb and approached the holy man.

"You've left your feather behind you, then?" he asked, Parisian accent thick.

"Of course," Sophia replied, grinning as the heavy robes came off, showing a slim figure in leather breeches and a vest. A wig of thick, dark hair was thrown with the robes into the bed of the haularound.

"The Red Rook!" they heard one of the thirteen whisper. "*Le Corbeau Rouge!*" Their murmurs of fear had shifted instantly to excitement. Sophia glanced once in their direction and switched to a softer voice and the language of the Commonwealth.

"Is all well? You got my message?"

The gendarme who was not a gendarme stepped closer, taking

his cue for the change in language. "Yes, and it scared the life out of us. Cartier agreed to man the second boat. How did you manage?"

"Waited until the alarm sounded and the gendarmes had gone running, then took them all out Gerard's office window and left the coffins behind. We were lucky to switch the wagons. The child came out under the robes. The poor holy man developed an abscess in his leg, I'm afraid. A horrible infection. The watchman at the prison said he must have sinned."

The tall man's face broke into a brief, perfectly formed smile, then fell back into worry. "We're late, and there are too many. You shouldn't have taken them all. I don't think we can be out of sight of the coast by dawn."

Sophia frowned, running a hand through curling brown hair still damp from the wig, shaking it out once like a dog. A girl of seventeen or so, one of the Bonnards, had been watching this intently, her eyes large and staring through shorn strands of dingy blond hair that was much like her little sister's. She stood so close, the starlight showed a spatter of freckles through the prison dirt on her nose.

Sophia turned away, quickly tying her brown curls back in the way of an Upper City man as the girl was bundled onto a horse. "It was not possible to take some and turn the key on the others, Spear," Sophia hissed.

"Not possible for you," Spear sighed, clicking the loose board into place across the back of the haularound. The horses with the Bonnard family and two other prisoners cantered away from the clearing. The other six residents of hole 1139 clung to one another on the ground, family or no, waiting for their turn.

"Send the twins to lay the usual false trail," Sophia said, climbing up into the seat, "though it may not help us this time. If LeBlanc is clever, he'll ride straight to the coast. And I think he is clever. Don't try to leave together. Push off and get them out to sea as soon as you can. Have them lie down in the bottom of the boats. And tell Cartier to use the fishing nets. Maybe LeBlanc won't know what he's seeing. You'll . . ."

"Wait." Spear's chiseled face, level with her own despite the climb into the haularound, narrowed to a scowl. "You're not coming in the boats?"

"No room." Sophia lifted a brow at his expression. "You think I can't get back to the Commonwealth on my own?"

He stepped closer to the haularound. "I know you can. I just don't like that you have to, that's all."

Sophia picked up the reins. "As if I'd be late to my own engagement party!" she whispered. "What would the neighbors say?" But this only made the young man's face darken further. "Move them as fast as you can, Spear. LeBlanc will be on your heels. Be careful." Leather snapped, and the horses jerked forward. "And save me some cake!" she said over her shoulder as the haularound lurched away down the track.

When the woods ended, Sophia took the turning to the sea and picked up speed. The Désolation had not been desolate for many generations, not since the turbulent centuries following the Great Death, and for two miles the horses ran past harvested fields on one side, cliff and booming sea on the other, any ruins long ago hidden by time and turf. Then the haularound turned back inland, drove through a small, sleeping village and straight into the open shed behind a wheelwright's house. It was not dawn but the sky was paling over the roof tiles, the north lights gone, a sea fog wisping past dark and silent windows. Sophia hurried.

The horses were left to hay and water on one end of the shed, where a fresh, bridled mare stood waiting, already hitched to a tradesman's cart. The robes of the holy man came out of the haularound, now turned inside out to show a soft green cloth, and the pins of the wig were pulled, releasing a woman's long, dark curls.

Soon after the arrival of a haularound full of potatoes, a trader's daughter drove out of the wheelwright's shed with a cart full of lettuce. Long, dark hair, honey-colored skin, wearing the distinctive green of one with permission to barter in the Sunken City. Sophia clucked to the mare and took the fast road to the coast.

LeBlanc ran his lathering horse down the road to the coast, lifting two pale eyes to a sky that had become a gold-red glory, an escort of gendarmes jangling fast behind him. It was dawn, and they were nearing the sea. Then his gaze came back down to the road and he jerked the reins to one side, only just missing the small cart driven by a girl in trader green, coming at him fast from around the bend. The cart carved a path through his galloping escort like a ship's prow, the young woman at the reins winking boldly at his men. Then they were off again, never slowing until the road ended suddenly with a cliff.

Horses fanned right and left, but LeBlanc brought his heaving mount to the edge, its breath steaming the air, bending sideways in the saddle to peer down at the rocks and empty beach below. He straightened, pulling an eyescope from his pocket and yanking it to full length. The glass end of the eyescope roved, searching the sea and thinning fog, pausing at the sight of two small boats riding the waves near the horizon. A single figure sat in each bow. One was rowing, the other throwing a casting net, a spiderweb of black against the glowing, orange sunrise.

LeBlanc clicked the eyescope shut against his palm. Then he reached into his pocket and removed a single potato he'd found in a clearing in the woods. He tossed the potato up and down, up and down, a thin smile creeping out from the corners of his mouth.

There would not be many places they could land. Luck had been with him. The Red Rook, it seemed, was only a man after all.

2

S*ophia* Bellamy leaned over the rail, looking down at her engagement party with disgust. The ballroom below her glittered with candlelight and wineglasses, alive with people and music and the excited chatter of distant neighbors and her father's friends. Ribbons, elaborate hair, billowing skirts, and embroidered coats jumbled into a riot of color, every garment she could see copied straight from *Wesson's Guide to Paintings of the Time Before.* The Parliament of the Commonwealth did not choose to print the *Wesson's Guide.* Because a printing press was a machine, and machines were technology, and because technology clouded minds, weakened the will, and took away the self-reliance of the Ancients— or so their Parliament said—such dangerous items could be used only by a special license. And since the last license for private printing in the Commonwealth had been removed from the Bellamys, taking their sole source of income with it, the *Wesson's Guide* was a thoroughly illegal item, leaving the power to cloud minds firmly in the hands of Parliament.

But for a book that no one had ever seen or read, and had certainly never purchased in the undermarkets of Kent, its contents had been well attended to. The copied clothing made the party opulent, decadent, a spectacle of Ancient curled wigs, face paint, and billowing dresses that was also an understated protest of

Commonwealth law. It should have thrilled her. The party should have thrilled her. This was a night she was supposed to have longed for all her life, her Banns, the celebration of her engagement to the son of a Parisian businesswoman. He would be down there somewhere, part of the light and music. Sophia stepped back from the rail. For now, the dark and dusty peace of the gallery held more charm.

"You're not happy, Sophie," said a voice from just behind her. A low, rich voice, much like her own. Sophia flipped out her fan and turned, giving her brother a raised brow.

"You thought I'd be up here giggling with excitement, Tom?"

He shrugged a shoulder, his walking stick tapping twice as he limped forward to stand beside her. Tom was not her twin but he could have been, had he not been fourteen months older, male, and she painted and bedecked like some sort of sacrifice readied for the marriage altar. His scarlet coat was pressed and perfect, unlike the bones of his leg, which were not going to unwrinkle in any way that would make him a soldier again.

"You look well," Sophia said. "What have you been doing this week?"

"Nothing as interesting as you." Tom glanced once around the gallery before he said, "You were late. And how were the explosions? Spear said he thought they went rather well."

"They were brilliant, thanks to you. And I was only late because Orla thought I had prison lice in my hair."

"Again? And did you?"

"Not much." She elbowed him once when he tried to lean away. "Don't be such a git, Tom. I don't have any now! And I got there in time for the introductions."

"Father's the one being the git. He's been so worried something would go wrong with your Banns he didn't even realize you weren't here. You've had a cold, by the way."

"He's not worried, he's afraid," Sophia said. "He'll lose the estate without this marriage fee and everybody knows it."

"Do they?"

"Well, they suspect it, anyway. How could they not? And what's worse, he suspects that they suspect it."

They peered over the rail, moving a shared gaze through the crowd to the man that was Bellamy, their father. Bellamy was small and bent, thinning hair tied neatly back, exuding an atmosphere of defeat in his conversation with Mr. Halflife, their county's member of Parliament—one man who was not dressed according to *Wesson's*, Sophia noted. Bellamy was desperate for this party to go well, she knew that, down to the gluttony and the wine and the overexposed bosoms. Then everyone, including Bellamy, could pretend that her engagement, and the money it would bring, was not the last thing standing between him and a debtor's prison.

"Do you think Father knows that man wants our land?" Sophia asked, eyeing Mr. Halflife. Tom sighed.

"I talked to him about it again while you were gone, about the river and the rumors of a new port, and why Mr. Halflife would have no interest in helping either him or me keep the estate. I told him that taking the printing license was likely Mr. Halflife's particular way of not helping. But . . . it's hard to know what Father understands these days and what he doesn't."

"He probably isn't understanding anything of that conversation at all," Sophia said. Mr. Halflife's posh Manchester accent was very thick.

Tom gave her a small smile, and Sophia smiled back, agreeing that the joke was not particularly funny. The more debt that had accrued, the more muddled their father's thinking had become. The solution should have been easy. If Tom could prove his fitness to inherit, as the laws of self-reliance required, the estate would pass to him and out of their father's mismanaging hands. All Tom had to do was amass enough money or assets on his own. For generations, Bellamy fathers had been quietly aiding their eldest sons in this, helping them earn the legal right to an inheritance by creating jobs, business opportunities, or even a clandestine windfall of cash. But their father had seemed unable to grasp that Tom was no longer ten years old, or that the time for his help was long overdue. He'd been hurt and confused by Tom's decision to join the militia, even when it began to produce the badly needed savings.

Sophia looked across the dark gallery. Tom's injury had put a stop to all that, or very soon would, when the colonel found out Tom's leg was never going to heal properly. If Tom could not prove his fitness to inherit before the age of twenty-five, then the Bellamy estate would go to Parliament, which would make Mr. Halflife very happy. If Bellamy didn't pay off his debt in twenty-six days, then he would go to prison with no proven heir, and the estate would go to Parliament. Which would make Mr. Halflife very happy.

"Well, I think the whole thing is unfair," Sophia said lightly. "If I'm the one earning the money, then I think the land ought to go to me."

Tom gave her a look of mock offense. "You're younger than me."

"Eighteen is not all that different from nearly twenty."

"My extra months of life imply clear superiority. And in case you've forgotten, you are also a daughter."

Sophia shook her head. "That is irrelevant. Obviously." She'd meant to go on with the teasing, but she knew Tom had caught the bite beneath her words. The one fact on which Bellamy remained perfectly clear was that he had a daughter old enough to marry a man who would pay for the privilege.

Tom leaned against the railing. "So tell me what you thought of him."

"Who? My fiancé?" Sophia glanced downward, searching through the rising haze until she found a young Parisian in a coat of gold brocade. He was surrounded by a gaggle of women, their smiles and their fans fluttering like bird wings. She'd thought him remarkably good-looking, even if it was in a very polished, Upper City sort of way. But that was before he'd said anything. "I've decided that Monsieur René Hasard will be a very manageable sort of husband."

"So the introduction went well?"

"I suppose. He went on and on to Father about his tailor and the fashion for *Wesson's* in the Sunken City and spoke barely two words to me."

Tom smiled. "Oh. Now I see. You're not unhappy, sister. You're ticked."

Sophia frowned and forced herself to examine René Hasard. His hair was powdered silver-white, like many in the room, though with him, the contrast of two very blue eyes and the gold brocade was striking. His gaggle of women certainly seemed to think him charming, and he seemed rather comfortable in the knowledge that they did. She saw him kiss the hand of the daughter of an ink-maker from Canterbury, watched him smile as Lauren Rathbone sidled much too close with her smudgy eyes and the blue plastic earrings dangling down to her neck. She was hanging on René Hasard's every word. And his arm. Sophia felt her painted brows draw together. She detested hair powder.

"Tell me what you're thinking," said Tom.

"Nothing. Just . . . I just never thought I would marry, that's all."

Tom gave her a sideways glance, deep brown eyes identical to her own. "Then you're as big a git as Father. I'll have to let you borrow my stick, I think." He paused. "To fend off all your lovers."

Sophia laughed before she whacked Tom once with the fan. Below them, René Hasard made an elaborate gesture and an eruption of feminine squeals and giggles floated up through the candlelight to the gallery shadows. He was smiling with only half his mouth. She couldn't look at him. She stared instead at the red and white brick arches that ringed the ballroom, then at the "Looking Man," as she'd always called him, a larger than life, round-bellied bronze statue of some Ancient man gazing upward in a blowing wind, presumably to examine a sky he could never see.

She kept her eyes on the statue and away from Tom when she said, "I've been thinking this could be an . . . arrangement. I would keep my rooms, and he would stay in the north wing. He could do as he pleases and so would I. So nothing would change. Not really."

They both knew everything would change. When she was little, she had wriggled her body into the metal folds of the Looking Man's coat, hiding from the world. Or Orla. She was half considering trying it again tonight. Tom rubbed a hand across the back of his neck.

"And this 'arrangement,'" he said, "is that what Hasard wants, too?"

"I'll make sure it's what he wants. That's all."

She stared down into the noisy party, so her brother couldn't see her thoughts. After she was married and the debt was paid, there might be just enough left to fund a business for Tom. She'd been doing the numbers while Orla did her hair. Men of the Commonwealth were notoriously leery of working with a man who'd made himself dependent, even if it was just on a stick, but Tom was clever. If they could just last long enough to get Tom solvent, then the estate would pass to him and they would be free of her father's mismanagement. The land would be safe.

Sophia felt her determination solidify. Money was the only thing to set all this right, and she was the one to provide it. She would pay her father's debt, every last quidden of it, and hand the rest to Tom on her wedding day. He would refuse, of course, but she would make him take it. At sword point, if necessary. Maybe they would fight over it. Maybe Tom would have to kill her before her wedding night. This thought made her smile. She snapped open the fan.

"Time to go be brilliant, I think. Wouldn't want to disappoint Father's investor." She picked up her pouf of white skirts, a faithful copy of *Wesson's* page thirty-eight, and moved toward the stairs.

"Come down to the beach tonight, Sophie," Tom called after her. "You've been tight with your sword arm lately. And your parry and thrust could use a bit of work, I think."

She didn't answer, just threw him a look from the top of the stairs. Then she was descending, down grooved metal steps so old their middles were slightly shorter than their edges, leaving the comforting dark for the dazzle and noise of her Banns. Her hair was black tonight, piled high and sparkling with jeweled combs, the soft brown curls that were like Tom's hidden beneath the more vivid locks. The music paused. She smiled at everyone and everything, looking anywhere except at the face above the gold brocade coat that waited for her at the bottom of the staircase.

"Mademoiselle Bellamy," said René Hasard.

Two words and she understood exactly what game he would play with her. He was going to be the gallant suitor, the sophisti-cated man of the city that girls like Lauren Rathbone oohed and ahhed over in smuggled Parisian magazines. He would have to play that game by himself. She fixed her gaze on one of the intricately cast silver buttons, the second one down on the gold jacket. He took her hand and kissed it.

"You are radiant tonight," he said, very Parisian, and very much for the benefit of the crowd around them. "A bright star fallen to the earth."

She smiled. "Why, you offend me, Monsieur. Isn't that what the Ancients said about Lucifer?" *Parry, Monsieur*, she thought. Even the vicar was laughing.

"But unlike the devil," René replied, "I am certain your beauty reflects your nature."

She eyed the button in the midst of all that gold brocade. "If you keep trying to flatter me, Monsieur, I will grow brighter still. So bright that your tailor will be disappointed."

"Disappointed, Mademoiselle?"

"That his most extravagant work should go unnoticed." And *thrust*, Sophia thought as a titter went through the delighted crowd. René's voice was unfazed. And possibly amused.

"To be eclipsed by you, Miss Bellamy, could only be an honor."

Oh, he was good, she thought. Just as glib and empty-headed and Upper City elite as Lauren Rathbone could have wished for. Sophia took his arm, careful not to disturb the balance of her hair, allowing him to charm her neighbors and her father's friends as he led her through the congratulations and well-wishes and more than a few looks of envy. She smiled until her face hurt, nodding at the appropriate times, her mind not really on any of it. She was thinking how unfair her brother's last words had been. She'd thought her parry and thrust were in quite good order.

—

Sophia danced twice with René, circumventing any possibility of being charmed by staring only at his second jacket button. His movements were lithe across the dance floor, her request to go and find cooler air their only conversation. Now she sat on a cushioned window seat in one of the bricked arches, taking refuge behind a row of potted ferns, fanning madly as the tottering heeled shoes of the Ancients went clacking across the floor tiles, keeping time with the drums. She wished she could throw open the window behind her, let the sea wind blow away the smoke and sheets of music, muss the shining curls and the hair ribbons, drive out the smell of perfume with fresh brine. But she couldn't. Not without ruining the Bellamy show. And the window was probably stuck, anyway.

The sudden plop of a body onto the seat broke her reverie. She turned to find Mrs. Rathbone beside her, the woman's sharp, wrinkled face glistening in the candlelight. Mrs. Rathbone seemed to have combined several pages of the *Wesson's Guide* at once, choosing one of the straight, white, one-shouldered styles worn in the pictures by both women and men, pairing it with a heavily embroidered corset and random sprays of flowers and lace. A dusting of hair powder drifted down onto her shoulders. Sophia resisted the urge to wrinkle her nose.

"There you are!" said Mrs. Rathbone. "What are you doing hiding back here? Why aren't you dancing with your young man? He is a fetching thing, I must say. Quite a catch!"

Sophia started to say what she thought, then opted for discretion.

"Well!" Mrs. Rathbone said, dabbing at her forehead. "I'm certain I would never have been so sour at my Banns. When I was your age I could dance all night, among other things. I've just done a turn with your future partner, if you can believe it. Why don't you go dance with Spear, then, poor boy, and console him?"

Sophia forced her smile. Usually she liked Mrs. Rathbone, but she was not in the mood for her tonight. "Don't you think the room is rather hot?"

"I think it's rather fascinating. I suppose you've heard about the Bonnards?"

"The Bonnards?"

"Yes, the Bonnards! Everyone is talking about it. The execution was not carried out!" Mrs. Rathbone leaned closer. "They were rescued. The entire family."

"Were they?"

"Spirited right out of the prison. By *him*. Or that's what everyone is saying, anyway."

Sophia twisted a large ring set with a pale white stone around her forefinger. "'Him,' Mrs. Rathbone?"

"Really, Sophia! You might get away with that act with the others, but I'd advise you not to sport with my intelligence. I'm talking about 'him,' of course. *Le Corbeau Rouge*, as the Parisians say. The merciful spirit. The Red Rook!"

Sophia smiled. "Now you're talking about a myth."

"Myth, my arse," stated Mrs. Rathbone. "Someone is unlocking the doors of the Sunken City's prison holes and I doubt very much that it's Premier Allemande, my dear. They say there wasn't a head left to cut off. Rooms bursting full of rook feathers! But listen . . ."

She breathed so close that Sophia could make a guess at the color of her wine.

". . . if the Bonnards have escaped then they will be trying to put their feet on Commonwealth soil just as soon as may be, isn't that so? And here you are, my dear . . . right across the Channel

Sea." She whispered this last part, tapping Sophia's arm with each word, as if the location of Bellamy House was a diplomatic secret.

Sophia looked at her carefully. "Mrs. Rathbone, are you suggesting that fugitive members of the ousted Parisian government have escaped both prison and death just to attend my Banns?" She was beginning to enjoy this conversation.

"Well, I shouldn't think so," the woman replied seriously. "They wouldn't have a thing to wear, now would they? But why, then, do you think that he is here?"

"Who, Mrs. Rathbone?"

"Him! Well, not 'him,' of course, not the 'him' of the first time . . ."

Sophia fanned her face. Just how much wine had Mrs. Rathbone consumed?

"I mean him! In the blue coat, chatting with your partner to be."

Sophia followed the woman's gaze, through trousers and skirts and false hair, dragging her eyes to where the gold jacket now stood beside a Sunken City blue. She had been avoiding looking at René's part of the room, a weakness she now paid for with shock. Just beyond her fiancé's shoulder was a face she had never expected to see in her home, on her land, or even on her side of the Channel Sea. A face she associated with misery and blood, so incongruent in the celebratory surroundings that its presence left her stunned.

The face belonged to LeBlanc.

3

"*Allemande's* Ministre of Security, is he not?" Mrs. Rathbone was saying while Sophia stared. "Now there's a man what's seen a head or two roll."

"Yes, he has," Sophia replied, not bothering to sugar her revulsion. She studied LeBlanc in his plain coat as he listened to René talking about she knew not what. LeBlanc was much shorter than her fiancé, an odd streak of white running through the sleek, dark hair. Spear Hammond stood with them, towering over both men like a tall blond statue, an empty plate in one hand, his furrowed brow the only betrayal of what had to be a considerable amount of alarm. LeBlanc was in Bellamy House.

"What does he think he's doing here?" Sophia said, more to herself than the lady beside her.

Mrs. Rathbone turned on the window seat. "You're not sporting with my intelligence after all, I see. You seem to have lost all your own! Your young man's grandmother . . ."

"He is not my young man."

"I apologize," said Mrs. Rathbone. "I thought I was attending your Banns. Your . . . *person*, his grandmother was a LeBlanc. They are second cousins once removed, or some such. Haven't you even looked at the pedigree of the family? What are you thinking of?"

Sophia shook her head, watching Spear's blue eyes widen slightly at whatever René was saying.

"But the question is, of course," Mrs. Rathbone continued in a confidential whisper, "why has Allemande's right-hand man come to his father's aunt's grandson's engagement party?" When Sophia did not give the required answer, Mrs. Rathbone supplied it. "I mean the Bonnards, of course! The coast! LeBlanc must believe they've landed nearby. He must think that *he* is nearby."

Sophia turned to Mrs. Rathbone. "Who do you mean?" she asked innocently.

"I mean the Red Rook, of course! He could be here right now, even as we speak. Wouldn't that be delicious?"

Sophia looked away, just lifting one bare shoulder, causing Mrs. Rathbone to huff once as she got to her feet. "I think you need a long moon's sleep, Miss Bellamy. Being engaged seems to have addled your wits. Good night."

"You, too, Mrs. Rathbone. Do come to dinner," Sophia replied absently. As soon as the lady had flounced away she stood and adjusted her bodice, pulled so tight that anything extra was in danger of being squeezed out, her forehead drawn to almost the same degree of tension. Then the fan snapped back open and she was gliding across the Ancient tiles of the ballroom. By the time she reached the three men her face was serene.

"René, there you are!" Sophia said, gazing at the second button. She held out a cheek for him to kiss. He obliged, but not before she'd caught a hint of a smile in one corner of his mouth. He seemed to think he had scored a point. He was wrong. Spear looked away, because of the kiss or because she was voluntarily approaching the snake that had slithered into her home, Sophia did not know. She stepped away from the hand René had left on her bare back and stood a little closer to Spear. Then she turned to LeBlanc.

"Monsieur LeBlanc, isn't it? I understand you are a Hasard relation."

"I have been remiss!" René said. "Please accept my apologies, my love. This is my father's second cousin, Albert LeBlanc. And this, Cousin, is my fiancée, Miss Bellamy."

"*Enchantée*," said LeBlanc, his long smile curling. She watched two pale, almost colorless eyes look her up and down as her hand was kissed, noting the man's meticulously manicured nails. She had half expected to see them bloodstained.

"And you have both been introduced to Mr. Hammond?" Sophia asked. She gave Spear's empty plate a significant glance. "You've forgotten to save me some cake, I see." Spear's face vacillated somewhere between amusement and anxiety as she turned to smile at the others. "Mr. Hammond is a very old and dear friend of the Bellamys."

"By which Miss Sophia means that her brother and I have been taking care of her since her days of tree climbing and scraped knees," Spear said.

"Scraped knees, you say?" said René, examining the contents of his glass. "How interesting. And tell me, when was the last time you had to bind her up, Monsieur?"

Sophia said quickly, "I understand you live in the Sunken City, Monsieur LeBlanc."

"I am the Ministre of Security in the *Cité de Lumière*. The City of Light. That is its new name, Miss Bellamy."

"A new name or an Ancient one, Monsieur?"

"An Ancient name that is becoming new again." LeBlanc's voice was oily slick, so soft Sophia had to lean forward to hear his next question. "Do you study the Time Before, Miss Bellamy?"

She shook her head. "Oh, no. My brother is the scholar."

"That is good. Technology and the Great Death are not amusing subjects for a young lady. Does your brother seek the lost London?"

"Don't they all?" Sophia kept her smile in place, trying to puzzle out whether LeBlanc thought young ladies should study only what was amusing. "But do let me thank you for coming, Monsieur LeBlanc. I am so flattered that you would come all this way for my Banns."

"I only wish that were so, Mademoiselle. I am here on the business of Allemande."

"Tedious business," René commented, gaze wandering the room. Spear looked down at him askance.

"And what sort of business is that, Monsieur?" Sophia asked. "I hope it is more diplomatic than your usual tasks as Ministre of Security."

LeBlanc's smile was indulgent, as if she were an adorably curious child. "I am sure you would not wish to spend the entire evening learning about politics."

"Oh, it would take the entire evening, would it?"

"Your pretty head is much better suited to your party, Mademoiselle."

Sophia felt her brows go up, lips parting to say something sharp, and then René cried out, "My love! They play McCartney!"

Three heads turned to the powdered one.

"You must come and dance with me, Miss Bellamy! It is too good an opportunity to miss, yes?" He offered a hand.

"No, thank you." Sophia looked back to LeBlanc, politeness restored. "And do you believe your business will keep you here until . . ."

"More wine, my love?" asked René.

"No. Thank you. How long did you say you would be here, Monsieur . . ."

"Cake?" René inquired.

"No. Please go on, Monsieur LeBlanc."

LeBlanc was just drawing breath when René said, "Sugared plums?"

Sophia turned. "Yes. I would love nothing more than a sugared plum. Why don't you go and get one for me?"

Half a grin was in the corner of René's mouth, over eyes that were an exceptionally deep blue, a blue that was the hottest part of the fire. She wasn't supposed to be looking at him. His grin widened when Spear said quickly, "I'll get it, Sophie."

LeBlanc's eyes roved between the three of them, his smile predatory. He said, "And now I am sorry to say I must go. My 'tedious' business, as my cousin says, takes me back to my city this very night." He bowed again over Sophia's hand, though his gaze was now on René. *"Ne sois pas stupide. Je pense que tu dois garder un oeil attentif sur cette fille,"* he said softly. "My congratulations to you, Miss Bellamy. Long may you rise above the city."

Sophia exchanged a look with Spear as Monsieur LeBlanc walked away, threading his way through the increasingly intoxicated crowd. Probably LeBlanc did not know that both she and Spear had spent most of their childhood summers in the Sunken City, spoke fluent Parisian, and were therefore perfectly aware of the advice he had just given René: to stop being a fool, and keep a close eye on the girl.

Sophia fanned her hot face. And what exactly had LeBlanc meant by that? Was he advising René to keep an eye on her as a fiancée? Or something more? She fanned harder, heart hammering against the tight bodice.

"My cousin," René stated, "takes himself too seriously in some matters, and not seriously enough in others. He dwells constantly on his duties, when the duty he should really be considering is a conversation with his stylist . . ."

Sophia looked away, so she would not make the mistake of meeting René Hasard's eyes again. She saw Tom standing not far away at the edge of the room, his gaze on LeBlanc's back as he whispered discreetly to Cartier. Cartier worked the Bellamy stables; he also worked for the Rook, and, she assumed, was about to be following LeBlanc. She let her glance pass over them, and then to the silver button, only then recalling that René had been talking to her.

"Do you not agree, my love?"

She had no idea what he was asking her to agree to. Was he aware that she was aware of LeBlanc's advice? Unknown. But if not, then she did not intend to enlighten him. Or let him keep any sort of eye on her. Sophia released her fan from its death grip and smiled.

"I've just remembered something I need to say to Father . . ."

"Do you want me to come with you, Sophie?" Spear's brows were drawn down again, causing one slight wrinkle in his forehead. He thought she shouldn't go alone, not with LeBlanc in the house.

"No need. But actually, would you do me a favor? Would you just ask Tom to check on those packages from yesterday? I wanted to be sure they were put away properly." Spear nodded as she turned toward the gold brocade.

"Gifts," she said to the button. "They've been arriving all week. Father's friends are so very generous. I'll see you later, Spear."

She turned away before either of them could speak, anger propelling her through the crowd, helping her push a path through the people that stood about watching the dancers. She felt invaded, violated. Contaminated by something vile, something she should have never had to experience inside Bellamy House. And she needed to understand just how much danger she was really in. She had her gaze riveted on the approaching back stairs when she felt a hand on her arm.

"You are leaving, Sophia?"

The lined face of Bellamy, her father, looked up at her, full of concern. Bellamy had been sitting at one of the little tables set up along the walls, eating cake with Mr. Halflife and Sheriff Burn. They both nodded at her, a little grim. Sheriff Burn was probably worried he would soon have to arrest the man he was having pudding with; Mr. Halflife was probably worried that the coming wedding would prevent the arrest.

She looked back at her father. Surely he knew what sort of family he was chaining her to. Allies of a government that had legalized mass murder in the Sunken City. That had taken the very real injustices of locked gates, and poverty, and the fear that a return of technology would steal livelihoods and starve children, taken them and used them, whipping the Lower City into a mob of frenzied hate against the Upper. Execute the rich, seize their assets, disenfranchise their religion, use terror to control the people and create new laws to justify their actions. That was Allemande's so-called revolution. And this was the family she was being sold to, blood relatives of the man that had sentenced people she loved to die beneath the Razor. And all because her father could not face reality or balance his own bank account. But Bellamy looked so uncertain, so miserable and guilt-ridden as he searched her face, that all at once her temper left her. Without it she was empty, bereft.

"Of course I'm not leaving, Father," she said. "The party is beautiful, and everything is going so well." She squeezed his hand, offering him a brief, false smile that she knew would make him feel better, seeing it tentatively returned before she moved away. She waited until Bellamy was distracted by the vicar, then made a dash up the back stairs.

She hurried through the gallery, clicking heels unheard in the din of music and reveling, past the Looking Man, up again, and then she was welcoming the quiet of a deserted corridor. Around she wound, through doors, past corners, and up more stairwells, some of them wood, some of them Ancient concrete, until she was in the long hallway of the north wing.

The hall was silent, a single candle left to illuminate the age-blackened paneling. Sophia took the taper from its sconce, poufy skirt rustling over the threadbare carpet, and quietly approached a door set back in its own columned recess. She stood still, listening. The Banns downstairs had everyone occupied, but René might have brought a manservant with him. He seemed the sort that would think himself incapable of carrying his own luggage. When she heard nothing but her own breath struggling against the restricting bodice, she reached up into the piled hair on her head, removed a silver key, and put it to the lock. She slipped inside René Hasard's door without the first creak of a hinge.

It wasn't long after that Sophia was opening the door to her own rooms, on the other side of Bellamy House, having seen nothing worse than three more jackets in the style of the gold one, shirts, breeches and pants, various articles of underclothing, reserves of hair powder, two razors, a book of questionable Parisian poetry, and some very dull correspondence. Nothing to connect him with the crimes of his city or his cousin. Or the Red Rook. René was a prat and that was all. The revelation made her both relieved and unhappy.

St. Just the fox barked once as she shut her door, his sharp ears pricked while he sniffed her skirts. She patted his head, and then

Orla was there, reaching up for the heavy dark hair. She had it off Sophia's head in an instant, setting it aside on the dressing table before spinning her round to unlace the bodice. Orla had been her nurse as a child, somehow going on with those duties long after Sophia had outgrown them. Mostly, Sophia supposed, because no one had ever told her to stop.

She relaxed, both from the relief at the lack of weight on her head and Orla's ministrations. Her room, at least, felt unsullied. She pulled out hairpins one by one while St. Just completed his investigation of her shoes, approved, and returned to his basket.

"Your Banns was tolerable, then?" Orla asked.

"Intolerable, I'm afraid."

"And Monsieur?"

"My father's choice of business partner is very handsome, knows it, and does not possess an intelligent thought. And he has some very nasty relatives."

"Your father or your fiancé?"

"Very funny, Orla." She felt uncharacteristically close to crying. "He brought one of his cousins to visit me tonight. Would you like to guess who was just downstairs?" She caught sight of Orla's questioning face in the mirror. "Albert LeBlanc."

Orla's fingers paused on the laces. "And he came as a relation, I suppose? Family duty?"

"I think not." Sophia watched worry press down on Orla's mouth. "Well, at least now we know why the Hasards haven't lost their heads to Allemande. Or their business. It's good to have friends in high places, don't you think, Orla?"

Orla didn't answer; she was too busy frowning. Sophia pulled the last pin from her hair and ran a hand through the damp, thick curls, shaking them all out once like a dog. The sight made a little line appear between the paint on her eyebrows. Jennifer Bonnard had been so young when Sophia saw her last, with those wide eyes and that freckled nose. Sophia wouldn't have dreamed Jennifer would recognize her, dressed in a man's clothes and with her hair cut like a boy's. The other Bonnards certainly hadn't.

"And what else has happened?" Orla asked. St. Just lifted his rust-colored head and whined once from the basket. He knew her moods as well as Orla.

"I think Jennifer Bonnard might have recognized me last night. She . . . It's very possible that she knows who I am." The Bonnards were half a mile away, and LeBlanc had walked right into her house.

"Are they safe?" Orla asked.

"For tonight. Spear is making certain."

"And where is LeBlanc?"

"He said he was going back to the city, I would guess on the ferry that leaves at highmoon. Tom was watching, and Cartier will follow. We should know where he goes, and when he leaves." Sophia grimaced. "It's all quite lovely, isn't it? A dream come true. Perhaps René and I will send the children to spend their summers."

Orla ignored the bitter tone. "Well, I suppose you've had a relative or two with a bad name, child, if you're wanting to cast stones."

"There haven't been any thieves in the family for two hundred years, Orla." Sophia rolled her eyes. Three centuries earlier, every Bellamy in the Commonwealth had been a pirate, before they stole enough to turn to more civilized trades. "Or not the bad sort of thief, anyway. So I hardly think that counts."

"You know best," said Orla, in a voice that meant the opposite.

Sophia shook her head. Orla really could be too practical. She put a finger beneath the edge of her dressing table and a drawer that had not been there before sprang out from the decorative carving.

It disappeared again with a soft click, the ring from her forefinger and the silver key with it. The bodice finally fell away, and Sophia breathed deep.

"Now, then. I've left your newspapers on the table and your breeches on the bed," Orla said. "And you can be shaking the sand out of them yourself this time, if you please. I plan to be in my bed when you come back. Where decent people ought to be by this time of night."

Being excluded from Orla's definition of "decent" made Sophia smile in spite of herself. "And what makes you think I'm going down to the beach tonight?"

Orla had a sharp face, a sharp nose, and now a voice to match. "Just what do you think I've been up to for the past eighteen years, child? Do you think I don't know you at all?"

The highmoon was rising above the secluded cove, making a pale, undulating path across the surface of the sea. A dense growth of bushes and salt-stunted trees made the cliff edge hard to find, the narrow strip of sand below almost hidden by overhanging rock and jagged rows of tumbled stones. Over the rolling surf and spray came a faint clang on the wind, steel on steel, and a silver flash that was the glint of metal catching the light. Parry, thrust. Parry and thrust.

"She works on her parry, Benoit," said René, his Parisian very quiet. He was flat on his stomach, surrounded by the thick branches, holding an eyescope trained on the beach below. Benoit sat beside him, a small man, nondescript, dressed as a servant, elbows balanced on knees. "The room was searched?" René asked.

Benoit nodded. "Very neatly done, nothing out of place. But the thread across the doorway has been broken."

"The lock was picked?"

"No scratches."

"Ah. And the hinges oiled before we arrived. That is excellent planning." He passed the eyescope to Benoit. "Tell me what you think of the brother."

"He trains her with the arms only, as he should," Benoit said after a moment. "But the leg, it changes its stance some, I think?"

"Perhaps it pains him?"

"Or pains him not at all. Who can say?"

René took the eyescope and turned it back to the beach, where he watched Sophia expertly relieve her brother of his sword. He smiled.

"I think we should follow Cousin Albert's advice, Benoit. This Miss Bellamy seems a much more interesting fiancée than I had first thought."

4

*S*pear Hammond stepped down out of the landover, looking left and right, making certain there was no one else on the road. A slate-colored sky hung low over the trees, and the wind gusted, tearing at his long coat, air whipping past with the feel of a storm on it. He didn't like this plan; it was risky, more so than usual. But he also didn't have a better one. He left young Cartier in the driver's seat of the landover, holding tight to the nervous horses, and hurried across the A5 lane, approaching a structure that had at one time been called a bungalow. Now it was a ramshackle tumble of stone and scavenged concrete, the roof caved in on one side.

The doorway of the ruin stood black and empty, but when Spear reached it, the tip of a sword appeared from one side of the darkness, just touching his chest. He paused and held out his hand, palm open, showing a single red-tipped feather. The sword lowered, and the face of Ministre Bonnard appeared in the opening, a frightened boy peeking out just behind him.

The Bonnard family was herded quickly into the landover, the door shut, the window curtains closed, and Cartier cracked his whip over the heads of the horses. Rooks cawed from the treetops, protesting the noise. Spear watched the wheels of the landover rattle fast down the lane, toward the turning to the Caledonian Road, where the buildings and fields of the Rathbone farm sprawled out along the banks of a wide river. He shook his head, promising himself again that this would be the last time. He knew he wouldn't keep that promise. Sophia would only have to ask him again. When the road was empty, he walked away past the bungalow, taking long, fast strides down the A5.

Sophia Bellamy took leisurely strides down the A5, away from the Caledonian Road and the Rathbone farm, picking her way around the massive ruts that were the result of dozens of landovers parading to her Banns the night before. Before the printing presses were taken, most of their friends would have been able to walk to Bellamy House. Now the road was lined with deteriorating bungalows.

Brown leaves blew past as she peered up, gazing at the steel sky beyond the oak trees, one hand holding a straw and ribbon hat on her head. The wind was sharp. She wondered if she could smell a storm, or if the rooks could. They were making an unholy noise. She adjusted the basket on her other arm, and then she paused, seeing what was disturbing the peace of the rookery. There was someone else on the lane. Her hat came off, dangling by the ribbons as she waited for the man's approach, one hand held near the filigree belt she wore around her waist. The rooks screamed.

"Monsieur LeBlanc," she said when he stood before her. She made her face look pleasant. "I thought you were sailing back to your city last night." She'd thought it because Cartier had followed him all the way to the ferry in Canterbury.

LeBlanc bent over her hand, allowing Sophia to study the odd streak of white hair in the natural light. He wore a large signet ring on his smallest finger. "Good day, Miss Bellamy. I had meant it to be so, but while on the boat I inquired of Fate and the Goddess most unexpectedly directed me to stay in the Commonwealth." Sophia felt one of her eyebrows rise. "Do you walk alone? Is that wise? Where is René?"

Sophia forced a laugh. "Your cousin is likely flat on his back with an aching head, Monsieur. And I often walk here alone. This is my land."

"Your father's land. Is that not so?" When she did not answer, LeBlanc said, "I believe I saw Monsieur Bellamy's landover drive by a few moments ago. You do not take the landover?"

"No." She kept her smile neutral while her pulse picked up its pace. "It was going to the smith for repairs, I believe. And I like to walk."

"And where do you walk to, Mademoiselle, when the weather threatens?"

"I'm bringing a basket to one of our neighbors." She lifted the arm with the basket slightly.

"And which neighbor is this?"

"Mr. Lostchild," she lied without hesitation. "He's very old, and one of the few we have left. We like to take care of him."

"And what do you bring him?"

"Cake. Left over from the Banns." Sophia tilted her head. "Would you also like to know exactly when I left the house?"

LeBlanc laughed very softly. Sophia hid an involuntary shiver. "You will forgive me for being so inquisitive, Miss Bellamy. It is my nature to ask questions. Would you allow me to walk with you to see this Mr. Lostchild? It would ease my mind if you were not alone."

Sophia inclined her head, trying to hold an agreeable expression while every muscle in her body rippled with tension. They began walking down the A5 together, Sophia keeping one hand unobtrusively behind her basket, near the filigree belt.

"I am surprised to hear that you bring food to your elderly. Does that not go against your Commonwealth doctrines of self-reliance, Mademoiselle?"

"Only if Mr. Lostchild is liable to become dependent on cake, Monsieur."

LeBlanc gave her a sidelong glance, as if trying to decide whether she'd meant to be impertinent. She had. "May I say you look very well today, Miss Bellamy. I think I prefer it to your more formal attire."

He was approving of the ringlets in her hair and the neckline of her shirt, which was significantly higher than her Banns dress. Sophia said, "I take it the fashions of the Commonwealth offend your Allemande tastes? If so, then your cousin must be a puzzle to you."

"It is true that in the *Cité de Lumière* we do not prefer the new ways."

"You mean the old ways that have become new again?"

He nodded, acknowledging the reference to his words the night before. "In the city, we do not see the need for excess. We prefer sensible dress and the honest work of the human."

"And yet machines are the work of humans, aren't they, Monsieur?"

LeBlanc's smile was once again indulgent. "Machines take away the means for the poor to earn their bread. And eventually, as it did with the Ancients, dependence on technology takes away even the most basic of skills, like the ability to find one's own food. That is not something Premier Allemande can condone."

No, he just condones cutting off the heads of those with the money to fund such technology, Sophia thought. Whether they had ever thought of funding it or not. She wondered just how often Premier Allemande found his own food.

LeBlanc was frowning. "You speak like a technologist, Miss Bellamy, as if you would see the world go back to the weaknesses of the past. Has your father or your brother been teaching you this?"

Sophia gave him a pretty, false smile. "Oh, no, Monsieur. Technologists are not popular here at all. I think the Commonwealth dislikes proponents of machines even more than the Sunken City does." She watched LeBlanc's expression smooth back to tranquility.

"I am glad to hear you say so. René has gone rather wild of late, as young men often do, and his mother hopes for a marriage that will tame him. Are you . . . how do you say it here? Are you 'up for the job'?"

She laughed again, but did not answer.

"It is a gamble, is it not?" LeBlanc continued. "We hope that you will teach René his responsibilities and bring strong blood to the family, while you hope the Hasard fortune will save the Bellamys from ruin."

Sophia stopped their stroll and turned to face LeBlanc. Behind him, across an overgrown yard, stood a ruined bungalow with half a roof and an empty front door. "Exactly what do you want to say to me, Monsieur?"

LeBlanc's smile spread slow across his face. "I would like your help, Miss Bellamy."

She waited, the hand that was behind her basket on the filigree belt buckle.

"I want information on the man known in my city as the Red Rook."

Sophia smiled, and then she said, "Are you also looking for landovers that drive by themselves? The Rook is only a story."

"The Red Rook is not a myth, Mademoiselle. He is a man, and . . ." He lowered his oily voice. ". . . I know he is near."

Sophia blinked. "You interest me. Go on."

"I know that he has landed two boats within three miles of this estate, boats I believe to have been filled with traitors to Allemande. I know he speaks two languages, for how else can he blend so well into the people of our different cultures? I believe that he is a man of some wealth, or that he is supported by one, so that he can come and go as he pleases. I believe he has a group of men around him that will obey without question. And your father's estate, Miss Bellamy, must be near where such a man might live on this isolated stretch of coast."

A small silence followed this speech, interrupted only by the cawing from the high branches of the oak trees. Sophia smiled.

"I believe your imagination has run away with you, Monsieur." She took a step away, but LeBlanc reached out like a striking snake and grabbed her arm.

"You do not understand me, Miss Bellamy. When I said I wanted information from you, I was not making a request."

Sophia pulled her arm away and stepped back, the basket now hiding the small knife that had been secreted in the filigree of her belt buckle. She held it loose in her hand. LeBlanc's smile spread.

"Let me explain to you. Your father is in need of the ten thousand quidden your marriage to a Parisian will bring him. But perhaps you do not know that the Hasard fortune is not at all secure? Premier Allemande does not like such inequalities of wealth in his city. The Hasard money has only remained intact because of his . . . benevolence."

Which meant that LeBlanc had made sure it stayed intact. For himself.

"I can ensure that the goodwill of Allemande continues," said LeBlanc, "but I will wish to receive something in return. Give me the Red Rook, and you can be certain that René will bring your family a marriage fee, and that your father will not see the inside of a debtor's cell."

Sophia stood stock-still on the road, wind whistling through the rubble of the empty building, the smooth handle of the knife in her concealed hand. "You would have the fortune of your own family confiscated?"

LeBlanc shrugged. "We have never been close."

"Monsieur LeBlanc," she said, "I am very sorry to disappoint you, but I know nothing of this matter. I have nothing to give you. Nothing at all."

"But I think you do. Or that you very soon will. You will see. You will discover. You will listen to the talk in the kitchen. Women can do these things. Succeed, and you will have your marriage fee. Fail, and you will lose your father and your home. I trust that these instructions need no more explanation?"

When Sophia said nothing, he bowed his head slightly and turned to walk away down the lane.

He was several steps away when Sophia called, "Have you spoken to your cousin about this?" LeBlanc spun slowly back around.

"Do you believe in Luck, Miss Bellamy? I do, most fervently. Luck is the handmaiden of Fate, and I think I will try my luck with you." He began to walk again down the A5, calling over his shoulder, "You will find me at the Holiday, Mademoiselle. For one week. That is all the time I can spare!"

Sophia watched LeBlanc's retreating back, wind stirring little tornadoes of dirt and fallen leaves, waiting until the rooks had hushed and the lane was empty again. Only then did she slide the knife back into her belt, its handle part of the buckle's decoration. The trees behind her rustled, and she turned her head.

"You heard?" she asked as Tom came limping out from the undergrowth.

"Yes," he replied. "Enough."

He stood beside her as they both stared down the empty road. "I'm thinking misdirection," Sophia said quietly. "You?"

"Yes, possibly. But we are going to have to play a very careful game, my sister."

"Do you play, my love?"

Sophia glanced up at René standing beside her father's chess set as if he were posing for a portrait titled *Parisian Rake*. She went back to stroking St. Just's head, the fox settling deeper into the gauzy pink of her gown. It was full dark outside, the storm that the wind had promised now lashing for its third day at the windowpanes. Bellamy slumped in his chair—he never stayed awake for long after dinner—while Spear and Tom sat on either side of the fire, Spear reading a legal newspaper, Tom thumbing through his illegal *Wesson's Guide*. Tom's interest in *Wesson's* was less about clothing and more about what the subjects of the copied drawings might be doing, and where they might have been doing it. Proving the theory that Wesson had copied Ancient paintings in abandoned London before it was lost was Tom's constant pastime.

Sophia wanted a pastime, or at least one that could be done in a sitting room, where sword fighting was frowned upon. Three days of torrential rain had left her cooped up and testy. René Hasard had been haunting her steps, paying her unearned compliments, stating his opinions on music, magazines, Parisian actresses, and, most memorably, an endless dissertation on his particular preferences in nursery carpets. Tom had nodded sagely while listening to this, asking her fiancé such detailed, serious questions that Sophia thought holding in the laughter might actually kill her. And if she did manage to be without René's presence for the odd moment or two, up he would pop unexpectedly, full of a restless, boundless energy and incessant talk that, good looks or no, stretched her patience to the limit.

St. Just lifted his head from her lap, sniffing at her foul mood. René's suggestion of a game was not appealing, but then again, Sophia wasn't certain he could have suggested anything that was. Her father snorted, startling belatedly from his doze.

"What?" Bellamy said. "What? Play my Sophia, Mr. Hasard? Oh no, I don't advise it. I've been playing her since she was ten years old, and the child has trounced me every time."

Tom smiled from his armchair, adjusting the cushion beneath his leg. "You'll make Hasard afraid of our Sophie, Father."

"And you think that a bad thing, Tom?" Sophia said sweetly. "Do go on, Father. What were you saying?"

René laughed, a little too loud, a sound that grated across every raw end of her nerves. He said, "And now I must insist on the game or be thought a coward." He turned back to Sophia. "Or you shall."

She set her mouth, put St. Just on the carpet, and marched over to the chessboard. Spear's newspaper lowered, and she could feel his eyes following as she sat herself down at the game table. René was in the green coat tonight. She found a silver button, the second one down, and fixed her gaze there.

"White first, my love," René said.

"I prefer black."

He turned the board while St. Just settled his bushy tail over her feet. They played in silence, she taking her time and with her attention on the board, he with quick, haphazard moves and his face turned toward the rest of the room. Sophia moved her sheriff and stifled a yawn. She was six moves from taking his king.

"My cousin says that he walked in the lane with you the other day," René said loudly.

"You've been to see Monsieur LeBlanc?" She glanced once at Spear. He and Cartier were supposed to have been watching, making sure René didn't leave the house. Spear almost imperceptibly shrugged a shoulder.

"Oh, yes," René said, "I went to see him early, before breakfast."

"In the rain?"

"It was a refreshing journey. But my cousin made me quite jealous." René ignored her sheriff and unwisely moved a pawn. "Perhaps you might like to walk with me next time, when the weather improves?" When she remained silent, René said, "Do none of the young women from your Banns ever come to walk with you? I would not mind seeing Mademoiselle Lauren again. I thought she was very . . . pleasant."

Oh, Sophia thought. So that's what sort of husband he would be. She supposed it shouldn't matter to her. She tried to imagine strolling down the A5 with Lauren Rathbone and failed.

"Bellamy has invited my cousin to dine with us tomorrow," René went on. "That was thoughtful of him, yes?"

Sophia looked over at the armchair, where her oblivious father was again snoozing. She lowered her voice. "I am surprised that Monsieur LeBlanc stays in the Commonwealth. What can he possibly have to do here?"

"I believe that tonight he was intending to ride the coast."

"Really? An impractical plan. Why would he want to do that in this weather?"

"I wish I could say he was riding out to have his hair dyed," René sighed. "That streak is not in fashion."

Sophia stared at the water streaming down the window glass. Sometimes it was hard to believe the man sitting across from her could possibly be serious. And then she did believe it, and it was depressing.

"But Cousin Albert does not share his reasons with me," René continued. "I only saw his horse being saddled."

"He'll have found somewhere else to stay, I would think. In Forge or Mainstay, if he got that far." For once she let her gaze rest briefly on René's face. "If the weather holds, maybe he won't be able to come to dinner after all. Maybe he'll have to go straight back to where he came from."

René laughed, again much too loud. "What a teasing little minx you are!"

This remark carried to the fireplace, earning her a surprised glance from Tom and a long look from Spear. Sophia felt a bit of heat rise to her cheeks. René had made it sound as if she was flirting with him. It threw another log of fuel on her smoldering temper.

"Such a shame Mrs. Rathbone couldn't come eat with us tonight," Sophia said to the room in general. "What did she say she had to do again?"

Spear immediately shifted in his chair, ready to accommodate her, but Sophia could see by the line of Tom's mouth that he disapproved. Still, she couldn't help it. She was ticked.

"Mrs. Rathbone mentioned something about a few unexpected duties that had come her way," Spear said. "Five of them, I think." He grinned, a thing of beauty and symmetry in the firelight. "And she mentioned old Mr. Lostchild. You did hear that he was no longer with us?"

"Yes, and I'm sorry for it," Sophia replied. Tom had assured her that Mr. Lostchild's death appeared to be from natural causes; he'd been very old. But the fact that she'd said his name to LeBlanc three days beforehand did not sit well with her. "Such a nice man," she continued. "Always a cookie to spare when we were children. But I had hoped Mrs. Rathbone might come. She was telling me the oddest story at the Banns, about how the Bonnards had escaped prison on the very night of their execution. Was there anything about it in the newspaper, Tom?"

"I'm not certain." Tom was frowning now.

Spear leaned his large frame back into the chair, his white shirt crisp and unblemished. "I saw something about it. They say it was the Red Rook. Isn't that what they call him?" This last had been to Tom, but Tom did not respond.

Sophia said, "Yes, I've heard of him. He's done things like this before, hasn't he, Spear?"

"I believe so. The Parisians seem to think he's some kind of ghost."

"They say he is a saint sent by God," said René unexpectedly. "Or at least those who do not believe that Allemande is God say it."

Sophia blinked once before she said, "Mrs. Rathbone said he was the talk of the Sunken City. If he's not a ghost or a saint, then who do you think he could be, Tom?"

"Whoever he is," Tom replied, eyes on his book and his words measured, "I think he is getting too bold."

Spear winked at her conspiratorially, but Sophia looked down at the board, supposedly to move her rook, really to absorb the shame brought on by the remonstrance she'd heard in her brother's voice. It was one thing to give in to temper in the sitting room after dinner; it was another thing entirely to disappoint Tom. St. Just whined, stretched his back, and exchanged Sophia's slippers for René's buckled shoes. What a little traitor.

"Do you believe that?" René asked. Sophia's eyes darted up, but he was speaking to Tom. "Do you believe *Le Corbeau Rouge* grows too bold? Do you think he will be caught if he tries his tricks again?"

Tom lowered his book, his brown eyes regarding René with interest. "I'm sure I don't know. But if Allemande would stop murdering his own people, then I suppose he wouldn't have to."

"You are against the revolution, then?" René said, moving a chess piece with barely a glance. "You believe the rich have the right to fund technology and build their own machines?"

Sophia met Spear's eyes, frowning a little. LeBlanc had asked her something very similar in the lane, whether or not she was a technologist. Tom folded his hands across the book in his lap.

"I'm not against the building of machines, Hasard, if that's what you're asking. Spain has broken the Anti-Technology Pact, as has China, and the Finnish Confederate. The loss of trade with those countries is crippling the Commonwealth. But I suppose that whatever your city does about technology is not really any of my business."

"But you are a student of the Time Before," René countered. Sophia looked up sharply from her queen. René's voice had lost just a bit of its Parisian sophistication. "Do you not believe that machines made the people weak, that the Great Death, as you call it, came about because the Ancients were dependent on technology, and did not know how to survive when they lost it? That making heat and light, traveling, fighting, that these things were impossible for them, because of their dependence?"

Tom tilted his chin. "There is some truth in that, though I could argue that the wealthy of both our cultures are becoming weak and idle without any machines at all. But I believe the Great Death was caused by shifts in our planet just as much as technological dependence. Did you know that in the Time Before, north was what we would now call northwest? That has been proven with archaeological finds. At the university in Manchester they teach that when the magnetic poles of the earth shifted, the protective layer around the earth was damaged, allowing the radiation of the sun to destroy the technology that the Ancients depended on. What I think, though, is that this same solar radiation caused the first wave of the Great Death. Sickness killed the people first, technological dependence second, that's what I believe.

"But that was more than eight hundred years ago, and the Anti-Technology Pact our two countries signed has far outlived its time. I think it more than possible to use machines without making the mistakes of our ancestors. That we could build a clock or a mill or play a piano without losing our ability to survive without them."

René leaned forward and spoke, still in the lower, less Parisian voice. "And the fact that your Parliament has taken the license for the printing press, does this affect your opinion?"

"The entire South Commonwealth would be better off if the Bellamys still had the license to print. We were putting books in every chapel and school. Instead Parliament reserves that power for themselves, controlling everything we read and driving one more industry to the undermarkets."

Sophia knew her brother thought Parliament was actually hoarding technology, using a much larger, more complicated printing press than was allowed by law. They were producing too many newspapers, and too quickly.

"But whatever I think," Tom continued, "I would never say that I don't obey the laws of my land. Or yours."

Sophia moved her rook across the chessboard, setting the next prong of her attack. Tom was helping her disobey those laws every day. He just wouldn't be so stupid as to say so, of course. Their father snored softly from his chair, and René moved a sheriff, his mind obviously elsewhere.

"And what about you, Hasard?" Tom said, turning the tables. "Do you agree with your city's revolution? Do you think technology will make the poor poorer, and the rich richer? Do you think the people of the Upper City are being executed for funding the return of technology at the expense of the Lower City, or for merely having the money to do so and owning property your government wants? Or is it because of their religious beliefs, because your cousin wants to replace the chapels with a cult? Or are they being put to the Razor because they do not agree with Allemande's absolute power, and the way he executed your last premier?"

For a few moments it seemed as if René wouldn't answer, and then he leaned back in his chair and began to laugh loudly, like the man of her Banns ball. "Oh, no," he said. "You have me, Monsieur! Here I was, hoping to impress my fiancée with lofty questions, when to say the truth, I never think on these things myself. Benoit is always telling me I should."

Sophia stared doggedly at the game and moved her vicar.

"But one thing I know to be true," René went on, recovering from his laugh. "No machine could make a better coat than my tailor. Now there is an opinion I can stand behind."

Really, the man could not have annoyed her more if he sat up at night and planned it.

Tom was still smiling. "But isn't a loom a machine, Hasard?"

"Or the Razor?" Sophia added.

René thrust his vicar across the board before he threw up his hands. "Please!" he cried in mock distress. "No more! I am defeated! Benoit was right again. As usual."

Sophia ran a hand through her ringlets, wondering how she could ever survive a lifetime of nights like this. There might have to be sword fighting in the sitting room after all. Spear rustled his newspaper, but she did not look his way. She moved her queen. Two moves and she would win.

"My love," René said, voice miraculously lowered. "Do you not think we should choose a date for our wedding? I really should write to my *maman*."

"I'm surprised you ask me, Monsieur," she replied. "I thought you would have banged out all those details with my father already."

He jumped his sheriff. "You could call me René." His voice was softer, but the amusement in it was loud and clear.

"I will call you 'monsieur' until you earn something better. And since you bring it up, I'll also thank you to drop this silly pretense of 'my love.'"

Spear was pretending to read his newspaper, but Sophia could see where his attention lay: on the conversation he could no longer hear. She moved her rook and René immediately moved after her, almost as soon as she had taken her fingers from the black-carved wings. She considered holding back her words, and decided she could not.

"And while we're speaking freely, Monsieur, there is something I have been meaning to ask you. I wonder what sort of proof you've offered my father that your inheritance is intact."

"You think I am a . . . what is the word? A 'con man'?"

"I think I shall know you are not before I make any plans with the vicar."

René laughed, not the one that set her teeth on edge, but something deeper. "Oh, Sophia," he said, shaking his head. "You see so much, and yet you only see so far. Shall I tell you why?"

She crossed her arms, staring down at her queen.

"It is because you do not choose to look."

And it was then she saw it. She sat forward, staring at the board while the wind howled, lips parted in a silent gasp. Before her was a trap, subtle yet effective. It was not his king but her queen that was lost. The game was lost. She had been a fool.

She raised her eyes, and for the first time gave René Hasard's face her full attention. He was still leaning sideways in the chair, their candle putting half his expression in shadow as he looked toward the hearth. Square jaw just showing the end of the day's stubble, straight nose, and eyes that were an intense blue, a fire in the forge blue, an almost unnatural color against the powdered hair. The brows were drawn down, thoughtful, not black or brown, she saw, but a dark russet. Did René have red hair?

Who was this man who never contemplated the matters of his city, but who could so easily out-strategize her on a chessboard, apparently without even trying? And why had he really gone to see his cousin that day, his dangerous, murdering cousin, the cousin that was threatening her father with jail unless she brought him the Rook? And then she saw where those hot blue eyes were looking: straight at her brother's bad leg, propped on the cushion.

A blast of wind whistled past the chimneys, smacking a branch sharp against the windowpane. "Oh!" Sophia squealed, leaping from her chair and upsetting the table. St. Just yelped and René caught the board before it hit the floor, chess pieces rolling to the far ends of the carpet. Bellamy woke with a snort.

"Blimey, Sophie," Tom said. "What's the matter with you?"

"I'm sorry," she said. "Stupid of me. The wind has me nervous, I think." She saw the surprise on Spear's face; she didn't dare look at René. "It's been such a long day, I think I should go to bed. Good night, Father."

Bellamy was still looking about, blinking in confusion. René had righted the table and was on his feet, taking her hand to kiss it as usual. But this time Sophia felt her own eyes dragged up to meet his, two wells of knowing over half a smile before his lips touched her hand. She could not fathom what lay behind that smile. Then he whispered, *"Je pense que nous pouvons dire que ce jeu est un match nul, n'est-ce pas?"*

Sophia pulled her hand away, only just keeping her walk from breaking into a run as she crossed the room to the door, where St. Just was already waiting for her. She shut out the light of the sitting room with a slam and leaned against the heavy oak.

René had offered to call their game a draw, when they both knew full well that he had won. And he'd said it in Parisian. She was unsure whether that, or his unsuspected skill at chess, or the way he had been looking at Tom's leg was the most unsettling. Or maybe it was the way he'd been looking at her. St. Just ran down the corridor, unperturbed by the dark, while Sophia shivered, waiting for her eyes to adjust and her heartbeat to slow. She'd forgotten a candle, and the corridor was not heated. They only heated the rooms they had to in Bellamy House.

She heard feet approaching from behind the door and slid a few steps down the hall, but it was only Spear coming out of the sitting room with a light. He moved down the corridor to lean against the wall opposite. Spear was built like a fighter, or a footballer, so tall she had to tilt her head back to look at him in the chilly, narrow hallway.

"So what happened?" he asked quietly.

"Nothing," she said. Or at least nothing that she could explain to Spear in a few stolen moments in a corridor.

"He's lying about LeBlanc," Spear said. "I swear he didn't leave the north wing until he came out to find you this morning."

Sophia wrinkled her forehead. "Why lie about that? It makes no sense."

"It doesn't make sense. Which is why you shouldn't go tonight."

"I think it's the exact reason why I should go."

"Put it off, Sophie. Please. Just for a night." He reached out and straightened one of the sleeves on the gauzy pink dress. She shivered again. The corridor was freezing. "You know Tom is going to agree with me," Spear said.

She bit her lip, thinking. "Are you sleeping here tonight, or going back to the farm?" Spear had had his own room a floor up from Tom ever since they were children.

"I can stay here."

"Then between you and Tom, let's make very certain that my fiancé does not leave the north wing."

5

"*I'll* do as I was told," Orla said stoutly.

The hotelier of the Holiday folded two meaty arms across his chest. "I've no instructions about any shirts. The man said no one in his room till he's coming back."

"Then Monsieur LeBlanc has made a mistake. He specifically asked to have his shirts cleaned before tomorrow."

"And you've come to get them in the rain."

"I have no control over the weather."

"And where do you come from again?"

Orla drew herself up straight, pulling her coat close around her, the picture of female dudgeon. "I don't see how that is any of your business."

The hotelier sighed. "Come back in the dawn, if you must."

"Is that when Monsieur LeBlanc said he would return?"

"At the soonest. Now be on your way. I've things to attend to."

"On your own head be it, then," said Orla. She pulled her coat even closer and stepped out of the Holiday, into the inky rain and a waiting haularound. From the dark corner of the common room, where the firelight did not reach, Benoit lowered his mug.

LeBlanc lowered his eyescope. He was standing in the stable, watching sheets of rain batter the house of Mrs. Rathbone. The house was large and respectable, the light of oil lamps shining out from the windows onto a recently harvested, now soggy field. The horses whinnied, kicking at the stall doors, upset by the storm and the scent of wild dog on the cloth that LeBlanc had been waving before their noses. A house door opened, as he had hoped, and a small figure stepped gingerly into the rain. LeBlanc moved back into the shadows.

The figure entered the stable, unwrapping a shawl from around a blond head shorn short about the ears. The girl set a covered lamp carefully on a shelf, its light showing a spatter of freckles over her nose, and went to lay a hand on the nearest horse. The nape of her neck glowed bare and pale in the lantern light. LeBlanc's smile crept wider. Luck truly was with him. He'd taken one step toward the girl when the stable door burst open. LeBlanc slid back into the gloom of an empty stall.

"Jennifer!" It was Ministre Bonnard, now shaved and looking considerably more clean, though no less fearful. "What are you doing?" His eyes darted over the interior of the stable, and he lowered his voice. "What are you thinking of, coming out here alone?"

Jennifer frowned. "It's raining, Papa, and the horses were frightened. No one is going to be out here looking for us in the rain . . ."

LeBlanc shook his head. Women were so foolish.

". . . and I thought I would go mad inside. The walls are too close . . ."

"It's not safe, Jen, rain or no. Come back to the house. Quickly, now."

Ministre Bonnard took the lantern in one hand and his daughter's arm in the other, pulling her away from the stamping horses. They left the stable in darkness.

LeBlanc rose up from his crouch, still smiling, and when the door to the Rathbone house had closed, he stole out into the rain and back to the woodlands beyond the fields, where he'd left his own horse tied beneath a thick canopy of branches. Fate, he sensed, was moving her divine fingers.

Orla flexed her cold hands, a towel beneath her dripping steel-gray hair. "I argued with the man, but there was nothing doing," she said.

Sophia was tugging her boots over tight breeches while the rain beat the roof tiles. "LeBlanc is being cautious, that's all," she said. As he should be.

"I don't like it, Sophie." Tom leaned on his stick, frowning at the pale pink, gauzy gown she'd left in a heap on the floor. He said no more words, but Sophia discerned the rest of his thoughts clearly. Too bold. "What Hasard said tonight was odd," he continued. "There's too much here that we don't know."

"Which is exactly why we must know what LeBlanc knows," Sophia said, now tying back her hair. Her ringlets were brushed away, a knife worn sheathed at her side. With a very deliberate fit of shirt, she stood on the hearth rug looking for all the world like a slightly younger copy of her brother, and she understood his hesitation; she was feeling it, too. A net, coming from all sides, and drawing tighter. "Really, Tom. You know there's no choice."

The truth was, she'd been hoping Orla's part of the plan would fail. Counting on it. She'd been sitting in the house playing polite for far too long. She wanted nothing more than to be out alone in the night and the rain. She tugged on an oil-slicked coat. "Do you have Mr. Lostchild's gloves, Orla?"

Orla handed her a package wrapped in a freshly laundered piece of wool with leather over that, the bundle tied tight with string. Sophia tucked it into her vest.

"And here, child," said Orla simply, holding out a leather string.

Sophia nodded, twisting her ring from her forefinger, its large, pale stone winking in the lamplight. She strung it on the leather and pulled it over her neck, letting it dangle beneath her shirt.

Tom sighed and turned the iron latch on Sophia's window, letting in a wet and salty wind. "The rain is unfortunate," he commented. "Cartier won't be able to start his run until it lets up or the foxes might lose his scent. He won't have enough of a start."

Cartier had been born in the Sunken City, along with an elder brother who'd gone beneath the Razor a year earlier. Tonight Cartier was running all the way to the hills above Mainstay in Mr. Lostchild's shoes, coat, and pants, leading LeBlanc on a chase that would hopefully turn the man's gaze from Bellamy House.

"Cartier's fast," Sophia said. "And willing, and you know as well as I do that the storm will have blown itself out before dawn. It's a good plan, Tom."

"I think we should be sending Spear."

"Spear drinks at the Holiday much too often for this!"

Orla shook her wet head. "Do you think your sister is going to pass up the chance to have all the risks to herself?"

Tom's frown deepened, and Sophia nearly stomped a foot. "Stop being such a grandmother, Tom! When will we have another opportunity to search LeBlanc's room and put him off the scent?"

Tom shook his head. He knew there might not be another opportunity. "By dawn," he said. "And don't be reckless."

"Reckless? Of course not!" She hopped onto the windowsill. "And keep an eye on my fiancé!"

"Two of them," Tom replied.

Sophia gave them both one last grin, and jumped out the window.

The roof tiles were slick with rain, but the slope was gentle, and even in the dark Sophia knew exactly when to turn and how far to slide to the edge. She made another jump and landed softly on the flatter roof over her father's study, ran across this, shinnied down a gurgling drainpipe, swung herself around to a window ledge, and dropped. Her boots thumped on a flat stone, placed there years ago for the purpose by Tom. She had the instinctive urge to move to one side so Tom could jump down after her. But there was no need for that, not anymore. She knew he missed it, the same way she missed him now. It had always been the two of them. And Spear.

The sea boomed on the edge of hearing, churned by the rain, filling the air with the smell of brine. Sophia lifted her face, letting the water pelt her cheeks until they stung. Then she took a deep breath and ran full tilt through the night, splashing across the lawns, around the derelict print house, taking the fence in one leap. She sloshed her way toward the woodlands, where her horse stood sheltered, saddled, and waiting for her.

It was well after middlemoon when Sophia tied her horse in another woodland, this time in a thick copse well off the road. The rain had finally poured itself out, only the occasional fat drop smacking against her shoulders and back. She left her wet coat on the horse, making the final part of her journey on foot. There was little danger in this. To come down the A5 was to take the long way around to anywhere unless you were headed to the Holiday inn, and even that was more of a pause than a destination, a place to stop on your way to somewhere better. No one ever used the lane except the vicar, and that was only after chapel, because he liked to shuck off his robes and have a dip in the sea on his way to the pub.

She was passing the last of the empty printer bungalows, at the place where the sea cliffs had eroded nearly to the road, when a glow caught her eye, up in the sky and far out to sea. Sophia slowed, and then stopped. There was a faint rumble, a short pop of very distant thunder, as if the storm had returned, and then the glow grew brighter, sharper. All at once a ball of light shot beneath the clouds. Sophia ran to the side of the road and jumped up to the first branch of a short, stunted tree, watching yellow fire make a streaking arc across the blackness.

She'd seen paintings that looked like that. On the walls of Parisian chapels. Fiery streaks of light that had led the dying to the underground of the Sunken City, sent to them by the saint that took the form of a rook. They were drawn as symbols of hope on those walls, like the black feather. But not long before her mother died, when Bellamy had been a different man, her father had told her that during the Great Death the nighttime had been filled with such streaking lights. That when technology failed, all the Ancient machines of the sky, the satellites, burned as they fell, rushing to the ground in pieces of flaming metal. So many machines that they'd fallen for years.

And she'd looked up into her father's face and asked him why the satellites fell. He said he didn't know. So she'd asked him what they were for, and why the Ancients had put machines in the sky at all, and he said he didn't know. Did they keep them on the moon, to be tidy? And how could the Ancients climb a ladder high enough to put a machine up there in the first place? He'd said he didn't know. And so she, in her seven-year-old wisdom, had decided that if he did not know, then she did not believe him.

Now she was not so sure. She watched the blazing light narrow to a pinpoint, falling away somewhere beyond the horizon. What would it be like, she wondered, to live in a world where everything that must have seemed so permanent was suddenly stripped away?

Where the things you'd built dropped like fiery rain on your head? Would it be like waking up and finding no sea beyond the cliffs? Or that Bellamy House had disappeared in the night?

Sophia climbed down from the tree, feeling the chill of the wind now that she had been still. She stole quickly down the lane, wondering if she should take that streak of light in the sky as a sign of hope, like some had, or a sign of despair? Or maybe it wasn't a sign at all; maybe it was just a streak of light, and the difference between the hope and hopelessness was entirely up to her. On her left she could just see the outline of the Holiday coming into focus, standing well back from the road. She decided that it was up to her. But that didn't mean the light had no significance.

She cut across a field to the yard of the Holiday. The inn was dark, no lights showing, the squelching of mud beneath her boots the only sound beyond distant surf; even the fox kennels were quiet. Sophia circled the building, counting the second-story windows. Orla may not have gotten into LeBlanc's room, but she had found its location. When Sophia saw the window Orla had described, she drew out a pair of gloves—her own, not Mr. Lostchild's—and a thin rope with a small iron hook from beneath her vest. She tossed the hook lightly upward, landing it in the roof thatch.

She dragged the hook, looking for purchase, and on the third time the hook found a piece of the wood framing beneath the thatch directly over the window. Sophia leaned back, testing the rope. When she was sure it was snagged well she slid one foot from a mud-caked boot, snaked the rope around it, and pulled herself upward, using the wrapped rope like a stair. She pushed off the other boot, and then she was climbing, quickly, rewrapping her foot, scooting and pulling herself up the rope until she had reached LeBlanc's window.

She got one stocking on the casing, then the other, and crouched, a hand still clutching the rope. She drew her knife from the sheath and slid it down between the two panes of glass until she heard a click and felt the latch give. The windows pushed inward, and Sophia dropped silently into LeBlanc's room.

Even with her eyes adjusted to the night the room was black. But it was also empty. She could feel that. Or maybe hear it, or smell it. Sophia hauled up the rope, winding it carefully into a pile on the windowsill, and again went to the supplies she kept beneath her vest. She would have to risk a small fire, and a light. As soon as she had a taper lit, she smothered the flame she had begun in the hearth and drew the curtains over the slightly open window. She tucked away the steel and flint and went straight to a traveling trunk in the corner.

Careful to put her damp knees on the matting, Sophia opened the trunk and sifted through LeBlanc's clothes—much less interesting than René's—and then a box containing his correspondence—every bit as dull as René's. The box was expensive, plastic that had been melted and reformed, its color dull and without a name. Something Ancient and irreplaceable had been destroyed to make that box, which was yet another crime of the Sunken City, in her opinion. At least the Commonwealth didn't allow melters to operate within its borders; everyone would know it if they did. It was impossible to hide the stench.

She set the box away, studying the room. Bed with curtains, no canopy, small table with an empty drawer, plain chair. Nothing under the mattress, no wall hangings, just an imperfect cube of plaster riddled with tiny cracks. Nowhere to hide anything. Maybe LeBlanc kept important things with him. Or maybe he kept everything important inside his head.

She went back to the plastic box, took the papers out again in a precise stack, and held it close to the candle. The outside of the box was satin smooth to her fingertips, and so was the inside. Except at one end. Her finger paused, pushed, and the bottom of the box flipped up and open, showing a shallow compartment underneath. Inside was a stack of letters. Sophia smiled, and then she froze, one hand full of papers. A board had creaked in the hallway, just beyond the door.

She lifted her other hand to the candle, ready to grab the telling light and blow it out if a key went into LeBlanc's lock. But the moments passed and there was no other noise. The old wood settling, most likely. She went back to the papers, scanning each one quickly. She needed to be gone.

The letters were written in Parisian, just like the rest of LeBlanc's papers. One was from Allemande, making LeBlanc aware of governmental minutiae, and one was from Renaud, his secretary, with the city's most recent list of traitors. None of her relatives or childhood friends were on the list this time, but seeing the names made her fingers itch for a set of picklocks all the same.

The next letter was an ill-written report from Gerard—the Gerard of the Tombs, she realized—giving LeBlanc a somewhat sketchy description of the Red Rook. Young, medium to smallish height, and in the robes of a holy man. Sophia cursed once beneath her breath. The holy man was not her only disguise, but it had been one of the most useful. She wondered what Gerard had promised the poor wretch who'd told him this. Freedom? The freedom of his family? But promises or no, now that Gerard knew he hadn't just been bribed, but bribed by the Red Rook, whichever prisoner had given this information would surely go straight to the Razor. The fact that Gerard was even mentioning it to LeBlanc made her feel certain this was already a truth.

She shifted the papers. The last letter was half-finished, and written in a hand that had to be LeBlanc's. Small, precise, and some-how ferret-like, just like him. Her eyes widened, nose moving closer to the paper as she read.

> *My dear René,*
> *I am certain your instincts are correct, and your ingenuity is appreciated. But let me suggest yet another step in your plans. Gain the young lady's trust; befriend her. Use your charms as you always do and I am sure you will get the information we seek. I will try to do the same. Taking the traitor Bonnard back to the City of Light is preferable, but as you say, it is the Red Rook that must be snared. The divine authority of Allemande and the Goddess cannot be questioned. I am happy to know that you are willing to sacrifice so much for the cause if this comes to marriage, but do not take such drastic measures too soon. The Red Rook is close. Write as soon as you have information. And tell your mother I . . .*

Sophia stared at the words, barely resisting the urge to crumple the paper. Instead she put the letters in the same order inside the false bottom and pressed it closed. She replaced the stack that had been on top, shut the lid, and set the box exactly where she'd found it. Then she stood, breath coming hard, candle held high to check the room. Her hand was shaking. Not from fear, or even a bout of temper. This was rage.

René and his cousin had planned this from the beginning, never intending to have René marry her at all, or at least not for the reasons they had assumed. René had come for the Red Rook, and was using her father's financial circumstances to do it. LeBlanc must have already had his suspicions before the night she'd rescued the Bonnards. And then he'd played her from both sides, actually threatening her with the loss of René's fortune when he knew she was never going to get the marriage fee in the first place.

She took a long breath. How ironic to be so angry that there would be no marriage, when marrying René Hasard was what she had so desperately not wanted in the first place. She thought of him playing games in the sitting room—what a time to give in to pique and spout all those things about Mrs. Rathbone!—and the way he'd been looking at Tom's leg, as if trying to judge its fitness. And LeBlanc thought the Red Rook was a man. Sophia bit her lip. A net, indeed, and it was closing tight around her brother.

She blew out the candle, replaced it in her vest, unwrapped Mr. Lostchild's glove, and dropped it on the floor below the window. Then she gathered up the rope and stepped out onto the casement. The night sky was still overcast, very dark, a stiff breeze gusting as the remnants of the storm passed. She left the window open, climbing hand below hand down the rope, her mind going much faster than her descent.

With the rain gone, Cartier should be on the run by now. He would have a decent start before the glove was found and they set the foxes on the scent. That was good. But would it be enough to divert suspicion from Tom? It should be easy enough to prove Tom hadn't gone anywhere near the Holiday. Especially since he hadn't. She thought of that subtle trap on the chessboard. Did René think he had engaged himself to the sister of the Red Rook, or could he have the first inkling that he was actually engaged to the Rook herself? And what were they going to do about it if he did?

A soft swish startled Sophia from her thoughts, a whisper of metal slicing through the air. The swing of a sword. She kicked at the wall and pushed off, turning half around, gasping as she caught what should have been a hack through her spine as a glancing cut to one side. The rope swung crazily, spinning the world in circles around her head. She let go and dropped beneath the next swing of the sword. The blade struck the wall of the inn with a dull tang, severing the rope, and Sophia hit the muddy ground as if she'd landed on ice. Her stockinged feet flew forward and out, the back of her head slamming hard into the limewashed stone, and suddenly the cloud-black night was full of stars and fire and lights that exploded in red and green before her eyes. Like they had in the Sunken City, confusing the gendarmes, making the mob around the bloody scaffold panic and scatter. Then the lights were gone, and it was black.

Sophia came back to herself in the dark, mind as thick and slow as the ground she could feel beneath her. The Holiday. LeBlanc's room. Someone had tried to kill her when she climbed down the rope, and now the foxes were barking. Her eyes snapped open. She must have been out for only an instant because a candle or lantern was just beginning to glow from a window above her head, spilling out in a pool of curtain-filtered light. A form lay beside her, prostrate in the shadows, a man with a face she'd never seen. He was flat on his back, very still, sword in one hand, a knife handle-deep in his chest.

Sophia scrambled to her feet and her vision blurred. She swayed. There was pain in her head, a horrible pain in her side, and a commotion starting in the inn, sleepy voices raised in alarm. The foxes would be loose any moment. She grabbed the knife and wrenched it from the dead man's chest, thrusting it quickly through her belt. Then she picked up her boots and ran, hand pressing her side, blood running through her fingers as she slipped and stumbled across the muddy yard of the Holiday inn like a drunkard.

6

Sophia slid down from the saddle, the jar of landing making her skull ache and her stomach sick. She was back in the woods of the Bellamy estate, she realized, in the little shelter she and Tom had created for stashing a horse. The horse had known to go there even if she hadn't. Her head was fuzzy, the trees stretching and bending in odd ways, the light of a yellow sun cresting the horizon behind ragged clouds. There was something about dawn that needed remembering, something Tom had said, but she couldn't think what.

She threw the reins over a post, and noticed that something was wrong with one of her hands. She opened her palm. Red. And sticky. Her whole left side was wet and stained, and it hurt. She left the mare to its hay, breaking out of the tree line in a slow, lumbering walk.

Bellamy House rose up before her in a mist, a mismatched hodgepodge of stone and concrete built around decorative arches of red and white brick from the Time Before, a building mostly made beautiful by its age. She could see the roof, and the ledge and lattice path that led to her bedroom window, but for some reason the drainpipe seemed daunting. She would climb it later.

She chose an unobtrusive little door instead, sunk into the wall stones around the corner of the house, its weathered wood half-hidden by ivy. Slowly, and with panting breath, she drew out a loose stone from the house wall and retrieved the key beneath it. She unlocked the wooden door, replaced the key and stone as she always did, ducked beneath the ivy, and pushed the door shut behind her.

Stairs twisted downward, spiraling round and round in the dark. She took the steps one by one, unaware of time, until they ended in a room that was a cold blackness, smelling of earth and underground, wind moaning from blocked tunnels beyond the walls. But she didn't need a light; she could walk this room blind. She knew exactly where the little cot was, and that there would be a blanket. Tom always had a blanket. It would be a good place to rest. Just for a little while. She sank down onto the chilly straw mattress and closed her eyes.

When she opened them again she knew immediately where she was. Tom's sanctuary, as he called it, deep beneath Bellamy House, a room that was nothing but Ancient. Light moved over walls tiled with white and artificial red—the red seen only in artifacts from the Time Before—arched doorways blocked with gray stone making dull, ugly scars in the otherwise bright surfaces. The pillars that held up the ceiling were also arched, some with their steel exposed beneath chunks of missing concrete. Tom was very careful with that steel. He oiled it regularly, so it couldn't, after all this time, decide to rust and let the roof collapse.

Sophia let her eyelids fall shut again. Her head, her side, everything hurt. She tried to move but there was a heavy blanket covering her, and something tight around her middle. And then she stopped any movement at all. There had been light. And she smelled fire. Her eyes flew open.

Flames were dancing in the little brick hearth just a few feet away, driving away the chill, and across the expanse of cracked and patched floor, a little farther down the tiled walls, there was a star of light flickering in the dimness. A man stood with his back to her, tall and lean, illuminated by a candle, white shirt untucked over brown breeches, boots to his knees, and hair loose to his shoulders. He was running a hand over the display shelves, where Tom stored the objects he'd dug up from the grounds around Bellamy House.

The man picked one up, such a vivid blue it could be seen from across the room, bat-shaped and the size of a hand, with some sort of knob on one side, a gray cross, and four small circles inlaid with yellow and unnatural red on the other. She'd watched Tom puzzling over this item many times. He thought the cross and brightly colored pieces were meant to be pushed, though for what purpose neither of them could imagine, and he'd had no success looking for the word "Nintendo" in the university archives. It was beautifully worked, though. Like a piece of art.

The man held up the artifact, examining it carefully from all sides and underneath. Then he looked over his shoulder.

"Bonjour."

Sophia sucked in a breath. It was René. The René who was her almost-fiancé. The René who had come here to catch the Rook. And his hair, she saw, was indeed red. A dark russet in the candlelight. She hadn't even recognized him. She turned her head on the pillow, making it ache. Some of her memories were clear, straight lines; others were blurred and smudged around the edges like cheek paint.

René laid the blue object back in its box and picked up the artifact next to it. He held up a round, flat disk, speared on his finger by the hole in its middle, flashing like a mirror as it caught the glow of flame. Sophia clutched harder at the blanket, torn between the desperate need to know what René knew, and hoping he was not about to break one of Tom's precious things.

"Do you know what it is?" René asked without turning around.

"No," she replied. Maybe she could get rid of him before he discovered she was hurt. She needed to get to Orla. And Tom. She struggled to sound more like herself. "But you should put it down. It's made of plastic, and it's delicate."

"Yes, Mademoiselle. I am aware that this item is made of plastic." She could hear that note of amusement in his voice. "I think I will tell you what my *maman* says about these disks. She says that her *grand-mère* told her that her *grand-mère* said there are messages hidden inside these, thousands upon thousands of pictures and words, so well concealed that we shall never find them."

He glanced over his shoulder again. "Do you think that could be so? Do you think there are a thousand pictures inside this disk? Or were my ancestors only very imaginative?" He gazed at the artifact. "I think perhaps they were. My *grand-mère* was a terrible liar. She used to say . . ."

Maybe she should kill him first. "What are you doing here?" she demanded.

"Ah." He set the disk down in its nest of soft cloth. "It was very curious. I was walking your grounds, watching for the sun, and then I see there is someone coming across the lawn . . ."

Her fiancé wasn't to have left the north wing; Spear and Tom were supposed to be watching him—she remembered that. So he couldn't slip out to LeBlanc, like the dawn before.

"I thought it was your brother. I thought he was unwell, that he had been . . . what do you call it in the Commonwealth? 'Out for a bender'?"

Sophia did not correct him. How was he moving in and out of Bellamy House?

"I watched him take a key and unlock a door. And so through the door and down the stairs I came, thinking to be a useful future brother, and who is it that I find?" He turned fully around then, a grin on one side of his mouth. "And how are you feeling, my love?"

Some of the more hazy recollections in Sophia's mind were taking on their proper shapes. The rope coming down from the window. The man with a knife in his chest. She must have done that, though she didn't remember. The strange, foggy journey on the horse. But the memory she was having the most difficulty reconciling was the man holding the candle on the other side of the sanctuary. The voice was different. Deeper, not as smooth, and not nearly as Parisian. As it had been for just a little while in the sitting room the night before. And that was the only thing about René Hasard that was anything like the night before.

She lifted a hand to touch the back of her head. A large knot had risen at the base of her skull, just inside the hairline. She said, "I took a fall, I'm afraid. From my horse. I think I've hit my head rather hard."

"Yes." René was moving across the room now, lithe, and with very little noise from his boots. He used his candle to light an oil lamp that was hanging from one of the exposed crossbeams. "And you also seem to have fallen on that knife you were carrying."

Sophia reached down to her side. The sword cut. Who had the man with the sword been, and was he still alive? Surely not. And just how much had she bled? She looked beneath the blanket. Her vest was gone, her knife gone, and there was a gash in her shirt, the cloth around it soaking in a large, dark circle. Blood had also run down the side of the breeches, all the way to the knee. Then she saw that another strip of cloth had been tied tight over the wound beneath her shirt, circling her waist. She lifted her eyes to René.

"Did you bandage me?"

It was not an inquiry; it was an accusation. He had taken off her clothes. Or at least taken them off a little. The line of René's jaw flickered as he bent over another candle, a grin lurking again in that corner of his mouth.

"Please don't think me impertinent, my love. We are betrothed, after all. And Monsieur Hammond was not here to do the job this time."

Sophia clutched the blanket, watching René closely. He lit more candles, flame to flame from the one in his hand. The words KINGS CROSS ST. PANCRAS spelled inside a circle of Ancient red leapt to visibility on the side wall. Even the way he held his body was unfamiliar, controlled, with no embellished movements.

She tried to think. The rope and hook would be found, and the glove. That was to plan. The wounded—or more likely dead—man was not. And neither was this living one. They would have the foxes following the scent on the glove, the scent Cartier was leaving in a zigzag trail across the Commonwealth. But it would not take long for news about the events at the Holiday to reach Bellamy House. The net had drawn tight, and now she was the one caught.

"It does seem careless of you, my love," the different René said, still grinning as he moved toward the cot. "Riding alone, in the dark, with a knife out of its sheath. Will you make a habit of such things after we are married?"

She'd spotted her knife now. It was on the floor beside her vest. Well out of reach. "I don't know," she replied. "Do you often take walks before dawn?"

He stood over the bed. "I do not know. Do you often go riding past nethermoon?"

Sophia raised her eyes. René Hasard was dirty and mussed, with an open collar and stubble around his mouth, as unpredictable as his hair color. She raised one arm over her head, covering her eyes. The best shield she had at this moment was her charm, and, if he was anything like his cousin, the belief that a female would be incapable of climbing up a rope, sinking a knife into a strange man's chest, and spiriting innocent souls out of the Tombs. But surely even René was not this stupid? She was beginning to be afraid that he wasn't. She had to keep him distracted, at least long enough to find a way out of this room.

He pulled up a stool. "Are you in pain?"

"Some," Sophia whispered, giving the word the tiniest tremble.

"Look up at me, and watch the candle."

He held up the light and put a finger to her chin, peering down into her eyes. She watched the candle, but mostly she was watching him, trying to see any remnants of the man she thought she'd been engaged to. Even with the polish gone, René Hasard still looked more than capable of flirting with a girl at a Bann's ball. He raised and lowered the candle, moving it from side to side, the wandering light and shadows making the fire-blue gaze into something wild. Sophia revised her earlier assessment. This René would definitely flirt with a girl, but then he might also nick her purse. He sat back suddenly, and Sophia let out the breath she'd been holding.

"You have some concussion, I think," he said, setting the candle on the little table beside the cot. "Your eyes, they do not change quickly for the light." He reached for the edge of her blanket, and Sophia gripped it harder. This time his smile was a little sly. "You will permit?"

She permitted. She'd thought better of it, anyway. She watched as he pulled down the blanket, bashful through her lashes. The act of being coy was costing her, but at least she wasn't manufacturing the embarrassment; that much was real.

"And turn," he said, adjusting her body so that she was almost completely on her unwounded side. Sophia winced, this expression also unfeigned. He lifted the end of her bloody shirt, exposing the bandage and also her skin from her breeches to about halfway up her rib cage. She concentrated on the movement of the flames in the hearth as he undid the knot in the cloth.

"Where did you get the bandage?"

"My shirt, it is not as long as it once was," he said. "It is very sad."

She glanced at his face, but it was inscrutable in shadow. Then the air hit her cut and she hissed. She tried to raise her head up to see, but that was painful as well. She dropped it back onto her arm, and remembered to use the tremble. "How . . . badly am I hurt?"

René didn't answer, and still she could discern nothing from his face. He began probing the wound, cool air and warm fingers gently moving across her skin. His palms were calloused. She tried not to shiver. The fingers left her, and when she looked up, there, all at once, was the René she knew, the one from her Banns. If not in dress, exactly, at least in expression.

"Well, my love," he said brightly. "I am guessing that you would like to keep this little accident to yourself, with no one the wiser, yes? Do tell me if you disagree."

Warning bells went off in Sophia's head. "Yes, it would be better," she replied, casting her eyes down in a way that she hoped was demure. "My father would worry so."

"And your brother?"

"Yes. He would worry." What she really wanted was for Tom to come banging down those steps with his stick and tell her what to do with this enormous package of enigmatic trouble that was René Hasard.

"And what about my cousin? He comes to dine with us tonight, does he not?"

The warning bells were at full tilt now, and Sophia's head throbbed. She had completely forgotten LeBlanc's intended presence at their dinner table. Perhaps he would be caught up in his cross-country pursuit and not make an appearance. But that, she knew, was too much to hope for. She lifted her eyes to René. The blue was almost hidden by heavy lids.

"I do not see why this cannot be our little secret, my love." He leaned close and gave the end of her nose a tap with his finger. "When we are married you will keep all my secrets, yes?"

Then he was on his feet. Sophia bit her lip, watching him move to one of Tom's cabinets near the workbench. It was amazing that he could look so different, so different she was having a hard time looking elsewhere, and yet still manage to be so incredibly irritating. And dangerous. Very, very dangerous.

René was bent down now, rummaging inside the cabinets. He seemed to have already explored the place fairly well because he straightened almost immediately, emerging with a bottle in one hand and a glass in the other. He bit the cork, pulled it out with his teeth, and spat it onto the floor. Sophia felt her eyebrows rise.

"I do not share your brother's taste in drink, I fear," he said, wrinkling his nose. "But this should 'do the trick.' That is what they say in the Commonwealth, is it not?"

It certainly would "do the trick." The bottle was one of Mr. Lostchild's homebrews, used for cleaning the artifacts Tom dug up on the estate. Sophia had never known anyone to drink it but Mr. Lostchild, and he was no longer living.

She shook her head, meaning to refuse, and was immediately sorry. The pain in her skull quadrupled. She put a hand over her eyes. Her side burned like a hot poker had been applied, vomiting was not entirely out of the question, and her recently turned rogue fiancé was trying to get her drunk, or possibly decapitated, she wasn't sure which. She wanted her bed.

When the wave of pain eased, she found a glass of clear golden liquid on the table beside her head, and René with his untamed hair behind an ear, hunched over the candle. He was running one end of a needle back and forth through the flame. It took a moment for the significance of the needle to set in.

"Oh, no," she said. "No."

"You are in no position to refuse me."

"What do you know about stitches?"

"Enough."

"And what do you mean by enough?"

"I mean that my *maman* always let me help with the mending. You should drink what's in that glass, my love."

"You are not giving me stitches." Sophia had forgotten all about coy and moved straight on to temper.

René took the needle from the candle fire and considered her. "Should I bring your father, then? Call the nearest doctor? That Sophia Bellamy runs about the countryside in breeches falling on knives in the dark will make for excellent conversation, especially at dinner tonight. Tell me I am wrong."

There was that other voice again. Who was this man? René began threading the needle with a thin silk.

"I am an only child," he said, holding the needle close to the light. "Perhaps you did not know that, Mademoiselle. But I have many uncles. Six of them, and they are always in need of repairing, I assure you. The cut is not deep, and the muscle will not need my attention. You will have only the smallest scar to mar all that beautiful skin."

She opened her mouth, and found nothing to say. She'd forgotten how much of her skin was on display at the moment. René was smiling at her again, something slightly devilish. No, this René Hasard wouldn't be stealing a woman's purse, Sophia decided; it was the daughters that needed locking up. His smile widened, and now she was going to flush, and that made her angry.

She picked up the glass and drained it. It wasn't much, but the whiskey went gliding down her throat like soft, hot coals. She set down the glass, won a mighty struggle not to cough, and, still on her side, raised her arms carefully to get a good grip on the iron bed frame.

René folded her shirt up one more time, to keep it clear of the wound. The rough palm of one hand was pressed against her ribs, fingers bringing the edges of the cut together, and somehow she could feel the heat of this burning in her face.

"So you carry needle and thread about in your pockets, do you?" Sophia asked.

"My tailor insists. You can be still, yes?"

She nodded, head swimming even more after Mr. Lostchild's poisonous concoction.

"Relax," he said. "It will hurt some less if you do." He paused, waiting to feel the tension leave her body. She wasn't sure that was going to work, since he was the one creating it by having his hands on her skin. "Tell me about this room," he said. "Do you know what it was used for?"

"No, not what it was used for Before," she replied. "But the Bellamys used it for contraband, a long time ago. Tom calls it his sanctuary."

"Because of Kings Cross and St. Pancras, the words on the wall?"

"Yes." She sucked in a breath at the first jab and pull of the needle.

"Who was St. Pancras?"

"No idea . . . Mostly Tom calls it . . . that because he . . . likes to spend time . . . here."

"And the shelves?"

"He digs . . ." She breathed. René was going very fast. He had already tied off two stitches and was starting another.

"And what does he find?"

"He has buckets . . . of bits and pieces. Plastic, but sometimes cast metal and . . . carved stone . . ." The pain was doubling with each fresh prick and pull. "He thinks we must be on top of a town . . . or a city. You can't dig a well . . . or plow a field without hitting . . . something. Especially at the beach."

"And the tunnels that are blocked?"

"They go out to the sea, drop right away in . . . the middle . . . of the cliff face. You have . . . to climb down. The cliffs . . . must not have been . . . there . . . Before."

"Did Tom block them up?"

"Yes, there was too . . . much wind to use the room. But he was careful. The stones can come . . . back out . . . without hurting anything." Unlike René, who was killing her.

"And your brother keeps his finds? He does not give them over for study? Or sell them?"

Sophia took a moment to grip the bed frame. "Tom thinks it's a . . . crime to . . . melt such things. He'll donate . . . give them to the Commonwealth, all at once . . ."

"And they will either put them in a box or lose them."

"That's why he . . . wants to study them first. He writes down what he . . . learns."

"And what of all those powders on the far wall? In the kegs. What are they for?"

She held the cold iron harder. Those kegs contained Bellamy fire, her father's discovery once upon a time, most recently used to panic the mob in the Sunken City. It was Tom who had learned to give them sparks and colors, to make the explosions small in order to frighten, not kill. But Sophia was beyond thinking of a lie to tell about Bellamy fire. For the moment, she was beyond speaking.

"There!" René said, running a sleeve across his brow. "Twenty-two. That is not so bad. I am a marvel, am I not? My uncle Émile says I am the fastest in the city."

Sophia didn't answer. She was sure her face must be white.

He dabbed at the newly bleeding wound with the bandage she'd been wearing, and then leapt up, wiping his hands on the front of his shirt. Her eyes followed as he retrieved Mr. Lostchild's bottle, then widened as he got right on the bed and straddled her, one knee to her back and one to her stomach, pinning her legs down with his weight. Sophia realized what he was about, allowed herself a sigh, and got a tighter hold on the bed frame.

"Apologies, my love," he said, right before he tipped the bottle over the wound. Her body jerked of its own accord, but he had her held tight beneath him. She squeezed her eyes shut. He poured once more, liquid running down her stomach and back, not unlike the tears she could feel leaking down each side of her face.

She stayed still, panting as the weight of him left her and she heard the bottle being set back on the table. When she opened her eyes again he had taken off his shirt, ripping methodically, tearing away another strip from the bottom. His back was a little tanned, muscled, like the men of the Lower City. Not what she would expect from the Upper. And equally unexpected was the sharp glance of fire-blue curiosity she intercepted when his eyes darted toward hers. But the expression was gone almost before she'd known it was there, and he came back to the bed, standing over her with no shirt and a smile that came straight from the Bellamy ballroom.

"May I?"

She watched as he knelt down, lifting her body just enough to slide the strip of cloth beneath her, almost formal as he wrapped the wound again, and again, tight. While he was tying, Sophia reached cautiously, respecting the pain in her side, and grabbed the bottle from the table beside the cot. She emptied the rest of its contents into the glass, turned her face to brush the wet streaks from her cheeks, took a small sip, and then silently held out the glass to René. He laughed once before he took it, and by the time she'd gotten herself painfully upright, the last of Mr. Lostchild's whiskey was gone.

René sat next to her on the bed. "And how is your head, my love?"

It was awful. He reached over and ran a finger very delicately over the bump at her hairline, and when he put his arm back down again, it was behind her on the mattress. Sophia only just kept one of her eyebrows from rising.

"You never told me of the kegs," he said, voice much closer. "What does the powder do?"

Tom had said those kegs could blow Bellamy House right out of the ground, and now Sophia was thinking it was a good thing René hadn't gotten a candle too near. But either way, there was no one, she feared, who would be coming out of the sanctuary unscathed. She remembered to be coy and peeked up at René from the corner of her eye. "I'm sure I don't know. Tom is the scholar."

"Do you curl it on purpose?"

She drew her brows together in question and René again lifted a finger to one of the little spirals behind her ear. She was fairly sure it had dried mud on it. "Sometimes," she replied.

"But not when you ride?"

"No, not when I ride. You are so full of questions, Monsieur."

She was on high alert now. René had a look about him, something about the slightly parted lips. It was dangerous. And fascinating. She forgot her pain for the moment and waited, curious to see what he would do. What he did was lean in closer, loose hair brushing her shoulder, his eyes half-closed. He smelled like wood and resin; she'd thought it would have been perfume.

"You have such pretty skin, Sophia Bellamy. Like sugar on the fire. What do you call it?"

"Caramel?"

"Yes, caramel."

A draft moved across the flickering room, but Sophia didn't.

"And now that we have been so intimate," he whispered, voice low in her ear, "do you not think we should discuss that wedding, my love? Or . . ." He still had fingers on the other side of her face, playing with her hair. "Or do you need a statement from my banker first?"

Sophia didn't breathe. He was going to kiss her. She ought to say something, back away, tell him to stop. But she didn't. Instead she wondered what it might feel like to be kissed by a daughter stealer. Turn her head just a little, and she would find out. The air hummed, full of static, stubble just brushing along her jaw. Her eyes closed on their own. And then René's cheek slipped to her shoulder, leaning there for just a moment before falling straight down onto the bed like a stone.

She opened her eyes and waited, drawing a shaky breath, and when she was sure he was not going to move she lifted his arm from her lap and scooted off the bed, wincing as she stood. She looked at René as he lay facedown on the mattress, running a hand through the curls behind her ear, brushing away a few small grains of white powder that had stuck to her fingers. The same white powder that had been hidden beneath the pale stone of the ring that was hanging around her neck. The same white powder she had poured from the ring into René's whiskey glass.

Then she walked slowly to Tom's worktable, dizzy and a little sick, found the glass vial, refilled the cavity in her ring, clicked it shut, and one by one blew out the lamp and the candles. It took a long time. When the only light left was the fire, she looked again at the bed and sighed. With difficulty and not a small amount of pain, she got onto her knees and managed to put René's booted feet on the mattress, pushing one of his shoulders around so that he turned onto his back. No, definitely not Upper City. He had the body of a man who'd been working a ship. She threw the damp and bloody blanket over his chest. The sanctuary was going to get cold, especially for as long as he was about to sleep.

She banked up the fire, retrieved her vest and knife, breathing hard, and then paused again. For someone who had made it a point not to look at René Hasard's face, she certainly had stared at it enough today. He was still something wild, dark red hair everywhere, wrapped in a blanket smelling distinctly of homemade bevvy. But the daughter stealer had been replaced by someone different. A bit like Tom when they were little. Almost innocent, but not quite. And he was beautiful.

Sophia stepped back. René Hasard was not innocent, and therefore could not be beautiful. He had blood under his nails, not just hers, but the blood of the hundreds—maybe even thousands—who had gone beneath the Razor. Like anyone who chose to ally themselves with LeBlanc. And he would not be sharing anything he'd seen in this room with that particular man tonight.

She climbed the steps one at a time, a hand over her bandaged side, and when she reached the bright sunshine beyond the little door, she looked back down the curving stairs. She had almost let him kiss her. She should never, ever think about that again. She turned the key and locked René in the dark.

7

"**I don't** know, Tom. What should I have done?" Sophia leaned back into the pillows, having just vomited for the second time into the bowl Orla held out for her. She was glad she had at least waited until now for that humiliation.

"Let her alone," Orla chided. "She'll rip that cut open if she keeps this up."

Tom stopped limping about his room and sat down in the armchair, thumping his stick to take out his frustration. His room was on the ground floor, in the oldest part of the house, thick-walled, gloomy, and away from the nicer apartments. Which was the way he liked it. It was as far as Sophia had gotten after she left the sanctuary.

"It is well sewn," said Orla, peeking beneath the blanket, where Tom could not see. She handed Sophia a wet cloth for her face.

"I'm shocked a man like that would know how to do it," Tom commented. "And how in the name of the holy saints is he getting out of the north wing?"

Sophia shook her head. She didn't know. There was much, she now realized, that they did not know about René Hasard. They might not know anything about him at all. "And where is the other one?" Tom continued. "What's his name?"

"Benoit," Orla replied.

Tom turned to Sophia. "Did Hasard mention where he was?"

She shook her head. They'd been careless about Benoit—watching René, or trying to, but not his manservant, misjudging Benoit's potential in the same way they had always depended on others underestimating Orla. A stupid mistake. The kind that could get someone's head cut off.

"Then the question is," Tom said, "how soon might there be a hue and cry over his missing master?"

Sophia sighed. "Orla, go to the north wing and see if you can find Benoit. Tell him that René sends word that he's with his fiancée, and might not return until just before dinner. Make it seem . . . you can make it seem as if he's in my rooms, if you want. I doubt Benoit will question you then." Sophia ignored the soft swearing coming from Tom's chair. "We'll think of some other excuse before dinner. Perhaps Monsieur will be ill." Likely he already was. She looked to Tom. "Do you agree?"

He nodded. Orla, grim as ever, patted her head once and hurried out Tom's door. Tom leaned back in his chair, rubbing a rough chin. "LeBlanc knew the Red Rook would come. It was a trap."

"But I think," Sophia ventured, "that he did not expect the window."

"Perhaps not."

Sophia closed her eyes, trying not to remember the way it had felt to pull a knife out of a dead man. "Is there news from the Holiday?"

"Oh, yes. It's all over the countryside. Burglary and murder. They're tracking the scent west. Spear is with them. He was worried sick when you didn't come back. I thought he was going to tear the house down." Tom waited, but Sophia didn't say anything. "And the dead man was a stranger to you?"

"Yes. Was he LeBlanc's?"

"Must've been. He was a stranger to everyone. And who do you think killed him?"

Sophia's eyes opened. "Wasn't it me?"

"Did you clean your knife?"

"No." Sophia thought back to the fuzzy dark with the foxes barking and the unnatural silhouette of a knife sticking out of a chest. "It wasn't my knife," she said suddenly. "The handle was too thick. Did I have two knives when I came in here?"

"No, only your own. Where is the other knife, then?"

"I don't know."

"And more to the point, whose knife was it, who put it into the stranger's chest, and who else might have seen you climbing out a window of the Holiday?"

They were questions neither of them could answer.

Tom said, "We are in a fix, my lovely sister."

She nodded.

"But I am very glad you're not dead."

She smiled wanly from his pillow. She had considered long ago what might happen on one of the Rook's missions, what was sure to happen if she was caught. She had thrown her death on the scale, weighed it out against her future, and made a choice. And that choice had been a secret shame to her. It hadn't been that many generations since the chaotic centuries following the Great Death, when all that could be expected from life was feuding, war, and the struggle to survive it. Personal fulfillment just wasn't one's top priority when the children were starving or raiders were cresting the hill. But Sophia Bellamy had not been born into those dark times. She had been born into an enlightenment, an age of privilege, art, education, living in a way that her Bellamy ancestors would not have dared to dream. And she'd been more than willing to risk it, everything her forebears had struggled to achieve, for nothing better than adventure and a challenge to her wits. When it came down to it, Sophia Bellamy simply feared boredom more than she feared death.

But all of that had changed the first time she crawled into the Tombs. Being the Red Rook hadn't been about adventure then. Suddenly it was about blood and disease and death and the children who watched their parents' heads being tossed into coffins. It was about injustice and a city possessed. It was about stealing from Allemande and cheating the Razor. And knowing that, in her opinion, only made her actions all the more reprehensible.

What sort of person went to the lengths she did to dam a flood of evil, and then lay awake at night dreading when there would be no more evil behind the dam? Without the Red Rook, she would be nothing but the girl she was before and the girl she would become: a wife, doing just as her mother and grandmother had, doomed to managing a house and dinners with Mrs. Rathbone until the end of her days.

The truth was that Sophia Bellamy went to the Sunken City because she didn't know who she'd be anymore if she didn't. If she was caught, she wouldn't be sorry. She would only be sorry that the people she loved most would bear the pain of it.

"Tonight," Tom said, "let's go on with this dinner as planned. Can you do it?"

Sophia nodded. She had to.

"Hasard will be sick, and we'll send Benoit for Dr. Winnow just before dinner begins."

She nodded again. Winnow lived fifteen miles away and was nearly deaf.

"Then, after dinner, we can go to the sanctuary and deal with your fiancé." Tom sighed. "A shame, really. He seemed so harmless at first."

He was not harmless now. Sophia stared at the finely woven fibers of Tom's linen sheets. Either the motion of her head or Tom's words were making her ill.

"Blimey, Sophie," Tom said suddenly. "Don't look like that. I wasn't planning on murdering the man. I definitely prefer to bribe him. What do you think he wants?"

Sophia let out her breath. What did René Hasard want? She remembered the way his words had moved the curls near her ear. Had he wanted her to turn her head? That the thought had even crossed her mind seemed like treachery; that she was thinking it yet again was a capital offense. She'd never kissed anyone before. Had never wanted to. And the peck she'd given Spear Hammond when she was six definitely did not count. She felt her face flushing and blinked long, in case Tom could see her thoughts. She said, "I have no idea what René Hasard wants."

"Then that's what we have to find out tonight. What will be enough to get him to betray his cousin and his city? And to drop this marriage contract."

Sophia looked up sharply. "What about Father?"

"Father may just have to face up to it, Sophie. I wish we could've kept things going until I could prove for the inheritance, though God knows how I was going to do it . . ." Tom glanced once at his leg. "And this fee is mental, anyway. It's supposed to keep us from marrying outside the Commonwealth, when really it just makes certain that every strapped-for-cash father on the island gets in a ruddy boat to go find a son-in-law."

Sophia shut her eyes, heart aching like her head. If René was working with LeBlanc, then maybe there would have never been a marriage fee in the first place. But the letter had said he might go through with it. She thought about Bellamy House, every beloved and cobwebbed inch of it, and the money she would have given Tom, for a business. What price would she have paid for those things? "Tom . . ."

"Please, Sophie. It's one thing for Father to sell you off to a prat. It's another to sell you off to spend your holidays with the likes of LeBlanc. All in all," Tom said, "if it's between the land and my sister, I'd much rather keep my sister."

She didn't know what she wanted anymore. "And so Father will go to prison."

Tom played with the head of his walking stick. "For five years he did little, and for three years he's done nothing. I know he's lost without Mother, but . . . they're his mistakes, Sophie. Not mine, and not yours."

Sophia sighed. Then her fiancé would just have to be bribed. But if she pulled out those scales again, weighing the things René Hasard might wish for against what she and Tom could give, she was very afraid that the Bellamys were going to come up wanting.

They were going to come up wanting no matter what.

The waiting hall outside the Bellamy dining room was small but formal, awash with soft, mirrored light that did not show the shabbiness of the upholstery. They only used this room when important guests came to dinner, and when Sophia entered, that guest was already there.

Albert LeBlanc was again in his blue jacket, a white shirt and meticulously arranged necktie beneath it. Sophia smiled brilliantly over his offered hand. All of her was brilliant; she and Orla had made sure of that.

It had been tedious and exhausting to get all the mud and blood off her skin and hair, especially without soaking her still-oozing cut. She'd spent a good part of the day in bed. But she was back in the dark hair now, black paint around her eyes and plenty of powder to cover paleness and shadowed circles. Her dress was a rich burgundy, a color originally chosen to set off her skin, tonight chosen to not immediately show a bloodstain. She'd never been more grateful for a tightly tied corset, though there was nothing she could do about the terrible ache in her head.

"Good dusk, Miss Bellamy," said LeBlanc.

"You look quite pretty tonight, Sophia," said her father. He seemed sad about it, and a little surprised, as if he'd just remembered that she was not a child, and that he was marrying her off to a stranger. Sophia kept her manufactured smile in place, raised her eyes, and saw that Spear stood just beyond Bellamy, filling one corner of the waiting room like a blond and marble statue.

"Hello, Spear. I thought you were away on the hunt. After a criminal, wasn't it?"

He came to take her hand. "The chase was called off." His eyes bore back into hers, as if he would tell her something, but couldn't.

"Didn't the foxes have the scent?" she asked.

"They did," LeBlanc answered. "But I chose not to pursue the matter, and so left the chase. Petty thievery is not worth my time."

"But . . ." Sophia glanced at Spear, and then back to LeBlanc. "I thought Tom said that a man had been killed?"

LeBlanc gave a dismissive wave. "Nothing was taken, Mademoiselle, and why should I be concerned with a quarrel among thieves?"

"The dead man was a thief, then?"

"Really, Sophia," said Bellamy. "I wonder at Tom putting these stories in your head. It's not decent conversation. I should speak with him, I'm sure . . ."

While her father talked, Sophia leaned just a little toward Spear, to catch his low, quick words. "He rode straightaway from the hunting party on the flatlands. No way to follow without being seen. Missing from just after highsun until now. And are you all right? I . . ."

"And where is Monsieur Tomas Bellamy?" LeBlanc was inquiring. "I was disappointed not to be greeted by him. I had wished to . . ."

Tom came into the room then, his stick tapping, brown hair curling against the scarlet of his uniform, and if Sophia had not happened to glance at LeBlanc at that very moment, she would have missed it. LeBlanc's colorless eyes had widened just slightly, the forehead betraying a crinkle of surprise before shifting back to its unruffled exterior.

Sophia turned her head, frowning, causing a nauseating ache in her skull. She found the nearest chair and sat. Obviously, LeBlanc had been surprised to see Tom. But why? Why would he think Tom wasn't going to come? Because Tom wouldn't be able to attend? Because Tom was wounded, perhaps? She drew a sharp breath. Wounded last night, while searching LeBlanc's room at the Holiday?

She heard LeBlanc giving Tom an overly polite, very Parisian welcome. She must have left blood on the ground. Or something had been seen. But surely LeBlanc could not think her brother capable of climbing up through that window? The rope, the height, and the scent moving west, all of it should have exonerated Tom. Unless LeBlanc thought Tom's bad leg a ruse? One of the few things about the Bellamys that wasn't!

"Sophie?" It was Spear's voice, whispering from behind her chair. He had a hand on her shoulder. "Are you sure you're all right?"

Sophia lifted her eyes to LeBlanc, his face smug as he gazed languidly at her chatting brother. How careful they had been all day, planning every detail to give her an alibi, to protect her from René's dangerous knowledge, and all the while doing nothing for Tom because they'd thought it was done already. Sophia set her mouth. She was at peace with paying for the crimes of the Red Rook with her life, but she would never allow them to be paid for with Tom's. LeBlanc was just going to have to think again about the identity of the Rook.

". . . my young cousin?"

Sophia's gaze jumped up, Spear straightening just behind her. She had lost the thread of the conversation.

"Oh," said Tom. "I believe Monsieur Hasard is . . ." He looked to Sophia.

"Sick," Sophia finished for him. "Not feeling well at all. Such a . . . tiring day, and he was looking so—" She struggled for a word that wasn't "knackered." "—so overcome, I convinced him to stay in bed. I was concerned he might have . . ."

She paused, eyes darting to the door. Fast footsteps were coming down the corridor.

". . . that he might have . . . caught something . . ."

Someone was running down the hall, the clack of shoes distinct against the multicolored floor tiles. She sensed Spear's sword hand move. He must have a knife somewhere in his clothes. Then the door to the waiting room burst open, the resulting space filled with a green coat, complete with silver buttons.

"Ah! Here you all are!"

Sophia held her face still, hoping at least she hadn't made LeBlanc's mistake of showing her shock. René Hasard stood in the doorway, unshaven, unpowdered hair pulled back into a hasty tail, but with the heavy Parisian voice and smooth manners in full force, brimming with that oblivious cheerfulness she found so annoying. But it didn't matter now if René vexed every nerve she had. Not anymore. Not when the game was over. No time to discover how he might be bribed, no way to bring him to their side. The Bellamys had just lost. Utterly and completely.

"Tell me I am not late?" he said.

Sophia let the realization settle. Maybe this was for the best. This way it would be her neck bared for the Razor, not Tom's. And any proof LeBlanc needed was standing in rather handsome dishevelment in the waiting hall doorway, and bleeding just a bit into the bandage beneath her corset. Why could René Hasard never, ever be where he was supposed to be? Sophia threw her shoulders back. Despair made her angry.

"I was just telling your cousin I thought you were sick," she said to René. "Why, exactly, aren't you sick?" He must have the constitution of an ox; he should have been sleeping until the middlemoon. Tom cleared his throat, but Sophia just narrowed her eyes at René, daring him to answer. A grin quirked at the corner of his mouth.

"Such a darling," René said to the room. "And so considerate of my health. You'd have me abed all day, wouldn't you, my love?"

The discomfort this statement left behind had everyone frowning except Bellamy, who was still trying to work it out, and Sophia, who had been obliged to press her mouth tight against an unreasonable urge to laugh. What a parting shot.

"Always," she replied slowly, "my love." Though the look she sent clearly added her preference that he be in an unconscious or perhaps a non-breathing state. It made his grin leap onto both sides of his mouth. She saw Tom's scowl deepen, felt Spear's resentment in the air behind her. Then LeBlanc laughed, a sound like snakes slithering across a carpet.

"Well, isn't that nice," said Bellamy finally, fidgeting with his coattails. "Young people, so nice . . ."

Nancy, the cook, appeared in the doorway. "Your dinner is on the table, Miss Bellamy," she said.

Sophia jumped to her feet, as if she had nothing on her that could hurt, ignoring all the things that did. "Thank you so much, Nancy." She faced their little party. "Shall we all go through?"

The dining room was Sophia's favorite in Bellamy House, and she pointed out all its details with minute attention, since it was likely to be the last time she ever saw it. The ceiling and one wall were made entirely of metal and triangular panes of glass, very old—though it did not have the telltale lack of bubbles to make it truly Ancient—the pattern of triangles spreading up and out like a fan, curving to create the ceiling. At some point a singularly uninspired Bellamy had built more of the house right over and around the glass wall, ruining the room with darkness. But her mother had had lights installed into the empty spaces behind the glass, with sconces and hooks for oil lamps, so that on nights like tonight, points of light glittered from every direction, reflecting again and again through the triangular panes.

"Please find a seat, everyone," Sophia told them. They arranged themselves, Bellamy on one end of the rectangular table, Sophia on the other. René and Spear to her immediate right and left, LeBlanc beside Spear and Tom beside René. Lovely.

She shook out her napkin, then reached over her plate and passed a heavy platter of sea bass and potatoes to Spear, a move that hurt her side intensely. She gave the pain none of her attention. René

Hasard had her well and truly on a hook, but she was in no mood to let him watch her wriggle.

"Monsieur Hasard," she said. "I am so curious about how you're feeling, and how you spent your time today. No more teasing now. Please tell us all about it."

"Yes, tell us, Hasard," said Spear in the resulting pause. "I'd like to know that myself." Sophia thrust a bowl of carrots at Spear. He was like St. Just at her heels, always the faithful friend. Only this time he had no idea what she was trying to do. If he had, he definitely would not be helping.

"But the answer is so dull, my love," René replied, as if Spear had not spoken. "Did you not think the night before so much more . . . stimulating?"

So, Sophia thought, he was getting straight to the point: her whereabouts last night. It was just as well, because she was tiring of the games. She glanced at Tom for the first time and met his startled eyes. This was going to hurt him, but better this pain than the Razor. She gave her gaze back to René.

"Tell them," she said.

"Sophie . . ." Spear reached for her arm but she put it under the table.

"Go on," she encouraged, holding her back straight against the throbbing in her head and side. "Tell your cousin what I was doing last night. He will be so interested."

There was a soft clank as LeBlanc set down his fork. Again she exchanged a glance with Tom, and there was an expression on his face that she'd never had occasion to see. Her heart slammed rhythmically in her chest, so hard she feared that it was breaking. That look on Tom's face made her sure that it was. She turned again to René. "Well?"

René's smile had gone, his lips opening slowly to speak below two very blue, very inscrutable eyes. She didn't look away this time.

"Well, do tell, Mr. Hasard," said Bellamy. "A father should never be the last to know." He chuckled to himself in the silence.

"Miss Bellamy was out of her room last night . . . ," René began.

A sharp twinge shot through Sophia's head, but she met René's gaze without flinching.

"She was out of her room because . . ."

That corner of his mouth was quirking. How odd that she could be sitting in the Bellamy dining room, her life crumbling into ruins at her feet, wishing just a bit that the person doing the ruining had kissed her after all.

René broke into a sudden smile. "Sophia was out of her room all night . . . because she was with me."

Sophia blinked. René ate a carrot. She looked to Tom, who seemed to have deflated in his chair, while Bellamy, having paid attention to the conversation for once, set down his wineglass, distinctly miffed. Spear had not moved a chiseled muscle.

"Oh," René said, bringing a napkin to his mouth. "Oh, I beg your pardon!" He was playing Parisian magazine René now, minus the hair powder. "But, please, do not misunderstand!" He leaned over his plate to look down the table at Sophia's father. "Monsieur Bellamy, I would never wish to stain the reputation of my betrothed. Sophia and I were up all night . . ." His face turned back to hers. ". . . playing chess."

"Chess?" Spear repeated.

"Why, yes," Sophia replied. "Chess." She offered Spear a bowl. "Creamed peas?"

Spear took the bowl, visibly confused, though not nearly as confused as she was. René was very deliberately removing her from the hook, and she could not fathom why. But by pulling her off, he was also sticking another straight through the chest of her brother. LeBlanc had lost interest in their conversation, his pale eyes watching every bite that went into Tom's mouth.

"Yes," Sophia said again, addressing René and the whole table at once. "You have caught me out, I'm afraid. I couldn't wait to tell them. It must have been humiliating to be beaten so many times. And so thoroughly."

René smiled. "Except for that once."

"Yes," she agreed, meeting the blue fire of his eyes, "except for that once. Isn't that right, Tom?" Her brother looked up from his plate, where he had been deep in thought. "Tom was acting as chaperone, poor man."

"He has always been an excellent son," said Bellamy.

"Thank you, Father," Tom said.

"Did you ever get any sleep, Tom?" Sophia continued. "There was that one game, it must have been just before nethermoon?"

"Just after, I think," Tom replied. He looked from Sophia to LeBlanc, who had stopped eating his own creamed peas and was now intent on the conversation. Tom's brows came down, and Sophia knew he had just seen his danger.

"Yes, just after nethermoon," Sophia agreed. "Tell them about it, René."

René launched into an explanation of a game that Sophia recognized to be the only one they had ever actually played, after dinner in the sitting room. This speech was so boring in its precise description of every piece and move, and at the same time such a perfect homage to René's own cleverness, that Sophia had to admit the whole thing was a stroke of genius. She watched Spear's face go from incredulous to blank, saw LeBlanc cutting his potatoes into painstaking fourths, her father yawning behind his napkin. She wasn't sure anyone even remembered what they'd been talking about.

Sophia pushed the food around her plate, trying to pretend she had eaten some of it. The pain in her skull was increasing, the smell of the fish making her ill. And she had no idea what was happening.

"That is all so very instructive, René," LeBlanc interrupted suddenly, dabbing at his mouth. "But as a member of your family, I think I must point out to you the bad manners of bragging, especially at the expense of your fiancée. You would be sorry, I'm sure, if I had to speak to your mother about it."

It was the first time Sophia had ever known Spear and LeBlanc to be in agreement. But when she turned to René, she was surprised to see that this mild threat had actually carried weight. René's smile had tightened, like the grip on his fork.

"My apologies, Cousin," he said quietly, "and Miss Bellamy."

His gaze ran once over hers. He looked away again, but not before she had noticed his look linger pointedly for just a moment on her side, the side closest to him. Sophia wrapped her arms around herself, as if she were chilly, squirming her fingers around until she felt a wet patch. Blood. Not much, but it was soaking through. She wiped her fingers discreetly on her napkin and folded it inward, smiling at them all, her head full of words she could not politely utter.

"Though I am glad you brought the particular subject to mind, Cousin," LeBlanc was saying. "Because I wished to ask—"

"Monsieur Hammond," René interrupted. Spear looked up, scowling. "Would you find a shawl for Miss Bellamy? She is coming all out in . . ." He turned to her. "What is the word, my love? Swan skin?"

"Gooseflesh, I believe he means," Sophia explained. "I'm afraid I didn't dress warmly enough." She ignored the instant glances this statement caused to be directed at her bosom; she was too busy try-ing and failing to understand why René was shielding her. A shawl would cover the spreading bloodstain at her side.

"I have always thought my daughter should dress more warmly," Bellamy muttered.

René was still talking to Spear. "Perhaps the woman Nancy, or . . ."

Sophia supplied the name. "Orla. Would you mind finding Orla, Spear? She'll know which shawl to send."

"Of course," Spear said, looking much less thunderous now that Sophia was the one asking. He left the room in a fast, booted stomp.

"I was saying," LeBlanc continued, taking in every moment of their little drama, "that I would also like to discuss last night." He took a sip of wine, his signet ring with the seal of the city flash-ing in the light. "I would like to discuss the person who was in my room."

The clink of plate and glass stopped. Tom spoke first. "But I thought you weren't interested in that, Monsieur LeBlanc. You called off the hunt."

"So I did," he replied. "But that is because we were hunting the wrong man."

"How so?"

"Because the man I am looking for is wounded, Monsieur, and there was no blood trail to go with the scent."

"Wounded?" said René incredulously. "Really, Cousin."

"And what makes you say this man was hurt?" Tom asked.

LeBlanc's grin curled. "Because there was blood on the dead man's sword. And I do not think this man stabbed his own sword into his own lung, do you, Monsieur Bellamy?"

"I don't like such conversation," Sophia's father said, frowning. "Especially at dinner . . ."

Sophia watched Tom set down his glass, a little smile playing over his face. Of course he had already thought of this. And of course there was blood on the man's sword. Her blood. The blood that was seeping through her dress at that very moment. She should've taken care of the sword at the time. Would have, had she been in a fit state. But she had not been in a fit state. Blimey, she was tired. Her head was pounding to a beat of its own.

"Am I right in thinking this man, this thief who was killed, was a Parisian, Cousin?" René was asking.

LeBlanc nodded. "You are correct."

"Then perhaps you are the victim of a plot from our city, and should be looking for another Parisian? A traitor to Allemande?"

"Why, yes, René. It is indeed an enemy of Allemande that I seek. But it is a Commonwealth enemy, I think, not a Parisian one. Which brings me to an uncomfortable question, Monsieur Bellamy."

This time he was addressing their father, who Sophia was certain had not been paying attention since the talk of a stabbing. She leaned back in her chair. The lights behind the glass were wavering, blurring her vision.

"I apologize for asking during your excellent dinner," LeBlanc continued, "especially as we are to be family. But I have a witness who will swear to a Bellamy horse riding away from the inn after the murder of the Parisian. And this witness will also swear to a Bellamy being on the back of this horse."

More silence at the table. Sophia's pain multiplied, a persistent pressure trying to split open her forehead. Not Tom. Anything but Tom. She knew she had to do something, but she couldn't think what.

"A horse . . . ," said Bellamy, voice trailing away in confusion.

"Sophie, are you all right?" Tom said, at the same time that René spoke something soft and harsh beneath his breath. The word had been "liar."

LeBlanc leaned forward. "What did you say, Cousin?"

"I said I believe your witness to be a liar, Monsieur. I have already said that both Monsieur and Mademoiselle Bellamy were with me last night. Unless you are accusing their father, of course?"

Spear's boots came back into the glowing dining room, their noise an extra ache in Sophia's head.

"I think, young René," said LeBlanc, "that we should be very careful who we are calling a liar here. And I also think you should perhaps look to your fiancée. She appears to be in distress."

Sophia felt herself sliding from her chair. The world had shrunk to little pinpoints of glass and light, fear and fractured thoughts. Then there were arms around her.

"No, Hammond. I have her. Put that shawl over her."

She smelled wood and resin. Good. René knew not to rip her stitches. Not to show the bloodstain. No one could see the bloodstain.

"Women," LeBlanc said from some distant place, "are always prone to such things when upset . . ."

The starry pinpoints of light behind her eyes shrank, brightening once before they went out.

One of the flames behind the glass over LeBlanc's head went out, a puff of smoke glazing the triangular pane with a thin film of black. Tom watched René carry Sophia out of the dining room, Spear and their father following close behind. Tom kept his hands beneath the table. Then he turned back to LeBlanc.

"We should have a conversation, I think," Tom said.

LeBlanc's smile came slow. "Indeed."

"Here?"

"There is no such time as the present. And there is someone I would wish for you to meet. Paul!" LeBlanc called loudly. "Paul! You may come in now."

The other, seldom-used door to the Bellamy dining room opened. Out of a long-abandoned pantry came a large man dressed in rough cloth, and he was dragging a girl behind him. Her short blond hair was bedraggled, freckled face tear-streaked, blood running down both her lower arms and dripping onto the rug. Paul ripped the gag from her mouth, her sobs becoming louder as four more men came into the dining room, swords drawn.

"You've been making free with my house, I see," Tom said.

LeBlanc shrugged. "The Goddess has sent Luck to me in abundance."

Tom shook his head. "Don't cry, Jennifer."

The girl cried harder. LeBlanc continued to smile, a livid, swollen thing on his face, and no one noticed Tom replacing the table knife onto the cloth beside his plate. The tip of the knife was now one more thing in the dining room that was bloodstained.

*S*ophia opened her eyes to a late, slanting sun shining through the windows. But it was sun coming from the wrong direction. And the mattress was wrong—sheep's wool, not feathers—and the sheets smelled like wood. Cedar, now that she thought about it . . .

She sat up, gasping at the instantaneous pain in her side. She was in the north wing. A pile of clothes, male clothes, lay strewn across the seat of one of the great window arches, her burgundy dress over a chair, a sheathed sword flung onto the floor nearby. And there was a stranger, his hair just turning to gray, startling awake on a chair beside the bed.

"Who are you?" Sophia demanded.

The man scrambled to his feet. *"Je ne vous souhaite pas de mal, Mademoiselle . . ."*

"Dites-moi votre nom!" she said again. Then she realized she was in some sort of nightgown and snatched up the covers. *"Allez-vous en tout de suite!"* They both turned at a voice from the door.

"I thought you must speak my language, Miss Bellamy. Let me congratulate you on a very passable accent."

René leaned on the doorjamb, hair down and a little wild, arms crossed over the shirt he'd worn the night before, now untucked. Sophia scooted back until she was fully upright, breath coming fast. She considered giving him a dose of her Lower City accent, though she doubted he would congratulate her on that.

"This is Benoit, by the way." René turned his head to observe the man making his escape through the open door. "I think you have frightened him." He peeled himself from the wood casing and strode into the room.

"Where is Tom?" she asked. "And Spear?"

"Hammond is out."

"And where is Orla?"

"With your father."

"And why am I in your room?"

"Because not knowing exactly who my dear cousin Albert wished to drop into a prison hole next, it seemed best to put you where you shouldn't be instead of where you should. And where someone could keep an eye on you. Are you always this irritable when you wake, Mademoiselle?"

"When I wake in your bed with no idea how I got there? Yes. And I don't believe you. Orla would not have left me here."

René sat almost exactly as Benoit had, boots on the coverlet, chair leaning back against the wall on only two of its legs. Daughter stealer. "Your Orla is an excellent woman. We have had a very useful talk." He stretched his arms up behind his head. "I think that irritation becomes you, Mademoiselle. It puts the pink in your pretty skin."

Sophia gripped the blanket harder, feeling whatever pink might have been in her cheeks heat up to scarlet.

"I told you yesterday you had some concussion," he continued. "Why did you not tell the others when you got back into the house?"

She shook her head, a movement that, to her relief, caused very little pain. "They may have been distracted by my bleeding."

"Ah. I would have explained to them myself, but I was detained."

"Yes . . ." She was waking up enough to remember caution. "And why exactly were you late to dinner again? You never said . . ."

"Oh, no." He shook his head, the late light streaming through the window glass, making the red in his hair gleam. "No more, Mademoiselle. I know a sword wound when I see one, and I know better than to drink anything that comes from the hand of the Red Rook. I thought perhaps you were trying to drug me, and so you were. Thank you for doing away with my doubts."

She blinked slowly, taking this in. "And you got out of the sanctuary how?"

"Benoit, of course. Eventually. If there was one place he knew I wasn't, Miss Bellamy, it was in your rooms." A grin crept into the corner of his mouth. "But, please, let me congratulate you on your climbing skills. I have been going out the windows since I arrived, and yet never did it occur to me that windows might be your favorite way to come and go as well. How pleasant to find that we have things in common. Perhaps when we are married, we will not need doors. It was most unfortunate that I climbed out yesterday without my picklocks. But it did give me the opportunity to finish exploring . . ."

Sophia moved, snatching up the sword from the floor and pulling it from its sheath before René could get his boots off the bed. She straightened, barefoot on the oak planks, and held the blade out in front of her, relieved that it wasn't too heavy. René stood slowly, guarded, his smile gone as she circled her way around the foot of the bed, toward the open door, sword pointed at his chest. He took a step closer, then back as her blade made a flat arc through the air not far from the buttons of his shirt. He raised his hands. It was only a few more steps to the door, but René's legs were much longer.

"Let me go," she said.

"Not yet, Mademoiselle. We have things to discuss."

"There is no discussion."

René had inched forward, but he leapt back again as the metal swished past his middle. He grabbed the chair he'd been sitting on, putting it in front of him like a shield.

"When I go back to the Sunken City, it will be by my own choice," she said. She dodged to one side and René stepped with her. "All I want is to leave this room, and for you to leave my family . . ."

He threw the chair at her head. Sophia ducked and the chair collided with the wall behind her, smashing the water ewer, and while she was avoiding a second concussion, René darted to the bedchamber door and kicked it shut. He stood in front of it, arms open wide.

"Run me through. I give you my permission."

Sophia raised the sword, wary.

"But if you do, you will never hear what I have to say." He paused. "Just think of the curiosity you will suffer."

Sophia opened her mouth, unable to form a reply, when René tossed up both hands in frustration.

"You! Why must you ruin all of my shirts!"

Sophia glanced down. She had made her stitches bleed again. Just enough to stain her clothing, which was, indeed, one of René's white shirts, and not near as much like a nightgown as she could have wished. The sword tip lifted to where it should be, her other hand creeping up to her open collar.

"Listen to me, Sophia. I know you are the Red Rook. But LeBlanc does not. He has taken Tom."

The sword point lowered an inch. "What?"

"He has taken Tom to the Sunken City, where he will be executed for crimes against the Allemande government. There will be no trial. Tom has confessed."

Sophia held the cloth about her chest, the sword in front of her, the worn oak planks solid beneath her feet. And yet she had the sensation of falling, falling with the wind rushing past and no bottom in sight. It was several moments before she found the breath to say, "What do you mean, he confessed?"

"To save his sister, unless I am wrong. And I am not wrong." René reached over to the window seat and held out his gold jacket. For once there was no tease or grin around his mouth. "Put down the sword, Mademoiselle. We must talk."

"Jennifer Bonnard went missing sometime after highsun, when the foxes were tracking your man on the chase, just before the family was to have left Mrs. Rathbone's for their new location. Jennifer admitted to seeing your brother flee the Holiday on horseback, and identified him as the holy man who helped her family and eight others escape the Tombs."

Sophia stood at Tom's wardrobe, wrapped in the gold jacket, calf length on her, a new bandage and René's bloody shirt beneath it, staring into one of Tom's open drawers. He'd taken nothing with him. Did Jennifer really think it had been Tom in the holy man's robes instead of her? Or had Jennifer chosen between them? Sophia glanced over her shoulder at René, waiting calmly in the doorway with his arms crossed.

"What did LeBlanc do to her?"

"Hammond says her arms were cut. Some places were burned."

Sophia lifted her eyes to the window, where the last of the daylight was spinning the bracken field into autumn gold. She was going to break Albert LeBlanc, break him into a thousand tiny, evil pieces. She slammed shut the drawer that held too many of Tom's things and pulled the next, nearly empty drawer all the way out of its slot, setting it aside. She reached an arm into the cavity, grimacing at the pain from her stitches. "And you said Tom was bleeding?"

"Yes. But I am certain he cut his leg himself. There was blood on the knife at the dinner table and on his chair."

"And LeBlanc thinks a fresh cut made from a table knife is the same as a sword wound from the day before, does he?" She pulled out a packet of papers from their hiding place behind the drawer. Maps of the Sunken City, meticulously drawn by Tom, Spear, and her over several summers, plus a bag of Parisian francs and Commonwealth quidden. She was furious with Tom. How could he do this? But she was so much angrier with herself. "And Tom's bad leg; I suppose that's all just part of the disguise?"

"LeBlanc has a witness, and a wounded man in the right place at the right time who has confessed. He believes his Goddess has smiled on him, and he looks no further."

She wanted so much to cry that it really was infuriating. She left the wardrobe and passed René with her handful of money and maps, walking as fast as she was able down the corridor. Which was not terribly fast. René came along behind. "Do you plan on following me everywhere I go?" she snapped.

"Since you never stand still, it is the only way to have a conversation with you, Mademoiselle. I have stopped fighting it."

She rounded a corner and started up a stairwell. She had to get back to her room, get dressed, get Spear, and go get Tom. When René had also come around the corner, she said, "Did Spear follow LeBlanc to the port?"

"Yes. My cousin brought an escort of twenty Parisian gendarmes. You should be flattered he thought so many would be needed."

Sophia stopped and turned. René paused midstep just behind her, looking up from where he'd been running a hand over the Ancient, pitted metal rail. She caught another glimpse of that intense scrutiny she'd seen in the sanctuary before he smoothed it away. Sophia held the gold jacket tight, the cold of the concrete step seeping through the matting to her bare feet, and asked, "Where is my father?"

René's brows drew together, and then they both looked down the stairwell. There was a voice somewhere below them, deep, male, and near the front hall, insistent words bouncing off the paneling along with Nancy's vague protests. But the name "Miss Bellamy," spoken in a thick Manchester accent, was coming clearly up the stairs. Sophia clutched the bag of money and maps, the other hand going to her hair.

"It's Mr. Halflife!"

"Who?"

"From Parliament! He's heard about Tom. Is our wedding canceled?"

"What?"

"Your cousin is trying to execute my brother!" she hissed, holding her exasperation to a whisper. "No heir, and no marriage fee! Mr. Halflife has come to take the house!"

René's brows came down farther. "I thought Bellamy had some time before that happened?"

"If Tom is executed, there's no heir and they take the land anyway! And Father will be considered dependent because of the debt. Halflife will be wanting me to sign . . ."

René said something that Sophia had heard only in the back alleys of the Lower City, grabbed a flickering taper from the wall sconce, sprang up three stairs, and held out his hand. "Come!" he said, and then again. "Come!"

She went. Up the stairs, painfully, leaving the sounds of a full-blown argument behind them, and then René turned left down an unlit corridor ending in a large window, where another stairwell led to an upper floor. "What is in here?" he asked, throwing open a door opposite the stairs. He pulled her inside and shut the door.

It was a bedroom, one of its corners a small, round tower that looked over the cliffs to the sea. There'd been a time when all these bedrooms were in use, when an entire clan of Bellamys had lived under one roof, adding the rooms as they added the children. They'd been doing the opposite the past century. Closing the doors as they closed the coffins. The door to this room had been closed for a long time.

René was looking for another candle, but there wasn't one, only an empty, rusting iron holder. He shoved the candle he had into it, doing little to illuminate the gloom of coming dusk and dark-papered walls. He picked up a blanket folded across the bed and shook it, making a dingy cloud before he held it out.

"Take the blanket, Mademoiselle. You are not dressed, and the room is cold."

She was "Mademoiselle" and "Miss Bellamy" now, she'd noted, never "my love." She wondered if this meant they weren't playing games. She laid the maps and the money bag on a dusty table, took the blanket he offered without meeting the blue of his eyes, and went to stand in the round-walled tower. Outside the windows, the lower roofs of the house slanted downward to the lawns, and beyond that were the cliffs and the sea, a gray dark coming down on the whitecaps. She hardly recognized the view from this room. She hardly recognized herself. Tom was gone, and here she stood, hiding in her own house from a member of Parliament, half dressed in the half dark with a half-wild Parisian with red hair and almost all her secrets.

"You should stop moving," René said after a moment. He'd chosen the floor instead of a chair, resting his back against the wall, elbows on his knees. "Or perhaps you would like for me to sew you up again?" A smile tugged at one corner of his mouth. "I would not mind."

Sophia turned back to the window, hoping it was dim enough that he could not see her flush. It had not escaped her that if René Hasard had never drunk Mr. Lostchild's brew, then he had never been drugged. And that meant he had known exactly what he was doing in Tom's sanctuary. Saying those things in her ear, making her think he wanted to kiss her. Making her wish he had. He was good. Very good. She vowed to look only out the window. Looking at René was not safe.

"Is it canceled, then?" she asked, eyes on the sea.

"Tell me about this Mr. Halflife," René said instead of answering. The tease was gone from his voice. "Are you certain he is not here to help your brother?"

"Very certain. Parliament wants the land. There is a bay just down the coast, with a tidal river. They want a new port. Tom thinks it was Mr. Halflife who made sure the printing license was taken, to drive us into debt. He'd be more likely to put Tom on the boat than take him off, I think."

"And what about Hammond? He has been a colleague of the Rook, yes? Is it possible that he will not let your brother leave these shores?"

She shook her head. "He won't risk twenty gendarmes. He can't call the militia without Mr. Halflife or the sheriff, and the Commonwealth would say it's your own business to make sure you can't be carted off, anyway. So says our doctrine of self-reliance." She smiled slightly. "A convenient excuse for Parliament to be weak, that's what Tom says about the doctrines."

"Tom was militia?"

"Until he broke his leg. He still is, officially."

"And is that where you got your training, Mademoiselle?"

"He brought most of it home, yes." Tom had been training her regularly since she was twelve years old. And if LeBlanc thought she had worked her parry on the Bellamy beach for the last time, he was sorely mistaken. She looked back over her shoulder. "How do you know I have training?" Waving that sword around in the north wing definitely did not count.

"I notice things. That is all."

Sophia ran a hand through her hair, which was sticking out in all directions. What else had René Hasard seen that she was unaware of? "So, is it canceled, then?"

"What? Our wedding?" His face took on an expression of mock hurt. "How could you think me so ungallant?"

"You don't consider lying ungallant?"

"But I am so good at it, Mademoiselle."

"And you wonder why no one trusts you."

"Do you trust me?"

"Of course not."

"Then why are you here?"

"Because you have a dagger in the inside pocket of your jacket." He smiled with that same corner of his mouth, the corner she really shouldn't find so interesting. She'd forgotten she wasn't supposed to be looking. "And I would hate to suffer and die from that curiosity you warned me of."

René leaned his tousled head back against the wall, fire-blue eyes a little sly. "You are curious, Mademoiselle? Tell me what you are curious about."

She was curious about why he had really come to Bellamy House. She was curious about what they were doing right now, alone in this room. She wanted to know about this game he'd been playing, why his hands were rough, what red hair felt like, and what would have happened in the sanctuary if she had turned her head. No, Sophia thought, her curiosities were one thing she definitely would not be sharing with him.

Then all at once René was on his feet without a rustle, cocking his head toward the candle. Someone was coming down the corridor. She pretended not to know what he wanted for a moment, then sighed and stepped around the flame, shielding the candlelight with her body and the blanket. René took one of the pillows from the bed, its rotting case leaving a trail of gray feathers, and pushed it along the crack below the door, so their light would not show.

". . . can't have lost the both of them. That is very careless . . ."

Sophia's eyes darted up. Mrs. Rathbone. Was the entire county running about Bellamy House today? René met her gaze and put a finger to his lips.

". . . and I have something very delicate to say to her. It's no use asking me what."

"Mrs. Rathbone, Sophie is resting. She isn't well . . ."

Spear, and he sounded tired.

"And so where is she, then?" said Mrs. Rathbone, her voice quite close. They must have been standing on the back staircase, just outside the door. "And where is he, and what have they been up to? Tell me that! You'll have to keep a much better eye on her from now on. Could she be up here? And when are you going to stop being such a coward? Stand up for yourself, young man! Why don't you just ask and be done?"

"I don't know. I will! Just . . . Leave it alone!" Those last words from Spear had been a shout, coming from a distance as they moved to the upper floor. Sophia bit her lip. Spear usually kept his emotions under tight command. Not today. She closed her eyes. If Spear was back, then Tom was on the Channel Sea, sailing in chains to the Sunken City.

René turned from the door. "Your neighbor seems to believe that you are now Hammond's responsibility. That is interesting. I think she has also assumed that our wedding is canceled."

Sophia lifted her gaze. "How could she think you so ungallant?"

"I cannot imagine." The grin tugged again at his mouth.

Sophia looked away and pulled the blanket tighter, wincing at the pain from her side as she went back to the safety of her tower corner. Dusk had come. Their candle was already brighter in the room than it had been. She said, "You asked what I was curious about. I want to know why you didn't tell him. You came here to help him. You knew where I'd been the night before. But then you didn't tell him."

"I assume you are referring to my cousin. And if that is so, Mademoiselle, I will tell you that I came here to help him do nothing."

Sophia turned to him again, ready to protest, thinking of the half-finished letter. But then she held her peace. LeBlanc had left that letter to be found, of course, just like he'd left a man to watch his room. What better way to bait Tom than insinuate his sister was being used? Perhaps she had been. Perhaps she was.

René had settled into his place on the floor, open collar hanging loose, hair untied, elbows back on the knees of his breeches, but now his expression was thoughtful. "It is time to speak plainly, I think, Mademoiselle. I came to the Commonwealth for two reasons. First, because I had been ordered by the head of my family to marry a young woman named Sophia Bellamy. And since I am being truthful I will tell you that this was not any more agreeable to me than I think it was to you. But the head of my family happens to be my *maman*, and she is a woman . . . difficult to refuse."

Sophia could not tell if he meant that as an insult or a compliment. His gaze was on the carpet.

"And then my cousin comes to me, a man I have never seen in my life . . ." Sophia raised a brow at this. ". . . but high in the Allemande government, and he says, 'I have been told you go to the Commonwealth to be married to the daughter of the Bellamys. Then I will offer you a bargain. The Red Rook is on the coast; perhaps he is on the Bellamy land. Find this Rook for me, and I will let your *maman* out of prison.'"

Sophia felt her mouth open. "Your mother is in the Tombs?"

"I am the last of my father's line. Without me, the Hasard fortune goes to LeBlanc. But, like a miracle, Maman's freedom will be restored just as soon as she signs away my claim and makes Albert LeBlanc her heir. Which she will never do. Or, like a miracle, if I bring him the Red Rook, then my reward shall be Maman's release, and LeBlanc will allow the Hasard fortune to stay with the Hasards. Which, you can be assured, Mademoiselle, he will never do."

Sophia watched René closely, her vow to keep her eyes elsewhere once again forgotten. She doubted her ability to catch him lying, but she did know anger when she saw it. His fingers were clenched together, jaw tight.

"He ought to challenge me for it, if he wants my inheritance. The laws of dueling are not so hard to understand. But perhaps my cousin does not like his odds. So he takes the easy way, thinking to use me in the Commonwealth while he waits out Maman. That she will crack in the Tombs like underfired glass. LeBlanc is an idiot about women. As if Adèle Hasard has not run the business of our family for the past eleven years . . ."

"Your mother runs Hasard Glass?" Sophia asked. "Herself?" She'd assumed it was one of René's uncles, or a manager, since René's father had died. Such a thing was unheard of in the Commonwealth, and must be nearly so in the Sunken City.

"Yes, she runs the glass factory. Some of her brothers are part owners, but we all know that Maman has the head for money. But . . . we have other interests as well." René's blue gaze finally lifted to find hers. "As we are laying our cards on the table, Mademoiselle . . ." He shrugged. "Mostly, the business Adèle runs is smuggling."

"Smuggling?" Sophia repeated.

"We are smugglers, Mademoiselle." His smile quirked.

Sophia turned back to the darkness of the tower window and leaned against the wall, her legs shaking just a little. Of course they were smugglers. Why shouldn't they be smugglers? She was considering just how much it might hurt to slide her back down the wall and sit when she realized that René was standing right beside her.

"You will permit," he said before he scooped her up, carrying her the few feet to the end of the high bed. "No. No more," he said before she could voice any indignation, or anything at all. "You not only endanger my excellent stitches and all my best shirts, but now your refusal to stay still jeopardizes my gold jacket. It is what they call the last straw."

Sophia closed her mouth. She was so tired, and she liked the way he smelled. He must pack his clothes with cedar. She'd been smelling it on the jacket ever since she left the north wing. Which was not at all what she should have been thinking about. He laid her down carefully along the wrong end of the bed, adjusting the blanket over her legs.

"And in any case, Mademoiselle, you did not mind so much when I carried you last night . . ." He dragged a nearby chair to the edge of the mattress and sat on it backward. "To say the truth," he said, looking elsewhere, as if to spare her embarrassment, "we had to pry your arms from my neck."

Again she was hoping the dimness of the room hid her flush. What a ridiculous habit this was becoming. Sophia turned to face René on her unstitched side, head propped up on her hand. "And perhaps you might remember, Monsieur, that I was suffering from a head injury at the time? Is it any wonder that I would act insane?"

Both corners of his mouth were turned up now. And there it was again. Daughter stealer. She wished he wouldn't do that. She looked at the fraying coverlet. It might have once been dark green. "So, the Hasards are a family of smugglers. I assume my father doesn't know about this."

"I would think not."

"And what do you smuggle?"

"Plastics, Mademoiselle." He leaned over, elbows on the mattress. "It is noble. The city has allowed them to be melted down and reused for many years, but how are we to understand the past if we destroy it? And when they are gone, how shall we ever get them back? So Maman, Uncle Émile, and Uncle Francois, in particular, are noted collectors—purely a pastime for the owners of Hasard Glass, you understand—but we assist in the buying and selling of artifacts, entertain other collectors and investors, host showings and arrange transactions with . . . certain individuals who we know will appreciate them. Sometimes a discreet removal is necessary. Or, if an item is in danger of falling into unappreciative hands, we might feel the need to . . . liberate it."

"You mean you have people steal them for you."

"Ah. Uncle Andre and Uncle Émile used to do most of the liberating, but . . . well, I am better at it than they are."

Sophia blinked long. Of course he was.

"One must buy and sell something, and we are saving history from destruction."

"And I suppose acting like a first-class git gets you a better price, does it?"

"You wound me, Mademoiselle!" He appeared completely unwounded. "Our clients find me charming. And I find out things Maman and my uncles never could . . ."

"Because people think you're an imbecile."

"Being . . . how do you say, underestimated, that is never a bad thing." He shrugged, looking every inch the scoundrel. "It could be that I enjoy it overmuch."

She'd noticed. And yet he'd deliberately shown her something different during that chess game. She wondered why. "And so it's clients that you've been entertaining, then, ever since the night of our Banns? Is that right? Or were you hoping Tom would underestimate you so badly that he would be compelled to sell you his artifacts for half their worth?"

"Ah." René shifted on the chair, showing the first tiny glimpse of shame she'd ever seen in him. "I said I would speak plainly, and so

I will. I told you before that I was not happy with this arrangement between us. I thought that perhaps if I made myself very distasteful, that you or your father would break the marriage contract."

It almost made her laugh. Almost. She wished she could have told Tom. No bribery necessary to get rid of René Hasard after all. What had truly been underestimated was the desperation of the Bellamys.

"Don't look like that, my love," René said. He very carefully removed a long curl from her face. "Lovely as you are, you did not strike me as a particularly sweet-tempered wife." He paused. "At first."

Sophia met his gaze, forge-fire blue in the dim of their flickering candle, for once not immediately looking away. He was teasing her, she could see that, but there was something else behind it, and she could not tell what that expression meant. She studied the coverlet again. "So, your mother sends you to the Commonwealth to marry a girl you've never seen because . . ."

"She says I need a firm hand."

". . . to tame your wicked ways. But then she is imprisoned, and your cousin offers to release her if you find the Red Rook. And you do not agree to this because . . ." She left the question in the air.

"Oh no, Mademoiselle. I told you that LeBlanc is not going to release her either way, but my *maman* has taught me much better than that. I accepted LeBlanc's offer. I told him I would find the Rook, and so I did. But do not reach for my dagger." He sat back, grinning. "I agreed because I wanted the Red Rook for myself. Perhaps Adèle Hasard will not give in, but that does not mean I will let her rot out her years in an Allemande hole. It is possible I could break her out myself, of course, but when the opportunity came, I thought, why not go to one who has had, may I say, such spectacular success?"

Sophia played with a thread from a hole in the coverlet.

"And so I sailed to the Commonwealth to engage myself to a girl I may not have the inheritance to marry, to find the identity of the Red Rook and convince him that Adèle Hasard should be the next prisoner on his list. All so that I could have the inheritance to pay the fee for this same girl that I did not so much wish to marry." He put his elbows on the mattress again, and she looked up to find the blue eyes very close, gazing at her from beneath heavy lids. "Imagine my surprise."

Yes, she could imagine it. It had to be almost as extreme as hers was right now.

"Make a bargain with me," he said, voice low. "You are thinking to bring out your brother, yes? And Jennifer Bonnard? Get Adèle out of the Tombs as well, and I will help you. And there are many ways that I can help you, Mademoiselle."

Sophia frowned down at the bed, considering.

"Come to the city as my fiancée and you can travel openly. Nothing would be more natural, and my connections in the . . . less than legal circles of the city are many. I can give you the flat to operate from. I can get you whatever you need. I can even smuggle them out. I can smuggle you out." He waited before he said, "I think you will not be able to rely on the methods of the past. LeBlanc will be careful with this prize, and this will not be a mission the Red Rook will wish to leave to chance." He straightened the edge of the blanket. "I believe that you will need me."

He was right. On every single count. She'd been upset earlier, barreling about as if she were going to ride for the next ferry, when she knew this was going to take careful planning. Planning she'd never done without Tom. She kept her eyes down as she said, "If LeBlanc does confiscate your mother's fortune, and if you were to scrape together everything you had left, would you have enough for the marriage fee?"

"No. But if Maman is out of LeBlanc's reach, there may be things we can do. I could force my claim, make LeBlanc fight me. But what do the laws of the Sunken City mean now? LeBlanc may take it anyway. Or it may be that we gather our assets and flee. But I will not do so without Maman. She is head of the family. The flat, the ships, they are in her control."

Ships. Maybe that was how he'd gotten the physique of a sailor. "But if she gets out? What then? The assets that are in her control, without the money. Would it be enough for the fee?"

René met her eyes. "I do not know. Possibly."

But still, "possibly." Then getting Adèle out could save her father, and Bellamy House. Possibly. And what would she do, what would she risk, for even the slimmest chance to set all this right?

"Mademoiselle," he said. "Sophia." She watched him hesitate. "I would suggest that we leave the discussion of our marriage until after your brother and my mother are out of the Tombs. There is much here that is not known. Do you agree?"

Sophia looked down at her own hand, showing creamy tan against the rolled-up edge of the gold brocade. Two weeks ago she would have never believed that she would go to such lengths to marry anyone, especially an admitted liar and thief with a half grin and hair that shone like dark red fire in the candlelight. She knew she couldn't believe a word he said. She nodded.

"And Adèle?" he asked.

Maybe René could be trusted where his mother was concerned, but for everything else, she would have to be on her guard. The truth was that she found him fascinating, down to the tiny little pulse that she could see beating at the base of his neck, just beyond the open collar. And he could trick her so easily. He already had. She needed him, but she was vulnerable, and she could never let him know it. She could not allow him to manipulate her. She looked up.

"Yes. Help me get Tom and Jennifer out, and I'll get your mother, too."

This smile came slower onto René's face. He took her free hand and lifted it to his lips, like he was the one wearing the gold brocade, like they were standing in the Bellamy ballroom. His mouth was warm on her hand. "Agreed," he said. "And you may even enjoy it, Mademoiselle . . ."

Sophia jumped hard as the door to the bedroom flew open. René's gaze darted up, and Spear stood looking in at them, a stampede that had come to an abrupt halt in the doorway. Feathers from the decrepit pillow floated gently to the carpet. Sophia pulled her hand from René's and pushed herself upright.

"Spear, we . . ."

But her irrational need to explain was interrupted by Mrs. Rathbone forcing her way around Spear, a feat that took considerable strength, especially considering the size of her flower-trimmed hat. A *Wesson's* page seventy-four.

"Right! You said there were voices, and . . . Well, really!" exclaimed Mrs. Rathbone, taking in the room, the bed, and specifically Sophia's attire, which obviously all belonged to René. Then she dismissed the situation with a wave of the hand. "Sophia. I had no idea. But I'm sorry to say I was only too happy to be part of Tom's schemes, not knowing it was Tom, and that I would do it again. So to say the truth, not sorry at all."

Sophia laid down her head.

"And now I think it might be good for my health to visit my sister in the Midlands, don't you think? And you should come with me. Especially now . . ." She gave René a sidelong glance. He came across the room and bowed over her hand, the man of the magazine despite the disarray.

"You bring spring into the autumn," he said, the heavy Parisian accent back. Sophia saw Spear's eyes open wide before she threw an arm over her head.

"I've always said you were a charmer," Mrs. Rathbone giggled. "Remember that I was the one that said it. Now listen to me, Sophia. People are going to be beastly. They were holding off on the beastly before, but now that Tom is caught it's ten times worse and there will be no holding back at all. And Mr. Halflife was here, wanting you to march down the stairs and sign over the deed—at once, I should say. I know you won't. Not yet. That's why I've come to say that I think you should sell me the house."

Sophia moved the arm from her eyes.

"I can't give you near what it's worth, of course, but I think you could come close to the debt and keep Bellamy out of jail. We can't have the whole family locked up. It would be indecent. Especially with the state your father's in . . ."

Sophia sat up instantly, gasping as she pulled on her stitches. She looked to Spear. "What about Father?"

"That's why I've been trying to find you, Sophie. Orla says you need to come. Now."

9

"*Father?*"

Bellamy sat in the armchair of his bedchamber, facing the window that looked out over the sea. There was nothing there to see but blackness. His hair, once exactly like Sophia's and Tom's, was a thin, disheveled mass over his head, his hands folded carefully on top of the blanket Orla had laid across his lap. But his room was destroyed. The furniture toppled, pictures flung from the walls, broken glass crunching into the rugs beneath their feet. Sophia had put on Bellamy's slippers just to enter. Now only his breath and the occasional blink showed that he was even alive.

Sophia knelt on a pillow beside him, a hand on his arm. Orla stood just behind her, Spear near the door, hands in pockets, towering over a tearful Nancy. Sophia said his name again, but Bellamy didn't respond.

"It's Sophie, Father. I just want you to tell me that you're all right."

Bellamy never took his eyes from the window, but this time rasping words came from his mouth. "You did this."

Sophia looked around the room and then up at Orla, perplexed. Orla's heavy brows were pushed together. Bellamy spoke again, his voice as broken as the glass.

"You think because I do nothing that I know nothing. You think that I don't know what it means when your face doesn't appear for days, that I believe every lie Orla tells me. That I don't know what is happening when footsteps run across my roof. That when I read that foul Parliament newspaper, I don't know where you've been."

"Father, I . . ."

"And now they will kill my son, the last of the Bellamys."

"Father . . ."

"They will kill him because of you. Everything is lost because of you."

If he had slapped her, Sophia could not have felt more of a blow. She sat back on her heels, breathing hard.

"And what would you have had me do, Father? Take up painting and visit the neighbors while the people of the city suffer and die?"

"I would have had you remember your duty! Tom always remembered what he owed to his family."

The injustice of this cut through the reserve that usually stilled her tongue. "How dare you remind me of my duty? I have not forgotten what I owe my family. I was sacrificing my entire future for this family. And that is your fault, Father!"

Bellamy did not answer, only moved his arm away from his daughter's hand.

"You sold me off because you did nothing. Nothing! For me or Tom! And what duty did you remember when Aunt Francesca was taken to the Tombs? Mother's own blood! You would have let them cut off her head!"

His face crumpled. "It is my own son's head they will take now. My dear son's . . ."

She stood up, holding her hand against her side. "I am not like you. I can't sit in my chair, doing nothing. Wasting my days wallowing in grief. I will not . . ."

"I will always grieve."

"You have thought of nothing but your grief since Mother died. But you have children, Father. Two of them!"

"I have only one child now. And he is to die."

Sophia stepped back, feeling every ounce of force from this second intended slap. Bellamy stared out the blank window, a single tear rolling down his cheek.

"Say to your mother that I have sent you to your room," he said. "And that she is to tell Orla you're to have no dinner. Mind that you do that, Sophia! Tell your mother I said you must do as you're told!"

Sophia felt Orla's hand on her back, tugging gently on the musty blanket she still held around the gold jacket. "Come away," Orla whispered. "Come, child."

Sophia turned away from her father and walked carefully through the debris, Orla's arm around her waist. Spear moved toward them but Orla held up a hand. "Let me," she said simply. Spear stepped back, running a hand over his unmussed head. Nancy was still standing in the doorway.

"I'll watch over him tonight, Miss Bellamy," Nancy whispered. "And, Miss Bellamy . . ."

Sophia looked up. Nancy had been cooking her meals since she was eight years old, her face as much a part of Bellamy House as the red and white bricks.

"I just wanted you to know that it's a shame . . . a terrible shame that I couldn't hear a word that was said just then."

"Thank you, Nancy," Sophia said, kissing her once on the cheek. She hadn't done that since she was little.

Orla guided Sophia away from her father's room and through the dark hallways of Bellamy House, walking slowly. Neither of them spoke for a long time, until Orla said, "He doesn't know what he's saying. He hasn't been right since your mother died. His mind has been failing for a long time, and this business has pushed things to the edge. You know that's so."

Sophia nodded. Knowing did not make the pain of it any less. "What do I do?" she whispered. "I don't know what to do."

"First is to eat. Second is to sleep and let that cut heal," Orla said sensibly, her no-nonsense approach to life unshaken. She pushed open Sophia's door. "I'll sit by your bed until you do. And third, we'll just see about bringing him his son back."

LeBlanc pushed open the door to Tom Bellamy's cell. The sound of Jennifer Bonnard's screaming rang from her prison hole, echoing through a round, open space carved deep within the Tombs. There were just five cells here: Fate's special place for special prisoners.

LeBlanc waited, examining his manicured nails as Tom Bellamy struggled down a long winding set of stone stairs, his bad leg bloody, only kept from falling by the two gendarmes that were escorting him. It took a long time before they got Tom to the open cell door and tossed him through. He landed on his bloody leg with a grunt. When he was shackled LeBlanc shut the door and Gerard turned the key.

But LeBlanc did not go. He stood still, frowning at the sandy floor while Jennifer cried and Gerard and his gendarmes waited. Renaud, standing just a few steps behind, ran a nervous finger beneath his collar, sensing the disquiet.

LeBlanc said, "I think I would like to hear again from our informant in the Commonwealth, Renaud. Send the message tonight with the fastest rider we have, and I will require an immediate reply. And, Gerard, have one of your gendarmes quiet that girl."

Gerard nodded to his men, Renaud bowed, and LeBlanc seethed until well past nethersun the next day, when the answer from his informant arrived. He read the contents, read them again, then hurled the message into the fire, watching the paper writhe until it blackened and disintegrated into ash.

He walked out his office door, waving Renaud away, and stepped into the lift, taking it all the way down the center of the white stone building, through the ground level of the Upper City and down through the cliff itself, where it stopped at the first level of the Tombs. He walked alone through the tunnels, listening to the burble of misery that was the music of the prison, and unlocked a metal door. Down the steps, down and down again to Fate's special cells, savoring the quiet in which he would vent his anger. He turned the key, and the door of Jennifer Bonnard's prison hole swung open.

Spear pushed open the door of his farmhouse, hinges creaking in the dim. He strode forward to light a lamp while Sophia waited, the others filing in behind, bringing the sharp air of an autumn night with them.

When Sophia had finally opened her eyes earlier that day it was to Orla packing her things in the light of a sun that was long past its height. Her fiancé, Orla had informed her, had not slept the day away. Instead he had met early with Spear, and then had a talk with Mrs. Rathbone, asking the woman to do him the personal favor of letting it be known that Sophia Bellamy and Monsieur Hasard would be traveling with her the next day to her sister's home in the Midlands—when, in fact, they wished to remove to an undisclosed part of the Commonwealth to "discuss their options."

Mrs. Rathbone had been more than happy to be included in one more piece of subterfuge, René had reported, especially if it meant keeping Sophia away from Mr. Halflife. If Mr. Halflife couldn't find Sophia, then no deeds could be signed, and Sophia could consider Mrs. Rathbone's offer to buy Bellamy House and its lands.

"She's better off selling it to me than giving it to Halflife," Mrs. Rathbone had said, "but don't forget, there's not many days left, and they'll take Bellamy to prison no matter what he says or what he doesn't . . ."

Bellamy had stopped speaking, Nancy had said, and did not move from his chair.

". . . and she can't hide forever. So don't be away for long! You leave at dawn, I presume? Or middlesun? And where are you going again? I can recommend some excellent little places in Manchester . . ."

But René had only smiled, not choosing to divulge that "remove to an undisclosed part of the Commonwealth" meant a mile trek down the A5 in the dead of night, taking the turn onto Graysin Lane, and stepping through the door of Spear Hammond's farmhouse.

Light blossomed from the lamp in Spear's hand, showing a strong, plain sitting space, low-ceilinged and timbered, an Ancient piece of steel girder forming the fire lintel. A fishing rod hung across the chimney, hawk feathers gathering dust in a vase in the window. Very much a man's room. Spear stood with the lamp in one hand and now a candle in the other, shifting his feet while the sound of Cartier riding a horse with padded hoofs thudded softly away down the lane. Orla had insisted that Sophia should not walk. She was probably right.

"Wait here, Sophie, and I'll go light the bedrooms," Spear said finally, leaving the candle and taking the lamp.

Orla and Benoit followed, arms laden with bags, St. Just's claws skittering after them up the stairs. Sophia sat straight-backed on the overstuffed couch, making a study of her hands while René dropped into a cushioned chair beside the hearth. He had his hair tied back, unpowdered, and she wondered vaguely where the plain black jacket and tall boots he was wearing could have been hidden when she searched his room. Was this version of René the real one, she mused, or just another persona he took on and off with the season? It was still safer not to look at him.

"So, Mademoiselle," he said into the quiet. "You have made your grand escape. Now tell me what you are thinking. How long will we need to prepare before we sail to the city?"

"I need the numbers of the prison holes. Two days, maybe three, and we should know where they are." The normal waiting period for execution was fourteen days, to extend the period of misery and suffering, Sophia supposed. She wanted her brother out in five. The thought of Tom in a prison hole was unbearable.

"You have ways to get this information, I assume."

"Of course. The message went on the dusk boat."

René had his brows drawn down. "You will need more time than that to heal, Mademoiselle."

She lifted a hand to the bandage under her shirt, just above the waistline of her breeches. She was sore, scabbed, and a little swollen, though not in terrible pain, not as long as she was tightly bound. And the knot on her skull was shrinking. But it was true that as the Rook, she would be limited. She went back to studying her hands. The things she'd seen in the Tombs were true, too, and she'd not forgotten Jennifer's arms. Time for her to heal might not be a luxury that either Tom or Jennifer, or perhaps even Madame Hasard, could afford.

René leaned forward in his chair, elbows on knees. "Allemande is a man of . . . let me think of the words . . . a man of standards. He cares for the look of things. Murder is all well, as long as it has the appearance of the law, yes? And the execution of the Red Rook, that will be an event for everyone's eyes."

Sophia looked up. René was telling her that no matter what happened, LeBlanc would have to ensure that Tom looked well enough for a public scaffold.

"Have you ever been inside the Tombs?" she asked. He shook his head, and Sophia kept her silence. There were many, many things that did not show. It was good of him, she supposed, to try to reassure her. She would be smarter to discern his motive, not trust in his goodness.

René's fingers tapped restlessly on the chair. They could hear Spear moving about upstairs, and Orla and Benoit. "How long has he lived here?" René asked. He meant Spear.

"Since birth, I think." Spear's father had put back money for his son very early. Between the two of them, Spear had saved enough to prove his fitness for inheritance on the day he turned eighteen. "But he's spent most of his time at our house since his father died. Father practically raised him." At least as much as Bellamy had raised anyone.

"Ah," René replied.

Sophia felt the little line forming between her brows. "'Ah,' what?"

"Raised like your family, but not your family. That would explain it."

"Explain what?"

"Why he thinks that you belong to him, Mademoiselle."

That made her lift her gaze. "He does not think that."

"I only talk of what I see."

Sophia opened her mouth to protest further, but then heavy steps came down the small staircase. Spear and his lantern were back. He was huge in this room, Sophia realized. He had to stoop strategically to avoid the ceiling beams. Spear set the lantern on the mantel and came to the couch with her shawl in his hand, the same one he'd fetched during the disastrous dinner with LeBlanc.

"Orla said to bring you this until we've got the fires going." He laid the shawl on her shoulders, his hand lingering, brushing across her bare neck before he moved away.

Sophia shivered, though not with cold. She watched as Spear moved about the room, a small smile on his statuesque face, setting this and that to rights, putting an extra cushion on the couch. For her. Sliding a bowl of shelled nuts a little closer on the table. For her. Now moving down the passage and into the kitchen to boil water for willow bark tea. For her. Just as he'd always done.

Her eyes went to René, who was uncharacteristically still in his chair, the deep blue of his eyes watching her think. Sophia stood suddenly, letting the shawl cascade over the cushions.

"Would you tell Spear I'm going to bed?"

René's expression was inscrutable. "Another grand escape," he said. "Perhaps I will try going to bed myself, the next time I wish to run away."

She had absolutely nothing to say to that. She was nearly to the stairs when Spear called out, "Sophie, wait." He had come down the passage from the kitchen, ducking under the door frame. "Let me . . . Orla says you have to drink this tea. For pain."

"No need. I'll have some in the morning."

"Then I'll show you your room."

"It will be the one with Orla and a fox in it."

"But . . ."

René leapt to his feet. "Monsieur Hammond, if you wish to speak to Miss Bellamy, please do not let me stop you. I will give you my chair." He was across the floorboards before Spear could answer, pausing beside her at the bottom of the stairs. "I think I should go to bed," he said near her ear, "as fast as I can. Don't you think I should, Mademoiselle?"

Then he was away and Spear was waiting. Sophia went again to the couch, wrapping herself in the shawl before sitting back down. It was awful when the people you didn't want to be right always were. Spear sat in the chair René had vacated. It looked too small for him.

"Thank you for the use of the house," Sophia said before he could start.

"I'm glad to . . ."

"Did I tell you the Bonnards were safely delivered? They will be called 'Devereaux' now." She did not mention their pleas for their daughter.

"Yes, I . . ."

"Durant—or the former Ministre of Defense—is only a few miles away. I'm glad they will have at least one person they know. They . . ."

"Sophie, it seems like you don't want to hear what I have to say."

She bit her lip and lowered her eyes.

"I wanted to tell you that I spoke with Tom. Before he left."

Her gaze jumped up to meet Spear's. His face was so extremely perfect she found herself wishing it had a blemish.

"We only had a moment, but he told me about getting the marriage contract broken. In fact, he told me to make sure it was broken. No matter what I had to do." He paused, gauging her reaction before he said, "And it makes sense, Sophie. You can see that, can't you? Tom said to tell you to let the estate go. To break the contract, so we can start fresh when this is over."

Something about the word "we" made her look at Spear sharply. "Is that what he said? That 'we' will start fresh?" Sophia waited while

Spear looked uncomfortable. "Tom meant all three of us? He knows I'm coming to get him?"

"I think he assumed you couldn't be stopped, Sophie. But he meant . . . I think he meant just in case . . . things don't work out." Spear reached out and took her hand. "Actually, when he said 'we,' Sophie, he meant you and me."

Sophia stared at her hand in Spear's, numb with surprise.

"And that makes sense, too, don't you think? I think it does." When she didn't say anything, he continued, "And I've been thinking that if all that's so, then there's no need to include Hasard in any of our plans now. You don't owe him anything. Or his mother. We can get Tom and Jennifer out without him."

"But . . ."

"The last thing Tom said to me was that Hasard couldn't be trusted. He's a liar, and he's playing his own games, Sophie. Let's get Tom, and let the rest of it go. There's still this house, and the farm. We'll move on, like Tom said . . . together. You know that would be . . . a good thing. Don't you?"

"Spear . . ." She shook her head, gently removing her hand and putting it in her lap. "Listen to me. If Tom said that, then . . . he was talking out of turn. I'm not . . ." She took a breath. "I don't think now is the time to be talking about it."

"You know it's what everyone expects."

Sophia felt her eyes widen. Did they? "Spear, I gave my word to René, to help him get his . . ."

"You gave your word," Spear repeated. The acid in his voice took her by surprise, just as much as the way he'd held her hand. "And what about the marriage? Did you give your word on that, too? Because I thought that was Bellamy's doing."

Sophia stood up a little too fast. She wrapped an arm tight

around her wounded side. "Actually, Spear, I don't particularly fancy marrying anyone at the moment. And I think you'll find that my fiancé was no happier about being engaged to me than I was to him. But I don't intend to discuss it again with anyone, not until Tom, Jennifer, and Madame Hasard are out of the Tombs. Is that clear?"

Spear didn't answer. He was still, fingers tented over his perfect face. He looked so cast down, like when she was small and had acted unreasonably petulant because he'd won their race to the top of the oak tree. She'd felt guilty then, too. She softened her tone.

"I have to concentrate on getting them out. Nothing else. Surely you can see that?"

Spear looked up. His eyes were a cool, clear blue, as far from the smoldering fire of another set of blue eyes as could be. And they were very sincere. "Let's go on our own," he said. "Like we always have."

"I'm not going to break my word. Not without reason."

Spear sat back, chair creaking in the quiet. The look on his face made her heart twist. Tom was a brother to him, too. He couldn't be worried any less than she was.

"But I will be careful. Very careful. I can promise you that. All right?" She waited, and when he didn't reply, she put a hand on his shoulder and kissed the top of his head, the same as she'd done after the incident of the oak tree. She left him in his chair, taking the stairs as fast as she could with heavy limbs, hand against the pain in her side.

She made the turn at the narrow landing and saw a figure in the dim, hair so red there could be no wondering who it was. René leaned against the wall at the top of the staircase, arms crossed, waiting for her. She came up the last step before she whispered, "You were eavesdropping, weren't you?"

"Yes. But I am a very honest eavesdropper, as you can see." He was also holding his voice low, but she could hear the anger in it, loud and clear, like she'd heard in the dilapidated bedroom. "Do you think I am lying to you?" he asked. "Do you?"

"Yes." She was surprised by the question. He had to be lying about something.

He took a step closer, voice a growling whisper. "I had a part to play, Mademoiselle. As did you. But I am not playing one now, and I have told you nothing that was not true. I swear that." The fire-blue eyes searched hers. "Do you believe me?"

She didn't know what she believed. She was tired, and upset, and this anger of René's seemed to have come out of nowhere, just like the direction of Spear's conversation below.

"Do you believe me?" he said again.

The only light was from a ceiling lamp hanging farther down the corridor. Much of his face was in shadow, but something about the line of his jaw was making her thoughts pause, like in the sanctuary, when she'd forgotten pain in favor of inquisitiveness. She wondered what stubble would feel like beneath her palm.

"Listen to me. I told you once that you do not see because you will not look. Open your eyes. Why might Hammond tell you Tom said those things? What does Hammond want? Think!"

She shook herself awake, wishing she could take a boot to her own shin. What was wrong with her? "Spear would not lie to me. Not about Tom."

A smile moved across René's mouth, a smile that did not do one thing to lessen his fury. She was instantly angry that she'd noticed it at all. "Then tell me this," he said, the words barely a whisper. "If I handed you your precious marriage fee right now, would you take it? Or no?"

She met his gaze. "No."

"Then I would say, Miss Bellamy, that between the two of us, I am not the liar here."

And now it was anger rather than embarrassment heating her face. "I think you should listen to me, Monsieur, and let me give you a word of advice. You wish to be believed? You wish to appear trustworthy? Then maybe you should get out of my bloody way and stop listening in on other people's private conversations!"

She pushed past and marched down the corridor, opening the first door she came to. When she found St. Just inside, she turned and slammed the heavy oak behind her, shaking the walls. In another moment, René had done the same to his door directly across the hall. And done it a little more thoroughly.

The floorboards shuddered beneath Benoit's feet as he peeked out his door. His questioning gaze met Orla's, who was just emerging from the dark end of the corridor, where the hanging light could not reach, a water pitcher in her hand. They considered each other in silence, and then together looked down the hallway, toward the two doors that had slammed.

"*Ce sera une longue séjour,*" said Benoit, who spoke no Commonwealth.

"I agree, Mr. Benoit," said Orla, who understood no Parisian. "I think we are in for a very long stay."

Spear stayed in his chair for a long time after the doors above him had slammed, watching his hands, where a piece of paper, much folded and marked with the seal of the Sunken City, now rested between two fingers. He turned the paper over and over, thinking of lips in his hair, listening to the groan of Sophia's footsteps moving across his ceiling.

—

LeBlanc pulled the heavy wooden door of Jennifer Bonnard's prison hole shut, listening to it echo in the Tombs. An unfamiliar shudder traveled down his limbs. It was unthinkable that this was fear. The girl must be lying; what she had said wasn't possible. It was inconceivable that he, Albert LeBlanc, could have made such a mistake. And if he had? Surely Fate had not removed the blessing of Luck from him?

He dropped to his knees, disregarding the filth and his pressed suit, and drew a hasty circle with his finger in the sandy, torchlit dirt. From his pocket he removed a coin and a small stoppered vial, then pulled the cork from the vial, hands shaking, and tossed Jennifer Bonnard's blood across the circle. He held the coin between two clasped hands, bowed his head in supplication, and flipped it high into the air. The coin turned, LeBlanc watched, breathless, and then the coin landed, the bronze relief of Allemande's profile looking up at him from the blood-spattered dirt. Face. Fate's answer was yes.

LeBlanc dropped to his elbows in the bloody, dusty grime. Luck was still with him; his mistake was not insurmountable. But he would need to retain the Goddess's favor. From now on he would be careful. He would inquire often. And he would take Bellamy blood as well, so that such a misstep could never be repeated.

He shuddered again as he stared at the coin. Fate was not a merciful Goddess. But if he moved forward with his plans to honor her, to give her all the Sunken City as her own, with victims and destinies to choose, if he brought the Red Rook to her altar, then surely Fate would not fail to bless him further still.

Perhaps she would even give him Allemande.

10

Sophia set one of her black boots and a knife on the low square table in Spear's sitting room while Orla settled in front of the fire. Orla was sewing up the gash in Sophia's vest, the bloodstains washed out, while Sophia worked on sawing off her boot heel. Her boot heel would be a good place to stash something useful, she'd decided. And it would keep her hands busy and mind occupied while Spear went for the post.

Before breakfast, Spear had knocked on her bedroom door, insisting on taking her up the hill behind the house. A short, easy walk, he'd said, too early and foggy for anyone to be about on his land. Orla had given her a scolding for it. She was supposed to be resting and therefore healing. But she'd been so afraid Spear would be angry after their conversation the night before, was so relieved when he'd sought her out, that she'd taken one look at his faultless smile and done as he asked.

And the view had been worth it. The hills were rolling green and autumn orange-brown; treetops still blushed with color, floating in a bed of white mist in the lower glens. She'd smiled, St. Just had leapt about and barked like mad, playing at being a wild fox, and Spear had been very pleased. But now she was alive to things she would have previously missed. Spear had wanted her to see those hills, this new, aware Sophia realized, not because she would enjoy them, or even think them beautiful. It was because he wanted her to love his farm. Because he wanted her to live there. With him.

For always being so assured of her own cleverness, Sophia Bellamy—she was discovering—could be extraordinarily stupid. She had always, always thought of Spear as a brother. He was fearless. Like Tom. And handsome. Like Tom, though in a colder, cut-marble sort of way. He was loyal to her. Like Tom. Her cohort in crime. Like Tom. And she had thought his feelings on the subject of her wedding were the same as Tom's, too. Indignation, a general wish for her future happiness, the desire for Bellamy House to go on as it had been.

But last night had changed all that. There had been nothing brotherly in the plans Spear had suggested to her. And now she was remembering certain comments dropped here and there by Mrs. Rathbone, their neighbors at the Banns, and even Tom, words she'd taken as silliness and teasing and never thought of since. Evidently she was the only person in the county who hadn't been looking on Spear Hammond as her right and natural suitor. At least before her engagement. Even René had realized. The whole idea left an uncomfortable, uncertain place in her middle.

She'd tried to think it through all night, pacing the wooden floor, staring up into the spidery shadows around Spear's ceiling beams. René made her uncertain, too. But for being the same word, "uncertain," the two feelings couldn't have been more dissimilar. Nothing about René was remotely brotherly. But by the time the sun rose she'd been able to draw only one conclusion: Neither Spear Hammond nor René Hasard needed to know what she felt about anything. One because it would hurt him, the other because it would give him the power to hurt her. René was much too good at the game, and there was too much at stake to be playing games with anyone. She ran a hand through her hair, pushing through the tangle where she'd felt René's words moving the curls near her ear in the sanctuary. And he wanted her to think he didn't lie.

"Is that cut difficult, Mademoiselle?"

Sophia bit her lip, absorbing her start of surprise. René's tall boots and brown breeches were standing right beside her, and she'd been staring aimlessly at a window too filmed with salt spray to be seen through, her knife halfway through a boot heel.

"That's not what our Sophia is finding difficult, Mr. Hasard," said Orla, pulling a long thread.

"I'm being punished," Sophia said quickly, in case the all-seeing Orla had a mind to elaborate. "For walking too much when I was supposed to be resting. I have to sit still until highsun."

"Or I'll take my hand to her," Orla stated.

"I envy you, Madame," René said, folding himself into his chair from the night before.

Orla snorted once with laughter. Sophia was about to express her righteous anger in some clever way she'd yet to devise when René held up a hand.

"Can we have peace? For a short time? I have brought you news." He tossed a newspaper onto the table, the *Monde Observateur*. "Benoit has just brought it from Bellamy House. I have been having them sent on since I came."

Sophia snatched up the paper, and then paused. "Did he speak with Nancy?" She was asking about her father, but realized instantly that it was a nonsensical question; Benoit did not speak Commonwealth.

"He went to see himself," René said. "There is no change."

Sophia nodded, and unfolded the paper as Spear came down the passage, filling up the doorway to the sitting room, a steaming mug in one hand. Sophia read aloud, the Parisian falling quickly from her lips, occasionally pausing to translate for Orla, who had left her sewing in a forgotten pile. The entire first page was about the execution of the Red Rook. Sophia looked up, wrinkling her forehead.

"Sixteen days from capture? Why do they wait?"

"Keep reading, Mademoiselle."

She did, her eyes widening until she raised her head again. "He's insane. LeBlanc, Allemande, they're both mad!"

"Yes, they are mad. The whole city is mad," René agreed. "But they are also clever." Sophia could hear the anger again. He leaned forward in the chair. "First, they take advantage of the unrest in the Lower City. They promise bread, and equality, and an open gate, and that technology will never return to replace the tradesman. They point to the Upper City and say these are your oppressors, these are the ones who look down from their high flats, they lock you in, they fund machines, feeding the hatred with lies until they have a revolution and the hatred feeds itself. Then they use the mob like a weapon, bring down the premier, seize the government and the chapels, anything with power. They kill all who oppose them, man, woman, and child. All in the name of revolution, and justice. But they cannot keep the mob rioting forever, and the list of traitors who have not fled the city grows short, yes?

"So now they say this revolution has been decreed by a Goddess, that Fate has chosen new recipients for her blessings. And the poor will follow, because Allemande has promised them all they wish to have, and because now those promises are backed by a deity. But even if they do not believe, they will follow, do you not see? They will follow out of fear of the Razor, and they will follow because there is no responsibility. For anything. All can do as they please, because all is as Fate has willed. There is no wrong. It is madness!" He threw up a hand. "A very clever madness."

Sophia watched him, mesmerized. Just a few days ago she would have bet Bellamy House that there weren't any such ideas in René Hasard's powdered head. Now it was as if he'd been possessed by Tom.

"Allemande will only take now," he continued, "as the Goddess decrees, with LeBlanc as his 'holy man' to make her wishes known. He will keep himself in the chair of the premier, hold the poor of the Lower City exactly where he wants them, and execute Jennifer Bonnard and the Red Rook in a ceremony of thankfulness to the Goddess."

No, they will not, Sophia thought. She glanced down at the newspaper. "And they will draw lots from the prison. Fate will choose one out of three. One to live . . ."

"And the other two will die," René finished. "Two-thirds of the Tombs will lose their lives on an altar. The gutters will run with the blood." The fire settled, the weight of this news doing the same in Sophia's mind.

"La Toussaint," Spear said from the doorway. He'd been so quiet Sophia had almost forgotten he was there. "Sixteen days from Tom's arrest will be the end of the festival honoring those lost in the Great Death."

René sat back, thoughtful. "That is so."

"La Toussaint is also when the saint in the form of a rook led survivors to the underground, before the city sank," Spear continued. "That's why they wait to execute Tom. LeBlanc has shut down the chapels, but Sophie has been leaving rook feathers. He wants to disprove the story."

"Hammond is right," René said, showing only the slightest surprise.

Sophia thought of that rumbling thunder, and the streaking ball of fire she'd seen moving across the sky the night she'd gone to the Holiday. The same as the iconography on the chapel walls. "It's also the night the Seine gate will be open, so the Lower City can visit the cemeteries," she mused. She'd never been in the city for La Toussaint. They'd always returned to Bellamy House by the equinox. But she knew there were coffins, and music and a parade, and that the graves were decorated with flowers. And feathers. She looked again at the paper. "Allemande will provide free landovers, hundreds of them, so that all may come to the Upper City and attend . . ."

"He is turning the mob loose on the Upper City," Spear commented. "No one is going to put on a parade down the boulevard, much less show up for one."

"And two out of every three will die . . . ," Sophia whispered.

"The gutters will run," René repeated.

Orla picked up the vest again and started sewing. "Allemande is not mad," she said. "He is evil."

"I believe he is both, Madame," René answered. "Every day the execution bells ring, and if I raise the windows of our flat, I can hear the noise of the mob echoing out of the Lower City, chanting while families are put to the blade. Half the children I went to school with are dead, along with their families, their property given over to supporters of Allemande or the ones that denounced them. When you live in the Sunken City, you look evil in the face." He paused. "But you, Mademoiselle . . ." The blue eyes lifted until they found Sophia's. "You can see the . . . possibilities?"

"It will be chaos," she said thoughtfully. Her mind was already humming.

"Sophie," Spear said. "We can't delay. We should go as soon as the twins get the number of Tom's cell, do it as we've done before. If we're ready to go when the information comes, we could have both Jennifer and Tom, and even his mum . . ." He jerked his head at René. "We could have them out in two days."

René kept his gaze on Sophia's face. "Take your best chance, Mademoiselle."

"Can Tom wait that long, Sophie?" said Spear. "And how long will Jen last?"

"They are sacrifices now," René countered. "They must walk to the scaffold. And if you go before you are ready, perhaps you will not be able to stop them from walking to the scaffold. Or the Razor from coming down for their heads."

"If you wait two weeks, you leave no room for mistakes, Sophie."

"That wound must heal, Mademoiselle."

Orla picked up her sewing, keeping her opinions in her head, while Sophia stared down at the printed words of the newspaper. Death for two out of three. What would LeBlanc do? Draw lots? Number them randomly? René leaned forward again, elbows on knees, almost coming out of his chair.

"Take your best chance and I swear that I will help you. Do you believe me?"

She met his eyes again. Whatever else he might be, she did believe that he would help her in this, especially where it concerned his mother. But René could not know that in the past ten heartbeats, her thinking had changed.

She got up and went to the hearth, running a finger along the steel girder, a part of some long forgotten, Ancient building incorporated into the new. But what she was seeing was cell number 1139. Not only had the Bonnards been there, blinking and starving and dazzled by her dim lamp, but a teacher who would not repeat the oath of Allemande, a smith who had taken five francs to repair an undermarket clock, along with four of his grown children, who had apparently done nothing at all, and a set of grandparents unlucky enough to have raised their children in a moderately nice flat near the top of an Upper City building. A flat someone else wanted.

Sophia felt her anger rise, a pressure cooker of rage that had been simmering inside her every day since the first time she entered the Tombs. Now it was turning her resolve into something diamond hard. She hadn't been able to turn the lock on the people of cell 1139, and she would not leave two-thirds of the prisoners to their deaths this time, either. It might kill her. It probably would. The land would be gone, there would be no respite for her father whether he got better or no, and nothing left for Tom. The Bellamys would be undone, but she wasn't sure that mattered anymore, not in the light of LeBlanc's planned bloodbath. What was the point of emptying three small cells? She was going to walk into the Sunken City and empty every stinking hole in the Tombs. Let LeBlanc's Goddess explain that to the mob.

"Spear," she said slowly, "when was the last time you went to Mainstay?"

"Yesterday. For supplies. Why?"

"Then we'd better go into Kent. Is the woman who forges our paperwork still in Brighton?"

"As far as I know. But, Sophie . . ."

"Would you be able to go to the undermarket? I'll have a list, and I can't run into Mr. Halflife. We're supposed to be in the Midlands."

Spear's shoulders sagged just a little. "Yes, I can go."

She turned to René, and again met his gaze. She had a feeling his had never left her. There was a grin beginning to show on one side of his mouth. "Do I remember that you have a ship, Monsieur?"

"Yes. I do have a ship."

"And do you have two ships?"

"Yes, I do." The grin had stretched to both corners before he added, "Mademoiselle."

"Sophie?"

She looked around to Spear. He was leaning back on the door frame, holding a mug gone cold, blue shirt tucked into darker blue pants, not one hair straying from its fellows. He would try to stop her if he knew what she was going to do. He probably should. The whole idea was ludicrous.

"You're sure this is what you want?" he asked.

"No, I'm not sure it's what I want. But it's what I think I should do. And, yes, I am absolutely certain about that." There would be two plans: the one everyone knew, and the one known only to her. Spear was still gazing down into his mug, wrinkles in the marble of his forehead.

"Are you with me, Spear?" she asked. When he didn't answer immediately she said, "You don't have to be. Hasn't that always been our bargain? Your choice, either way, and no blame."

Spear's face showed her nothing. "I've always been with you, Sophie. You know that."

She hid her breath of relief. For a moment she'd been afraid Spear wasn't coming. And she was going to need him; she'd never been to the Sunken City without him.

"Then we should plan to be in the city in something like twelve days. Orla, would you mind popping up to my room and getting Tom's maps, since you won't let me on the stairs?" Sophia was already sitting carefully at the low table, moving her knife and mangled boot and swiping away the bits of leather heel, purpose making her movements swift. "Spear, why don't you come and sit down. And you, Monsieur," she said, "what can you tell me about smuggling?"

—

Sophia did not have to force herself to remain at Spear's table until highsun; she was still there at dusk, and long after nethermoon, sometimes with Orla, sometimes Benoit, always with René and Spear. Spear's table was littered with sketches and lists, mugs and plates, but there was an acknowledged plan now, simple yet elegant. And there was an unacknowledged plan, too. Perhaps just as elegant, Sophia thought, but not at all simple.

René was stretched full length on the floor, hair undone, one arm behind his head, spinning a coin on the wooden planks, or sometimes tossing it to the air and catching it on an open palm. Sophia had been schooling herself not to notice this, even though his coin had been landing with Allemande's face up ever since the moon set.

Spear rubbed his chin, voice scratchy and hair miraculously in place. "I don't know, Sophie," he was saying, "I'm just not sure it will work."

The coin glinted and landed face up. "It will work, Mademoiselle," René said.

"How are you doing that?" she asked him, curiosity too piqued to stop herself.

"The coin is weighted," Spear replied for him.

René sat up on an elbow. "That is true. The spin is easy, but there is skill in the toss. I will show you sometime. If you wish."

Sophia sensed danger and looked quickly back to the maps in front of her. "Well, I think the plan is brilliant, Spear. And, anyway, you're forgetting our biggest advantage."

Spear sighed. "And what is that?"

She smiled as she blew out their candle. "If LeBlanc thinks he has the Red Rook, then he won't have any reason to expect that the Red Rook is coming."

LeBlanc blew out his candle. Dawn was filtering through the tall stone windows, throwing yellow light on the plain, polished floor of his office. There was a light knock at his door. "Come," he said softly.

Renaud ushered in an elderly Parisian in a neat black suit, the scent of the Tombs still hanging faintly about his clothes. LeBlanc stood, his politeness oily.

"Dr. Johannes," he said. "Thank you for coming so early. Please, sit." He gestured to Renaud, who brought a wooden chair before LeBlanc's desk, the same chair Gerard had used ten days earlier.

"I'll admit it was a surprise to be asked," replied the doctor, who had woken to four gendarmes breaking down his door. He sat stiffly, mouth in a straight line. LeBlanc smoothed the long, black, white-collared robes he now wore instead of a jacket, positioning them so as not to wrinkle when he slid into place behind the desk.

"And what is your opinion of the prisoner?"

"A little dehydrated, nothing that access to water would not correct, and crawling with vermin, which is no different than the others. There is significant bruising, and three ribs on the right side are broken. I have wrapped them, and he will need to be still and left strictly alone if he is to walk upright, especially with the leg."

"And what about the leg, Doctor?"

"A bad break that did not set well. Nearly two years ago, according to him, and that seems right. Still gives him a good deal of pain, I am sure."

LeBlanc's fingers tapped the desk. "So in your opinion, Dr. Johannes, could a man with a leg such as the prisoner's perform . . .

certain tasks? Sword fighting, for instance? Jumping, running, or climbing a wall?"

"There is nothing wrong with the arms, but anything that involves agile movement of the legs is in my opinion impossible. The limb will not bear the weight."

"Could the prisoner walk without the limp? Even for a short distance?"

"No. The leg is physically shorter now, after the injury."

"And the more recent cut? It was made by a sword?"

"If so, it was a small and dull one. There is no infection, though how that's so I cannot say. But the edges of the skin are ragged, not clean. I'd say a knife. Serrated."

"Like a table knife."

"Just so. I have wrapped that wound as well."

LeBlanc glanced toward the back of the room, where Renaud stood along the wall, his long face impassive, then at the doctor, grim and assured of his facts, hands on the bag of medical tools in his lap. LeBlanc smiled.

"Thank you, Doctor. Just one more question, to appease a little curiosity of mine. Some of these tasks we were discussing, could the more . . . arduous of them, could they be performed by a woman?"

"They could be done by anyone with the proper strength."

"Even sword fighting, Doctor?"

"Size and muscular development make a difference, of course, but both the male and the female respond to training, Monsieur."

"And the mental training that goes with such skills? The agility of the mind?"

"No difference under the sun."

"I see. And others in your profession, would they say the same?"

The doctor, whose brows had gone up at the odd line of questioning, frowned now, confused. "Of course they would. Why shouldn't they? The idea that women are not fit for certain tasks is based on cultural expectations, not the science of fact. It is an old-fashioned belief coming from the less civilized centuries after the Great Death, and has nothing to do with medicine. Any man of science knows that."

"Oh, that is unlucky," LeBlanc said. He waved a hand toward Renaud, who moved quietly forward. "Thank you, Doctor, for giving me so much to think on. Renaud will take care of you. And, Renaud, when you are done, I will need another message sent to our informant in the Commonwealth."

LeBlanc drummed his fingers on the desk, contemplating one or two things he would have to say in his letter while Renaud came up behind the wooden chair and, with quick and silent efficiency, slit the doctor's throat.

11

"*Now*, Mademoiselle," René said, adjusting the angle of her body carefully as they stood in front of the sitting-room fire, the slanting rays of nethersun glowing through the filmy windows. He was in his linen shirtsleeves, the plain jacket tossed onto a chair, hair tied. "Hit with an open palm, and aim for here."

He put her fingers against the lower edge of his cheek. She'd wondered what that would feel like. It prickled.

"Do not hold back," he instructed. "There must be no doubt that we are having a fight of passion. That will be essential. Unless you are pulling on your wound?"

She shook her head. She was going to slap him with her right and her cut was on the left, but overall she thought this situation particularly unjust. What she wouldn't have given to do this one week ago, and René was ruining it with sheer willingness.

"Hit him hard, Sophie," Spear said, chuckling as he watched from the couch. Even Benoit had come to see, a man-shaped outline easy to overlook in the corner.

René waited, almost daring her, while she was trying to ignore the little pulse beating at the base of his throat. It was beating rather fast. She took a deep breath, pulled her arm back, and slapped. Her skin on his made a solid, but faint, smack.

"Oh, no," René said, shaking his head. "I do not think you meant that."

"And he would know when a woman slaps him and means it, Sophie, don't you think?" said Spear, still chuckling. He put a hand to his shirt pocket, as if checking to see that something was still there.

René was looking over his shoulder toward the couch, an amused half smile on his face, and something about the expression put Sophia in mind of their Banns, and Lauren Rathbone, and that gaggle of women he had so expertly flirted with.

This time her slap turned his head.

"Ah," René said after a moment, hand to his cheek. "That was much better."

He rubbed his face, where a patch of skin was beginning to show the shape of her hand. Sophia would have sworn the blue fire in his eyes was pleased. She almost smiled before she could stop herself.

"This will be about the timing, I think," he said. "You should come across the room, pause, step one, two, three, and hit. Let's do that, Mademoiselle, without the hitting . . ."

They did it without, and then they did it with, adding dialogue, working for the actions to be automatic, for René to turn slightly just in time to deflect the worst of the blow, until Benoit could tell them the level of preparation was not obvious. René would accept no one else's opinion on that subject. She was afraid she must be bruising his face, but René's enthusiasm, she discovered, was a force of nature, not to be diminished or controlled. They kept at it.

Spear seemed to forget that there was a rehearsal going on, and it made him bold. He flattered her, shielded her when it wasn't needed, sat too close when she let René's cheek have a rest. "Staking a claim," that had been Orla's single comment in her ear. Sophia did not want to be "staked." And René was aware of it, too. He kept giving her that knowing look, as he had that first night in the farmhouse, which made him much easier to hit. Especially when she called up the image of the way he had smiled at Lauren Rathbone's smudgy eyes.

The candles had burned low before Benoit finally gave his blessing. Spear banked the fire, thoughtful, while Sophia trudged up the stairs, tired and with a hand on her side, Orla behind her. Benoit and René were both out of sight. Spear allowed himself a smile. Things were going well. Sophie seemed to like the farm, she'd sat with him on the couch, and she'd been slapping the stuffing out of Hasard. Since dusk. And he knew Sophia Bellamy well enough to see when there was anger on her face. She'd never been that good of an actress. He had nothing to fear from Hasard. The knowledge lifted a weight from his mind. Spear put the poker back in place, still smiling, checked his shirt pocket once more for the rustle of paper, then headed toward the kitchen to blow out the lamps.

Hasard was just entering the narrow passage from the kitchen door, head down and preoccupied, barreling down the hall to stop only just short of a collision. They circled each other, Hasard's hands going up in mock apology before they both moved on in their opposite directions. Spear smiled again. The man's left cheek had been a very satisfactory reddish-purple.

René grinned as he walked away down the kitchen passage, rubbing his sore cheek, slipping the folded piece of paper from Spear Hammond's shirt pocket into his own.

"What do you think, Benoit?" René's Parisian was very soft as he knelt at the little table in his room, where Benoit was taking advantage of a strong lamp. Benoit ran the end of the eyescope over the now unfolded piece of paper, then held it up, peering at the light shining through.

"It is an official document of the Sunken City," Benoit said. "Not a forgery, I would say."

"And why would Hammond be carrying this particular document with him, do you think?"

Benoit didn't answer. René had not expected him to.

"And where did he get it, Benoit? Had Tom Bellamy already acquired it, or did he get it from LeBlanc, perhaps?"

But René did not expect an answer to this, either. He scratched his stubbled chin, frowning once as he grazed his bruised cheek.

"She slapped you very thoroughly," commented Benoit. "What did you do to her?"

"Teased her. About Hammond. But only a little. She is an interesting girl, do you not agree?" Benoit just shook his head, and René picked up the document. "I suggest we give it back, and see where he leads us. Do you agree to that?"

"I do," Benoit said, and soon after, when Spear left his bedroom to investigate a noise at the front door, there was a folded piece of paper on the floor of his bedroom, just where it might have fallen from a shirt's front pocket.

Tom glanced down and saw a piece of paper in the dirt beside him. He got a hand on top of it, only just clinking his chains, studying the two gendarmes that had come to his prison hole with Gerard. Which of them had dropped the paper while he'd been dazzled by the lantern light?

The younger gendarme of the two was carrying the water bucket, which he managed to bump and slosh onto Gerard's shoes. Tom hated to see any of the water go, but they would have left it just out of his reach anyway. While Gerard fussed and the three of them argued, Tom unfolded the paper beneath his fingers and his eyes darted down. Very small, in red ink, was the shape of a feather.

Tom wiggled the paper into the dirt beneath his hand, stiffening as the younger gendarme approached. He'd drawn his knife. Gerard and the other gendarme, a man with a small, brown mustache, waited by the door. The young man squatted beside Tom, his back to the others.

"A pinprick, that is all," he whispered.

"No talking to the prisoner!" Gerard snapped.

The young man winked, pushed up Tom's filthy sleeve, and made a quick stab into his forearm with the knife tip. Then he held a small glass vial to the wound, squeezing and pushing a little to help the blood run into it.

They left him in the dark soon after. But Tom, having quickly learned to memorize the position of his water bucket, had seen the young gendarme nudge it to just within his reach. He listened for the metal door to bang shut from far above, and as soon as it did he called, "Jennifer?"

His voice echoed in the dark, oppressive quiet. A primitive sort of panic swelled in his chest.

"Jennifer! Are you there?"

"I'm here, Tom." Her voice came through the little barred window of her door into his, and it was shaking. "Are they gone?"

"Yes, they're gone." He didn't mention his bleeding arm; he was just now beginning to notice the sting of it. He found the tiny piece of paper and made for the water, drinking straight from the bucket, heart beating hard against his cracked ribs.

Sophie was coming. That's what the paper meant. Part of him wished she wouldn't, but surely he'd known she would. He wondered what she'd done about René Hasard, who seemed to be operating under his own flag, and if Spear had done what Tom had asked right before LeBlanc dragged him out of Bellamy House: to find out who had denounced the Bonnards. It could have been anyone, he supposed. But he wondered . . .

And why had LeBlanc sent in a doctor, and taken a vial of his blood, as Jennifer said he'd taken hers before? The doctor must have seen his limitations, which meant LeBlanc must know them now, too. LeBlanc had to at least suspect that he didn't have the Red Rook. But then who did he think the Rook was? And why wasn't LeBlanc down here right now, dragging information from his screaming mouth? So far their favorite way to torment him was to make Jennifer scream, which was very effective; he'd bit his lip bloody and pulled the hair from his scalp just trying to endure it. But no one had ever asked him any questions.

"Jennifer?"

"Yes, Tom?"

"Tell me about the time you went to Finland."

She began to talk, hesitant at first, eventually losing herself in the story.

Now that he'd thought it through, it was clear that if LeBlanc had sent his cousin to them, then he must have been looking at the Bellamy coast long before the night that Sophie emptied the Bonnards' prison cell. And someone must have given LeBlanc a reason to do so. It was this unseen enemy that frightened him. He hoped that his sister was being smart. That she was trusting no one.

He leaned his head against the rough stone, listening to Jennifer describe trees frozen like ice sculptures in the snow. He tore the piece of paper with the red feather into tiny pieces and ate them bit by bit.

Sophia ate a piece of bread at the table, tearing off chunks while looking out the kitchen windows, where the salt wind had been prevented from mounting a direct attack on the clarity of the glass. It was the quiet time after dawn, when the birds were awake and most other animals too sensible to be so. But she thought she'd seen movement on the hillside, a branch bobbing where there was no breeze.

The daylight grew, the remnants of mist lifted, and the woods remained tranquil. Spear's horse whinnied in the stable. She wiped the crumbs from the table, moved softly down the passage, through the sitting room, and knocked once on Spear's bedroom door before she poked her head in. She'd heard him moving about for some time.

"Spear, can I ask you something?"

Spear looked up, startled. He was on the edge of his bed, pulling on his boots. "Yes, but just let me . . ."

She slipped in and closed the door behind her, feeling rather daring, while Spear checked the order of his hair. She'd never seen Spear's bedroom. It was neat. Spartan, even. And she had a suspicion there would be no stray balls of fluff roaming beneath the bed, either.

"Do you remember last year, when the three of us were in the undermarket at Kent, and we went to the blacksmith's?"

Spear finished his bootlace. "The one who had clocks under the floorboards of his mother-in-law's potting shed?"

"That's the one. Do you remember seeing this?" She pulled a paper from the back pocket of her breeches as she came across the room. On it was a drawing of a clock, an odd sort of arm apparatus attached to the top.

"Yes. I do remember," he said, taking the paper. "He called it a 'firelighter,' right? Because the flint on the top would strike a flame at a certain time, depending on how you set the clock?"

"Exactly so. I want to buy it."

"That was a lot of money, Sophie. Hard to imagine somebody paying so much not to light their own fire."

"I know. That's why I hope he still has it, and that he will bargain. Do you think you could talk him down on the price?"

Spear studied the picture. "I could make this, I think. If I had the clock."

"Could you really?" Sophia sat next to him, looking at the drawing. Spear was good at that sort of thing, but it had never occurred to her that he was *that* good. "Are you sure? How long would it take? Can you do it in ten days?"

"I think so. It's just flint and steel, and the parts for the top. And it would be much cheaper to buy the clock alone. What do you want it for?"

"Oh." Sophia smiled. "I was just thinking it would be safer not to have someone standing right there, lighting the Bellamy fire. This could be set to light a greased fuse ahead of time. No one near it at all."

"I thought you were using the explosions for a distraction, like before?"

She nodded, her brown eyes open and earnest. His narrowed.

"Well, that's a lot of trouble for a distraction. What are you not telling me, Sophia Bellamy?"

What she wasn't telling him was that she was going to put that firelighter in barrels of Bellamy fire and blow a great ruddy hole in

LeBlanc's prison. And that she was going to usher out hundreds of sick and dying prisoners first. And that it was very likely she wouldn't be coming back out again.

"Really, Spear," Sophia said. "When did you get so suspicious? What would I not be telling you?"

She looked down at the floor, so he wouldn't see her face, and noticed a piece of paper, much folded, peeking out from the space beneath the bed. An anomaly in such an orderly room. She leaned over and picked it up.

"Here," she said. Spear took it from her, tucking the paper into his shirt pocket without meeting her eyes. "So will you make the firelighter for me?" she asked. "If you can?"

"Yes," Spear replied, "I can do that."

A completely unreasonable part of her wished he had slapped that drawing right back into her hand and for once in his life denied her a request. "Thank you. And . . . maybe we should keep this between ourselves, if you don't mind."

That brought a tiny smile to his face. He nodded, and she stood up to go, wincing a bit.

"Sophie," Spear said, "what are you doing for money right now? Are you able to pay Nancy and Cartier?" Without waiting for an answer, Spear opened a drawer in the table beside his bed and took out a small cloth bag. It clinked. He held it out to her.

Sophia shook her head. "I can't . . ."

"Yes, you can."

"But where did you . . ."

"I came into a little money. You can pay me back when we get all this sorted."

She smiled ruefully as she took it. "That really is good of you, Spear. I . . ."

"Or," he went on, "we could just consider the money ours. No need to pay it back. We could say it's for a common cause, couldn't we? For you and me."

Sophia stood still, the bag heavy in her hand.

"I know you said you don't fancy marrying anyone right now. And I know that's because the timing is bad. But it's always been us, hasn't it? And when this is over, no matter what happens, I'll make sure that doesn't have to change. I can promise that."

Silence settled over the room, and Sophia still had not moved. Her eyes were stinging, and she was willing herself not to blink, not to spill any tears. How did you tell someone that you loved them, truly loved them, but not in the way they wanted you to? How could she tell him that one way or the other, whether she came back or not, the future he'd planned was never going to happen? You didn't, and she couldn't. Not now.

She turned to walk away, but Spear caught her hand, lifting it to his lips and kissing it once. She left, the bag jangling, tears finally spilling as she climbed the farmhouse stairs. She heard another person coming down.

"*Bonjour,*" said René.

"*Bonjour,*" Sophia whispered. She could feel the blue of his eyes on her back as she hurried around the turn of the landing.

Spear sat on the edge of his bed, thinking about Sophia's silence. The most important words came hardest to her. She'd always been like that. She needed someone to take care of her. Spear stood and left his room, the folded paper with the seal of the Sunken City back in the pocket against his chest.

"*Bonjour,*" said René as they crossed paths in the sitting room. René's left jaw was a faint purple. Spear nodded, picking up speed as he moved down the passage to the kitchen. He pushed open the back door and walked fast through the farmyard, scattering a few slow-moving ducks, taking long strides through the uncut stubble of the cornfield until the plow land gave way to brushy trees and an overgrown path. He disappeared into the woods of the hillside.

And like a shadow where it shouldn't be, Benoit also entered the woods, his eyes on Spear Hammond's back.

It took the better part of two days to make the preparations for Spear's trip. None of the rest of them could be seen outside the house, not a terribly difficult thing on Spear's isolated farm, but they couldn't just pop over to Forge for bread, either. So Sophia wrote lists and instructions, planning for their needs both now and in the Sunken City, and all the while Spear had not been exactly forward, but behaving as if things were . . . settled between them.

She'd thought she'd been right not to tell him, that the whole tangle of the future could wait until she brought Tom home, as René had suggested. Tom would be on her side, she knew that, no matter what Spear thought her brother had said. And if she didn't come back, there would be nothing to tell Spear anyway, would there? Now she was thinking that this perfectly logical line of reasoning was really nothing more than an excuse. An excuse for being a bloody coward.

She watched Spear gallop his horse down Graysin Lane, carrying her list, money, and a letter to their forger, the back of her hand still warm from his kiss. It was a relief to have him go, which made her sad. And guilty. She'd never been glad to see Spear's back before. But wisdom or cowardice either way, for however long Spear took in Kent, she would not have to look into his sincere eyes and think about how she would hurt him.

"So tell me about the water-lift shaft," Sophia said.

It was nearly middlesun and she stood at the sink, washing the pan she'd been frying eggs in, all the dishes they hadn't done the night before teetering in a pile to her left. She was feeling rather cheerful about doing dishes. It was uncomplicated work, with no expectations she could not fulfill, results seen instantly in a growing stack of clean plates. St. Just prowled about her feet, devouring scraps, and Orla was behind the toolshed, plucking a duck for their dinner, well away from the laundry blowing in the autumn wind. Benoit had not shown his face. Probably following Spear, if Sophia had to guess.

René sat at the kitchen table, writing out the invitations to their second engagement party, this time in the Sunken City, all one hundred and thirty-eight of them. The invitations were his curse for having the best handwriting in Parisian, and they had to be in the post by the next highsun. He leaned back, stretching ink-stained hands behind his head and into the air, left cheek just showing a faint bruise. Sophia's scrubbing slowed. René was definitely a filcher of purses today, working his way up to daughters. She went back to her pan before she got caught staring.

"The water-lift shaft," he replied, still stretching, "is twelve floors down and narrow. You will be able to get your back and feet on the walls, if you wish."

"It will be dirty," she said, considering.

"Very. But you will enjoy it, Mademoiselle, especially if the bucket on the other side is full."

"What do you mean?"

"Because if one bucket is full, and you are certain to take the opposite rope, you will get such a ride to the bottom! Just do not stand on the bucket."

Sophia smiled, amused. "And why ever not?"

"Because then you will get such a dunking at the end of your ride! And LeBlanc will track your wet footprints right across the Lower City." He leapt up from his chair. "Here, give me that towel. If I do not do something else, I will explode."

"You want to dry dishes?"

"I have done it before," he said, expression serious. "It was Maman's most particular punishment."

"You must have done it every day, then."

"Once again, you wound me. It was only five or six times a week."

She laughed before she could help it and tossed him a towel, which he caught on his way to the sink. "Have you ever been down it?" she asked, going back to the water lift.

"What do you take me for, Mademoiselle? I have climbed both up and down, though not for some time. There has been no need of escaping my tutors."

"And the rope?" she asked, handing him a dripping plate.

"It is replaced from time to time. But it should be tested, I think, before you go down."

For a little while there was just the slosh of water and clink of stacking dishes, until René said, "Tell me what you are thinking of."

Sophia had been watching the wisping steam rise off the water in the rinsing bucket, and realized she'd been smiling. She ran the dry part of her arm over her forehead, pushing back hair gone mad from the heat, and shook her head. "Nothing."

"It is not nothing. Tell me. I am suffering."

Nothing made René Hasard suffer more than information he could not have. It was a good thing he wasn't aware of just how much she denied him. She let him fidget for another few moments before she said, "It's just that I was nearly killed by an old rope once, that's all."

"And this makes you smile?"

"Yes." She bit her lip, smiling even more. She knew she needed to be careful, that she was vulnerable, that keeping René at arm's length and focused only on the business at hand was the best thing for her. But one glance at the grin in the corner of his mouth and she succumbed.

"Tom stole a rope once. He was going to bring it back, of course, but he wanted to measure exactly how far the Sunken City had sunk, to know how high the cliffs were for our map."

"You went to the city every summer?"

"Yes. Tom and Spear and I. Father took us. Since I was too small to remember."

"And you often climbed down into the Lower City?"

"Nearly every day. I had . . . there were people there, Mémé Annette and her son Justin, Maggie and the baby, they were like family to me. I think I was all of eight years old before I realized that Mémé Annette wasn't actually my grandmother. I used to help her sell oatcakes on Blackpot Street."

"Oatcakes," René repeated. "On Blackpot Street?"

"Oh, yes. I thought it was great fun. Do you know the market there?"

"I do."

She glanced at him again from the corner of her eye, a little surprised, though perhaps she shouldn't have been. Smugglers might very well know the Blackpot market. René had stopped drying and was just watching her talk, all his energy focused on her face.

"So the three of us climbed the fence, snuck past the guards at the Seine Gate, where there is a little path down to the waterfall . . ."

"Yes, I know the place."

"And Tom dropped his rope over, only it was a cool night, and there was so much fog coming off the river we couldn't see if the rope had reached the bottom. So Tom decided to climb down and find out. Spear and I were to let out more rope if he tugged once, and pull him back up when he tugged twice. Or Spear was supposed to, anyway, since he was so much bigger . . ."

"How old were you?"

"Nine, maybe. I think Tom was ten, Spear eleven. But Tom never tugged the rope. And I was so jealous that he'd gotten to do the measuring down the cliff . . ."

"You went down after him," René said.

"We had a bet on how far it was, and I was afraid he might cheat. But when I got near the bottom I found out why Tom hadn't tugged. He was talking to a woman, telling her the most ridiculous story about night fishing."

"In the Seine?"

"I said it was stupid. But then I realized the rope above my head was fraying, untwisting bit by bit. I tried to climb back up above the weak place, but the rope snapped, and if I hadn't landed on Tom's head, I probably would have broken mine. As it was, I left us in a pile on the ground."

"And what did Tom do?" René asked, grinning.

"He picked me up, dusted me off, and apologized beautifully to the woman. And then, being the helpful sister I was, and because no sane person would believe the story he'd been telling, I told the woman that we were actually in secret training for the circus."

René laughed, which made her smile. "Who was she?"

"No idea. But she was Lower City, and she must have known we were Upper. Tom's hair wasn't cut. She could have called the guards, though I don't suppose they threw children into the prison in those days. Instead she told us to climb back up and practice more or we'd be the worst circus act the Sunken City had ever seen. Tom gave me such a smack when we got back to the top."

René laughed again, and Sophia laughed with him. It felt good to laugh. But the feeling died away as she rinsed another plate. What would she do without Tom? He should be here right now, at the kitchen table, correcting the details she'd gotten wrong, telling her when she was being an idiot. And when she wasn't.

René said, "Sometimes, Mademoiselle, it is a torture to me, trying to decide what is inside your head. And then at other times, I can see just what you are thinking." His voice lowered. "Should I tell you what you are thinking now?"

She rinsed the same plate again, suddenly aware of proximity, of the arm next to hers, the smell of cedar wood and that little beat of pulse at the base of his neck, just at the level of her eyes, close enough to touch. He'd moved up to daughter-stealing before she'd realized. No. She really didn't want him to tell her what she was thinking.

"I will say, then, and you will tell me if I am wrong. You fear that this plan will fail, that this will be the first time the Red Rook does not come out of the Sunken City with her quarry, and that this is the one time you cannot live with such a failure. But that is not so difficult to see, is it? Who would not fear that in your place? But I think I will tell you what you truly fear." He paused, and when he spoke again, his voice was even softer. "You fear what will happen if your plan succeeds."

She stood still, her fingers dripping. She didn't dare look up.

"If your plan succeeds, will you come back to a father imprisoned and a home lost and a life that is uncertain? Or no? Will there be a marriage fee, and a husband instead? And if there is, what will you do with them, this husband you did not ask for, a brother who cannot provide, and a father whose mind is not whole?"

Sophia let her wild hair fall about her cheeks where it would hide her face, her body paralyzed. How could he know that? These were things she hardly admitted to herself.

"But even if none of that were so," he went on, "if there was no husband, your father restored, and home secure, if Allemande fell on his own sword and the Tombs were empty and the Razor torn down tomorrow—if you could have everything you have ever allowed yourself to wish for, you would still lose, would you not? Because you would go back to being Sophia Bellamy before the Red Rook, and I think you fear that just as much as failure. Now tell me I am wrong."

She could not tell him he was wrong. And it was mortifying. He reached up a finger and hooked a long curl, moving it away from her face. She felt her gaze pulled upward. René's hair was russet and mahogany in the window sun, his expression serious, the blue eyes heated and focused and intent on hers.

"Do you know why I know these things you do not say? It is because you are like me. That is why I can see. I know what it is to live as someone else, where others can never know you." He was making free with her hair on one side now, letting the strands spiral around his fingers while he ripped secrets straight from her soul. "But have you never thought that there could be a life you would want after the Rook?"

She should go. Some part of her mind knew this, was telling her to put an end to it, that she'd been caught in his spell unawares, that she was allowing what had happened in the sanctuary to happen again. But she couldn't speak. She breathed in as his hand moved to her neck, thumb running along her jaw, tilting her chin to steady her gaze.

"Shall I say more truth to you? You have never thought there would be a life you would want, because you think all that is possible is only what you have seen. That anything sweet is like the honey in a trap."

The universe had narrowed to the inches around Spear's kitchen sink, to the lack of space that was between them. He brought his other hand up to her neck, cradling her head so she could look nowhere else. Her pulse was racing, the feel of his hands, the path of his thumb along her cheek negating her will to move.

"But what if Sophia and the Rook did not have to be two separate people, but could be one and the same?" His gaze looked hard into hers. "You are a risk taker, Sophia Bellamy, and I wonder, if you believed anything I am saying to you now, what would you risk for such a life?"

If she believed. Hadn't she entered into this arrangement with René Hasard knowing she could not believe? That he could bewitch her like this if he wished? That she could not afford to be taken in just because she was aching to know what would have happened if she'd turned her head that day in the sanctuary, what would happen right now if she leaned forward just the slightest bit?

"But you do not believe me, do you?" he whispered. "Do you?"

Her lips parted, but she had no words. And then he stepped back a pace, dropping his hands, the smile in the corner of his mouth now bitter.

"Or do you choose not to believe, Sophia Bellamy?"

And she fled. Out the back door and into the muddy yard, crisp air hitting her panting lungs, clearing away the cobwebs of her trance. She looked left past the well, at the small barn and the loo and various sheds, and then to her right at the harvested cornfield, brown and crackling with stiff, dead stalks. The hill to the view was straight ahead, but she rejected all of these and instead turned and took hold of the house stones.

She pulled herself up, the flinty rock rough and still cold from the night, finding purchase for her side-turned feet as she grabbed, clawed, opposite leg, opposite arm, pushing her body away from the ground. She felt the ache in her muscles, so pampered the past nine days, and a protest from the wound in her side. She welcomed it. Again and again she stretched up, and then there was roof thatch in her hand. She got a leg over, rolled, and found herself lying flat on the roof, heat pouring down on her from a bright blue sky. She put a hand to her stitches, but she was whole.

What had just happened? What had she nearly allowed to happen? Her skin was tingling, pulse still racing, and not from her climb. She closed her eyes, letting the sun burn the lids. When she was a child she'd seen molten glass once, a glowing, fiery mass that looked soft and moldable like clay, but amazingly translucent, lit from within, so alluring that she'd ached to touch it even though she knew it would burn. And that was exactly how she'd been thinking of René Hasard, something tempting but off-limits for her own good. But what if he did not burn? He'd just said truth to her, more truth than she'd known what to do with. She touched her neck where his hands had been. Or what if he was just that good at the game?

Then she was up on her elbows. The kitchen door had been kicked hard from the inside, bouncing back into the wall stones she'd just climbed. She craned her neck and saw René striding across the farmyard, untucked shirt billowing with his speed. He went straight into the toolshed, coming out again with a curved, rather wicked-looking scythe, his face hard and white as a chalk cliff. When he got to the cornfield he tossed the blade aside, stripped off his shirt, wadded it up and threw it on the ground, picked up the scythe, and took a mighty swing. Down came the cornstalks in a scythe-wide swath. Once more, and again, each new swing of his arm ending in a little Parisian *uff*. The muscles of his back stood out with the effort, smooth movements repeating over and over until he was shining with sweat, red hair blowing wild in the wind. It was true. He was beautiful.

Sophia lay back down on the roof thatch, listening to René cut the remnants of Spear's cornfield. *Swish, uff! Swish, uff!* What if he could be believed? What if she could believe him? She'd already pulled out those scales again, this time weighing her future against two-thirds of the souls in the Tombs. That was done. An easy choice. But did she really know what she was giving up? And what if, somehow, she managed to come out again?

She closed her eyes, feeling a finger move her hair, a thumb brush the skin along the edge of her jaw. No matter how many times she told herself that René Hasard was a liar, the simple truth was that she desperately wanted him not to be.

12

"*Tom?*" Jennifer called.

Tom brought his knees up to his chest, huddling for warmth, though he knew his leg was not going to like that for long. The cold down here had a way of seeping into the bones, making them ache. "I'm here."

"Are you afraid to die?"

"No," he said. "But I hate the idea of not living." He'd had Jennifer talking for a long time. He liked it when she talked. It kept her from terror and kept him sane. When she was quiet, he was consumed by the irrational fear that someone had spirited her away without him knowing.

"Tom," she said again. Tom concentrated on her voice in the dark. He could hear the change in it. "I . . ." She paused a long time. "I told LeBlanc that it was you. The day they cut me. I knew it was Sophie, but I told them it was you. I didn't want them to catch her, and I needed . . . I needed them to stop."

Tom sighed. He knew. But Jennifer hadn't done any different than he had, had she? "You did the right thing," he said. When she didn't answer he said, "It was right, Jen."

"But in here . . ." Tom leaned nearer the door, straining to hear. "When LeBlanc came, I told him it was Sophie. Because I couldn't . . . make myself live through that. Not again."

Tom lifted his hands, wrists heavy with the shackles, and rubbed his bearded cheeks. He'd thought as much. Then it was certain that LeBlanc knew the identity of the Red Rook. And he would be a fool not to know that the Red Rook was coming for her brother.

"Tom, I'm sorry . . ."

"Jennifer, listen to me. None of this is your fault. I don't want you to think about it again. Not for another moment." He didn't know if he would have risked her anger and resentment if the circumstances were reversed. It would be too much of a loss. "And if you don't stop thinking about it, I'll be forced to sing you a song."

The darkness of the Tombs pressed down. "Oh, no," Jennifer said, her voice small. "Please, Tom. Anything but that."

They laughed, a weird, incongruent sound in that place. But if LeBlanc knew Sophie was coming, Tom thought, then what was there to prevent him from taking her now? From her bed in Bellamy House, or the Channel ferry, or an Upper City street? What would keep him from just killing her on the spot? He couldn't think of a thing. And LeBlanc seemed to have allies in the Commonwealth that none of them had been aware of. His sister had enemies on every side, and there was nothing he could do about it.

"Now close your eyes, Jennifer," he said slowly, "and imagine you're on the balcony of your flat. The tiles are cold, but you've got a blanket wrapped around you. You're camping out, like you and Sophie did when you were little. The sky is black, and you can hear the water of the Seine falling down the cliffs. And I've brought you a light, so you won't be frightened . . ."

LeBlanc lit his last candle and stepped back, admiring his work. He stood inside a giant circle of fire, dozens of tiny, blazing flames that lit the polished floor of his private rooms, sending bright, flickering light onto the black-painted walls. LeBlanc's flat, connected by a door to his office, looked like the rooms of a holy man, or a hermit. Serviceable, plain, unadorned. But he knew Fate was soon to offer him better.

His new black and white robes rustled pleasantly as he moved to a table in the center of the circle, draped with a cloth that had been stitched together, half white, half black. It matched the streak in his hair. A coal fire burned in a small brass brazier, and swinging above this, suspended on a tripod, hung a burnished pot filled with water. LeBlanc looked up as Renaud entered.

"You have brought it, Renaud?" The secretary approached and presented a small vial of rust-brown liquid over the candle flames. "Good. Very good. The blood of the brother should be perfectly adequate."

He set the vial beside the pot. Tiny wisps of steam were beginning to curl into the air. Then he clicked the latch of a plastic box, not reformed, but Ancient, smoothly ribbed and shining black. Inside was a row of four small plastic bottles, also Ancient, two partially filled with a dark liquid, two with white, all fitted with a heavy wax seal. LeBlanc chose one of each color and lifted them to the light. Formed into the plastic of each bottle was the word HILTON.

"This is a dear sacrifice, but I think it is needed, Renaud. When to kill the Red Rook is a decision that lies heavy. But what will be, will be, and therefore has already been. The Goddess will show the path."

He set the bottles to one side, picked up the vial Renaud had brought, and began pouring Tom's coagulated blood into the pot that was just beginning to boil. And then the door to LeBlanc's office creaked open slowly. LeBlanc paused, paralyzed, still in the act of pouring Tom's blood, while Renaud slipped farther into his corner.

Premier Allemande stood looking at them, blinking at the dozens of candles dripping wax onto the floor.

"There you are, Albert," said Allemande, voice as soft as LeBlanc's. He was a small man, unassuming, in trousers that were just the slightest bit too long for him. He turned and waved a hand, instructing his escort to wait before he shut the door on them.

"You did not come to the viewing box tonight, Albert. And the last one was so lively, too. She gave us quite a show." He indulged in a muted chuckle as he removed his spectacles, cleaning them with a handkerchief. The viewing box had been built with such proximity to the Razor that occasionally there was spatter. "We can only hope your Red Rook will be half so entertaining," he continued. "I am disappointed you missed it. Very disappointed. Or perhaps you have lost interest in the justice of the city, Albert?"

"I apologize, Premier," LeBlanc said, steadying himself against the table. LeBlanc's reply was just as soft as Allemande's, only his voice betrayed a tinge of fear. "Forgoing something enjoyable is often a sacrifice required by Fate. The greater and more personal the sacrifice, the more the Goddess will attend us."

"While I am of the opinion that official executions should be attended by my ministres," stated Allemande, holding up his spectacles to the candlelight, "especially my Ministre of Security."

LeBlanc bowed slightly, a move of both apology and deference.

"I take it you have an important question to ask of your Goddess?"

LeBlanc glanced once at Renaud, and then at the boiling pot, the edges now ringed with brownish foam. If Allemande discovered that the man rotting somewhere deep below them was not the Red Rook, then it would be the Ministre of Security's head that the officials of the city would enjoy watching roll across the scaffold. He could always allow Tom Bellamy to die as the Red Rook, of course, have the sister quietly killed, and Allemande need never be the wiser. Sophia Bellamy could be dead by the next dusk if he chose. But would that displease the Goddess? Or no? Fate had not removed Luck from him, and he would not choose the death of the Red Rook without consulting her. Who he would not be consulting was Allemande. He set down the vial.

"Yes, Premier. I do have a question for the Goddess."

"Well, by all means," Allemande replied. "Let's hear it, then. I am always in need of amusement."

Renaud stiffened in the corner where he had retreated, watching his master carefully, but LeBlanc only smiled, a creeping crack that widened across the bottom half of his face. He stood a little taller. What did he have to fear from an unbeliever like Allemande? Was he not fated to become all that Allemande was, and more? Was he not marked by the sign of the Goddess in his own hair?

"I will be happy to, Premier. Perhaps you would allow me to show you." LeBlanc picked up the Ancient plastic bottles as Renaud seated Allemande in a chair. "Yes," LeBlanc said, holding up the bottle of white liquid, "and no." He raised the bottle of black. "Life and death. Those are the answers of Fate. One of these answers she will give us, and show us what is to be."

He looked to the air, where the steam from the pot was rising. "Goddess, is it your will that I kill now, while the Red Rook is in my hand? Or do I wait, and grant life until the proper time, that the Rook may become a sacrifice to you?"

He waited, bottles raised to the Goddess, then dropped them simultaneously into the bubbling pot.

Sophia paused on a small stone bridge, water churning and splashing beneath her feet, rushing on its way to the sea cliffs. She thought she'd heard a faint rustle in the trees to her left, but the noise did not come again. She looked skyward. The north lights were muted tonight, faint undulating waves of pale green and a bit of red, the sky behind them spangled with the last of the stars. That's what Tom had always said: spangled with stars. The stars, he said, were from Before. She wondered if Tom had gotten her note, if he knew she was coming for him. If he didn't, then he didn't know his sister at all. But she'd wanted to make sure he hadn't forgotten to hope, like their father. Their father had forgotten everything but despair.

She'd sat for a long time on the floor of Bellamy's room, coming up through the trapdoor beneath his rug—Bellamy House was full of such oddities—watching his back as he gazed out the black and empty window. It had been very quiet, only Nancy snoring faintly in the other room. She thought her father had been asleep as well, but it was hard to tell. Nancy said there wasn't much difference either way.

But strangely enough, she'd felt better sitting there, huddled on the floor. Her father was ill in his mind and becoming so in his body. Seeing that had made it easier to let go of words that reflected nothing more than sickness and grief. She decided not to remember them. And so instead she'd thought about what René Hasard had said in Spear's kitchen, just as she'd thought about it while he swung his scythe in the cornfield until there were no more stalks. The way she'd thought about it when he sat down in the kitchen, doggedly finishing the invitations, while she made her escape from the roof and into the toolshed, where she'd spent the entire span of highsun sharpening her sword and every one of her knives. After that she'd shut herself up in her room, sewing her picklocks into the seams of her gloves, not thinking about what René Hasard had said at all. Instead she thought about what he'd done: his slightly calloused hands on her hair and her neck, the way his thumb had moved, as if he liked the feel of her. She paid zero attention to Orla's shaking head and knowing looks.

And when she finally had encountered him, coming up the stairs as she was going down, she hadn't been able to think about anything at all; her eyes had dropped immediately to her feet. "I owe you an apology, Miss Bellamy" was all he'd said before moving past her up the stairs. Thinking about that had kept her restless and kicking the furniture until, when the much too observant Orla had finally fallen asleep in her own room, Sophia had thrown open the window, dropped out a rope, and taken off to Bellamy House.

The water beneath her feet was noisy, the rookery sleeping and quiet, the north lights fading almost to nothing. There were no portents, signs, or balls of fiery machinery shooting across the sky, either. Mostly there was the wind, which smelled just a little like the sea. And winter. Sophia pulled her coat closed over the filigree belt she wore, just in case, and glanced once at the trees on her left.

"Benoit," she called, raising her voice, though not enough to wake the rooks. "Come walk with me." She waited, standing still in the breeze, then switched to Parisian. "Wouldn't it be easier if we just walked back together?"

She heard the faint rustle of leaves, and the rustle became the shadow of a man materializing from the woods. Sophia smiled as Benoit stepped into the road and followed her across the footbridge. They walked side by side down the A5 lane.

"I've been to see my father," she said, still in Parisian. "Though I'm sure you know that already."

Benoit didn't say anything, just walked, hands in pockets.

"I've wanted to . . . I should have said it sooner, but I wanted to thank you for what happened at the Holiday."

She saw the movement of his nod. Benoit was thin, unremarkable, perfect for his job, but his walk struck her as unhappy. She said, "You didn't do anything wrong, you know. I didn't know you were there. I just assumed that one of you must be. I wouldn't have let me go sneaking off in the middle of the night on my own." Benoit shuffled along beside her, silent. "Your master really should let you get some sleep."

"René does not sleep. And he is not my master."

"I see." Sophia considered this as they made the turn onto Graysin Lane. Parisians were usually so clear about the lines between classes, but nothing about René seemed to follow the usual. "If he doesn't sleep, then why doesn't he follow me himself?"

"Because he is being a fool."

"Oh, so he thinks I don't need following? And this upsets you?"

"I am not used to seeing a Hasard act like a fool."

Sophia smiled, thinking of René running about Bellamy House, finding ingenious ways to be annoying so he wouldn't have to marry her. "I would've thought you'd be quite familiar, actually."

Her words had been teasing, but Benoit's were not. "Now you are being the fool, Mademoiselle."

She looked at him sidelong. Probably he'd be surprised to know that, generally speaking, she agreed with him. "I don't think you like me, Benoit."

"No. I do not."

"And why is that?"

"Because you care for nothing but the money."

Sophia stopped in the road. "Once you get going, you are very free with your opinions."

"I am truthful. That is all."

"You may think you're being truthful, but you are just being wrong."

"As you say." He started down the lane again, hands in pockets.

Sophia caught up to him. "I didn't ask for this, you know. No more than he did, and of course I care whether my father is in a debtor's cell and if we lose our land. But I will get Adèle Hasard out of the Tombs whether there is a marriage fee or not."

The trees thinned, the farmhouse looming dark on their left, one window showing a faint candle-glow. Sophia felt her spurt of temper evaporating. "I said I would get his mother out and I will. But whatever happens afterward, I don't mean him any harm, Benoit."

His soundless footsteps ceased. "And yet you are causing it, are you not? René does not show himself easily, Mademoiselle." And with that Benoit turned and walked away, taking a smooth, quick stride to the farmhouse, uninterested in anything else she might have to say.

Sophia looked up. The candlelit window was René's room, a figure moving back and forth behind the curtain. What did Benoit mean? And could she really have the power to hurt him? She'd thought any danger of that was the other way around.

She watched Benoit's shadowy form slip around the corner of the farmhouse, then turned and looked behind her. Branches were moving, and Cartier came out of the woods on the other side of the lane.

"You're lucky I got him to walk with me," Sophia said as he came trotting up.

"I reckon he would've spotted me for sure, Miss Bellamy."

Sophia grinned at the top of Cartier's mop-like head. You would never guess that Cartier was Parisian. He'd taken to the

Commonwealth like a little chameleon, embodying Parliament's ideal of the resourceful survivor better than most men she knew. Even though he hadn't quite hit his growth spurt.

"I've left you three more kegs," Sophia said. "In the print house, in the usual place. You can get all eight of them sent on to the city tomorrow? And they are all correctly marked?"

"Yes, Miss."

"And this is still our secret, even from Spear?" The boy looked so affronted she didn't wait for an answer. "Right, off you go, then. And . . . No, wait."

Cartier dropped out of his runner's stance and looked up at her inquiringly. She reached into her jacket and handed him a small sack of quidden.

"This isn't all of it. Money is . . . a bit scarce at the moment."

"Well, that's no secret, Miss Bellamy. My mum told me that."

Sophia sighed. That should not have surprised her. "Will your mother be all right? Until I can get the rest?"

"Not to worry, Miss."

She grinned again. Cartier was an absolute brick. "Careful, then!"

"Double to you, Miss Bellamy." He took off like a young fox into the trees.

Sophia looked up again at the farmhouse, the vague silhouette walking back and forth between the candle flame and the curtain. She supposed she'd always thought of things like marriage and love as a trap, like René had said, something clever girls didn't let happen to them. Mrs. Rathbone, for all her prattling, had never struck her as happy. Nancy she could envision nowhere but in a kitchen, and the loss of her mother seemed to have all but destroyed her father. Not, perhaps, the best of examples on which to form all her judgments. But now she wondered.

Leaves rustled, and Sophia turned her head, thinking Cartier had come back. But he hadn't. She went still, eyes scanning, hand to her belt buckle. She waited, but there was nothing, only trees combing the wind with half-naked limbs.

She took Benoit's route back to the farmhouse, watching black shadow arms stretch up high behind a head in a room filled with candlelight. She wanted to know if what René had said could be true, and if so, what she would risk to have it. She wanted to know if Benoit meant what she thought he might, that René was showing her something real. She wanted to know if he was real. Preferably before she risked death in the Tombs.

Life. Or Death. LeBlanc pressed his hands together, waiting for Fate to declare the Red Rook's destiny as the Ancient bottles bobbed in the boiling water, warping and collapsing in on themselves. It took some time, as if the Goddess was suffering a fit of indecision. But then, suddenly, a bottle broke.

LeBlanc straightened. "The water is white. The answer of the Goddess is life."

Renaud's face showed a slight eye-widening of surprise from his place behind Allemande's chair.

"I am of the same opinion, Renaud. I . . ."

Allemande got up, voice smooth and even softer when annoyed. "So you wait to send Tom Bellamy to the Razor until the last day of La Toussaint. That was the answer of your Goddess? Isn't that the date you have already set, Albert?"

LeBlanc ignored Allemande's pique and bowed over the pot. "The will of Fate is absolute."

"I think you will find that my will is also absolute. The Red

Rook dies at the appointed time, no matter how many more rituals you perform. Is that understood?"

Allemande turned to go after LeBlanc had directed another bow his way, spectacles flashing with the tiny flames of half-burned candles. But then he paused and turned back, using a voice so muted it forced the attention of the room.

"I am glad to have seen this little demonstration. I believe the idea of being fated to die will capture the imagination of the people nicely. Set up something especially dramatic when you reduce the population of the Tombs, Albert, and I don't think you'll have trouble filling the chapels with your believers. What think you of a lottery wheel?"

"A wheel," said LeBlanc quietly, "is not an object of Fate."

Allemande dismissed this with a hand. "Present your ideas to me, then. Tomorrow, if you please. I hope your paperwork is in order?" LeBlanc nodded, lowering his eyes. Allemande looked him over for a few moments more, then opened the door and left with his escort, weapons jangling as they filed out of LeBlanc's office.

LeBlanc waited until he heard the bell of the lift taking Allemande back down the center of the white stone building. Then his smile curled, long and slow.

"And now we let her come to us, Renaud. Every move that Sophia Bellamy makes is one step up the scaffold."

Sophia came down the steps of the farmhouse, turned at the landing, and immediately turned again and went silently back up. Mr. Halflife was coming through Spear's front door, and René was letting him in. Sophia froze on the stairs, out of sight around the corner of the landing, but trapped by the creakiness of Spear's floors.

"Good day to you, too, Monsieur Hasard!" Mr. Halflife's posh Manchester accent was strange in the house, especially in comparison with the ballroom Parisian René was affecting while inviting him in. "This is such a pleasant surprise, such a pleasant thing. I had thought you and Miss Bellamy were holidaying in the Midlands . . . discussing. I am happy to find I was wrong. Might I speak with Miss Bellamy? I have business with her that I want to conclude posthaste."

"I wish that I could help you, Monsieur. But Miss Bellamy still travels. I came before her, to stay with my good friend Monsieur Hammond. He is nearly a brother to me now, of course."

Sophia stood silently, hearing the pause this last sentence gave Mr. Halflife. She stuck one eye very carefully around the corner of the landing, where she could see the back of Mr. Halflife's slicked head sitting on the couch. He was wearing a gray jacket, very tasteful, the cut of which was not at all Ancient, René nearly facing her in the other chair. He was sweaty, wood chips sticking all over his shirt, and yet somehow managing to pull off ballroom René very well. She saw the blue eyes make a quick, general sweep of the room that included the stairs.

"Then, I am to suppose . . ." Mr. Halflife collected himself. "I take it you are still contracted to marry Miss Bellamy, despite her brother's misfortunes, and your cousin's . . ."

"But of course! We are so very in love."

"And what does Mr. Hammond think . . ."

Sophia watched René make an elegant gesture with his hand. He slid so easily from one role into another that it gave her pause. Then she felt her stomach tighten. Her silver shoes for the second engagement party, with the heels so high she'd had to practice walking in them, were still on the floor at the end of the couch, just out of Mr. Halflife's sight. She focused her gaze, willing René to see what needed to be done, and then she heard St. Just's claws come clicking down the stairs.

She reached out to catch his collar and thought better of it. He wanted out, and would have protested. Vigorously. Mr. Halflife began to turn at the noise and Sophia ducked back around the corner. She heard René get up from his chair as St. Just went yelping and barking into the sitting room.

"Ah, St. Just!" René cried. Sophia could hear her fox resisting having his ears scratched. He really was desperate to get out. "He is such a good pet, is he not, Mr. Halflife? But you must excuse his wild behavior. He is not a happy fox. He has the trouble with the . . . how do you say, the vermin."

Sophia closed her eyes.

"Monsieur Hasard, I would be so grateful if you could tell me when I might have the pleasure of speaking with Miss . . ."

"Oh, *pardon*, Monsieur! Please . . . No, no, allow me . . ."

Sophia peeked around the corner to see St. Just leaping about the room like mad, her silver shoes gone, and René pulling pretend fleas off Mr. Halflife's gray coat. She pulled her head back, biting her lip against an urge to laugh.

"We will have this attended to in a week or so, I am certain," René was saying. "But they are stubborn creatures to be so small. Very vexing. A thousand pardons . . ."

The front door was opening. "When does Miss Bellamy return from her . . ."

The voices and barking faded as everyone moved outside. Sophia waited, then hurried upstairs and into René's room, which had a view of the front. She put a finger to the wavering crack between the two curtains and watched Mr. Halflife practically on the run, brushing at his sleeves. A sleek landover stood waiting a long way down the lane. It seemed Mr. Halflife had hoped to catch someone unawares. He nearly had.

She heard boots on the stairs, and René came in, Benoit just behind him. René paused in the doorway. He'd been avoiding her when he could, and she had just made that impossible. Good. Sophia peered once more through the curtains. "He's at a trot," she said, speaking Parisian for Benoit. "I'd say that was very well done. And where are my shoes?"

"Under the couch," René replied, tossing clothes from the bed onto a chair, brows drawn down. He looked tired, as if someone had pulled the cork and let out all his effervescence. She glanced around. His room had so many foreign things in it. Large boots, an eyescope on the table beside the bed. A little bowl of soap for shaving a face. So was this the real room, she wondered, instead of the staged one he'd left for her in Bellamy House? Or only another carefully constructed set? She watched Benoit taking away the clothing René had put in the room's only chair.

"And here," René said, emptying his pockets onto the cleared bed. She came to look. Her necklace, a list of food items in her handwriting, a few letters, a brush with brown spiral hairs sticking out of it, and a pencil. She stared at the pencil.

"Because you bite them, Mademoiselle," said Benoit, answering the unasked.

"I did not know if Halflife would know that," René added.

She picked up the pencil, which did indeed have bite marks. She hadn't known she did such a thing. "Do you think he knew I was here?"

"He knew someone was here," René replied. "He heard me putting logs in the hearth. But the chimneys would tell him as much.

Perhaps he did not know you were here. Necessarily. Otherwise I do not think he could have been so easily dissuaded."

He sat down on the unmade bed and leaned back, one arm behind his head, propping all but the dirtiest end of his boots on the blankets. He was a mess. Sophia felt sure he hadn't slept. He'd been moving near dawn, when she saw him behind the curtain, and he'd been splitting logs not long after that. She'd heard him from the stable, where she'd gone with her sword to render unwarranted destruction on three bales of hay. He had his coin out of his pocket now, flipping it into the air and snagging it easily with the same hand. He opened his fingers, and the coin was face up. He made a mess look rather good.

"Did you tell her?" René asked. Benoit shook his head while René caught the coin again. Face. "Benoit says there is someone watching the house."

Sophia felt her forehead crease, remembering rustling, and branches that moved when there was no breeze. She looked to Benoit. "You think, or are you certain?"

"I watched a man leave the trees after you went into the house last night. He circled, and then went back through the woods. I did not see a man replace him, but there could have been one. I do not think there was."

So Benoit had not gone back to the farmhouse after all; he'd been watching her. She wondered if he'd seen Cartier. Probably. Likely the whole time, from the footbridge on. Benoit did not like her, but this might be the second time she needed to thank him for her life. She sat on the corner of the bed and ran her hands through her hair.

"What did he look like?"

"Large," Benoit said. "Muscled. Knitted hat. No beard. But that is all I can say."

"Who outside this farmhouse knows you are here, Mademoiselle?" René asked. Flip. Three turns in the air. Face.

"No one. Other than Cartier, of course." She tried to think. "Nancy and her husband must know I haven't gone far, and they might guess Spear's, but they wouldn't tell anyone. I'd stake my life on that. Could it be Mr. Halflife, do you think?"

"Then why is he not the one sitting on my bed, Mademoiselle, pen and ink in hand? This man that was watching, he was right behind you last night, Benoit says."

Sophia looked closer at René. He was tired, yes. But he was also ticked. What about, exactly, she was not sure. "LeBlanc, then?"

"Why?" he asked, without sarcasm.

She didn't know. If LeBlanc knew she was the Red Rook, wouldn't he also be right here in this room, with twenty gendarmes and a pair of shackles? Her gaze went to Benoit.

"What is your opinion, Benoit? Do we find out who he is? Or do we move?"

Benoit sat down in the chair. "It is my belief that men show more truth when they do not know they are showing it. When they know they are caught they will tell you all lies, everything lies. I have told René that I think we should go on as we are, aware that there are eyes, give them nothing to see, and see what they show us. And I will be watching back, of course. He is unhappy with this course, I think."

Sophia turned her head. "Are you?"

"Yes. But that does not mean I think Benoit is wrong, because he is not."

Sophia looked at him carefully. "Unhappy" was not near as accurate as her assessment of "ticked." Then a letter caught her eye, on top of the pile of things René had rescued from the sight of Mr. Halflife. It was that day's post, freshly fetched from Bellamy House. She snatched the envelope, tore it open, glanced through the contents, and looked up.

"I have the numbers of the prison holes."

"That has not been posted straight to here?" René sat forward to look at the address.

"Of course not. There's a . . . Never mind. It's forwarded twice." She read on. "And it's no wonder it took so long. Jennifer and Tom aren't in the normal tunnels. They're deep, in a separate shaft." Sophia bit her lip. That was a complication. She'd never been down to those cells. "And Madame Hasard is in a cell alone," she continued, "on the first level . . ."

"Have they seen her?" René asked, voice very calm. A certain sign, Sophia was learning, that he wasn't.

"They don't say. Probably not."

She watched him frown. He was elbows on knees now, rubbing a hand hard over his rough jaw. He'd been much gentler with hers, she thought. She looked back at her letter.

"We have two days before we sail for the city. I need to go to the sanctuary to get the last odds and ends, and it will take a good part of a night to mix up all the Bellamy fire." René leaned against the headboard, flipping his coin. "So," she said, looking back and forth between them. "Do either of you know when Spear will be back?"

The coin flipped, and René cursed softly at the minted silhouette of the premier's building in the Sunken City. Facade.

"I know you had him followed," she added.

Benoit replied vaguely, "I do not think we should be worried about Hammond."

Sophia sighed. That was all the answer she was going to get. And since she didn't quite think Benoit a murderer, she decided to be satisfied.

René said, "For now, none of us should be alone outside of the house." A thought of a smile hovered around that corner of his mouth. "And that means no more climbing out of the windows, Mademoiselle."

So he knew she'd gone out the window, did he? And what was it about her that he hadn't noticed? She said, "No more climbing out of windows, or just no more climbing out of them all by myself, Monsieur?"

That made him grin. A real one, and it gave her a secret little thrill.

"As for your tasks, we will all go," said Benoit. "A walk to Bellamy House for some of your things should not give anyone watching much to think on."

"And what about Mr. Halflife?" she asked.

"Ah," René said. The coin flipped to face. "We should not go until highmoon. Your member of Parliament will be sleeping well by that time, do you not agree?"

"I have no idea. Where is he sleeping?"

"Did I not tell you?" The grin widened. "Monsieur Halflife has invited himself to sleep at Bellamy House tonight."

13

It was strange to see the sanctuary—a place Sophia had always associated with secrets and shadows—so brightly lit and filled with people. The room was deep under Bellamy House, no danger of Mr. Halflife knowing they were there, unless he'd seen them coming across the lawn, which he hadn't. René had skirted around to Nancy's flat at the back of the house and found that Mr. Halflife was on the opposite side, near her father's wing. They hadn't spotted anyone watching their progress on the road, either, though it was impossible to know who might be wandering the woodlands. Mr. Halflife could be wandering, too, she supposed, but nighttime guests of Bellamy House tended to favor locked doors, an extra candle, and a blanket pulled up to their chins.

Sophia bit her lip, rolling her thick paper into a tube, ready for filling with her brother's recipe of powders. She wondered what Mr. Halflife expected to accomplish by staying there. If he hoped to find the deed to the Bellamy land lying about on her father's desk, he would not, as it was currently tucked into the hidden drawer in hers. Or perhaps he was waiting for her to appear one day at the breakfast table, where he could courteously convince her not to marry the man who could save her family and sign away her home instead. She might undo the Bellamys when she blew up the Tombs, but she was fairly certain she would not ruin them out of polite obligation over middlesun scones. And it was hard to seriously fear a man who was afraid of fleas.

She rolled another tube. Tom had left everything written down so they were able to work quickly and almost in silence, Orla waxing and gumming the tubes together, Benoit trimming and greasing the fuses, while René measured the powders and salts carefully per Tom's instructions. A good job for him, Sophia thought, considering how careful and precise he was being with her. Making sure they were not long in the same room, walking just a little back as they made their wary trip down the road. And he'd chosen the opposite end of the tall worktable now, sleeves rolled up and brows drawn down. It wasn't very different from the way she'd behaved their first days in the farmhouse, and somehow this seemed to make her paper tubes more uncooperative.

"Tom," Sophia commented, scowling at her unrolling paper, "is much better at this."

"These kegs are nearly empty, child," said Orla. "Go and fill them." She shoved two small kegs toward Sophia and went back to waxing the tube ends. Sophia knew exactly what this meant. It was, "We'll go faster without you, so go do something useful instead of something that isn't."

She took the kegs and went to the dim end of the room where KINGS CROSS ST. PANCRAS glistened in white and red, the bigger barrels of saltpeter and charcoal lined up beneath it. She ducked behind one of the concrete columns near the wall, taking advantage of a small sliver of privacy from the people across the room, and leaned back her head. Making Bellamy fire was the last thing she'd done with Tom before the Red Rook crossed the sea to rescue the Bonnards. It made her plans, the acknowledged and unacknowledged, seem very tangible.

Then she realized there were booted footsteps coming across the broken tiles. Too heavy for Orla, and Benoit she wouldn't have heard in the first place. She straightened as René came around the corner of concrete, ceramic bowl in his hand, though not in time to look as if she had some purpose for standing still in the near dark behind a column. He paused, looking her up and down.

"You are not in pain?"

She shook her head, failing to think of a single thing to say. His gaze moved away to the ground at her feet.

"If we are to make more I will need the sulfur as well." He waited. "Do you know which . . ."

"Oh, yes. Over here." She led him to the small cask of sulfur, sitting on top of the saltpeter, and pried open the lid.

"How did your brother learn this?" he asked, wrinkling his nose at the smell.

"Tom? He didn't. My father did." She glanced up as she poured a spoonful of yellow powder into the bowl. "Hard to imagine, I know. He must have been like Tom, I think."

There was silence before René said, "In what way?" She heard the caution in his tone. Interested, when he knew it would be better if he wasn't. She knew the feeling.

"They were both curious about the Time Before," she replied. "But for Father, it was the stories of guns that interested him, and the noises they were supposed to have made. He thought they must have needed an explosion of some kind to work. He didn't believe they were just stories."

"Sometimes legends can be true, I have found."

This made her smile. But she was afraid to look up, in case it might scare him away. She talked quick and spooned slow.

"Father studied about it in the Scholars Hall in the city every summer, and he experimented. Down here, I would think . . ." She hadn't really considered that before, her father in Tom's place in the sanctuary, actually striving for something. "And finally . . . he did it. He made a powder that would explode. He said it was what made a gun work, and that enough of it could blow Bellamy House right off the cliff. That's what he told Tom, anyway. When we were young."

René looked back over his shoulder at the worktable.

"That's why the lamps are covered," she said. "But it was Tom who learned how to make the explosions smaller, to mix the salts in for sparks and color."

"But, Mademoiselle." René had set down the bowl of sulfur and picked up one of her casks, moving to the open barrel of saltpeter as he talked. She followed him. "Would the Commonwealth not pay your father well for such a discovery? A weapon that is not a machine?"

"I think any country still honoring the Anti-Technology Pact would. But Father thought about what could be done, what had been done with such things and . . . he didn't want to tell anyone what he'd found. It's part of what torments him, I think. That if he had gone against his conscience, that maybe . . . that we wouldn't be in the predicament we are."

"I see." For a moment there was no sound but the dry, grainy swish of the black powder pouring into the wooden cask. René said, "But Tom could sell what his father did not wish to, is that not so?"

"Tom agrees with Father. He thinks the world is better off without it. And I agree, too, actually."

"But, Mademoiselle . . . ," René said again. She could see his curiosity. It was in the intensity of his gaze and the way he held his body, in the way he angled toward her, forgetting to fill the barrel. "Tell me this. What if the powder is the true thing, but it is the weapons that are the legend? What if a gun is a . . . a story my *grand-mère* would have told?"

"You mean the one who was a liar?"

He cracked a sudden half grin. "You did not have as much concussion as I thought. But how do you answer the question? How do you know what is real, and what is not?"

And wasn't that the matter of the moment, Sophia thought wryly, eyes on his. They were the same color as that tiny bit of blue in the bottom of her candle flame. She glanced over at Orla and Benoit on the other side of the room, working with perfect understanding despite the lack of a common language, and then back to René.

"If I asked you to go somewhere with me, would you come?"

He hesitated, as she'd thought he might.

"You don't have to, of course. But if you don't . . ." She smiled. "Just think of the curiosity you will suffer."

René followed her up the long, winding stair, out the door of the sanctuary, and onto the starlit lawns. She'd felt Orla's surprise when they'd gone, her excuse of "getting something upstairs" evidently not carrying much weight. And she'd seen the look exchanged between Benoit and René, reinforcing their agreement that no one was to go anywhere alone. She looked at the amount of light, and then at René.

"Long way, or the short?" she whispered.

René glanced at the expanse of wall they would have to walk around to get to a door, then the distance up, questioning.

"I've been doing some climbing already," she said. She didn't choose to tell him why. "My cut hasn't bothered me, and it's bound tight."

She watched him consider the presence of Mr. Halflife, but he only waved a hand. "After you, then."

Sophia took hold of the window ledge and was up on it like a cat. She scooted across, grabbed the drainpipe, and shinnied up, using the toeholds she and Tom had placed there as children. As soon as she was off the drainpipe and on the roof, René came up after her from the window ledge, taking every other toehold. Sophia crossed the flat roof over her father's study and started up the latticework that would get her to the more angular sloping gable below her window. She always jumped from the gable to the study roof on her way down, but gravity didn't allow for such an easy approach from the other direction.

At the top of the lattice she got a knee over the gutter at the edge of the roof, and only just bit back a scream. A hand had come out of the darkness, very near her face. She looked up and there was René, sitting on the sloping tiles, grinning like he'd just nicked her purse. She took his hand and let him pull her the rest of the way up. When she was on her feet she looked back down to the study roof. He must be able to jump to the eaves, she thought. Cheater.

"It is good to be tall, Mademoiselle." He was still grinning.

"Unfair, you mean." But she smiled when she said it.

They walked carefully up the gable. Sophia crouched before her dormer window, took a sliver of metal from a small hook under the gutter, and used it to trip her latch. She pushed open both window-panes, swung her legs through, and hopped inside, René after her. Her room was very dark, and with that slightly stale smell that meant no one had been living inside it for a few days; she hated it when a place that was hers smelled that way. She went to the mantel over the hearth—a formal thing of white marble, glowing ghostly in the starlight from the window—took the tinderbox, and put it in René's hands.

He accepted it without comment, and she walked across her rugs to the tune of flint on steel. She knelt and pulled a wooden box from beneath the bed. By the time she had brought it to the hearth there was a small fire just kindling, the mantel candles brightening their end of the room. René held one of them up.

"This is your room?"

"Yes." They were holding their voices low. The quiet seemed to dictate it, even though there were two levels and many layers of hallways and stairs between themselves and Mr. Halflife. She put the box on the hearth rug, settling herself down beside it. René was gazing at everything, turning a half circle with the candle, his hair coming loose from its tie. "What?" she said.

He looked down. "There are little blue flowers. Painted on the walls."

"Yes," she said slowly. "Did you forget that I'm a girl? Is it the breeches?"

"No, Mademoiselle, I had not forgotten." One corner of his mouth lifted. "And that is the fault of the breeches, I think."

Sophia decided not to ask him what he meant by that. She busied herself with the box, so her hair would hide her telltale flush. "My mother painted the walls, so I don't want to have them changed. And the curtains are lace, too, by the way. I thought I'd point that out first and save you the astonishment." When she peeked up, both corners of his mouth were turned up. "Sit with me," Sophia said, "and I'll show you what I made you climb a roof for."

He sat on the opposite side of the box from her, as if suddenly remembering caution, setting the candle on the safer surface of the hearthstone. What had she hoped to accomplish by bringing him up here? What she wanted was to understand him, and this was only going to reveal herself. He pulled up his long legs, waiting.

She brushed the dust from the box—her room was not as immaculate as Spear's—and opened the lid. Packed inside in soft cloth were pieces of clear glass, square, about the size of a window-pane, leaded together in sets of two. Trapped between the pieces were fragments of paper.

René lifted a pane, holding it near the candlelight. The paper inside the glass was brown, in bits and cracking. "There is writing," he said. "Printed." He turned the glass over. "On both sides. How old is this? Did the Bellamys print it?"

"No. It's much older than that. It's as old as Bellamy House, we think. My grandfather found them in the walls."

"They are from Before?" He touched the glass over the paper with a finger, as if he could coax it into speaking. Sophia felt her smile break free at his expression.

"Can you read them?" she asked. "It's a story."

He held the glass closer to the light. "St. Just! Is that why . . ."

She nodded.

"And Marguerite! It was my mother's mother's name."

"The one who was such a liar?"

"No, the other one." He grinned. "Who was also a liar."

"There are only bits of the story, but . . ." Sophia searched through the pieces until she found the one she wanted, scooting around the box to show him. He leaned in to see, caution lost. "This is what I wanted to show you. It says, 'The dull boom of the gun was heard from out at sea.'"

René took the glass in his hands, reading it himself, soft Parisian beneath his breath. "It is real, then," he said, more to himself than her.

"And look, they call it 'firing' the gun."

"Like Bellamy fire?"

She smiled. "Maybe. I don't know."

He gazed at the words. "Does it makes you wonder . . . what else . . ."

"What else your *grand-mère* said that might be true? Like hidden pictures on mirror disks and flying through the air and machines on the moon?"

"Yes," he said, "just so." Sophia watched him running reverent fingers over the glass, his hair such an extraordinary color in the candlelight. If he was an actor, he was the best in history.

"This is my favorite." She pointed at the words. "It says, 'The walls of Paris,' and right here, she calls someone 'Monsieur . . .'" She felt René's eyes dart up at that. "It's even spelled the same. And here, she—whoever she is—talks of being condemned to death, and that someone has hidden her children—and herself, I think—beneath some . . . things in a cart and helped her escape. And the driver is in disguise. He uses tricks to smuggle them out, you see, and he leaves something behind him . . ." She hunted through the tiny, dim words and pointed.

"What is a 'pimpernel'?" René asked.

"I'm not sure. Tom thought it might be a flower, or a drawing of one. But I think he uses it like a signature, so no one else will be accused of his crimes, which is rescuing the people from a prison before they can die. No one knows his real name, only the sign of the 'scarlet pimpernel.' That's about all Tom and I could make out, and it took us ages. It's very hard to read."

René's body had gone very still, the little pulse beyond his collar the only movement. The intensity of his gaze on the glass was something she could feel. "And so now," he said, voice low, "you go to the

Sunken City, which was Paris, and you bring the people out of the Tombs before they die. And you leave a rook feather painted red behind you."

She nodded. He leaned forward, and then all the energy of his gaze was on her.

"Why?" he said. "Tell me why you do it."

Sophia looked down. Their small fire was already smoldering in the hearth, making the room even darker.

"Come," he said, almost a whisper. "Tell me."

Without looking up she said, "Every summer we went to the city to stay with Aunt Francesca, my mother's aunt. She was Upper City, near the Montmartre Gate, about halfway up," she explained, referring to the level of the apartment flat, "one of the first women to teach history at the Scholars Hall. And she was busy, and Father absorbed, and Orla never came to the city, because she is afraid of boats. Tom always teases her about that, about her luck being born on an island . . ." She smiled just a little. "And so Tom, Spear, and I, we ran about like wild things, I guess. We climbed into the Lower City every day it wasn't raining." She ran a hand through her tangle of hair. "I loved it there. The rules were different, not so polite, and it was like a whole secret life, something that no one knew about but the three of us. I went with Mémé Annette to Blackpot Market, and Tom and Spear taught Mémé's son Justin to read, even though he was grown. They felt very important about that. And no one cared that we were Upper City. Maybe because we were young, or Commonwealth, or maybe they'd just gotten used to us. But that last summer before Allemande . . ." She paused. "That last summer everything changed. Our first day back we scaled the cliff wall. I'd brought grapes from the greenhouses for Mémé . . ."

She gathered her thoughts, and again the power of his focus was something she could feel on her face.

"Do you remember when the old premier broke the Anti-Technology Pact and lifted the embargo on simple machines, and a mill owner tried to install a waterwheel? How he told the grindstoners he'd sacked that they would be better off without their jobs, because the wheel would lower the price of their bread?"

"You were not in the Lower City during the Grindstoners' Riot?" he asked.

"The place had gone mad, like looking out a window at a view you see every day, only on this day the glass has warped, or been colored red. It was the place I knew, and then it was not. Tom was nearly killed, would've been if Spear hadn't fought so well. And gendarmes were everywhere, and they were just . . . hacking at everyone, rioters or no . . . We had to jump the bodies in the streets. I cut Tom's and Spear's hair with a knife behind the weaver's shop, just so we could get back to the cliffs."

"What happened to the woman Annette? Mémé?"

Sophia looked up. "She died. The night of the Grindstoners'. How did you know to ask?"

"I heard it. In the way you said her name."

She nodded. "And within a year there was revolution, the premier was dead, and Allemande was in power. People I'd called friends in the Lower City hated me because I was Upper. And the people I knew from Upper were going to the Tombs, to the Razor, students from the Scholars Hall, our neighbors, Aunt Francesca. They set fire to the chapel with the rook paintings on the walls, on Rue de Triomphe, where Father used to stop and leave coins. Everything was changed."

It was the sadness that had made her so angry, she supposed. Started her pressure cooker of rage.

"And so that whole first winter of Allemande, while Tom was nursing his leg, I dreamed up outrageous plans to break people out of the Tombs. It kept Tom's mind from the pain. But Tom said they weren't bad plans. In fact, he thought one might work, and then I remembered the pieces of the Ancient story, and I wondered exactly what I was doing that was so worthwhile, anyway."

"And so you did it."

"We got Aunt Francesca. She's Mrs. Ellington, now, living up west."

"And you did it again."

"And again, and again."

"And you loved it," he said.

She looked at her hands, dirty with dust and black powder, and felt the little line appear between her eyes.

"Of course you did what was right," he said, as if she'd argued. "They were innocents. It was justice. But justice was not the only reason you went back." He tried to make her look at him, his voice lowering further. "Come, Sophia." She lifted her gaze. "You loved taking them from the Tombs because you loved the challenge. You loved outwitting the ones who would destroy so much. And you love it now. Tell me I am wrong."

She bit her lip. She couldn't tell him he was wrong.

René breathed out a small laugh. "You act as if you have just confessed a crime. Why should you not love it? Do you not think I love snatching artifacts from the hands of the melters? Smuggling them to safety under the very nose of the gendarmes?" He looked down at the Ancient paper in his lap, touching the words "blood-thirsty revolution" behind the glass.

"Have you ever thought," he said after a moment, "that perhaps . . . all of this could have happened before? That the people of
the Time Before, no matter how weak we think them, that they were
only making the mistakes of their ancestors, and that we, in turn,
are only making the same mistakes as them? Technology or no? That
the time changes but people do not, and so we are never really moving forward, only around a bend? That the world only ever turns in
circles. Do you think that could be so?"

She met his gaze, fascinated. "I don't know," she said. "But even
if that's true, then don't you think there is always someone who can
change it? Who could break the pattern? Or who could try? If they
chose to. Don't you think that has to be true as well?"

"Yes," he said, "I do think that." The tiny fire went out, leaving
only the candles. "And I would help you."

"You are helping me," she said, voice small. "Isn't that our
agreement?"

"You know that is not what I mean. I would help you."

She did know. She knew exactly what he meant, and it was loud
inside her, like the shattering of glass, like the shifting of the poles,
swinging the world into a new alignment. He thought she was someone who could break the pattern of history. And he was offering to
break it with her.

And just like that, there were no more questions about games or
what was real or whether René Hasard was telling the truth. She just
knew he meant what he said. She chose to believe, and with her
belief came a pull to him, such an irresistible force, that she wondered if this was how it would feel to be an Ancient satellite, forever
circling in the sky. Always kept from flying away by that magnetic
draw, always kept from drifting too near by the uncertainties of the
atmosphere. She clutched her knees, breathing deep, and breathing

deep again, afraid to look at him, this time because she didn't know what would happen when she did.

Then René said, "I owe you an apology again, Miss Bellamy."

Her head jerked up. René had gone rigid, expression hard, careful as he set the glass panes back into their crate. He'd completely misinterpreted her silence.

"I have thought of what you said," he continued, voice still very low, "or what you did not say in Hammond's kitchen, and I want you to know that I think you are right. This arrangement is . . . insecure at best, and if another marriage fee can be had, of course you will be obligated. Of course you will do what is needed for your family."

Sophia stared at him, dumbstruck. Was he really talking about the money? She was sick to death of the money. "I don't . . ."

"No. Let me say. We agreed to leave these matters until after the Rook's mission is done, and it is wrong of me to . . . to put you in such a position. And the situation, it is . . . ridiculous, is it not? We do not even know each other."

They didn't? In some ways, he seemed to know her better than Tom. "But . . ."

"Do not concern yourself. You are right. There is no reason to discuss it again."

The glass with the Ancient fragments had all been replaced inside the box now. He reached out, lifted her hand, and kissed it, a frown on his forehead. She could feel the heat in her face, a pricking sting behind her eyes. If she'd been a satellite before, then maybe this was how it would be to fall through the sky in a blazing ball of fire.

"We should go and help the others. That would be best, no?"

No. No, that would not be best at all. He was setting her hand gently back in her lap, but she did not let go. The frown on his forehead deepened, she opened her mouth to speak, and then the back of her neck prickled, tingling with the pressure of a gaze. Sophia's head whipped around.

"Spear!"

René sprang to his feet as Spear pushed her bedroom door open a little wider and ducked inside. Sophia stood more slowly, that guilty, uncomfortable feeling in her middle warring with all her newly freed truths. How long had he been standing there? René slid his hands into his pockets, looking at Spear with the blue eyes heavy-lidded.

"When did you get back?" she asked. "I've been expecting you."

"I was on my way to the farmhouse now." His face was like a metal casting. "I just stopped for . . . Tom had oil in the sanctuary." He held out a bundle wrapped in sacking. "I've brought you our project." He'd looked at René when he said it, a particular emphasis on the word "our," before his cool eyes went back to Sophia.

"They're done downstairs, Sophie. Don't you think we should go now . . ." He nodded toward the dark corridor. "Before you run into someone you shouldn't?"

LeBlanc stepped carefully around the filth of the street, turned the corner, and was almost immediately confronted by the guard of Allemande. They surrounded their premier, swords drawn, standing at one end of an Upper City boulevard that no longer resembled a boulevard. Barricades that were equal parts scrap wood and pieces of fine furniture had been piled across either end of the block, one of them still ablaze, illuminating the bodies and broken glass that lay on the pavement.

The drawn swords parted, and Allemande stepped through. "Premier," LeBlanc said. "I have only just arrived. Could I ask for a few moments to assess the situation? And I would prefer to have you wait in my office."

Allemande's eyes blinked beneath the glasses, a few of the guards showing surprise.

"For your safety, of course, Premier. I would like to be certain the area is secure."

"Yes," said Allemande slowly. He looked about, and then chuckled. "I would like to be present for your interview with the commandant of the Upper City, I think. He has much to answer for. As do you." The premier put his hands behind his back. When LeBlanc had bowed he strode away with his jangling men, looking a bit like the runt of a litter. A very cunning runt.

LeBlanc watched him go. He had no need of a guard; he was in the hands of Fate. He put his pale eyes on a gendarme standing before a little stone and concrete chapel, unbroken, vibrant red glass showing behind the boarded-up windows. The greatest concentration of the dead were piled before its door, city blue scattered among the other varying colors of cloth. LeBlanc approached cautiously, holding his robes above the blood and muck.

"They tried to take back a chapel, Ministre," the gendarme said. He was young, voice a little high.

"Are there any live ones?"

"I don't think so, Ministre. They fought to the last."

How wise of them, LeBlanc thought. "And who are they?" He looked down at the body in a stained brown shirt near his feet and pushed gingerly with the toe of his shined shoe. The body turned, the man's eyes wide open and vacant, a gaping sword wound in his chest. Beneath the bloody grime on his face, painted on one of his cheeks, was a red and black feather. LeBlanc looked at the man for a long time, then raised his eyes to the shaking gendarme.

"Tell your commandant that he is to come to my office," LeBlanc said, voice oily soft. "That he may give me a full report on his failure to maintain order in the Upper City."

The gendarme scuttled off, nearly at a run. Renaud stepped up from the shadows as LeBlanc reached into his robes and removed a small black sack from the inner pocket. He emptied a single Ancient coin onto his palm, stamped with the year 2024, cupped his hands together, and shook. The coin inside his hands rattled against his skin while he closed his eyes, lips moving silently. Then he pressed the palms flat, the coin still between them, and slowly opened his hands, presenting them to the air like a supplicant. Renaud leaned forward to see. The coin was on facade.

"The will of Fate is no!" LeBlanc snapped. "The Rook lives until the appointed day." Renaud stepped back a pace, but LeBlanc's voice regained its preternatural calm. "I believe the Goddess wishes to increase my enjoyment of the Red Rook's death with each delay." He put the coin away and turned over another body, blotting the shine on his shoe, showing another face with a painted feather. This time it was a woman. LeBlanc stepped back.

"She is responsible for this," he hissed. Renaud nodded, aware that his master did not mean the dead woman. "She has begun this and she will pay. Get another report from our informant. I want to know when she walks from her door. Be certain I have an answer before highsun." He looked to a group of gendarmes putting out the barricade fire, and the little chapel with the red-glass windows and red-stained door. "And if there is an altar in there, tell them to bring it to me . . ."

Renaud raised his eyes. Faint and ethereal above the white running through the dark on LeBlanc's head, a yellow light streaked fire across the night sky.

—

René and Benoit were watchful as they took turns pushing a handcart of Bellamy fire—packed inside one of Sophia's traveling trunks—back down the A5. Spear Hammond was on his horse a little way ahead, his bags on either side and the bundle in his lap, Sophia and Orla with him. So far there had been no telltale rustles, no mysterious figures in the woodlands. The Rathbone cows lowed in a nearby field.

When they had dropped far enough behind, René said beneath his breath, "He has the project he was working on in Kent. He said it was for her, though I would say that he does not know what she really wants it for. She plays her game close. There is nothing new?"

"No." Benoit made room for René to slide over and take the handles of the pushcart without breaking the rhythm of the wheels. "Our man in Kent has seen nothing that should not have been, but Hammond may be more clever than you allow." Then Benoit went still and said, "Look."

The handcart paused. High above them, a light was shooting across the stars, drawing a yellow line in the sky. René watched in silence, then shoved the cart hard through a rut. Benoit shook his head, keeping pace with the cart.

"You, Monsieur, are a wreck. You know this?" When René didn't answer, Benoit said, "Is there nothing you can do about it?"

"No," René replied. "I think not."

Sophia walked with Orla down the lane, grateful for the dark even if she was stumbling over the ruts. It hid the fact that she had tears on her face. Why did she never, ever know the right thing to say? She certainly had no trouble speaking out when she should keep her mouth closed.

She pushed back her hair and paused. A light was streaking above her, a trail of fire across the sky, exactly as she'd imagined in her bedroom. She watched its path as she walked. René had asked her once what she would be willing to risk for a life she could want. She hadn't known how to answer him then, either, and now she knew why. She hadn't known how to answer because she hadn't known just how much she would want it.

"Really, child," Orla chided. "You're a mess. You know you are. What are you going to do about it?"

Sophia shook her head. She didn't know.

Spear was quiet as he rode down the lane, watching Sophia's slim back move wraithlike through the dark. What did Sophie see in this Parisian with his sly city ways? What could she be thinking? Sitting there alone in her bedroom, talking so close he couldn't hear. And he'd seen the way she looked at him. If Sophia Bellamy had looked at him like that just one time, he would have forced Bellamy to let him marry her, at knifepoint if necessary. And this man was cousin to LeBlanc!

What did she think was going to happen when Tom came home? Bellamy wouldn't live much longer; he felt certain about that. And sorry. But Tom wasn't going to let this marriage happen, even if Hasard did scrape up his blasted fee. Tom had said he'd let the land go first. That they would all start again. Spear adjusted his weight in the saddle, making a crisp, clean paper with the seal of the Sunken City rustle just a bit in his shirt pocket. He'd been right to be prepared. Sophia needed looking after, whether she knew it or not.

He watched her push the hair back from her forehead, watched her staring up into the sky as she walked. But it wasn't the Rook in the man's jacket and breeches he was seeing. He saw the Sophia of the sitting room after dinner, in gauzy pink with her feet tucked up beneath her, St. Just in her lap, hair done up in ringlets. She'd been happy like that; they'd all been happy like that. And she would be happy that way again. Add two or three children playing on the floor, and that was exactly what Sophia Bellamy would want. Just as soon as this Parisian was gone.

14

"*Jennifer,*" Tom called. "Tell me about . . . your first day of school." The dark of the Tombs pressed down. "Jennifer?"

The silence was so loud Tom wanted to cover his ears. But the shackles on his wrists were getting hard to lift. He was weakening, and he knew Jennifer was, too. He'd heard it in her voice the last time they talked. And now she wasn't answering.

She was sleeping. That was all. She needed to sleep, to slow her body down. It was the best thing for her. It was what he had to believe. Tom lay down in the dirt beside his dry water bucket, eyes squeezed shut though the dark remained the same. Was Sophie being smart? Had she found LeBlanc's ally, or had LeBlanc found her? Was Sophie dead? Or was she coming for him? And she would get Jennifer, too, wouldn't she? He wasn't going without Jennifer, or whatever was left of her.

"Jen?" he called. "Jen!" He was alone with his echo.

Before, he hadn't wanted his sister to come. Now he only wanted her to hurry.

Sophia came running down the farmhouse stairs. René looked up from the *Monde Observateur*, while Spear straightened from over a trunk, adjusting his position so his head wouldn't brush a ceiling beam.

"Sophie. Good," he said. "We should . . ."

"I need to see the firelighter," she said, hands on hips.

"Sophie, I don't—"

René interrupted. "You are well, Mademoiselle?"

"Yes," she lied. Orla had stayed with her the night before, rubbing her back until she could stop crying. Then she'd slept like a brick, felt awful for it, and woken up guilty. Cartier was coming to drive a load into Canterbury, so their bags could travel ahead of them to the Sunken City. The luggage had to be on the dusk ferry, the same ferry they would catch themselves at dawn, and now it was nearly highsun and the sitting room was still littered with lists and half-packed boxes and trunks.

But it had occurred to her midcry the night before that all her plans for blowing up the Tombs were based on Spear's firelighter working as they had discussed. What if it did not work as they had discussed? What if it did? To come out of the Tombs or not, she hardly knew which she wanted anymore. But what she did want was to understand her possibilities. She wanted to know if her scales had tipped.

"I need to see the firelighter," she repeated.

Orla came through and set down a basket of laundry for packing, shaking her head when Spear turned to René and said dismissively, "Sophie and I have plans to discuss."

Hot blue eyes met hers, and René inclined his head, a stinging smile in one corner of his mouth. He stood to move away just as Orla passed Sophia at the bottom of the staircase.

"Do something about it, child," Orla whispered as she brushed by.

"No," Sophia said. "Wait." Both men turned their heads, but it was Spear she was speaking to. "I think he needs to see."

Spear didn't say anything.

"It would be for the best. Neither one of us will be close by if something goes wrong, or if it doesn't go off . . ."

"It will go off, Sophie," Spear said stiffly.

"I know. But we haven't gotten this far by not having a plan B, have we?" She planted her feet a little more firmly, listening to Orla continue her trip up the stairs after a long pause to listen. René stood with his shirt untucked and hair undone, hands in pockets, watching Spear, whose practiced expression was impossible to read.

She must have looked a little fierce because Spear did not argue, only said slowly, "Of course, Sophie. If that's what you want."

Spear ducked through the open door of his bedroom while Sophia came to the couch and sat. René dropped into his usual chair, neither of them looking at the other. But she could feel him sitting there, like a redheaded, smoldering fire.

Spear came back with his bundle from the night before. They watched as he untied the sacking, and on the low table in front of the couch he set a small wooden box with an odd mechanism attached to its top. On one side was a clock face, painted with simple symbols for the times of the sun and moon, a skinny black pointing finger pivoting out and around from the middle. Spear sat down on the couch next to Sophia, and they all leaned forward. The box made a strange *tick, tick, tick* in the quiet room.

"You have to make sure it's wound," Spear began. "Use this key, here." He put a blunt-ended key in a hole on the side of the clock, and turned. The clock made a sharp clicking noise above the ticks. "Turn until it's tight, no more. Then start with the finger pointing to the time that is now." Spear glanced at Sophia. "You know how the symbols work? Dawn at the bottom, then around to middlesun, highsun, to nethersun, and then dusk, and the same for the moon, middlemoon, highmoon, nethermoon, and then you're back to dawn . . ."

Sophia bit her tongue. Of course she knew how time worked.

René was leaning forward, his curiosity on display. "Ancient clocks were marked with numbers," he said, "but I have never understood how time can be held to a number. Every night it takes a little longer and a little longer for the moon to reach its height, or else a little less and a little less, but a clock makes the same number of ticks each day to get to the marking of highmoon. It cannot be accurate."

"That's why clocks will never really work," Spear said. "Technology can't keep up with those kinds of changes. It does better with the sun, of course, the sun being more regular, and when the moon is full it's not too far off. We're only two or three days out from a full moon, so by the time we get to the city we should be able to go by the times marked, which is good. Another week and we'd be making guesses, especially at night . . ."

"Well, I think you're looking at it all wrong," Sophia said, chin in hand, eyes on the symbols of sun and moon. "I've always thought that the Ancients could have used the clock to mark the time of day, instead of marking the time of day on a clock."

René leaned back. "Tell me what you mean, Mademoiselle."

"I mean that a clock is precise, divided up into even ticks, right? What if the Ancients used the number of ticks to mark the time of day, instead of the height of the sun or moon? So highmoon could happen here . . ." She put a finger on the space between middlemoon and highmoon. ". . . or even here." She pointed to the area close to nethermoon. "That way highmoon is not the time; highmoon is happening at a different time every night. If you're counting the ticks as time."

Spear chuckled. "You mean that two Ancients could agree to meet at highmoon, wait until the clock says it's highmoon, look up in the sky, and see the moon still rising?"

"Hence the preference for numbers on a clock," she said, "rather than the symbol for highmoon."

"That's mad, Sophie," Spear said.

René stretched his arms up behind his head. "No," he said, holding Sophia's eyes for a moment. "It is brilliant."

She dropped her gaze back to the clock, so he could not see how ridiculously pleased that comment had made her.

"So, you start by pointing the finger at the time it is now," Spear said quickly, "and by that I mean the time it really is . . ." He glanced once at the filmy windows, and moved the finger to just past the full yellow circle, the symbol for highsun. "And then you turn the wheel . . ." He spun the clock around to show a small, flat wheel on the back of the box, sun and moon symbols also neatly painted. ". . . and point it to the time you want the machine to work."

Sophia looked at Spear sidelong, smiling a little, watching him turn the wheel to just past highsun. He really was clever to have made this, and it was obvious that he was enjoying the opportunity to show off the firelighter, whether he had wanted René to see it or not.

"Then pull out this knob here . . ." He put a finger on the knob beside the wheel. ". . . and the machine will be set."

"And what does it do, Hammond, when you set the time?" René asked.

Spear pulled out the knob instead of answering, the iron arm of the apparatus on top of the box moving upward on its own. They waited, listening to the rhythmic ticks, like a fingernail on glass, or sharp-heeled shoes clacking across the Bellamy ballroom tiles. Then there was a sudden bang and flash of fire. Sophia jumped, caught her breath, and smiled.

"Oh, Spear, that's really very good."

Spear grinned back at her. He looked just like he had when he was thirteen and her father had given him a colt for his birthday. "I put a little bit of the black powder from the sanctuary in it," he said, holding up a small bottle from the sacking. "It's loud, but it works much better that way."

René had recovered from any surprise and was on his knees at the table, peering at the mechanism closely in the sunlight. "And where did you put the powder, Hammond?" When Spear pointed, he said, "May I?"

Spear reluctantly handed over the bottle and René sprinkled just a little where Spear had shown him. He checked the time, turned the wheel in the back to only a little past where Spear had set it, and pulled out the knob. They waited. A whir, a snap from the iron arm, another startling bang as the flame flared.

"This is to light the Bellamy fire?" René asked, gaze still on the machine. He hadn't moved, even when it flashed.

"Yes, that's right," Sophia said when Spear didn't answer. The smell in the air was sharp in her nose. "It will catch the greased fuse on fire, so the tubes can explode while we're well away."

René straightened, sitting back on his boot heels. "I see."

Sophia tucked her feet beneath her, watching her hands. That story had sounded feeble even to her. The firelighter was going deep into the Tombs, where the barrels of Bellamy fire she'd been having delivered were disguised and stored. But she would not set it until the mob had cleared from the prison yard, and that could take a long time if they were expecting an execution, especially the Red Rook's execution. Especially an execution that wouldn't happen because the Red

Rook was not there. She might spend all night playing hide-and-seek with LeBlanc. And the Tombs would be swarming with gendarmes after the prisoners were gone. An anthill stirred with a stick.

Spear leaned into the couch beside her and threw an arm along the back of it, as if they were sitting there . . . together. Sophia closed her eyes, absorbing her frustration.

"You should think about how the firelighter will be packed," René was saying. "They may be searching at the gates, and they will not let this through, I think."

He was right. The firelighter had to be breaking at least ten anti-technology laws at once.

"And there is another thing we should discuss."

Sophia opened her eyes. Everything about him was fiery where the sunlight hit, but his tone had gone cold. He dropped into the chair again.

"You may remember that in the Upper City I am known as something of a . . . pleasure seeker. And Miss Bellamy will be coming as my fiancée, to an engagement party which my cousin must attend. It is essential that this part of our ruse is successful, yes? Or the plan will not work at all."

Sophia got up from the couch and went to the window, where she could see the vague forms of trees. "What are you getting at, Hasard?" Spear asked.

"I am saying that when LeBlanc hears my marriage to the sister of the Red Rook goes forward, he will be filled with suspicion. But when he hears that it is a match of love, he will be curious. And it is this curiosity that will bring the guests, and LeBlanc, to the door of my flat. Our upcoming marriage must be the talk of the Upper City. It must be in the newspapers. That should not be so difficult. Most of the reporters who write these things are . . . friends . . ."

Sophia wondered what Madame Hasard paid them.

"They know what to print and what to not. But they must have something to write about, yes? And we must give it to them. So I am saying that starting at dawn, at the dock, Miss Bellamy and I will have to behave in a way that is . . . very engaged. Can we do this?"

An uncomfortable silence spread. Sophia hadn't considered this part of their plan, especially in light of that magnetic force that she was currently trying to resist by standing at the window. René would go back to being the man of the Parisian magazine, and with a bride-to-be to show off. Should she pretend to like it, when she really did, all while pretending that she didn't? She fiddled with a shirt button. What a strange torture.

"But it is not only the papers that should concern us. We must assume we are being watched," René continued. "LeBlanc will be watching. On the ferry, on the road, every step we take in the city. No one must doubt my relationship with Miss Bellamy, not until the fight we have planned. To do otherwise would endanger the Rook and those that wait for her in the Tombs. So I cannot afford to have my behavior questioned."

"You are not to kiss her," Spear said. Sophia's head whipped around.

René was slouched into the chair now, his grin a little wicked. "As chaperone, you must feel it your proper duty to make such rules. But I wonder, Hammond, just how good you will be at enforcing them?"

Spear and René glared at each other like two boys with one cake between them. It woke her temper. Sophia left the window, snatching up her fluffy white underskirt from the laundry basket on the way, and sat herself down before the low table in a cloud of white cloth.

"I'll be the one making my own rules, thank you," she said, pulling out a knife. "And I think you both know I'm perfectly capable of enforcing them." What was wrong with them? What was wrong with her? Since when had she ever wanted to marry anybody? "Spear, I'll die happy if I never hear your opinion on this again," she said, mentally gauging the size of the firelighter. "And as for you, Monsieur . . ." The cloth of the underskirt made a soft ripping sound as she slid the knife through the seam. "Tomorrow we will be exactly as engaged as I say we are."

LeBlanc set down a goblet of wine and cut a slit beneath the seal of a small invitation. His desk was littered with reports of insurrection and red feathers, but his interview with the Upper City commandant had left him in a good mood. He read the invitation's neat Parisian, drumming his fingers on the top of the plain, polished desk.

"Well, Renaud. It appears the marriage with Miss Bellamy goes forward. Isn't that charming?"

Renaud was on his knees on the other side of the desk, scouring blood from the floor.

LeBlanc read through the invitation again, drumming harder on the desk. "They are to give an engagement party, on the eve of Tom Bellamy's execution, and we are invited. How kind of them." He chuckled. "I don't think we need to attend such a farce, do you? And what funds does my young cousin think to use for this marriage?" His pale eyes became slits. "Exactly whose side is he playing on, Renaud?"

Renaud always kept his opinions to himself. It's why he was alive.

After a time LeBlanc sighed. "It is unwise to tempt Fate, and I admit I am curious. We will have the landover road to the city watched, and a personal search at each gate, I think. The Goddess may have declared life for the Rook for three more nights, but there is no need to make that time easy for her, Renaud. And perhaps it is also time to have another talk with Madame Hasard. She may be very interested to hear this happy news about her son." LeBlanc's smile curled as he looked at René's looping script. "The love of a parent often affects good judgment."

Sophia lifted the trapdoor to her father's room and silently pushed aside the rug. It had been a difficult trip to negotiate. She'd had to go out the farmhouse window, onto the roof, across and down the outside of the chimney stones. And then she'd taken to the woods and fields instead of the road, ways that were almost as familiar, all of it armed to the teeth. For all she knew Mr. Halflife was still lurking about, hoping for that breakfast meeting with signatures and scones. But she would not leave the Commonwealth without seeing her father, and she wasn't in any mood to ask permission, or make the trip with fanfare and an escort.

Bellamy sat much as he had the last time she'd come, in his chair looking out the window. Dying firelight flickered on the walls, and the room was stifling. Just how many times a night was Nancy tiptoeing in here to build up the fire? She was glad Orla was coming to help her. Bellamy's eyes were open, hair combed, pajamas and robe clean, but he seemed to have shrunk beneath his blankets. Sophia put a tentative hand on his chair.

"Father? It's Sophia."

Bellamy blinked once, but did not change his stare.

"I'm leaving now," she whispered. "I'm going to get Tom. He'll come back to you in just a few days. I promise you that." She did not promise him that she would come back. She waited. "Do you understand, Father?"

The boom of the ocean was an undercurrent in the thick, stagnant silence. Sophia waited for ten of Bellamy's breaths, then laid a red-tipped feather in her father's open hand. She left the way she'd come, the stifling dark of the room settled deep in her lungs. The feeling didn't fully clear away until she was back at Spear's farm, up the chimney stones, across the roof, and in through her bedroom window.

Sophia turned the latch and threw her jacket on the bed. She was cold, but it was a clean cold, so much better than the horrible warmth of her father's room. St. Just cracked open an eye from his basket, then went right to sleep again, as if girls crawled through his window all the time. She supposed they did.

Sophia unbuckled the short sword she was wearing, the knife on the other side, pulled the smaller knife from her boot and the cheesewire from around her laces, making a pile of metal on the mattress. She kicked off her boots, and then paused, listening. She had heard one hard thump from outside her locked door.

She stole softly across the room, avoiding the third and fifth floorboards, where the creaks were hiding, turned the lock, and peered into the hallway. It was empty, dimly lit by the overhead lantern. And then there was another soft bump, as if someone had stomped, just once. The noise had come from René's room.

Sophia ventured into the hall and put her hand on the doorknob. She thought better of that, and was going to lift it away to knock when the door suddenly shook, an impact she could feel through the metal against her palm. And she knew exactly what that had been. A body hitting oak wood. She threw open the door.

A man in dark cloth, big, balding, and with bulging arms, had a rope around René's neck from behind, and they were staggering backward, struggling in a macabre sort of dance. René had managed to get a hand between the rope and his neck on one side, and he was trying unsuccessfully to get a foot behind to knock the man's feet out from under him. Sophia made a lightning scan of the room. No weapons she could see, no time to go for the pile on her bed. The two men lurched around again, and she did the only thing that occurred to her. She threw her body at the back of the stranger's legs, aiming low and behind his knees.

The man's feet flew over her side, a boot heel catching her hard in the ribs, and both men went down backward, slamming the floor with René on top. Furniture rattled, the man lost his grip on the rope, and as Sophia was rolling free from the tangle of feet, René flipped around, gasping in a breath as he got a knee on the stranger's arm. He brought up an arm to hit the man in the face, the rope now dangling from his hand, but then he hesitated, and so did Sophia, midscramble to get herself upright.

The stranger had gone still, his eyes open and unblinking, staring at the ceiling, the bald head raised slightly from the floor. He had landed on the iron grate surrounding the fireplace, a small pool of blood forming below it on the hearthstone. René put a hand first on the open mouth to feel for breath, then on the man's neck, searching for a pulse. He dropped the rope and climbed off the thick chest, coughing, looking around until he found Sophia. He shook his head.

Sophia let a small shock wave pass through her. It wasn't as if death was something unfamiliar. She wished it was. But she hadn't expected to encounter it here, tonight, on the floor of Spear's spare bedroom.

Instead of standing, René stayed on his knees, coughing spasmodically, and stuck a hand in the man's pocket. Sophia saw what he was doing and quickly did the same to the other side. Empty. She looked more closely at the clothes, the dark cloth, examined the bald head, shaved to remove any telltale sign of a hairstyle. He could have been from anywhere. He could have been from anywhere so deliberately that he must have come from somewhere significant.

"Do you know him?" Sophia whispered. St. Just was barking full force, clawing from the inside of Sophia's room, and footsteps were coming up the stairs.

"No," said René, voice gruff. "He was in the room, waiting . . ."

Then Benoit was through the doorway, candle in hand. He looked at the dead man's eyes, then spotted the reddening mark on René's neck. He turned to Sophia. "*Êtes-vous bien?*"

"I'm fine," she replied as Spear came at a run to the door. He stopped, Orla moving around him and into the room from behind. Sophia saw Spear's eyes widen at the sight of the dead man, his hand grab the doorjamb, and for a moment she couldn't decide why he looked so odd. Then she realized it was because his hair was mussed. Orla pulled her to her feet, lifting and pinching her arms, checking for injuries without comment.

"What happened?" Spear asked. He sounded dazed.

"A man has attacked me." René stood up. He was a little breathless, voice full of sand, but very calm, so much so that Sophia was not fooled. "We fell . . ." His gaze darted once toward Sophia. ". . . as you can see."

Spear did not miss where René's look had gone, and then he took in Orla, brushing off Sophia's clothes and checking her limbs.

"Sophie?" he said. Now he had both hands on the door frame, as if he might push the opening apart. "Were you in here?"

She narrowed her eyes at Spear's tone. "I heard a noise and came to see what was wrong." She glared back, defying him to ask her more. When he didn't, she turned to René. "Is he Parisian?"

But before he could answer, Orla said, "No." She stood looking over Sophia's shoulder. "He's shaved off his beard and what little hair he had, but that's the hotelier of the Holiday."

Benoit asked René for a translation, then knelt down, studied the man again, and nodded his agreement. Sophia turned to Spear. "Are they right?"

"Yes," he said, ducking beneath the door. "He looks so . . . I didn't recognize him. But . . ." Spear looked around at them all. "Why would he try to kill Hasard?"

Sophia stared down at the hotelier. She didn't even know his name. It was just coming home to her that if she hadn't stepped into the hall, it would have been René, not this man, lying dead on the floor planks. She looked to René, hands on knees, still catching his breath, and felt the pull she'd been resisting since that night in her bedroom become a tug, an ache so hard it made her put out a hand for the bedpost. What would have happened if she hadn't thrown open that door? She turned to Benoit, and found that he'd been watching her.

"Is this the man you saw in the woods?" she asked him in Parisian. Benoit scratched through his wispy hair, once more assessing the hotelier's dead body.

"It could be so," he replied. "The shape is not unlike. I would say, yes, it is so."

"This man needs to get off Spear's land as soon as may be, while it's still dark," Orla said, her Commonwealth cutting harsh through the Parisian. "Unless somebody thinks we ought to bring out the militia?"

If they brought out the militia, they would never be boarding a ferry to the Sunken City at dawn.

"Does he have a wife?" Sophia asked. "Children?"

Spear shook his head. Orla crossed her arms, expression severe.

"Spear and Benoit, go make certain we don't have any other uninvited guests in the house, and then Spear, go get a shovel. Two or three, if you have them. The other side of Graysin and over by the cliffs will do, I think. I'll change clothes . . ." Sophia realized with a start that Orla was in her nightgown. ". . . and bring something to wrap his head in, so he won't make a mess on the stairs. Sophie, take care of Monsieur's neck. Monsieur can take first watch while the rest of us are gone, and I'll get you a bucket and brush to be cleaning that hearth."

Orla discovered that everyone was staring at her, making the lines of her face deepen.

"You thought we were going to lock the doors and have a long moon's sleep?" she said. "Go!"

Spear and Benoit scurried, though Sophia wasn't sure Benoit knew what he was supposed to do, Orla marching out right after them. René watched Orla leave, then met Sophia's gaze.

"An excellent woman," he said. Then he coughed.

Sophia walked quickly around the dead man to René's washstand, poured water from the ewer into the bowl, and wet a cloth. She wrung it out and went back to René, who was now sitting on the edge of the bed. She knelt down. "Show me your neck."

"There is no . . ."

"Just show me your neck."

He raised his chin. There was a red mark circling his skin, a burn almost, tiny pinpricks of blood where the rope had pulled hardest, already purpling along the edges. She sponged at it carefully, the little pulse at the base of his throat beating strong. She imagined what his throat would look like without that pulse, and struggled with a hot burst of fury. "Tell me what happened," she said.

"Are you shaking?"

She paused, holding the wet cloth against the mark. "I'm angry. That's all."

"At who?"

She stared at him, incredulous. "At LeBlanc, of course!" René leapt up from the bed and began to pace.

"I do not think he was trying to kill me."

"But you're standing between him and a fortune!"

"No, no! I mean him." He coughed again, waving a hand at the dead man on the floor. "He was not even trying! He is here, waiting, as soon as I climb through the window, he has me unawares, he knows not to get his feet knocked out from under him . . ."

"He did get his feet knocked out from under him!"

René turned, his smile wry. "You are the variable in every equation, Mademoiselle. But I am saying he knew how to keep his feet back so that I could not knock them out, and that he had the advantage of weight. And yet this man cannot throttle me properly? He lets us thrash about the room with my hand beneath the rope? No, no, no."

He went to the pitcher and poured himself a glass of water, drinking slowly and apparently painfully. Sophia sat on her heels, cloth still in hand. "What do you mean you were climbing through the window?"

He set down the glass. "I mean that I have been on the roof, watching Sophia Bellamy come sneaking back into this house."

She opened her mouth once, then closed it.

"You have spent much time on the roof these past days. Do you think no one notices when you are gone?"

"I went to see my . . ."

René threw up a hand, the perfect impression of a red rope across his palm. "I know where you went!" Now she saw where all that restless energy was coming from. She was not the only one angry. He was furious. With her. "You know there is someone . . ." His eyes darted to the body on the floor. ". . . you agree there will be no more climbing out of windows, and yet you go anyway, alone, without saying . . . That is madness. Reckless!"

Sophia bit her lip, still kneeling on the floor, breathing hard against her own temper. Then before she could react, René came across the room, sat again on the edge of the bed, and caught her head in his hands.

"Look at me. Do you trust me?"

She looked at him. He was angry and wild-headed and unshaven and beautiful. "Yes," she whispered.

"Why?"

"I don't know."

There was the hint of an irate smile around his mouth. "Then prove it. Prove that you trust me and tell me your plans."

"You know all our plans."

"Stop lying to me! Do you think I do not see all the things you choose not to tell us, how you have placed the others and how you have so exactly placed yourself? Do you really think I am what I pretend to be?"

The room had gone still. And just as suddenly as he had in Spear's kitchen, René dropped his hands. "I am sorry," he said, and got up to go stand in front of the window, arms behind his head. She could see him struggling for control, deep breaths that were straining the linen of his shirt. She missed the warmth of his palms.

"Tell me your plans, Mademoiselle," he said, in the calm voice that was not, though this time the sound was full of gravel. "Tell me what the firelighter is for."

"To blow up the Tombs," she said. Just like that. How odd to hear those words coming from her mouth; it made her heart slam repeatedly in her chest. "I'm going to empty the prison holes, blow them up, and take down LeBlanc. If I can."

René had gone absolutely still in front of the window. She counted several more breaths before he said, "This is why you wanted both the ships. Not as a decoy. You are going to fill them with prisoners."

She didn't need to answer.

"And, like tonight, you go on your own, you say nothing . . ."

"I . . . didn't want to worry them," she whispered.

"What you did not want, Mademoiselle, was to be prevented. Tell me I am wrong."

She couldn't. And then he spun around.

"You do not expect to come out. That is why you do not say."

"I don't know what will happen." She jumped as he kicked a stray buckled shoe, making it bounce against the far wall, near the dead man.

"And Hammond does not know this, of course."

"No." Sophia got up, her temper back in control. "But this is not what we should be discussing." She ignored the way René threw up his hands, as well as the word he'd said softly in Parisian. "We need to know who our enemies are, or we might not get to the Sunken City to do anything at all. Was the hotelier LeBlanc's man?"

"I think he would have been anyone's man who paid him." René was pacing. "But you should consider that someone on this coast has been talking to LeBlanc. And for quite some time."

"Do you think it was him?"

The hands went up to his head again. "I do not know."

"And you think he wasn't trying to kill you, but . . . what? Incapacitate you? Dissuade you from traveling to the city tomorrow? Who doesn't want you in the city, and how did they find out where you are?"

He looked up. "It makes no sense. But I will say this to you, Mademoiselle. If this is LeBlanc's doing, if I am the only thing standing between him and the Hasard fortune, then the person I should be worrying for most is Maman."

LeBlanc twisted the signet ring with the seal of the Sunken City around and around his finger, light that was just past highmoon slanting in through the stone window. "I have finished waiting, Madame. Do we have an understanding?"

The woman nodded, flaming red hair still vivid beneath the prison dirt.

"One should never deny Fate, Madame." LeBlanc's smile came slow as he slid the pen and ink pot across his desk.

15

Sophia pushed out her breath, trying to endure Orla's tightening of her clothing. Only Orla could arrange one's traveling costume and bury a body in the same night, and with equal efficiency. It was still practically nethermoon. But they would need to leave soon to make the dawn ferry.

"You will . . . you'll take care of Father for me?" Sophia said. She knew Orla would, she just wanted to hear her say it.

"I'll be looking after Mr. Bellamy."

"And St. Just?"

"As if I wouldn't."

"And yourself?"

"Well, really!" said Orla. "You'd think you weren't coming back in just a day or three."

Sophia grimaced as the last string of her corset was pulled, but she also smiled. She wasn't positive she was coming back, of course. She never had been. She never was. But it seemed much more certain now, ever since René Hasard had pulled her out her bedroom window.

The others had been off dealing with the hotelier when the knock came on the glass; she'd nearly jumped from her skin. But when she threw open the window, René had merely stuck out a hand, offering to help her up onto the roof.

"What are you doing?" she whispered, once she'd gotten onto the thatch.

"I am on watch, remember?" he said quietly, his voice rough. "And I am guessing that you do not mind having a conversation on a roof, Mademoiselle." She'd pulled up her knees, hugging them from both cold and nervousness while he settled himself, careful not to be too close. He had a mug of hot tea, though how he'd managed to climb a roof with it she wasn't sure. He offered her a sip. Willow bark. For pain. Probably for his throat. Then he'd said, "I want you to tell me how you are going to blow up the Tombs."

"Is this where you try to prevent me?"

But he'd only shaken his head. "Tell me your plans, Mademoiselle."

And so she'd told him, about the Bellamy fire that should already be inside a cell, and the free landovers Allemande was providing for La Toussaint, taking the people of the Lower City to the Upper, and out the gates to the cemeteries. And René had listened, first with elbows on knees, and when his tea was gone, on his back beneath the stars, flipping his weighted coin while the highmoon made the lane a luminescent ribbon, twisting through the trees along the sea cliff. There was a darker circle on the skin around his neck.

And when she was done he took her plan and expanded it, adding detail, changing the timeline. They'd argued over it, and it had taken him some time to convince her. But in the end, René was to go back and set the firelighter when the prison yard was clear, after she'd gotten everyone away, including herself, eliminating her need to stay and play cat and mouse with LeBlanc.

"After all, Mademoiselle," René had commented, "you are no good to your family dead. Can we at least agree on that?"

And that had started her thinking. If she could rescue Madame Hasard, if she could take down LeBlanc, if she came back in one piece, what would stand in the way of a marriage fee, then? Unless René had completely decided against her. If. If. If. But at least there were possibilities.

Orla tied down her last lace, and Sophia turned and gave her one brief, ferocious hug. Orla kissed her cheek—which with Orla was not a particularly tender gesture—then pushed her away with a tiny smack.

"Now then. Don't you have a boat to catch?"

They left for the ferry in the dark, Cartier at the reins of the landover, driving around the ruts in the lantern light, and on the way, they passed Mr. Halflife's landover in the lane. Sophia peeked through the curtain of the back window, watching the sleek vehicle rattle away in its own sphere of yellow light. He was going to Spear's. In the dark before dawn. Poor Mr. Halflife. It would be a long time before there was a place wide enough for his driver to turn around, and by that time he would have no way of knowing which direction they'd gone. She let the curtain fall, and turned back to the Bellamy landover's slightly worn interior. None of them even mentioned it.

It was odd to see everyone in their finery after nearly two weeks of linen shirts and breeches at the farm. Even Benoit was in his more formal servant's attire. Sophia was wearing a navy dress Orla had altered for her, demure in color but with a cut that was a little more daring, the white underskirt—firelighter sewn in—underneath. The revival of Ancient voluminous skirts had made Sophia happy for very different reasons than other girls in the Commonwealth. They'd decided on natural, ringleted curls, and a small amount of paint around the eyes, all of it engineered to evoke a Commonwealth girl trying to assimilate into Upper City society, where being ostentatious was not in fashion. Unless, evidently, you were René Hasard.

He was back in the gold jacket, like at their Banns, and now that she could look at him without such trepidation, she could see what his gaggle of women had. If Spear Hammond was a marble statue precisely carved, then René Hasard was an Ancient painting out of *Wesson's*, foreign and yet so striking it was hard to look away. Or maybe, Sophia thought, it was because she knew there was a russet-headed daughter stealer underneath the hair powder.

And he made a scene at the Canterbury dock. From the moment she stepped down from the landover, they were *engaged*. He introduced her to the captain, whom he did not know, explaining his fiancée's specific need for a journey without many waves, chided Benoit about the baggage, was loud with his opinions about the cleanliness of the boat and overzealous in the arrangement of her cushions until the steward was exasperated. There was no one on the ferry who was not aware of their presence, and a man in the corner of the windowed cabin appeared to be scribbling down notes. It was very well done. When they finally settled on one of the bench seats, René pulled her close, arm around her waist, cheeks nearly touching, turning her to him as if they were in a constant state of whispering.

"I think the man behind us wonders if you are a victim of kidnapping, my love," he said, voice low and still gruff in her ear. "So you may want to act as if you are enjoying this."

She would have been offended if she had not heard the tease in his voice. She'd been trying hard not to show just how much she was enjoying it, this feeling of being held while they rode the waves, the smell of the soap he'd used to shave, the sun rising just beyond René's shoulder, making the salt spray sparkle on the glass. She lifted her hands to the white cravat around his neck and began to adjust it, so the edge of his bruising did not show. She was also enjoying the fact that he was not dead on Spear Hammond's floor. She made long, slow work of the cravat.

"Ah," he said, the breath on her cheek almost a sigh. "Now my uncle Émile will not have to be ashamed of me."

"And why would your uncle Émile be ashamed?" she asked.

"To have not taught me better, of course. This is his, how should I say . . . his area of expertise. You will meet Uncle Émile soon, when we get to the city." The arm around her tightened, voice a gritty whisper. "I have some advice for you, my love. Never sit next to my uncle Émile."

She laughed, and she could see the edge of his cheek crinkling above his jaw. She decided to be bold and stroked it once with the back of her fingers, a move she was sure made them look like happy lovers. His face was almost smooth this time.

"Oh, no," he said, twirling one of the ringlets. "Benoit is doing his best at distraction, but I think Hammond may murder me in my bed tonight. And you should arrange your skirts, my love, your fire-lighter is showing. I would do it, but . . ."

She was sorry to see the coast. She knew he was playing his part, doing exactly as they'd planned, but she wondered whether it would feel different when he was being the real René. Or if the two could ever be one and the same.

The dock at Berck was more of an arrival and departure point than a town, and it was thronged with people trying to make their way out of the Sunken City and off the Parisian coast. Animals, bags, carts, men shouting about their tickets and muddy streets all mixed with landovers coming and going. Somewhere in that crowd there would be another man from the newspapers lurking, and if nothing of their arrival was printed, it would not be René Hasard's fault.

Again he chided Benoit unmercifully about the baggage, took personal offense to a stranger's innocent glance at Sophia, and now was loudly insisting to the porter that planks should be laid from the pier to the landover, so that his wife-to-be's slippers would not be discolored by the dirt. Sophia held her skirt just above the mud, helping the underskirt take the weight of the firelighter, looking on adoringly while René explained that he was René Hasard (cousin to the Ministre of Security, but say nothing of that), that his fiancée's brother had just been condemned (he is the Red Rook, but please do not tell anyone, Monsieur), and that dirty shoes could be the final blow to the emotional well-being of his betrothed. It was difficult not to laugh. René did not possess the first ounce of shame, and he was loving every moment of it—when you knew to look. But she was also very afraid that Spear might hit him.

Sophia reached up and unpinned her navy hat as Benoit finally drove the hired landover lurching and rattling down the pitted road that would take them to the Sunken City. René adjusted the blanket over their laps and her dress—it was chilly, clouds rolling in across the sun—and again he pulled her close to him on the seat.

"I think that is unnecessary," said Spear from the opposite side, his features tightly controlled. He had not spoken since they got off the boat.

"I am not being impertinent, Hammond." René's lower, less Parisian voice was a shock after the one he'd been using on the dock. "I am keeping our heads safe. You would be surprised, I think, to know how many eyescopes are between here and the city."

Spear looked René full in the face. "Close the curtains, then."

"In which case we will not be seen at all. As we wish to be, or otherwise. You would rather our plan did not work?"

"Really, Spear," Sophia said, "it's nothing. And you know he's right."

René was right, but it certainly wasn't nothing. That aching pull she'd been feeling had been soothed all day; she wanted to be soothed again. Spear crossed his arms, leaned back his head, and closed his eyes, which, Sophia thought, was probably as good an escape as he was likely to get.

She scooted in to René, his arm still around her waist, squirming about until she said, "Corsets are of the devil."

"Sophia," said Spear, in the corrective tone of her father, once upon a time.

"Spear," she said, in the exact same tone. She'd felt guilty before; now she was irritated. "It's an item of clothing. An item of clothing that happens to be worn under a woman's clothes and happens to be of the devil. If you had one on, you'd say the same."

"Turn this way," René said. She could hear the amusement. And so, probably, could Spear. René guided her around until her back was to him, doing the same until his own was in the corner of the seat. She adjusted the firelighter beneath the dress and the blanket on her lap. She could feel René's chest behind her, his chin somewhere near her ear.

"Better?" he asked.

She nodded, staring out the window where the farms of The Désolation were passing, a few vineyards yet unharvested, purple grapes hanging under the clouded sky. She was aware of his breathing, in and out against her back, of the arm around her middle, holding her in. René's cheek settled against her curls. He was probably getting hair powder on her, but she didn't care. Then his other arm moved very gently beneath the blanket.

She darted a glance at Spear, but he was still head back, eyes closed, swaying with the motion of the wheels. René slid his arm around her from the other direction, his fingers lacing together over her middle, the warmth of him seeping through her dress. She breathed deep. There was no risk in this. This was safety. And nothing even resembling the feeling of being trapped. Did this sort of thing go on all the time when you loved someone? She felt René's breath slow behind her.

And then she opened her eyes. René was asleep; she could feel the relaxed stillness around her. She was pleasantly pinned inside it, and the light in the landover had changed. Slanting now, on its way to dusk. Spear was awake, looking at nothing somewhere near the floor, and she wondered how long he had been sitting there, watching the two of them sleep. Guilt snaked inside her; Spear hadn't deserved that. He didn't deserve any of this, really. She tried to imagine the situation reversed. Spear's arms around her middle, Spear's breath in her hair. She couldn't. She looked out the window, trying to understand where they were, and only then did she comprehend what was passing by them.

She must have stiffened, because René said near her ear, "What is wrong?" His voice was even more rough with sleep. She sat up, startling Spear from his reverie.

They were driving through the cemeteries that lay outside the gates of the Sunken City, but she was not seeing what she'd expected. Mémé Annette had told her all about the one day a year the gates opened, how she could leave the Lower City and go to the cemeteries for the last day of La Toussaint, decorating the gravestones with feathers and ribbons and autumn flowers; she saved all year for those flowers. Mémé had even whispered to her once, while tying a La Toussaint ribbon of satiny yellow into the long, wild braids she'd worn as a child, that some people would slip away from the cemeteries and never come back again. The gates would close on them forever. Sophia had made her promise never to do that, and Mémé had said she wouldn't.

But the last day of La Toussaint had not come, and yet the cemeteries had been decorated. Hundreds upon hundreds of blooms of white and black—were they dyed, or had someone actually grown a black flower?—and swaths of dark and light cloth. Masks with dual faces, one side ecstatic white, the other an anguished black, had been set up on poles among the tombstones, as far as the eye could see, ribbons trailing from beneath them and dangling in the wind, looking horribly like the staked heads the mob sometimes paraded through the Lower City.

"The answers of Fate," René said. "Yes and no, life and death." He sat back on the cushion of the landover. "Have either of you noticed that my cousin is a lunatic?"

This actually pulled a faint smile from Spear, which was saying something. But Sophia sat forward, watching the violated cemeteries pass in a rolling black and white sea, grave after grave, mask after empty-eyed mask. There was something ghastly about it, a wrongness beyond the obvious that she couldn't immediately put her finger on. And then she knew. It was because this stark world LeBlanc was trying to create was a lie; there was a spectrum of color between black and white, and many, many layers of choice between yes and no.

The nethersun was dipping low when Benoit rapped twice on the roof from the driver's seat, letting them know they were approaching the Saint-Denis Gate. Sophia pinned on her hat, René straightening his cravat and sleeves as the landover rolled to a stop. They should only have to show their papers through the window, but he was preparing to make as much of a commotion as possible.

Spear didn't move, even for his papers. René looked out the window and frowned.

"Benoit is talking with the guards," he said. "The baggage will be searched, I think."

Sophia sighed. They had anticipated the possibility. Spear ran a hand over his face, and finally started reaching for his things.

"And here they come," said René.

A gendarme with an eye patch and the blue and white uniform of the Upper City knocked once on the window and then opened the door. "You will please step . . ."

But René had already leapt out before the man finished speaking, formally extending his hand. "Please! Step carefully, my love!"

She took his hand. She had a knife in her bodice, just in case, but it was the firelighter that required some particular maneuvering as she made her way down the folding steps. Familiar buildings of carved stone rose seven, eight, and even nine floors high behind the walls of the Sunken City, lamps and candles beginning to twinkle in the windows. But as she raised her eyes to the rooflines, she saw that some of them had new construction on top, metal-lattice towers narrowing like pencils as they pointed to the sky, most only half-finished.

Spear crawled out of the landover—he had as much trouble getting his shoulders through the door as she did her skirt—and Sophia handed her papers to the guard with the eye patch while Spear asked him about the towers on the roofs.

"Lights" was the guard's terse answer.

Sophia looked up again. The City of Light. She wondered if Allemande thought the lights above would blind everyone to the ugliness going on below.

The gendarme handed back her papers and examined Spear's. They were their usual false ones, just in case LeBlanc had a mind to make the entry to the Sunken City difficult, but the forgeries were excellent. She was counting on fooling the guards without fooling any reporters that might be present. Not as tricky a business as one might think, given the general intelligence of reporters versus gendarmes, and the Hasard habit of putting money in the right pockets. The guard handed Spear his papers, stepped up into the landover, and began patting down the cushions while another searched the contents of their luggage. René stood over this one, complaining about what the damp air would do to both his fiancée's health and the starch in his shirts with equal vexation.

Sophia laid a hand on Spear's arm. Not only were they being very thoroughly searched, their landover was the only one waiting to enter the Sunken City, while a huge line of vehicles stood on the other side of the gates, queuing up for permission to leave. And the guards were sober, alert, two on inspection, three keeping watch on the perimeters. Not the outer perimeter, she saw, but the inner, guarding against a threat from within.

"Spear?" Sophia whispered.

That was all she needed to say. He nodded and strolled over a few feet to speak with one of the gendarmes on watch. René's argument with the other guard was taking on a more insistent note, some sort of objection to the handling of his fiancée's underthings. And if there wasn't a reporter here to recognize him and write that down, Sophia thought, the *Monde Observateur* had missed a golden opportunity for the gossip page.

The gendarme with the eye patch stepped out of the landover, and suddenly René called, "My love! I have found it! I have found your handkerchief!"

He came springing over to where she stood and, before she knew what was happening, had thrown his arms around her in celebration, one hand full of lacy white cloth. The gendarme's unpatched eye looked them over once, then the man made a sudden decision to go help with the luggage inspection. As soon as the guard was out of earshot, René said, "That hurt. Your skirt is very bumpy." He tightened his grip. "They say they will search you."

"Prevent them," she said in his ear.

René released her a little to swipe hair powder off her nose with the handkerchief. "What news, Hammond?" he asked beneath his breath, eyes still on Sophia. Spear was back beside them, jaw tight.

"The gendarme wouldn't say why everyone is trying to leave the city, or why we're being stopped," he replied.

"Ah." René held her gaze. "I will be back," he said, right before yelling, "Wait! You there, Monsieur! Do not touch those!" He strode quickly over to the rummaging guards.

"They want to search me," Sophia whispered.

"Looks like he already searched you himself."

She held in a frustrated sigh. Spear had no way of understanding why it would be such a disaster to have the firelighter confiscated. She watched René foment an argument with the gendarmes, the tempo of her pulse increasing. She might have to do something about this. And then she turned and found Benoit beside them. "Best to get back in the landover," he said quietly. "We will be leaving soon."

Sophia frowned, puzzled as to why Benoit would think this. One guard had already stripped René's jacket off, running hands along his shirtsleeves, and the gendarme with the patch was returning to the group with a determined step, his one eye on Sophia. She felt her back straightening. She could cause a scene just as well as

René; she could cry, or be sick, and she had her knife. She was not about to give up the firelighter.

Sophia felt a hand on her arm, light but restraining. Benoit shook his head once, his attention not on the approaching guard but on René. Sophia followed his gaze. The gendarme had moved down to René's legs, patting them for hidden weapons, and René, so fast she almost didn't see it, grabbed the man's head and brought a knee up beneath his chin. The guard hit the ground, out cold.

"Monsieur? Monsieur?" René said loudly, reaching down to slap the unconscious man's cheeks. The gendarme with the eye patch spun on his heel, hurrying back to the man on the ground. "Your friend here is ill!" René said, his expression all concern, and as soon as the man bent down to look at the unconscious guard he got the same treatment and joined him on the ground.

"Time to get in, Mademoiselle," Benoit said in his soft Parisian. "And Monsieur." Then Benoit called one of the guards on watch, beckoning him over to the scene, and as she was climbing into the landover Sophia could hear frantic conversation, the word "plague," and the sound of their luggage being strapped on. René jumped in just as Benoit clucked at the horses, readjusting the gold brocade of his sleeves.

"So," he said cheerfully, looking around. Beyond the rattle of the wheels and the clatter of the gates closing after them, it was silent in the landover. Spear had already resumed his stare out the window, but Sophia's gaze was leveled on René. He blanched.

"You did say to prevent the search . . ."

"All that time at the farm," Sophia said, "and you never thought to teach me that?"

He grinned with half his mouth. "How could I have neglected you so? Come and sit next to me." He'd almost put the words "my love," on the end of that sentence; she'd heard the hesitation. He lifted his arm to give her more room and she took her place. They were still speaking Parisian, Sophia noticed. It just seemed the thing to do once the gates of the Sunken City were closed behind them.

"Here, Hammond, look at this." René handed Spear a piece of paper with his free hand. "Monsieur with one eye must have been in charge, and this just happened to be in his jacket pocket, and I, of course, just happened to find it. We are taking a message about sickness to his commandant, by the way. I do not think it will arrive, do you?"

Sophia turned to look at him. "And what happens when he wakes up and finds his orders gone? Don't you think he'll remember a knee to his chin and the incredibly annoying young man whose papers he'd just read?"

"You insult me, Mademoiselle! Why would I hand a gendarme papers with my true name on them?"

She rolled her eyes at him, unsuccessfully holding in a smile, and then saw that Spear was staring hard at the words before him.

"The Seine Gate will be opened at middlemoon tomorrow," he read. "For La Toussaint, or the Festival of Fate, as they're trying to call it. But they will not be opening the outer gates. Not even for the cemeteries. Not without a pass."

Now the line of landovers, and even all the people at the dock made sense. Word had leaked out, as it always did. The Seine Gate would open from the Lower City, but none of the outer gates would. Allemande was not only turning the mob loose on the Upper City, he was cutting off the escape routes.

She exchanged a glance with Spear. His look told her clearly that he thought this was why they should not have waited to come. That they'd left themselves no time to adjust, no time for mistakes.

He was worrying about his part of the plan, of course, about getting Tom, Jennifer, and Madame Hasard out of the gates and to the coast; she was worrying about those three, plus hundreds of prisoners more. There was another way beneath the walls, but the tunnels were small and difficult, often wet. It would take much too long. Most would not have the strength for it. So it had to be the gates, even if the Upper City was in chaos. She turned inside René's arm and found that he had been watching her think.

"You pick pockets, don't you?"

"On occasion," he replied.

"Are you good?"

"My uncle Andre says I am."

"Can you steal a ring off a man's finger?"

"Ah. But do you want this man to know his ring has been stolen?" he asked. Sophia felt her brows draw together. "Perhaps what you really want is to borrow a ring, Mademoiselle? From my cousin Albert?"

"Yes," she said, brightening. "That is exactly what I want."

"Then you can leave that to me, I think." She turned, settling back into René's encircling arm.

"What are you thinking, Sophie?" Spear asked.

"That we'll drive them straight out as planned, and that LeBlanc is going to open the gates for us."

LeBlanc twisted off his signet ring, dropped it into the drawer, and opened a report from the Berck dock, laying the paper flat on his desk to read. He frowned a little, then opened three separate envelopes sent express from varying points on the landover road. His pale eyes widened, then narrowed. This was unexpected. And suspicious. And intriguing. Could his ridiculous young cousin really be so half-witted as to have fallen in love with the Red Rook? He took out his black bag with the Ancient coin, cupped the coin in his hands, shook, opened his fingers, and looked at the answer of his Goddess. Face. He was more surprised. He had not thought that even René could be this stupid.

LeBlanc picked up the invitation still on his desk, thoughtful, slipped it into the inside pocket of his robes, and left his office, Renaud stepping softly just behind. They took the lift down through the white building, then down through the cliffs, opening the door to the first level of the Tombs. But LeBlanc did not go into the prison. He passed Gerard's office and opened the door into the prison yard, where the scaffold and the Razor cast deeper shadows across the darkness.

On the far side, where partially derelict buildings created one edge of the space around the scaffold, LeBlanc opened the door to an empty warehouse, Renaud closing it behind him and turning the lock. Inside, in the orange flicker of torchlight, stood Gerard and a gendarme with a tiny mustache. Gerard appeared a little ill. The man with the tiny mustache did not. That was something to note. Behind them were two guards, both with crossbows, and on the far wall, six men and women, gagged, blindfolded, tied, beaten, and bloody. One still had the remnants of a red-painted feather on his cheek.

LeBlanc sighed. The Razor was a superior method. This was likely to take a little time. But Fate had instructed him to have it done this way, and she was a wise mistress. There would be no Allemande or other ministres to hear. He sighed again. Inefficient. He raised a hand, the crossbows aimed, and when he lowered it there was a soft swoosh of arrows.

He ignored the noises from the other end of the warehouse while the gendarmes reloaded. She would be here by now, wandering through his streets. The Red Rook was in the Sunken City. And it was time to move Tom Bellamy.

Just like in the cemeteries, Sophia was not seeing what she had expected in the Upper City. After dusk was when the restaurants filled, the last of the stores closing and theaters opening, when the fashionable people came out to see and be seen. It was the time she'd always been meandering back to Aunt Francesca's with Tom and Spear, so Father wouldn't realize where they'd been. But even though the sun had fallen away behind the buildings, these streets were empty, some unlit, more and more so as they followed the sloping pavements deeper into the Upper City, moving closer to the sunken center. They began passing windows that were boarded over, and charred barricades, broken glass, patrolling gendarmes, and a few buildings burned to an empty shell. The columns of the concert hall and the hospital were both splattered with circles of half black, half white. The sign of Fate. Obviously the *Monde Observateur* had not been reporting everything that was happening in the city.

René said, "I think I should ride outside with Benoit . . ."

"No," Spear replied. "I'll go. You're a target with that jacket." He half crouched as he left his seat, loosening his sword before pushing down the handle of the door and swinging himself onto the outdoor rungs that led up to the luggage rack. René pulled the door shut as the landover tilted and lurched until Spear got on top and evened out the weight.

"He is right," René commented. "But I think we may be a target either way." He settled Sophia back beneath his arm, staring out the window again. The city seemed to be in a state of unquiet calm, the kind that comes right before a storm. He pulled her a little closer and said, "Look, up on the high ground." She craned her neck to see an industrial building of dark, brown brick on the top of a hill. She could just make out the enormous sign across its front in the light from the upper floors of other buildings. Hasard Glass. "I am glad to see it still standing. I . . ."

He went quiet. Sophia saw that he was looking at a passing chapel with a boarded-over door. That in itself was not so unusual; all the chapels had been closed since Allemande's revolution. This one had been defaced on all its windows with the sign of the Goddess, but now, over each black and white circle, a long, curving slash had been painted, even brush strokes branching out on both sides of the main stem, red paint tipping the ends. It took Sophia a moment to realize that it was a feather.

"They are fighting back," René said.

"Who is?" she whispered, turning her head to watch the passing chapel. Someone was setting themselves against Allemande, and using her symbol to do it. But what were they trying to do? Did they want to show support for the Red Rook, scheduled for execution the day after tomorrow? Or were they trying to start another revolution?

"I do not know," René said, eyes on a smoking building. The landover wheels were bumping over debris and splintered wood. "But you may have more friends in the city than you thought."

They turned the corner onto a ruined boulevard. This was not the result of rioting. There had been fighting here, bloodstains showing on the pavement in the light of the landover lamps. Were people dying for the symbol of that red-tipped feather? The symbol that she and Tom had created together in the sanctuary, mostly because the paint was already there from some long-forgotten project? The idea settled over her, heavy. What had she begun? She leaned into the corner made by René's body and arm, breathing hard against the tightness in her chest, against the brokenness of this Upper City boulevard. She reached out without thinking and took René's free hand, twining her fingers with his.

She felt him go still, and so did she. That had not been for show. No one could see their hands through the carriage window. She should take it back, say she was sorry. But she didn't want to. She didn't want to face the debris on the streets alone. Then there was the tiniest squeeze from the arm that was around her. She let out her breath, and laid her head on René's shoulder.

They passed eight more red feathers, painted on shops and the gymnasium, one on the bottom of an air bridge. Then the landover turned onto a wide boulevard with planted trees, rolling to a stop before a building of white and gray carved stone. There wasn't much that was Ancient in the Upper City, and here there was nothing at all. No vestiges of concrete or steel, just cut stone and marble, baked tile and stained glass. Very modern. And very protected. Six gendarmes had stopped to eye the landover, four swords and two crossbows out and ready. René frowned at them.

"You have a knife?" he asked. It was the only time they'd spoken since seeing the first painted feather. Since she'd held his hand. Sophia nodded. "Easily reached?" She nodded again. "Then follow my lead," René said.

"Are those gendarmes here for me?" she asked.

"I do not know."

They could feel Spear clambering off the luggage rack above them. It was time to go. But René didn't move. Instead he lifted the hand that still held his and kissed it, holding it close against his lips before he let it go.

16

René pushed down on the door latch, and the blue eyes lifted to hers. "You are ready?"

She nodded, still feeling his mouth on her hand.

"Speak carefully before the bellman," he added. "He reports to Allemande." Then he leapt out of the landover and extended his hand with a flourish, not paying the slightest attention to the guards. "We are arrived, my love!"

Sophia allowed him to hand her out, holding up her skirts carefully for sake of the firelighter. Spear landed on the paving stones, and they both looked up. Stars were beginning to wink above the spire on the top of René's building, the upper floors shrinking in size as if stacked, a relief of flowers and vines decorating the foundation and twining upward. The curving roofline was cut with round windows, small from her vantage point on the ground, though she knew they must be huge. The gendarmes watched, but made no moves. Two green doors opened, and the bellman appeared. Sophia took René's arm.

"If he reports to Allemande," she whispered, "then why is he here?"

"Because he also reports to us. Yes, yes, Monsieur Hammond," René said loudly, as if Spear had asked. "It is, indeed, very tall. But, please, not to worry! My building has a four-man lift! Nothing less than a four-man lift for my lovely fiancée!" He spied the approaching bellman and began shouting. "Bellman! Bring help. At once!"

The gendarmes seemed a bit taken aback by all this, just as they had at the gate, swords dropping down and crossbows lowering. They were guarding only, evidently, not there for her. Sophia let a little tension out of her body, watching Spear's face become expressionless with anger as René harassed the bellman and Benoit, who was unstrapping the luggage. Sophia reached out and put a hand on his arm.

"He's doing what he has to, Spear. It's a persona. You know that. Try not to let it get to you. Please. For me."

The lines of Spear's jaw grew even more rigid as he looked down at her. "Has it ever occurred to you, Sophia Bellamy, that I might not be here for you at all?"

She moved her hand, but found herself smiling up at Spear's handsome face, which was for once showing its fury. "And that," she said, "is a long overdue first installment on a number of sharp words you owe me, Spear Hammond. But you're still far behind on your payments, I'm afraid."

They left Benoit and a bellboy to deal with the landover, the luggage, and the gendarmes, and stepped into the lift. It was mirrored and carpeted, the edges painted gold. René chatted on and on, bragging ridiculously about the four-man lift, meaning there were all of four men pushing the turnstile around and around, powering the chains that would haul them to the top, rather than only two or three. Sophia listened to the familiar rattle and squeak of the vast pulley system as they started up, a sound that said "city" to her ears. The Commonwealth didn't allow lifts. Too machinelike.

Since all René's babble was for the benefit of the bellman, Sophia jumped in, recounting how she and her brother had once seen a liftman when she was a little girl, a big man with very big arms, and how she'd been frightened at first but then found how jolly he was. It was true that she and Tom had once snuck into the cellars of Aunt Francesca's building to take the liftmen bread, and those men had not been jolly. But she struck a pose of confused sadness at the mention of her brother, and knew that this juicy bit of information—that the Red Rook and his sister had once lived in the Sunken City— would seep into every flat like the city smogs. A bellman was the best source of gossip there was. René gave her a grin from behind the man's back.

"All the way to the top, René?" she said idiotically as the lift doors opened onto the twelfth and last floor.

"Of course, my love! Now, please, watch your hem . . ."

The landing outside the lift was square, walls painted in pale green and blue stripes, the number 1250 in iron above only one set of double doors. René's flat must have the entire top floor. The bellman handed René a tiny covered lamp, to light the candles, and then yanked a silken pull. A bell rang far below, and the chains and pulleys clanked as he started down again, his expression rather eager, Sophia thought. When his head had disappeared down the shaft René put a key to the lock and pushed open the double doors.

Sophia walked into the flat first, Spear behind her, René locking the door again after them. The room was dim, only the smallest light coming from the lantern René held, but she could feel that it was huge and, to her surprise, semicircular, the entire wall in front of them a curving sweep of windows, showing a panoramic view of the Sunken City. Sophia moved silently across the polished floor, a floor spotted with reflected points of light from the buildings on the other side of the windowpanes. It was like walking the Bellamy ballroom, only with a few sparse pieces of furniture added here and there.

She stopped before the wall of windows, Spear doing the same just a few feet away, hands in his pockets. They were right on the edge of the cliffs, looking far down into the fogs of the Lower City, lights twinkling in the smoky darkness. She put a hand on the glass. Tom was down there somewhere, buried deep below that vast hole. And by highmoon tomorrow she would have him. Sophia lifted her eyes to the lights encircling the rim of the chasm, then turned her head to the lamps and flying bridges of the Upper City, spreading below and around them as far as the eye could see, a maze of streets in the air. Who were those others out there, leaving the symbol of the Red Rook across the city, weighing their lives on the scales for the same thing she was? This had been her own private war for a long time. She spun around at the smell of smoke.

René stood at a long table near the doors, now in a swath of light from a newly lit lamp, thumbing through a stack of letters. There was a glass bowl of fading flames near him, what she assumed were the gendarmes' orders now becoming ash. A small gallery hung above the doors and over René's head, a curved stairwell leading up to the second level of the flat. Beneath that was a familiar stack of boxes, the items they'd sent on from Spear's farm.

"Is anyone here?" she asked René.

He looked up and smiled, the white hair and gold jacket looking far less exotic in this setting than at Bellamy House. But he looked different as well. At his ease, more relaxed. "The staff do not live in anymore . . ." His voice was again a surprise, after the ride in the lift. ". . . and I wrote for them not to come until middlesun. They will have a long day tomorrow."

Sophia threw her hat onto a backless couch and kicked off her slippers. They went flying in two different directions, making Spear glance around from where he was gazing dourly at the view. She sighed in relief, done with being hemmed in by a boat and a land-over all day. She turned her back to both of them, hiked up her navy skirt, and quickly pulled the tie of the heavy white underskirt. She stepped out of it, careful not to let the sewn-in firelighter hit the floor.

"Really, Sophia," Spear said. "Can't you wait?"

"You haven't been wearing that weight since nethermoon, and I am perfectly decent, thank you." But she couldn't help smiling as she carefully folded the fluffy white material around the precious fire-lighter. That was three censures in one day from Spear. Somebody should write a song about it.

"Monsieur Hammond," said René. "Do you prefer that we speak in Commonwealth?"

"Parisian is fine. The luggage is coming up?"

"Benoit is on his . . ."

"Then I'd like to see the flat," Spear said. "All of it. Is there a way down other than the lift?"

Sophia saw a frown brush across René's forehead, but he only nodded and picked up the light. "Come, and I will show you."

They followed him through the echoing main room to a door that led into a long, bending corridor, carpeted in cream and mid-night blue, continuing the curved shape of the window wall. There were doors on both sides, opening onto grand, windowed rooms on their left, utilitarian, interior rooms on their right. The entire flat was almost a complete circle, spiraling on two different levels around the central lift shaft.

"Attic space?" Spear asked.

"Yes," René said, "but it is small and unused. There is a trapdoor in the ceiling of the linen room. You can get onto the roof from there, but it is steep. Very dangerous, and of no use unless you wish to fly or elude your tutor. But at the end of this hall is the kitchen, and a back stair that leads to the ground. That door will lock from the outside, and there is a drop bar on the inside. So you may leave that way, if you wish, but if for some reason you wish to return by climbing all twelve floors, you will have to make much noise until someone lets you in. And here is the water room."

René opened the door of a small, closet-like space that had a rectangular wooden panel built into one wall. He slid this up and there was the water lift, a bricked shaft, two ropes inside, a water bucket dangling from one of them. Sophia stuck her head in the opening and touched the rope. The walls were slimed from constant splashing, and it smelled a bit musty, but the rope seemed to be in decent condition. She couldn't see the bottom.

"Did you hear a door?" Spear asked from the hallway. The little room wasn't really big enough for him and anyone else.

"That will be Benoit with the luggage. He has a key."

"And where are you putting us to sleep?" he said. "I need to see to my things."

René looked at Spear closely, but again he only said, "This way." They left the water room and followed René back down the hallway to a set of stairs, also following the curve of the inner wall. At the top of the stairwell was another corridor, straight this time, the wall space that was not interrupted by doorways gleaming dully with hanging weapons.

"The rooms we use most often are here," he said. "This is my room." Sophia looked with interest at the closed door. "Benoit is the next door down, and you are the next from that, Hammond. Mademoiselle, across the hall. Take the last door, that is the better room."

Spear started asking about the roof again while she examined a sword hung near her head on the wall, a bit shorter and lighter than the others, with a hilt of twisted silver. The hilt had been worn smooth by hands.

"Sophia," said Spear. "I assume you're tired and going to bed. I'll have Benoit bring up your bags and something for you to eat." He started down the hall, then looked back. "Are you going?"

Sophia raised a brow. "No, I don't plan on locking myself in my room just this moment. Am I confined to quarters?" Spear hesitated. "Really, Spear, what is wrong with you? I'll go in a bit, when the bags come up."

He stood still, torn by some decision that Sophia could not fathom. "I need to see to my things," he said. And before she could close her mouth or even say a word, Spear was away down the hall and through the door at the end, the door she assumed led to the gallery and stairway she'd seen in the flat's main room. Never had she seen Spear behaving this way. She was surprised he hadn't ordered her to brush her teeth.

René watched Spear go, then put his gaze on Sophia. "Do you like that one?" he asked. She turned to the sword she'd been examining, with the twisted silver hilt. "You can try it, if you like. These are not decorations."

His eyes stood out bright in the dim. She smiled and lifted the sword from its hooks. She held it out, feeling the weight, swung it once, twice, and turned to find René where she had left him, only now the gold jacket was on the floor and he had a sword as well, loose and ready in his hand.

"Come. I do not think you wish to sleep. I think you would much rather hit something. Tell me I am wrong."

"You want to fight me? Right now. In the hallway?"

"Unless you are frightened, Mademoiselle."

"I'm wearing a dress. And you are much taller than me."

He tsked as he approached in his vest and shirtsleeves, looking every inch a gentleman thief. Or assassin. "Your disadvantages are many. I can understand your fear."

She smiled at him from beneath her lashes and raised the sword. So did he, fiery blue on either side of his blade. She moved forward, bare feet silent on the carpet, as if trying to ascertain his reach, and then she darted ahead quickly, getting her sword over his on the inside, but he was back and away before she could get it out of his hand. She cursed once beneath her breath. She'd wanted to take it on the first try. René's smile was devilish, and it was distracting.

"Oh, no," he said, as if sad and sorry for her. "That will not work on me, Mademoiselle. I have seen you do that before." He came at her and she blocked.

"What do you mean you've seen me do that before?" She blocked again.

"To your brother. On the beach, at Bellamy House. The night of our Banns."

He blocked her this time. So René Hasard had been watching her on the beach that night? That was cheating. She parried him once and then twice, but only just. She was in trouble. She knew it, and so did he. He was quick, had reach, and she was hampered by cloth even without the voluminous underskirt. His grin was even bigger.

He came at her fast again, and instead of meeting him head-on she ducked and turned, switching their positions. She stepped back, knocking his sword aside and then crossing with him again, letting him push her up against a door. His expression was a little disappointed from the other side of their blades. "You ran? I did not think . . ." She gave him a beatific smile, reached behind with her free hand, and pushed down on the door latch.

She'd been ready for the loss of resistance but he had not. She dropped to her knees and he went down to the floor through the doorway, though he managed to knock her sword from her hand on the way. There was a scramble in the dark as they fought over the loose blade, Sophia crawling right over his back to get it, her struggle becoming ineffectual from laughter. René was cursing up a storm in Parisian, a flurry of words that would have made any man on Blackpot Street proud.

Then he froze for just a moment, grabbed her hard by the arm, and thrust her behind him, both of them still on their knees. There was someone else in the room, moving with soft footsteps across the carpet. The window curtains were yanked back, the lights of the city and a rising middlemoon showing a tall woman in her nightgown. Even in the dim Sophia could see that the woman's hair was flaming red.

"Maman!" said René, in a tone rather close to his words from Blackpot Street.

"René," the woman said. In her voice, the name sounded like an accusation.

Sophia sat straight-backed on one end of the pale green settee in the main room of the flat, René on the other end, her discarded underskirt piled in fluffy disarray between them. Her hair was a mess but her dress was righted, shoes scattered somewhere on the floor near the windows. Madame sat enthroned in a gold-painted chair, regal in a dressing gown, looking pointedly at the underskirt. The silence stretched. Sophia wondered where Spear had gotten to. Then Madame Hasard held out a handkerchief from an outstretched hand.

"Miss Bellamy," she said, face unreadable, "you have hair powder on your . . . chest."

"Oh, please, Maman," said René, throwing up a hand.

Sophia took the handkerchief with a smile. "Thank you, Madame Hasard, for pointing that out." She made a show of tidying her skin before handing it back. "Is that better?"

Benoit came in with a tray, eyeing René with what Sophia thought might have been amusement. He offered a glass of wine to Madame Hasard, a mug to René, and a mug of the same to Sophia, then stepped away to hover in the background. Sophia peeked inside the mug.

"Warm milk," said Madame Hasard. "It promotes sleep, and discourages nighttime rambling."

"Enough, Maman," said René, slamming down the mug alarmingly hard on a tabletop of glass. "I apologize for disturbing you. But might I remind you that you were supposed to be in prison?"

She feigned surprise. "You prefer your *maman* to be locked away?"

"When did you get out? Are you on the run?"

"René! You will offend the sensibilities of Miss Bellamy."

"I do not think you are concerned with the sensibilities of Miss Bellamy!"

"If you were concerned with the sensibilities of Miss Bellamy, perhaps you would not have been ravishing her in the same room where your poor *maman* was trying to sleep!"

René loosened the cravat and then he was on his feet and pacing. Sophia's eyes bounced from one powdered white head showing streaks of red to one mostly red head showing a few streaks of white. She considered saying, "No, Madame, he was only trying to skewer me with a sword," but decided to hold her tongue. Benoit put his hands behind his back.

"Miss Bellamy," René was saying, "is my fiancée, Maman. And by your orders, if you will remember."

"What Miss Bellamy is remains to be seen."

That statement stopped René's stride. He turned on his heel to look at his mother. "Maman, why are you out of the Tombs?"

Madame Hasard sipped her wine. "I am out of that filthy place, dearest, because I signed away your fortune."

Sophia's eyes darted to René, and she watched shock hit him like a blow to the middle. He sat on the edge of the settee, elbows on knees, breath knocked out of him, expression uncomprehending. And then his head was down, hands on the back of his neck. When he finally looked up he said, "I was coming to get you, Maman."

"Were you?" She sipped more wine. She was thin beneath her dressing gown, but Sophia did not know her usual build. "It seemed to be taking quite some time."

"You signed?"

"Yes, René."

"And what do we have left?"

"Not a franc in the city."

"The flat?"

"LeBlanc owns the flat."

And that, Sophia thought, explained the guard at the street level of the building. René said, "What about the ships?"

"LeBlanc does not know about the ships."

Sophia breathed. That was good.

"And how long do we have the flat?" he asked.

"Two days, René."

Sophia let out her breath again. They needed only one. One day, and they could do what they had to. René's eyes met hers, but the fire had gone out of them. He leaned forward again, fingers tented over his nose, staring at the floor that now belonged to LeBlanc.

"You should feel privileged, Monsieur, to call this place your final home. Not many have seen it." LeBlanc's smile was long and wide.

He watched Tom push himself upright in the dirt, panting from where he'd landed on his broken ribs, then frowning as he tried to make sense of his surroundings. The room was circular, but the walls were made of bones. Old and yellowed, stacked in rise and fall patterns like layers of continuous waves caught in cross-section. The bones rose higher than could be seen, to a vast ceiling that was in shadow, hundreds of thousands of them. LeBlanc's smile lengthened. This was a place strong with those who had accepted Fate.

Two gendarmes, still with their training patches on their uniforms, fastened Tom Bellamy's chains around a stone pedestal in the center of the room. They backed away quickly, obviously wishing to leave.

"Where is Jennifer Bonnard?" Tom asked. His lips were cracked.

LeBlanc shook his head. He was not going to tell him that.

"Tell me where she is!"

LeBlanc turned and walked away with the lantern, the gendarmes behind him.

"Tell me!"

The echoing words gave chase as LeBlanc reverently walked pathways thick with Ancient dust, the shouts eventually dying on the air. He made a slow way back to the Tombs, the young gendarmes following soundlessly behind him. LeBlanc ordered them to stand, and when he finally stepped out of the lift and into the upper level of the prison, Renaud was there, waiting.

LeBlanc nodded. Renaud drew a sword and a knife and walked into the lift. LeBlanc listened as the young men died. Now let the Red Rook try to find her brother, he thought. And when she tried, he would have her. Exactly where she was supposed to be. As Fate had decreed.

—

Sophia smiled when Madame Hasard showed her to her room. It was huge and also sparsely furnished, the bed an afterthought in an ocean of pale gold carpet and a beautiful view of the Upper City. It also had an interior door. Connecting with Madame Hasard's. Benoit brought the rest of her luggage a short time later, but before he left he stopped, turned, took her hand, and kissed it. Sophia was so surprised she said nothing, only watched as he inclined his head just a little and shut the door softly behind him.

She opened her suitcases and hung her clothes, including the underskirt with its extra weight sewn inside, humming while she did it. She put both her knives and her sword under her pillow and climbed into bed, but she had not put on a nightgown. She was wearing breeches and a loose shirt of Tom's. She looked through exactly twenty pages of the *Wesson's Guide*, flipping them regularly before she blew out the light.

She stared into the dark, motionless, envisioning again the reaction she'd seen when Madame Hasard told René that the money was gone. The way his fists had clenched on the back of his neck, the roughness of his voice that had not been from the rope. It had taken her a little time to analyze, but now she knew. What she had seen was more than shock or the loss of money. More than just pain. What she had seen was the loss of hope. And to lose hope, you must have had hope in the first place. René had been hoping to pay the fee. He'd been hoping to have her. And without the money, he thought he'd lost her. How ridiculous. What could the money have to do with it? How could René Hasard think any such thing, when it was perfectly clear that he belonged to no one but her?

Sophia ran her fingers through the ringlets, letting her hair go back to some of its natural wildness. Now, finally, after all this, she knew exactly what she would risk. Not for any certain kind of future she might prefer, or Bellamy House, or even the Red Rook. She knew what she would risk to have him. And it was everything.

She threw off the blanket, picked up the dead candle, went softly to the door, and opened it. She knelt on the carpet, looking carefully in the light from the wall sconces in the hall, and there, at about the level where her knees would have been, was a single thread. She smiled, stepped lightly over it, shut the door without noise, and went down the silent hall to the last door on the left. But she didn't have to knock. René was coming up the stairs from the lower corridor.

He stood on the last step when he saw her, waiting for her to come to him, away from the closed doors of the bedrooms. "What is wrong?" he asked. He'd washed out his hair. It was loose and russet and still a bit damp, and he was back in his linen shirt, like at the farm, like the ones she'd ruined. He smelled of outdoors, and chimney smoke.

"Have you been on the roof?"

"Yes."

She could see him being careful. Afraid of her, because to be near her was pain. She knew exactly what that felt like. Only she wasn't going to be careful anymore. "Would you look at my stitches?"

He shot a glance down the dim corridor. "I thought perhaps you had taken them out yourself."

"No. But I think they should come out. Before tomorrow. And I can't see."

He hesitated, looking again down the hall with its rows of occupied bedrooms. Then his shoulders slumped a little and he said, "Come with me."

He went back down the stairs, Sophia pausing only to light her candle with one of the wall sconces, then moved quietly along the lower hall, opening the door across from the water lift. They stepped inside a storage room the size of a large closet, sheets and towels and tablecloths stacked on the shelves.

"The linen room?" Sophia said, a little amused. She set the candle on a small table for folding as he shut the door. "Couldn't we have just gone to yours?"

"It has been a long day, Mademoiselle, and still I hope to avoid fighting a duel for your honor before the night is out. I do not think we will be bothered in here."

"I brought you this," she said. It was a thin knife, tiny, for opening letters.

"You will allow me to look?"

She lifted her shirttail cautiously, and René got on his knees to untie the knotted bandage, unwinding it from her middle until he could see the bare swath of skin with her stitches. The air was cool, giving her goose bumps. Sophia tried to slow her breathing, not an easy thing when her heart was slamming such an unnerving tattoo against her chest. René's expression was controlled. Set. Like the day he'd cut the cornfield. He held the candle close, studying.

"Do they hurt?" he asked. "Even a little?"

"They itch like the devil."

"Good." He rose from his knees, more slowly than his usual spring, and picked up the small knife she had set on the table. He began running it through the candle flame, as he'd done with the needle. He smiled at her look of mild alarm. "We have done so well, no need to ruin all of my good work." When he judged the blade to be clean, he said, "Ready?"

She nodded, still holding up her shirt.

He knelt down again. "Be very still, yes?" He slid the knife carefully under the first knot, the metal hot against her skin, and, with a firm tug, pulled free the first piece of silk.

"Ow!"

René eyed the thread's tiny hole before he looked up at her. "You are ridiculous, you do know this? I gave you twenty-two stitches, poured alcohol straight into the wound, an act that has earned me a fist in the eye from my uncle Émile, and you did not make a sound. And now you cry out like a child?"

She shrugged. "That was pain, this is discomfort. It's hardly the same thing."

"Well, if you are not quiet now, we will have Hammond breaking down the door. Or my *maman*." He sighed in mock exasperation. "Hold back my hair for me. It is in the way and I do not have a tie."

Sophia moved the hair away from his face, gathering it into her hand, fascinated that it felt like hair—it was so red and male she'd half thought it might feel like something different.

He turned her body to the light, and then slit a thread and pulled, slit and pulled, and now that she knew what to expect, she was quiet. When he was done he sat back on his heels. A pinkish-red line, neat and straight.

"Finished," he said.

"Thank you."

René was still on his knees. "You should keep it well tied tomorrow," he said, "to be certain it will not tear."

Sophia didn't answer. She also didn't move, and neither did he; she still had his hair in her hand, the other holding up her shirttail. The candle flame wavered. René closed his eyes, brow furrowed. Sophia held her breath, and the hand with his hair pulled just a little, the smallest of tugs. The lines in his forehead deepened. She pulled him again and this time he relented, leaning in to lay his cheek on the new scar.

He sighed and she breathed, his face warm, prickling the sensitive skin, arms coming up around her legs as she held him in, both hands now full of his hair. Then he slid to his feet and took her head in his hands.

"Look at me," he said, the blue of his eyes blazing in the candlelight."You are sure?"

"Yes."

"There is no money."

"I don't care."

Her breath was so short she could hardly speak. She had one hand on his chest, the rhythm of it fast and hard beneath her palm. He was so beautiful, and so unsure, and she had never been more so.

"Sophia . . . ," he whispered.

She slipped her other arm around his bruised neck and put her lips on the pulse at the base of his throat.

He made a noise somewhere deep in his chest, and then he had his mouth on hers, hard, holding her head still as she was pressed back, rattling the shelves, and then back again until she hit the wall. All at once she was boiling, frantic, trying to kiss him more, hold him closer with fistfuls of his shirt, pinned by his body to the painted plaster. He seemed to have forgotten his worries about noise. It was a long time before his lips broke away and he put his forehead against hers, breath coming fast.

"Don't worry," she whispered into the pause, chest heaving against his. "We're betrothed."

He actually laughed before he kissed her again, this time exploring her neck, her ears, cheeks, and both her eyelids before wandering back to her mouth. Everything about him felt good: her head still resting in one of his hands, as if she might try to get away, his other hand tracing the curve of her side, her fingers through his belt loops, the foot she had hooked behind his knee. Sophia wondered how she could have ever wanted to be anywhere but inside a linen closet.

When he broke away again, his cheek was next to hers. "I do not know what will happen after."

She stroked his back. "It doesn't matter what happens after. Not anymore."

"You will stay with me?"

"Yes."

He leaned away to look in her eyes. "You believe me?"

"Yes."

"Together, then?"

She felt the smile on his mouth when she kissed him in answer, and this time she was able to feel how right this was. Like circling the earth, opposing forces all brought into balance. Then his warmth was gone and he had her hand.

"Come with me," he said, like he had a little while before, only now he was smiling. He took the candle they had miraculously not knocked over, leading her past the scattered pile of once-folded towels and sheets that they had, to the other side of the room where an iron ladder was attached to the wall. She followed him up through the ceiling and he took her hand again, helping her pick her way through a dim, dusty space that ended in a soot-stained window, one of the round decorative ones she'd seen intersecting the roof spire from the ground. She'd been right to think it was enormous. The window was taller than René.

The window creaked on heavy hinges as he pulled it open, and there was the leaded roof of the building, a gentle, curving slope ending in a gutter and a very long fall. And beyond that was the Sunken City, thousands of twinkling candles and lamps both low and high, mirroring the thousands of stars shining through the north lights, a hazy green and purple dome across the sky.

They sat on the attic side of the windowsill, an ice wind blowing from so high, but Sophia wasn't cold. René had her surrounded with his arms, and it was his lips instead of the breeze making her shiver.

"René," she said, "we can't tell Spear. Not until we get them out."

"I know it," he said from against her neck. "My love."

She leaned her head back. What a different meaning those words had now. "René?" she said again.

"Yes, my love?"

"I don't want to talk about anything else."

She felt him smile again when he kissed her. And the highmoon bells rang out across the city.

When the dawn bells rang, Sophia rolled over on her pillow, looking across the expanse of gold carpet at the empty room. There were heavy footsteps walking down the hall. She hadn't been in her bed until past nethermoon, stepping carefully over the thread strung outside her door. But someone else had been present while she slept. The thread she'd strung across the connecting door to Madame Hasard's room was broken, floating gently in the draft.

"The thread across the front door has not been broken," said Benoit softly and without preamble as he slipped into René's room. René lay fully dressed on a still-made bed, one arm behind his head, candle burning low.

"And yet Hammond has returned," he said. "I could not mistake those footsteps. The back stairs, then? Was the drop bar not in place?"

"It was in place. I would say that Monsieur thought to have paper, string, cord, and a metal hook in his pockets."

"Ah. I thought that was your trick?" René pinched the candle flame away as Benoit opened a curtain to the dawn.

"I keep telling you not to underestimate Monsieur Hammond."

"Did he go to him?"

"I do not know." Benoit scratched his thinning hair. "The bellman said he came from the other direction, but that might not matter."

"Or the bellman has been paid. What about Uncle Andre?"

"He missed him in the dark."

René swore. "How can you miss Hammond, even with the streetlights out?"

"I say to you over and over that he is more clever than you think."

"And yet I do not think he will hurt her. Me, yes. Her, I think not," René mused. "Sophia might be able to find out. Or it may be interesting to see what he tells her about being out of the flat all night."

Benoit looked at him closely. "You are very cheerful this morning, René."

"Can a man not be cheerful?" He was grinning from both sides of his mouth.

Benoit shook his head, but he was smiling as well as he pulled the rest of the curtains.

"So we watch him," René said. "As ever. Do you not agree, Benoit? There is only the day and the night left, and then she is beyond his reach."

17

Sophia found Spear and Madame Hasard on the dining end of the large main room, bathed in smoggy sunshine, having what seemed to be a very friendly breakfast. The staff had arrived, and the place was already busy, smells coming from the kitchen, a girl in a white apron arranging flowers on the table beside the door. René was stewing, she saw, or pretending to. He was unshaven, in the same clothes as last night, arms behind his head and feet hanging off the settee. It was difficult to hold in her smile. She left him to it for the moment and sat down to a table of Parisian coffee and rolls.

"This is a delightful young man," Madame pronounced, patting Spear's arm.

Sophia looked up and smiled at them both. "Mr. Hammond is like family to my brother and me."

"He has told me of this business with your brother."

"Yes." Sophia buttered a roll, trying to keep her tone neutral. "We don't like to speak of it. Do you plan to attend the party tonight, Madame?"

"René says that Monsieur LeBlanc has been invited."

"That's so."

"And so you ask me to celebrate my son's engagement beside the man who has not only had me imprisoned and taken my flat—

the flat in which we are celebrating—but also stolen the very francs that would make such an engagement possible?"

"I thought perhaps you wouldn't approve."

"I cannot think of anything I would enjoy more, Miss Bellamy," she said, spreading sarcasm like the marmalade on her breakfast roll. "Though I think it a strange time for a party, with your brother going to the Razor at dawn."

Sophia cringed inside. Tom would not be going anywhere near the Razor, but the words hurt just the same. "I believe René thought it would be a distraction for me."

"And we will have the mob on us tonight, when the Seine Gate opens," Madame stated. "Really, the timing in all this is impeccable."

Spear had been engrossed in the newspaper, which he now folded in half and handed to Sophia over the table. "Pages two and six," he said.

"My son, is it?" said Madame Hasard knowingly. "You have been making the papers again, I see!" she called across the room. "A trial to the heart of your mother!"

"I was taught by the best, Maman!" René yelled.

Sophia handed the paper back to Spear. "I'll just take him a coffee," she said. "He can be so irritable first thing, don't you think?" She ignored Madame's raised brow as she moved across the gleaming floor, skirt rustling and cup in hand, to sit on the edge of the settee next to René's prostrate form.

"She will come," René said quietly, hidden by the couch back, "and will put herself in the thick of things. So we must consider that in our plans." He put an arm behind his head and gave the cup she handed him a dubious glance. "Is it safe?"

"You are so witty." She let her loose hair fall down, hiding her face from the side view. "I dreamed last night that I was in a linen closet."

"Did you?" He stealthily took her hand, cup and saucer balanced on his stomach, and pressed her fingertips to his lips. "And was this a good dream, my love?"

She closed her eyes for just a moment, hoping no one at the table could see her expression. "You bruised my lips."

The corner of his mouth lifted. "I am very sorry."

"You are not sorry at all." She thought she could feel the gaze of Madame Hasard. And possibly Spear. "Your *maman* was in my room last night."

"And I was not." His tone was glum.

"It is so frustrating not to be able to hit you when I want."

"Just wait for the party, my love." He swung his dangling feet back and forth over the end of the settee. "Benoit says Hammond left the flat before the luggage came up last night, and that he did not return until dawn. Did he have business in the city?"

Sophia darted a quick glance at the table while René sipped his coffee. Spear and Madame Hasard appeared to be deep in conversation.

"There were some tickets to be taken care of. But I don't think he could have done that at night. How did he get in again?"

"The back stairs, which he unlatched. From the other side."

"Did he?" Sophia looked again at Spear. How had he managed that?

"I think you are very beautiful," René said, "especially when you are admiring mischief."

"You must think that every time I look at you, then."

He gave her all of his grin. "You admire me, Mademoiselle?"

She bit her lip against her laugh. "I am going to hit you whether your mother is watching or not." She stole another look at the table and found Madame's sharp gaze on her, watching their conversation. She moved her eyes to the other end of the room, where a tall display cabinet stood, taking up most of the wall. René nodded once, and Sophia got to her feet and strolled over to the cabinet to study its contents until he joined her.

Most of the cabinet showed pieces of decorative glass, plates, and goblets in jewel reds, blown into scallops and waving shapes like rippling water. There were even one or two fluid-looking human figures, some clear, some shot through with colors. But it was the plastic that amazed her. An entire bowl complete with lid in a beautiful, translucent green, a row of small, stylized human figures, and no less than eleven mirrored disks like Tom's. And there was a miniature house. She knelt in front of this. A little like Spear's farmhouse, only with a white roof and chimney, a large chunk missing from the upper corner. One side had faded almost completely, but where you could see it, the color was shocking. A vibrant pink, bright like a rose, or a hibiscus flower. What must the world have looked like in the Time Before, to have houses of such colors? You would have needed a shade for your eyes just to walk the streets. She felt René come up behind.

"Did you nick any of these?" she asked quietly.

"It is not wise to display what has been . . . acquired," he replied.

"Of course not. So did you?"

"The bowl, and two of the little blue men. Foreign sellers, and not collectors, so very little danger in showing them here. And they were getting cheated by the melters. The blue is much more valuable than they were told." He paused. "I spoke with Maman this morning about selling them."

Sophia glanced over to see his expression, but it was sanguine.

"Getting their full value would take time, of course, and we would have to look outside the Sunken City, but we could get half the price quick. Maman seems to think, however, that we will need the money to live on. She has shut down Hasard Glass. For the time being. There is some worry whether the Upper City will survive the mob that will come through the gate at middlemoon. Uncle Peter and Uncle Francois have been here already; they run the factory more than our . . . other concerns. They are not happy. And yet Maman is right in this, I think, if not in other things."

Sophia straightened from her examination of the plastic house, looking over the other items in the cabinet while the girl with the flowers passed behind them with another arrangement. When she had gone Sophia whispered, "Will you have trouble getting back to set the firelighter, if there is fighting in the streets?"

"I will get there, and you shall be tucked into your bed, exhausted by our very public spat, Tom and Jennifer and a throng of prisoners on their way to the coast. LeBlanc will never know that you have left."

"That will depend on the signet ring. I will have to seal the forged passes to get them all out of the gates, and in time for Spear to deliver them."

"It will be done by the party. How do you want me to set the firelighter?"

"For dawn, don't you think? Unless the crowd hasn't gone. The prison should be empty by highmoon, or a little after. The guards will be on the hunt for me. If there is no one to execute I hope the mob will be on their way."

"I will go to the prison just after nethermoon, to be certain before I set it. Then I will come back to the flat, we take our things, and by dawn we will be out of the city."

She looked around when he didn't speak again and saw his gaze set on one of the little human figures. There was an expression there she recognized. She saw it in the mirror when she thought of Bellamy House.

"René, I am sorry," she whispered.

"I had looked forward to showing you the flat," he said. "I had thought of you living here someday. With me."

She turned back to the cabinet, so no one across the room could see her face. Why would he choose her, and all the complications that came with her? It had not escaped her thoughts that there must have been many gaggles of women, fluttering their fans in the Sunken City, women who did not come with a price tag. And she still hadn't stopped being surprised that she had chosen him back. She wished they were in the linen closet again.

"I have been wondering," she said aloud, "what your mother's signature might be worth when LeBlanc loses the Red Rook, a Bonnard, the Tombs, and all its prisoners in one night."

"It will not matter if you are caught. You cannot be reckless. Promise me you will not be reckless."

"I won't have to be reckless," she said. The middlesun bells rang, a sweet noise echoing out over the city. Her smile was grim. "But I am going to break him, René. LeBlanc has no idea what is coming to him."

LeBlanc listened to the middlesun bells, pacing the black floor of his rooms, unquiet in his mind. He had decided to accept his cousin's invitation, curious to know what sort of game the Hasards played. It should have given him satisfaction. At dusk he would attend a party in a flat he had just acquired, a party given for an enemy he was about to destroy, celebrating an engagement for which he had personally removed the finances. And at the next dawn, he would end the Festival of Fate by putting the Red Rook to death along with her brother and the Bonnard, and by giving two out of three to the Goddess. The myth of the saints destroyed, and so many destinies to choose. Fate could not fail to put the city in his hands after such a gift. It would be as had already been decided, as he'd known it would be, ever since his mother crooned the words into his ear after his father had left them to shift for themselves on Blackpot Street. Since the white had grown slowly through his hair. He could not understand his lack of contentment.

He opened a drawer and picked up his pendant, a thick, round metal disk enameled half black, half white with the sign of the Goddess, suspended from a silken black cord. But one push of a tiny button on the side and the pendant flipped open to show a small clock, the symbols of day and night inlaid with onyx, pearl, and crystals of glittering yellow; the finger in the center pointed to middlesun. The secret clock made a satisfyingly soft *tick, tick* in his hand, like a heart. What was the Goddess trying to tell him? What was Fate prompting him to do?

Suddenly LeBlanc hurried to his wooden table, sweeping it free of books and papers, took chalk from a box of reformed plastic, and drew circles of white and then black, white and black, smaller and smaller, until the tabletop was covered with them. Then he removed a single eight-sided casting piece, molded in rare, solid white by plasticians, painted with the sun and moon symbols of his clock, one on each side. He rolled the piece gently between his palms, then dropped it onto the circles.

He smiled, his doubt draining away like blood from a severed neck. The Red Rook was to die at dawn. Fate had decreed it to be so. But neither Tom Bellamy nor Jennifer Bonnard was the Red Rook.

How could he have been so blind? Allemande would not be pleased, of course, but the premier's time was nearly over. Fate had decreed this as well. The Goddess ruled the city, not Allemande, and surely there was no need to inform unbelievers of these matters?

He gazed at the symbol on the casting piece. Highmoon. Tomas Bellamy would go to the Razor at highmoon, Jennifer Bonnard after him. The Red Rook would come, thinking to rescue her brother, but Tomas Bellamy would already be dead. Or she would search for him until he was. And then, at last, Albert LeBlanc, soon to be the premier of the Sunken City, would have her. The Rook would be his. Fate had spoken, he would obey, and the world had been nudged into place.

Sophia stood on the small gallery, looking down at her engagement party, if not with disgust this time, certainly with apprehension. The flat was sparkling with soft light and the dusk skyline of the Sunken City, the violins playing, the room below her more full of people than they had dared hope, though it was nothing like the boisterous celebration of her Banns. The newspapers must have done the trick, or people were too afraid to stay in their own homes. The gendarmes surrounding the building might actually be a draw, once the Seine Gate opened.

She stepped back, restless and unsure why. Spear had not been himself ever since they left the Commonwealth. He was distracted, and when she'd asked him where he'd been the night before, he'd said Aunt Francesca's, reminding her that it was good to have more than one plan B, and would say no more. She thought perhaps he was angry with her, after the ferry and the landover ride. If he was angry with her now, he would be furious with her later. He was never going to understand why she would take René Hasard with no marriage fee, when she could have had Spear Hammond for the same. But she could not think of that now. It was time to go down, to get Tom, to do what she'd come to. But for just a few more moments, the shadows of the unlit gallery held their own charm.

She started at a hand on her shoulder, and found René behind her. He was in full ballroom René regalia, though a bit more understated, as favored by the city at the moment. He didn't speak, just pulled her through the doorway to the corridor, where he turned and put a hand on her neck and his forehead on hers. Sophia closed her eyes, lifting his other hand and holding it to her cheek. The door to the flat opened and shut below them, a distance that for a little while seemed very far away.

"Are you ready now, my love?" René whispered. She nodded. He tilted up her chin and kissed her once. "Then I will see you downstairs. Give me time to come through the back hall."

She straightened, nodding again as she stepped away, watching as René disappeared into the dark hall. Her uncertainty was gone, doubt trickled away into nothing. She snapped out her fan, went onto the gallery, and waited in the shadows. When she saw René's white head in the crowd below she lifted her chin, and began taking slow steps down the stairs to her engagement party.

Spear wove his way through the crowd, glass in hand, ignoring the women who smiled, moving to a corner where he could watch Sophia's gray gown glimmering in the shadows of the gallery. She'd been just as easy to see at the end of the corridor, standing still with Hasard's white head against hers when he'd opened his bedroom door. So easy to see when she'd let him kiss her. And now she was coming down the stairs, head held high under the fancy, black curls, eyes painted dark, skin the color of honey. She was so, so naive.

He'd thought it all through, made his preparations, but still he'd been undecided, dithering like a schoolboy. But now he knew what was right, and he knew what to do about it. Would not be dissuaded from it. He could have forgiven her infatuation; such things went away. What he could not forgive was what he had just seen in the upper corridor of the Hasard flat.

Just like at her Banns, conversations paused as she came down the stairs, and ballroom René, or a version of him, was waiting for her at the bottom. He kissed her hand.

"Miss Bellamy," he said, so that only she could hear. "You are the brightest of stars fallen to the earth."

Sophia looked at him from beneath darkened lashes. "Isn't that what the Ancients said about Lucifer, Monsieur?" The familiar words caused a quirk at the corner of his mouth as she took his arm. "I am surprised you remember that," she whispered.

"I never forget your insults. They are so instructive. And it is good to be right." His eyes were mesmerizingly blue in the soft light. "Sometimes I do think you are the very devil."

She hid her smile behind her fan before putting on a more formal expression. Unlike at her Banns, these guests were queuing up in a line several feet away, ready to walk up one at a time and greet her. The violins began to play McCartney as the first in line, a woman with a turban on her head, approached.

"Madame Gagniani, stop! Please!" René said loudly. "You turn my thoughts from my fiancée!" Sophia returned the woman's amused curtsy.

"Smuggler," René whispered near Sophia's ear, as Madame moved away, "though she never uses the turban, which is strange to me. And this one coming is a collector, and a supporter of Allemande.

We watch him carefully." Sophia gave her hand to an older, very proper gentleman, and then to another man, large around the middle.

"My love, let me introduce you to the Sunken City's new Ministre of Trade." She smiled pleasantly at the man who had taken Ministre Bonnard's post. If this was the man who had condemned them, she wished him a slow death.

"And Louis!" René said. "Where is your *maman*? You know how she always longs to dance with me!"

There must have been some inside joke here, because Louis, a boy who could not have been much older than Cartier, dimpled a little when she held out her hand. To her surprise, she felt that he'd left something behind when he let go. "Smuggler?" she asked René beneath her breath, hiding her hand behind her fan.

"Fence."

"Is there anyone here who is not a criminal?"

His gaze roved the room. "Are you including us?"

Sophia smiled. Mostly criminals, then, and almost all of them armed, she'd noticed. She glanced down to see what was in her hand, and froze. It was a tiny black feather with a tip of red. This was for Tom, she thought. From the young fence. And for her, if he'd known it. She exchanged pleasantries with a sand supplier, and before their conversation was over, the tiny feather was down the front of her dress.

As the line thinned René said quietly, "I should warn you, my love, that you will meet all of my uncles before the night is over. But do you see the tall man with the lace on his collar, drinking wine with that foul melter, the one who is looking at us now? That is Uncle Enzo, and you must be particularly cautious around him."

"Will he garrote me in my sleep?"

"Not unless Benoit tells him to. But he is a lip-reader, and if he can see you, he will know everything you are saying. And if he doesn't stop listening to our conversation now, I will be the one to garrote him in his sleep."

The level of René's voice had not changed, but when Sophia looked over at Enzo, he made a quick strangling motion before he winked.

"But I am also noticing we are a smuggler short," René said. "We seem to be missing Maman."

And Spear, Sophia thought. They were also missing LeBlanc.

Sophia danced her requisite two with René, who then left to go do his requisite flirting. It had been hard not to look at him this time, rather than the reverse. She received five more token feathers, slipped surreptitiously into her hands as she moved through the dance, all of which went down the front of her dress. Then, finally, through the milling crowd of somber grays and city blues, she spotted LeBlanc coming through the front door of the flat. He was impossible to miss with long billowing robes like a holy man, the white streak in his hair, and a huge pendant with the sign of the Goddess dangling from his neck. And he was positively strutting, confidence surrounding him like a stench as he greeted the proper gentleman, the ally of Allemande from the receiving line. The noise in the flat died down just a little as the crowd noted who had arrived. LeBlanc had a young woman on his arm, a girl much too young for him, curls hanging limp on either side of her face. She appeared to be petrified.

"Hello, Sophia Bellamy," said a voice near her ear. "Welcome to the family."

She found herself looking up into a face that was René's, but not. This face was much more weathered, red hair that was not quite as rich, a pair of keen blue eyes regarding her beneath fine brows. It was René's face, she thought, but in thirty years' time. "Uncle Émile," she said. "Am I right?"

"My nephew has been talking of me?"

Émile was handsome, though not conventionally so. But he was most definitely dangerous, like his nephew. Though perhaps he'd be more likely to nick the mother rather than her daughter. She smiled. "He has talked of you, Monsieur, but only with the greatest respect."

Émile tsked quietly. "How sad that you should be a liar, and that I should come to know it so quickly. Now if you had said he praised my looks, then . . ."

He shrugged once and grinned. Actually, Sophia thought suddenly, Uncle Émile might not have any need for stealing any woman's anything of any sort; he might only have to ask.

"René seems to be besotted with you, Mademoiselle, but it is Benoit who has taken us by surprise. He has defended you to the skies. How did you bring him to your table, may I ask?"

"I did not know I particularly had, Monsieur." She looked at Émile curiously. Just who was Benoit? The respect he commanded in the Hasard family seemed unlimited. "Though I am glad to hear it. And why, exactly, did I need defending?"

"My sister, René's mother, she had certain questions."

Sophia flicked open her fan. "Well, she signed the contract, didn't she?"

Émile's mouth quirked. "Only too true. But let me say for all the family how sorry we are for the arrest of your brother. He will die a hero, Mademoiselle. May I kiss your hand?"

Sophia smiled and lifted her hand. Uncle Émile's mouth remained a trifle too long, but at the same time she felt something slip beneath her fingers and into her palm. Not soft like a feather but hard and metallic. She slid her hand away and switched her fan to it, so she would not be seen clutching what she now realized was a ring.

"What has René told you?" she asked, still smiling as she leaned forward to listen.

"Only that you were in need, and through you, him. But time, Miss Bellamy, will be precious to us."

"Did you get it off his finger?" she asked, darting a glance at LeBlanc and his wilted companion across the room.

"No. I did not wish to be dead. But it was not on his finger, nor was it in his pockets, which René has now picked twice. Would you have guessed robes have pockets, Mademoiselle?"

"What I don't wish to guess is how you got it," she said, looking at him through her lashes.

His mouth quirked again. "My brother Andre says the top left drawer of his desk. It should be returned there as soon as possible. Andre is here, and waiting to do so."

Sophia gazed at the man beside her. They must think much of their nephew if they took this kind of risk on René's word alone. "I need to go to my room," she said.

"You are next to my sister, I assume?"

"Yes."

"I am sorry for you. I will be there as soon as I can. Hurry, Miss Bellamy."

He bowed and walked away through the dancers, hailing a friend or some relative as Sophia turned in the opposite direction, clutching her fan and moving as quickly as possible. But progress through a crowd of René's business associates of collectors and criminals, all of whom wished to speak to her, was an impossible task, and time was slipping before she was able to plead the loo and escape into the corridor.

When the door was shut she ran the curving hall, grabbed a candle from the wall on her way—startling a young woman carrying a tray of cheese—found the back stairs, and then she was shutting the door of her room behind her and turning the lock. She slid a chair in front of the connecting door to Madame Hasard's, tossed an unlit taper from its holder, and put in her lit candle instead. Then she went to her suitcase, tripped a switch, and pulled out the false lining of the top.

Crammed against the interior of the suitcase were official documents, what Spear had brought back from the forger. She rummaged among them, finding the stack of gate passes and the stick of black wax she had brought for such an occasion. She spread out the documents, carefully melting wax onto the bottom corner of the paper without dripping the tallow of the candle. As soon as she had a tarlike blob she rolled LeBlanc's signet ring across the soft surface, impressing his seal.

She did it again, and again, and eight more times before there was a soft knock at her door. "Coming!" she said, hoping her voice would carry through the door and no further than Émile. The knocking came again. She rolled the signet ring on the last pass, wondering briefly what the Parisian gossips would think if Uncle Émile were seen sneaking in or out of her bedroom. She suspected he had a reputation that would do hers no good. She flung open the door.

"Spear!" she said, surprised and a bit relieved. "Good, you'll save me a trip and I'm in a hurry." She pulled him into the room, shut the door, and locked it again, running to gather up the papers that now bore LeBlanc's seal. "They got LeBlanc's ring, the scoundrels. This is for you." She thrust a gate pass at him, the signet ring on her forefinger, and began to hastily replace the false top in her suitcase.

"I need to talk to you, Sophie."

"So talk," she commanded. She was cleaning away any remnants of black wax now, trying to find a place to stash the telltale bits. "And where have you been all nethersun? We didn't do our last go-over. I know we've already done it a thousand times, but . . ."

"Sophia Bellamy." He grabbed her arm. "Stop and listen to me!"

She stopped and narrowed her eyes. Spear had yanked her arm, actually yanked it, and the bits of wax were now all over the carpet. She straightened. His perfectly chiseled face was drawn in, as if there were a string pulling too tight from the inside.

"What's wrong?" she asked.

"You think you love him."

Her stomach wrenched once. "Spear, this is not the time to . . ."

"Answer me. You're going to marry him anyway, aren't you? Without the fee."

She looked up at Spear's taut face, at the broad shoulders heaving as if he'd sprinted to her door. She owed him honesty at least. "Yes. If he will have me."

Spear just stared at her, hands in pockets. Then he said, "Sophie, you're being played."

She blinked at him, uncomprehending.

"By the Hasards. All of them. You're being played."

"Oh, Spear. Listen . . ."

"No. You are going to listen. For once in your life you're going to close your mouth and you will listen to what I have to say. Do you really think that Hasard was just pretending to work with LeBlanc, that he had his own interests, and that they just so happened to coincide with coming to Bellamy House to marry you? That Madame just happened to arrange some fool marriage that would bankrupt her family? There is no marriage fee, Sophia."

"Spear, we both know that. He told me himself . . ."

"Of course he did. But I mean there never was one. Ever. The Hasard fortune has been dwindling for a long time. Madame arranged a marriage to you for no other reason than to get her son and LeBlanc into Bellamy House. Somebody's been talking, Sophie. LeBlanc already knew where we'd been landing."

Sophia was shaking her head. "You don't know what you're talking about."

"How do you think they're planning on building their fortune back? How have they kept their business through the revolution? Do you really believe they just stole that ring you're wearing? Or did LeBlanc walk in here tonight and hand it to them? You're being played. You . . ."

"Just stop. Stop it!" she yelled. "You're jealous, Spear, and I'm sorry for it. But I don't have time for this and I don't believe a word you're saying."

The drawn look on Spear's face tightened. "I know you don't believe me," he said. "I knew you wouldn't. Because you want to believe what he tells you. You want to believe in him; you have almost from the beginning. I'm no match for his lies, Sophie. It's taken me time to realize it. I thought you'd come to your senses, but I know I'm no match for him. I've had to wait for proof, and now I have it."

He reached beneath his black jacket and pulled out a crisp piece of paper with the seal of the Sunken City showing through. He offered it to her, and Sophia came and took the paper reluctantly, reading the first few lines before she looked up again, confused.

"The denouncement of Ministre Bonnard?" she asked.

"Yes. Signed by a citizen of the Sunken City, swearing the Bonnards committed treason against Allemande. The reason the entire family was arrested and nearly executed, right down to their toddling children."

She read, her eyes glossing over the words until they reached the signature at the bottom. And when they did Sophia stepped back, and then back again until she bumped into the gold-papered wall. She stared at the ink, a hand reaching up to cover her mouth. The name on the bottom was René Hasard, the same looping signature she'd seen on one hundred and thirty-eight engagement-party invitations.

"I was surprised to see your name on my invitation, René. Surprised and pleased, of course. But where is your charming fiancée?" LeBlanc's grin was a long, thin gash in his face as he tightened his grip on the limp girl beside him; she made the slightest motion of leaning away. "I was so looking forward to seeing her before I go."

René drained a glass of wine. "But surely you will not go before the entertainment, Monsieur? We have made such special plans, and with you in mind." LeBlanc glanced toward the windows and their spectacular nighttime views of the Sunken City, where a full, rising moon hung low on the horizon between buildings.

"Yes," he said, smile becoming contemplative. "Fate has destined a very entertaining night for us." The girl at his side squeaked slightly as her arm was squeezed. "And the new Festival of Fate is also cause for celebration. Though those who set themselves against the Goddess may not find it so. Do you not agree, René?"

"Oh, yes. When the gates open, that will be very amusing. I

noticed the armed men at the street door. You are careful with our assets, Cousin, that they do not receive too much celebration."

"We worship Fate, René, but we do not tempt her. Your little fiancée should take those words to heart."

"I am certain she will."

18

Sophia slid down the wall, crouching on the floor, staring at the handwriting on the parchment until her eyes watered, aching to blink. The name on the page pierced straight through her chest. She could have countered Spear's arguments, every single one of them, disputed his interpretation of events. Except for the document in her hand. How could this be? And why? Someone knocked at the door, but she ignored it. She looked up at Spear, questioning.

"They're smugglers," he said simply, "and Bonnard was Ministre of Trade. He was going to shut them down."

The knocking came again. "Mademoiselle?" It was Émile.

Spear whispered quickly, "Tom was looking into Hasard's background before he ever got to Bellamy House. He made me swear to look out for you, to find the proof, and I promised him I would. But Hasard has been reeling you in like a fish on a hook ever since. He wants the Red Rook, Sophie, and he and LeBlanc, they know it's not Tom. They've known for a while now. They want you, and they want you in the Sunken City, with your hands dirty with prison filth. It's a . . . it's like a religious thing with LeBlanc, but the Hasards just want their fortune. Hasard convinced you to wait until La Toussaint because LeBlanc wants to make a ritual out of you. LeBlanc took Madame to the Tombs for insurance, and the price for getting her out was to bring you to the city. And little by little, Hasard convinced you to tell him everything . . ."

Some part of her mind registered that Émile was still knocking. "Mademoiselle? Are you there?"

She sat all the way down on the thick carpet, staring at the huge, looping R. She was stunned, blindsided, hit so hard she couldn't think. No matter what Spear said, no matter how she untangled truth from lies, the reality was that the man she knew as René Hasard and the man who had signed the paper in her hand could not coexist. He wasn't real. Nothing was real. This moment was unreal. And she'd known he was good at the game, known she was an easy target. She'd seen the danger and even guarded herself against it. And what had she done in the end? Chased him down. Offered herself up. He wasn't just good, he was a master. She'd known deep down that it didn't make sense. She had been incredibly stupid. Because she'd wanted to be. She'd wanted to believe. Because she'd wanted him.

"Did you send the hotelier?" she whispered.

Spear didn't answer. The room sat quiet, the knocking on the door long stopped. She discovered Spear's hand near her head.

"Here, Sophie. Come up here."

She took his hand and he pulled her to her feet, put his arm around her, guided her to the edge of the bed, where they sat, her face against his chest. He held her, his other hand stroking her back, up and down. Spear was so big you could drown in him. She wished she could drown.

"Here's what I think we should do, Sophie," he said quietly. She could feel the words in the chest beneath her ear. "LeBlanc will know exactly what you mean to do. He'll be expecting you to leave the party and come back, like you planned with Hasard. So let's go now, as soon as we can. We'll do what we've done before with the coffins, before anyone is the wiser. Did you ever mention the coffins to any of them?"

She wasn't sure. She didn't think so.

"LeBlanc knows you're coming, but he thinks it's from one direction and not the other. We'll take the tunnels out, and if something goes wrong, there's always plan B and the forged passes and the tickets to Spain. We'll get to the coast, just like we've done before."

No, Sophia was thinking. *You don't understand. You don't know what I was really going to do at the prison. What I thought René was going to help me do at the prison. Plans are in motion that cannot be undone.*

Or were they? If they involved René, then perhaps those plans were never going to happen in the first place. Spear had a finger on her cheek now, sliding it down to beneath her chin.

"We'll get Orla and Bellamy, take Jennifer to her parents, and then you and me and Tom, we'll all go away together, maybe up west, or to one of the islands, somewhere they won't bother to look for us."

She closed her eyes. She could save Tom and Jennifer, but what about the rest of them? How would skulking off to the coast save two out of every three prisoners? Running wouldn't break the pattern, and it wouldn't take down LeBlanc.

"Don't you think we could do that, Sophie?"

She was a burning thing, streaking fire and making thunder across the sky. The finger beneath her chin pushed upward, and Spear leaned down, touching his mouth to hers.

And she woke up. Sophia leapt away like a startled deer, the paper with René's signature landing softly on the floor. "What are you doing?"

"Sophia. Sophie . . ." Spear reached for her hand, but she moved it away. He was being incredibly gentle, as if she were a wounded animal. Maybe she was. "This . . . thing with Hasard. It's over now. It never was in the first place. You're free of it."

A bolt of white-hot pain shot through her middle, making her flinch. She had never wanted to be free of it. She wrapped her arms around her waist.

"And now that you're free, we can . . ." He hesitated, and her eyes snapped wide.

"We can what, Spear?"

"We can . . . be together."

Sophia felt her mouth open slightly. "Do you really think . . ." She breathed, searching for her words. "Do you really think that because I have been betrayed, been a fool, been the biggest arse the Bellamy family has ever seen, that because of all that I'm going to suddenly fall into your arms?"

Spear leaned forward from where he sat on the edge of the bed, fists clenched.

"Spear, I don't love you."

It was silent in the bedroom, and then all at once Spear exploded, jumping to his feet and kicking the table where she had been forging the passes to the floor. Sophia shrank back.

"Why?" he yelled. "Why the bloody not?"

Sophia watched him, hand hovering near the sword she had strapped to her leg. She'd beaten Tom in a fight, but she had never beaten Spear. She didn't want to try now. But when he just stood there, waiting, hands hanging loose at his sides, she went to him and put a hand on his heaving chest.

"What I said just then wasn't true. I do love you. I've loved you ever since I can remember. It's always been Tom, and Father, and

Orla, and you. No one else mattered. Just my family. And that is how I love you, Spear. Like my family. I don't know why it's different for you than for me. But you need to understand that it's not going to change."

She could feel the tension inside him, though whether fury or pain was dominant she could not say. Everything she felt was firmly under lock and key. She was like the firelighter now, moving toward the inevitable explosion, but until then, ticking on and on automatically.

"You're going to have to let this go, Spear. And if I don't do what is needed right now, Tom and Jennifer are walking to the scaffold at dawn. You know I'm right."

Spear nodded slowly, his cool blue eyes staring at the floor.

"Then what I need is for you to get those passes to the gates. You know what to do after that, and what to do if we don't come."

He nodded again. Sophia left the passes on the bed, picked up the paper with René's signature from the floor, and left Spear standing by the overturned table, shutting the bedroom door quietly behind her.

The corridor was a tunnel of dim, flickering shadows, only a few sconces lit. She stood still and dry-eyed, watching the light quiver. She hurt. In her chest, in her fingers, the backs of her legs, and behind her eyes. Every inch of her insides bruising and sore. But she knew this was nothing, nothing at all, compared to the pain and humiliation that awaited her when the ticking inside her reached its appointed time.

She took a step toward the water room, toward Jennifer and Tom, and then she paused, wavering like the candlelight. She was thinking of horrid masks and pale eyes and cemeteries full of the dead. Of the red-tipped feathers she had slipped into her bodice, and fighting in the streets, and the Razor, and LeBlanc's hands. His bloody, bloody hands. Fire replaced her pain. The blessed heat of rage. She was still going to break him. Without René. Or Spear. But there was something to be done before she left.

She folded the paper that had changed everything, shoving it far down into her dress with the feathers, adjusted the dark hair on her head, and slapped her cheeks, once each in case they were drained of color. Then she turned and walked fast down the hall, opening the door onto the gallery and her engagement party, a reckless smile on her face. She needed to see LeBlanc.

And as she was entering the gallery, Benoit slipped out of Madame Hasard's door. He went fast down the hall, away from the gallery, a crease in his forehead. He needed to find René.

Sophia came down the stairs, blinking in the dazzle after the dim. René's criminal friends were very cordial, and she smiled back at them, as if she were happy and brilliant and not a walking firestorm. She spotted her quarry—a black-as-death billowing robe and a streak of white hair—held up her skirts, and made her way through the crowd; she'd forgotten her fan somewhere.

"Monsieur LeBlanc," she said.

His eyes were nearly slits when they turned to her. "Mademoiselle Bellamy," he said softly. He reached for her hand, and she immediately offered him the other one. She'd forgotten she was wearing his signet ring, now hidden in the clutched fabric of her silver-gray skirt. Some part of her realized she was out of control, and that Tom and Jennifer were depending on her not being so. But she also didn't seem to be able to help it. LeBlanc's lips were cold evil on her free hand. "Allow me to introduce Amber," he said, "my . . . friend for the night."

Amber curtsied awkwardly, not looking up from beneath the hanging front curls. She was even younger than she had looked from across the room. Sophia saw Émile over to her left, inching just a little closer. Too bad, Émile, she thought. *The ring is on my finger, and this dress does not have a pocket.*

"What a pleasure it is to finally have you in the City of Light, Mademoiselle," LeBlanc was saying. "Now that you are here, I think that you will never leave it."

Sophia kept her face pleasant.

"It must be agreeable to your brother," he added, "to finally take credit for all his deeds. Do you not think that it must be very relieving, to give credit where credit is due?"

Amber raised her head a bit at this, but Sophia just stared back into LeBlanc's pale eyes. It was true, then. He did know she was the Red Rook. Of course he did. How could he not? She could hear René's laugh somewhere near. She smiled.

"What a strange thought, Monsieur. But I can honestly say that as long as the goal is met, I do not mind in the slightest if no one knows what I am up to. Or if they do."

LeBlanc's slow smile curled, and she matched it. He would be in a million tiny slivers by the dawn, and so would his prison. She glanced past his shoulder and saw René, his arm around a rather lovely young woman in a blond wig. Lies, lies, and lies, served up with more lies. Promises whispered in her ear, arms around her on the roof and just that middlesun, in this very room. *I had thought of you living here someday. With me.*

René was swaying on his feet a bit now, as if he were drunk. Just as they'd planned. It was almost time to slap him. Just as they'd planned.

". . . might injure your health, Mademoiselle?"

She jerked her eyes back to Amber and LeBlanc, who were both watching her curiously. She hadn't been listening. Émile inched closer on her left.

"I . . ." And then she gasped. A strong burst of laughter from the group around René made several heads around the room turn. René was leaning down to the young blond now, whispering something in her ear while she giggled. "Did you see that, Amber?" Sophia said loudly. "Did you see him?"

Émile went still, and both Amber and LeBlanc craned their necks to look behind them. As soon as they had both turned back to her Sophia yelled, "Oh, there! He did it again! Come with me."

She snatched Amber's arm with her left hand and marched past, wrenching the girl from LeBlanc's grip, pulling her at a trot toward René. René saw her coming and got ready.

"My love!" he called, much too loud for politeness, especially with his arm around another woman. Émile was sidling along, still on their left, Benoit now with him and speaking into his ear.

"Friends!" René slurred. "This is my fi . . . my wife . . . my fian-cée! Sophie, my love, have you met . . ."

"How could you?" she said. "How?"

It was what they'd planned for her to say. Ask him "how could you," step one, two, three, and slap. But now she meant it. The talk around them fell away, a rippling tide of silent air. She paused, still clutching Amber, then came forward one, two . . . and slapped René's face with everything she had. She caught him full force, LeBlanc's ring still on her finger, the sound of her palm on his cheek reverberating, snapping his head around, making the signed paper with his signature rustle against her chest.

He turned his head slowly back, hand to his cheek. She met his eyes, such a hot fire-blue against the white hair, and for one brief moment was confused by the confusion she could see inside them. His lip was bleeding.

Amber made a feeble attempt to move away, but Sophia didn't allow it. She was supposed to berate René now, to complete the scene they had created, but she couldn't. She couldn't do anything. Everything that had been making her tick was stuttering, all her inner workings grinding to a halt. And when they did, she would detonate. She walked away, forcing Amber along beside her, her high heels clacking on the polished floor.

"Comfort me," she ordered Amber, in barely a whisper. "Don't make me drag you. Do it. Now."

Amber whimpered, but she put an arm around Sophia's shoulders, walking her to the corridor door, the crowd parting for them like wheat in the wind. Sophia opened the door, shut it behind them, and then grabbed Amber's hand.

"Run," she commanded.

They ran around the curving hall, past the noisy kitchen full of people Sophia had never seen, and to the door at the very end. Sophia pushed up the drop bar, opened the door, and shoved Amber through it.

"These are the stairs to the ground. You can go all the way down to the street, or take the air bridge on the eighth floor." Amber stared at her, goggle-eyed. "Unless you want to stay here with LeBlanc?"

The girl shook her limp curls. Then she shook them harder.

"Do you have somewhere you can go? Can you hide, or get out of the city?"

"Yes, Mademoiselle, I . . ."

"Then go. And here." Sophia reached between the edge of her bodice and the top of her skirt and drew out one of her sheathed knives, shoving it into the girl's hands.

"Thank you," Amber whispered.

"Go!"

When Amber started moving, Sophia shut the door, dropped the bar back into place, and ran again, down the hall and up the back stairs, pausing before the corridor that led to her room. She darted her head around the corner. What she could see of the hall was empty, so she flitted quickly through the shadows, drew out the knife strapped around her ankle, put an ear to the door of her room, and then opened it cautiously. Except for the table on its side, the room sat ordinary and deserted, as if it hadn't just experienced the catastrophic collapse of her entire life. Spear and the forged gate passes were gone.

She jerked open the cupboard, found her fluffy underskirt hung among the other dresses, and drove her knife into the white cloth with a ripping tear. The firelighter was in a sack of burlap that was now in her hand, and there were men's voices coming to her door. Benoit, she thought, and probably Émile. She darted silently to Madame Hasard's connecting door and slipped through it just as hers was opening. When both men were in her room, she dashed out of Madame Hasard's and down the stairs, around the curve and to the linen closet, where she'd left a covered lamp burning. She shut the door behind her.

Sophia paused. It was excruciating being in this room; it nearly stopped her ticking altogether. She thought of Tom, and Jennifer, and pretended to be somewhere else. Pretended to be someone else. The wig came off and so did the dress, hidden quickly behind the hanging tablecloths, her black breeches and black shirt already underneath, cut low so as not to show beneath the lace of her former neckline. Her vest she fished out from the ironing pile, supplies already sewn in, the feathers from the party going into the bag with the others. The denouncement of the Bonnards she left in her shirt. Then she took her second knife and pushed the tip twice through the burlap that held the firelighter, making two holes, cut a cord from the washed curtains and strung the whole thing sideways across her chest. Her sword went from her leg to her back, for climbing; a soft black cap was pulled over her pinned hair; dark leather gloves onto her hands. And when the door of the linen closet opened again, the Rook peered out into the empty hall. She flitted across to the water room, shut herself inside, and opened the sliding panel to the lift.

She leapt up onto the ledge and looked down. The bucket was dangling one level below on the nearest rope. Hoping that meant the other bucket was near the bottom and full, she reached out, and that was when the door to the water room opened. Madame Hasard stood looking in at her, vivid hair piled high for the party, one red eyebrow raised.

Sophia met her gaze, grabbed the rope with both hands, and jumped. The rope swung out as she got a foot wrapped around, she bounced once off the bricks, and then she was gone, dropping down the shaft, water splashing somewhere below, leaving her stomach where she'd started. She passed the closed lift door for the flat below, and the next open one, showing a man's turned back, and glanced up. The top of the shaft was still lit and growing smaller, but no one was trying to cut her rope. Surely Madame Hasard carried a knife? But Madame wasn't going to have time to cut anything.

Air whistled around Sophia's ears. She wondered if she would be able to keep her grip when the rope came to a stop, or if she was about to take a cold, wet bath in a cistern. She hung on, saw the bottom coming, got her knees bent, and the rope stopped with a jerk that nearly wrenched her arms from their sockets. But she was able to swing her feet to the edge of a cistern and hop down, and as René had said, landing her boots on the stone floor of the building's cellar.

She looked around, wary, ready to reach for her sword, but no one was there. She took a moment to lean against the wall, the great turnstile of the four-man lift creaking somewhere behind it, probably taking people up to her engagement party. She had to think.

René knew her plans, and now through his mother, he would know she was gone. And yet the rope had not been cut, and there were no gendarmes waiting for her now. Which only confirmed what Spear had said, that they needed to catch her in the act, probably to satisfy Allemande's twisted sense of justice. She remembered the look on René's face just that middlesun, when he'd talked about losing the flat. What would she have done, what had she planned on doing, to preserve her family and home? Was it any different? Oh yes, she thought. What he had done was very different.

She walked quickly across the cellar and found the grate in the floor, just as he'd described, lifting it away to show a circular drain. The hole bore straight down into the ground, rungs of metal making a ladder down into a dark that was blacker than where she stood. One touch without her glove and she knew the surface was concrete, like some of the laddered tunnels in Bellamy House. Cool air wafted upward, smelling of earth.

She descended two rungs, dragging the grate back over the opening, and started her way down, thinking. The farther she went, the faster she went, rung after rung, quicker and quicker, despite the fact that it made no difference whether her eyes were opened or closed, or that she was in a deep hole that she couldn't see the bottom of. She was smiling again, the reckless sort. Because she had just changed the plan.

René picked up speed down the hallway, holding a cold wet cloth to his bleeding lip, his face like bleached stone. Benoit followed after him.

"Is Uncle Émile watching LeBlanc?"

"Yes," said Benoit. "He has told him that his lady friend is attending Mademoiselle Bellamy with a womanly complaint."

"Does Uncle Émile think he's telling LeBlanc lies or the truth?"

"Possibly the truth."

"And she's away down the shaft?"

"Madame says so."

"And she still has the ring?"

"The one she has just hit you with? I would guess so. I only know that Hammond has spoken with her, and there is broken furniture as a result. I arrived in time to hear that he wished her to make a new plan, and she would not. She was not herself when she left."

René let out a string of curses that would have made Uncle Émile blush. "Where is Hammond?"

"I have had Andre and Peter detain him. They have him in her room."

René opened the last door in the corridor. He walked past Uncle Peter, who had a split on his cheek that was going to bruise, and Uncle Andre, who was gingerly pushing upward on a loose tooth, going straight to Spear. Spear had his hands behind his back, arms and legs tied to a chair. Benoit shut the door and turned the lock while René leaned down over the big man's face.

"Tell me what you have done, you great, lumbering bag of filth, or I will cut off your ears."

Spear looked up, and then he smiled.

It was a long time before Sophia found the bottom of the laddered hole, the ground coming as a surprise beneath her boot. She looked up into the darkness and smiled. Too bold. That's what Tom would have said. She didn't care. She had to feel with her hands until she found the next tunnel. The opening was small, not a real opening at all, probably an erosion of concrete. She wiggled until she was through, careful with her sword and the firelighter, and then moved quickly, first stooping, and then crawling in complete blackness, until she came to a paler shade of night from a drain above her.

She counted three more of these, and on the fourth, instead of following the tunnel as they'd planned, she carefully pushed up the grate of the drain, panting from her efforts. She saw a back alley behind a squalid structure of ill-formed bricks, one of the buildings that formed the loose open square of the prison yard. It was also the building that squatted over the entrance to the Tombs.

She pulled herself up to the surface, hugging the dark, replacing the grate with the soft scrape of iron on stone. Then she slipped around the corner and crouched down, where the shade of the scaffold hid her from the rising moonlight and the gendarmes patrolling the yard. The scaffold had been decorated, she saw; there were shadows hanging from it, twisting around the timbers and fluttering in the breezes like tattered souls. She wondered if those decorations were for her. She waited for the guards to pass, then circled the building, slowly lifting her head to peek through a lit window.

A stout man sat with his back to her before a rickety desk, the fire low and smoldering in the hearth, his head tipped forward and still. Either sleeping or dead, Sophia thought. Silently she pushed open the window—why did no one ever think of the windows?— grateful that the holy man had had the foresight to grease it before rescuing the Bonnards. She dropped to the floor without noise, shut the window again, drew the curtain and her sword, and moved toward the man's back. He woke with a start, a red-tipped feather before his eyes and a blade at his throat.

"Hello, Gerard," she said, low in his ear.

Renaud slid to the rear of the crowd, where LeBlanc was standing, and whispered in his ear. A dark-skinned woman in a simple high-waisted gown was providing the singing entertainment for the Hasard engagement party, the cityscape twinkling behind her. LeBlanc did not like the woman; she was blocking his view of the moon. He straightened as Renaud finished his whispering.

"Then we can assume the Red Rook has flown, Renaud, and that she has taken my little bird with her." He laughed softly, though loud enough that a few heads turned, frowning at the interruption. LeBlanc glanced about him once, flipped open the top of his pendant, then shut it after a quick glance. More than halfway to middlemoon.

"It is earlier than I thought. I think I will spend a little more time in my flat, Renaud, at least until the execution bells. I am curiously happy. That slap was very convincing, wasn't it? And it is Sophia Bellamy's last night to fly. I will listen to the performance, and enjoy the thought of the Red Rook's struggles as she tries to find her brother." He sighed with satisfaction. "All is as Fate has ordained. There is no hurry."

Enzo sat on the other side of the room, not listening to the singer perform, instead watching the one-sided conversation between LeBlanc and his secretary. He frowned, leaning forward just a little, waiting for an opportunity to leave his chair. He had the sudden feeling that he might be in a hurry.

Gerard could not move from his chair.

"I have no time for negotiations, Gerard. Do we have a deal?"

He couldn't nod. The sword at his throat did not allow it. "How do I know I can trust you?" he whispered.

Sophia was using the gruff voice of the holy man. "Should you trust the one who puts the people in the prison, Gerard, or the one who breaks them out? I will cut your throat, but LeBlanc will cut you up, piece by tiny piece. How is your finger healing?"

Gerard glanced down at the bandage on his hand. "I will lose my job!"

"You will lose your head. And, frankly, you're due a career change, Gerard." The Red Rook waited, and when Gerard didn't respond she gave him a tiny prick with the sword edge.

"Yes, yes! I will do it!"

She eased the sword away from Gerard's throat. "Your wife will thank you. Now remember the rules. Clear the prison of gendarmes but for the two I have named, and then you are to unlock the doors. Understood?"

He waited in his chair, shoulders shaking as he breathed, the sword in her hand tickling the place between his shoulder blades. "Are you a man," he whispered, "or a spirit?"

The Red Rook smiled. "I am neither, Gerard."

"He knows you are coming."

She gripped the sword hilt harder, feeling a last tiny something shrivel up inside her. Where had that treacherous little bit of hope been hiding, and why had it existed? LeBlanc would have known she was coming for quite some time now. "I know he does, Gerard. But I am going to outsmart him, and you and your wife will have a new life in Spain. Now stand up. And leave your sword on the desk. Do it!"

He did.

"Call your man and give the orders. Stay behind the desk, keep him in front. Your man will not see me. Do you understand?"

"Claude? Claude!"

A jingling noise indicated a guard coming toward LeBlanc's door. The gendarme who had cut off Gerard's fingertip strode into the room, stroking his tiny mustache.

"We have new orders," Gerard said. "Bring the tunnel leaders to me. One at a time, if you please."

Sophia glanced out the window from where she was crouched behind Gerard's desk, the sword tip now at the back of his knee. A round, rising middlemoon was just cresting the edge of the cliffs.

19

Light that was almost to middlemoon poured through Sophia's bedroom window before Spear stopped talking. René stood still, inhaling five full breaths before he turned and went to the clothes cupboard, yanking open the doors and ransacking Sophia's dresses until he found the white underskirt.

Andre frowned, still worrying his tooth. "What is this man talking about, René? What is happening? And if you put that on, I'm telling Émile."

René didn't answer. He rifled through the cloth, going still when his fingers slipped through the fresh white rent made by Sophia's knife, where the firelighter had been.

Benoit opened the door to a soft knock and Enzo slid inside, taking in the scene with a swift glance before he crossed the room to his nephew. "René," he whispered, "why does LeBlanc think your fiancée is the Red Rook? I thought it was her brother."

René clutched the cloth in his hand. "He has said so?"

"Yes, to that little viper of a secretary."

René looked down at the golden carpet, his hand through the cut in the white cloth. Then he turned his face to Spear. Spear was still tied to the chair, defiant, ears intact but with blood flowing from the corner of his mouth.

"You understand that you have killed her," René said.

No one spoke. Andre and Peter shifted their feet, curious and impatient, while Benoit, who had been inexplicably searching Sophia's suitcase, suddenly held up a ring with a single pale stone. René threw down the white cloth, walked across the room, and kicked the legs out from under Spear's chair.

"Oh, really, René," said Madame Hasard from the doorway. She shut the bedroom door behind her. "Stop being so dramatic. Pick that man up again and we will discuss what is to be done."

"Yes," René replied, glaring down at Spear lying sideways on the floor, jaw clenched so tight he could hardly speak. "Yes, pick him up, Uncle Andre. And someone hand him a sword."

"René! I . . ."

"Shut up, Maman!" He threw off his jacket while Spear was cut loose from the chair, yanking off his cravat and tossing it to the floor.

"Great Death, René," said Peter at the sight of his neck. "Who tried to strangle you?"

"That," René said, eyes on Spear, "would be his fault, I think."

Spear just smiled as he got to his feet, wiping the blood from his mouth onto his sleeve, swinging some feeling back into his hands. "Not me." He took the sword Andre handed him, sizing it up. "But I wish it had been."

"Men," muttered Madame Hasard, though none of the men present paid any attention to her. "You cannot have a proper duel in a bedchamber. It is ridiculous."

"I will be happy," Spear continued, "to slice you to pieces, Hasard. But I want you to know I won't wait. I'm in a bit of a hurry."

René's grin lurked as he lifted his sword. "I also have an appointment, Monsieur."

"But it is certainly worth a few moments of my time," Spear continued, "to carve up any man who lifts a hand against Sophia Bellamy."

"How much we have in common."

Spear brought up his blade and they watched each other, blue gaze on blue gaze, one of ice and one that was fire. René struck first and Spear blocked with a clang of metal.

Gerard walked the subterranean passage, keys clinking, the heavy locks clanging as they were turned. Light from the ever-rising moon poured down the drains from a prison yard that was empty of everyone, even his guards. He was not whistling this time, or searching for the right door. He was unlocking them all. Silence spread from hole to hole as the people inside tried to understand what was happening. There would never be a promotion, Gerard thought, but it certainly was a fine night for an execution. His.

One brave prisoner finally pushed open her door.

Sophia found the door to prison hole number 522 deep within the Tombs and thrust it open, scattering the rats inside, panting from her run and from the stench. The prison was a maze, the numbers nonsensical, and it always took some time to stop smelling the tunnels; she'd never yet been able to stop smelling a cell.

But there were no prisoners in here. This hole was being used as a storage room, for distributing the little food that LeBlanc chose to dole out. Sacks of potatoes, a few evidently rotting, sat beside the door, a water cask and buckets in the corner, and an unusual number of barrels of the hard, almost bread-like *pain plat*. Most of them, Sophia knew, did not contain *pain plat*. They were full of her father's Bellamy fire.

She set the lantern far away from the barrels and drew the cord with the hanging firelighter over her neck. She was surprised to find the casks still here, but since René was the one who was supposed to set the firelighter—the task he had so carefully made sure was his—she supposed LeBlanc thought there was no danger. Or maybe he wanted to study the powder's uses for Allemande. Another very good reason for blowing it all up.

The noise of prisoners being released was coming to her ears, and the cries of those who did not yet know if they would join them. Time to go. She scanned the dim, dank room. Would René find the firelighter gone, and try to come in time to turn it off? She was certain he would. And she had no intention of making it easy for him to find.

Sophia turned the pointing finger to middlemoon, or just a little before, the time she hoped it was now. She'd told René to set it for dawn, so she turned the wheel to the full, silver circle of highmoon. They should be away by then, the prison yard still empty before the execution that was not going to happen, and that would give René the least amount of time to find the firelighter and turn it off again.

She pulled out the knob. When the moon reached its height, the Tombs would explode into chunks of rock and wicked dust, and LeBlanc would be explaining the loss of a prison to Allemande.

Or maybe it would be just a little before.

The entertainment was over, the low hum of conversation resuming. LeBlanc settled down on the settee, Renaud standing, as ever, just a few paces behind. LeBlanc leaned back, taking in the view of his city outside the curving windows. Almost middlemoon. The gates would be opening soon for the Festival of Fate, a few carefully chosen leaders of the mob given the addresses of those that still required removal from the Upper City. Quick work, and for what would have otherwise taken him weeks of paperwork for Allemande. He smiled, studying the windows, mentally measuring them for new hangings.

The guests were also watching the moon. They seemed reluctant to go, even if the couple they had come for had just publicly fought and now disappeared, perfectly content to drink and listen to music while the gendarmes guarded the street entrances downstairs. But there was a bubble of isolation around the settee, an aura of something unsavory that kept even Allemande's allies at a distance. Except for Émile. Émile made himself at home in the chair opposite, handing LeBlanc a glass of wine that had just been delivered by Benoit.

"Do you play games, Albert?" Émile asked.

LeBlanc's pale eyes flattened just a bit as he accepted the glass. "I believe that would depend on the game, Émile. What sort do you have in mind?"

"Games of strategy. Chance. You are a student of luck, are you not?"

"Luck is the handmaiden of Fate, Émile. There is no 'chance.'"

"So you do not play games?"

"Strategy is for implementing the will of the Goddess, not discovering it."

"Tell me," said Émile, "how do you determine the will of Fate? How does she make her wishes known to you?"

"Why, one only has to ask," said LeBlanc, as if he were sniffing out a convert. "Just this middlesun, I was uneasy in my mind. A decision weighed on me. And so I did the proper honorifics, asked my question of Fate, cast the die, and received my answer."

"And what was your answer?" Émile asked, sipping his own wine.

"That my timing was imperfect. That highmoon was the proper time for certain festivities. Isn't it fascinating, Émile? Fate reached out her finger and tipped the world into its proper position." LeBlanc's smile was smug as he drank. He sat back, the pendant dangling against his chest from its silken cord.

"Fascinating," Émile agreed, glancing at how much LeBlanc had swallowed. His eyes roved through the mass of people that were milling about the flat, unwilling to leave. He could not see Enzo.

The tunnel was in confusion, people everywhere, propping each other up, some carrying one another, all unsure of the way, all wanting out. Sophia pushed her way through the melee, her shouts ineffectual. Then there was a clang of metal up ahead, someone hitting two swords together rhythmically, calling the prisoners to the upper tunnel and the exit. The throng surrounding Sophia turned as one to the sound and gradually began a steady pace, the stronger moving ahead of the weak, an avalanche of humanity sliding sideways and up through the muck and dark of the rough tunnel.

If the gendarmes came back, if even one of them saw something they shouldn't, these people would have nothing but their numbers to defend themselves. But surely, Sophia thought, nothing could have been worse than what they were facing the moon before. She held up her lantern, steadying the arm of a woman stumbling next to her. The woman looked up once, glassy-eyed, but any curiosity Sophia saw there was quickly eaten by the panic to get out.

A gendarme stood at the highest bend of the tunnel, where there was a crossroads of sorts, and this caused a palpitation of fear through the prisoners. But when it was obvious that this gendarme was also holding a light, waving them on and up, calling that there were landovers arriving to take them out of the Sunken City, they moved on again. He must be one of her twins, Sophia thought; an ally she'd never even seen before tonight. The clanging was still going on somewhere beyond him.

She broke away from the stumbling herd into a side-branching tunnel before the gendarme spotted her. This passage went down again, ending in a locked metal door. Sophia brought out the key Gerard had given her, turned the lock, and started down a long, winding set of stone stairs. LeBlanc's special cells, for special prisoners. That's what the twins had written.

Cartier would be out there somewhere, helping the twins direct the prisoners to the temporary safety of the warehouse across the prison yard. The Lower City was emptying for La Toussaint. With no executions soon, he should be able to get the prisoners safely loaded into the landovers Allemande was so thoughtfully providing for their trip to the Upper City and out the gates. As long as Spear got out of the Hasard flat quick enough, delivered the forged passes to the gates, as long as she could get everyone out before René or LeBlanc realized the Tombs were completely empty of gendarmes . . .

She stopped on the stairs, stomach twisting as she looked at LeBlanc's signet ring, now filthy but still on her index finger. René knew about the passes, and he'd made sure the ring came into her hands. Or had he made sure she had the ring to fully gain her trust, and not told LeBlanc he was doing so? Such a double cross was not unthinkable. And then she felt another hard wrench in her middle. René was providing the ships. That meant there wouldn't be any ships.

The prisoners would just have to scatter; it was all she could do. At least she would have gotten them to the coast. She could only hope that René would not want to admit he'd helped her forge passes, and that Spear had gotten out of the Hasard flat with his life.

She doubled her pace down the stairs, boots making quick, tapping echoes against the shadowy walls, like her heart, like the ticking of the firelighter she'd left behind, a machine that felt nothing, knew nothing but the job at hand. And then the steps ended in an open space of rough brown rock. The dim light of her lantern showed five stone carved arches, all in random directions, heavy wooden doors with locks fitted into the openings. What this place had been Before Sophia couldn't imagine; there were faint traces of paint in the deep crevices of the walls. But if these cells had numbers, she could find no trace of them.

"Tom? Tom Bellamy?" she called. It was silent under the Sunken City. She took Gerard's keys and put one to a lock, trying each until she found a fit and flung the door open. Empty, except for the dirt. She tried keys in the second door, turned the lock when she chose the right one, and there was a crumpled mess of thin arms and legs and hair that might be blond.

"Jennifer," she whispered. The girl didn't move.

Sophia came inside with the light, and held it up. Low, rough ceiling, a floor thick with dirt and rubbish, and, oddly, a small hearth. Special cells, the twins had said. She guessed those hearths were not put there for comfort. Jennifer lifted her head, squinting her eyes against the light.

"Jen," she said again, coming close. "It's Sophia." Jennifer raised a dirty hand to cover her face. The cuts and burns on her arms were a mass of festering sores, red and running, streaking up beneath the skin and past her elbows. Sophia pulled Jennifer's hand away and touched her forehead. Dry, and burning hot. And she was shackled by both wrists. Sophia heaped a thousand silent curses on LeBlanc's head.

"I'll be back, do you understand?" she said "The door is open. I'm coming straight back."

Jennifer didn't answer. Sophia left her where she lay and put a key to the next cell. It was empty. And so was the next. And so was the next.

Sophia stood in a ring of open cell doors, heart beating faster and faster until it was slamming against the wall of her chest. Tom wasn't there.

René's back hit the wall of the bedroom hard, and hit it again, but he twisted away before Spear could get a real blow in. The men of the room were lined up against the window wall, while Madame Hasard sat on the opposite side in a chair, her legs crossed, looking both elegant and disgruntled. Spear was surprisingly fast for someone so big, as René had quickly learned, and he had reach. But at his best, René was faster. The room was quiet but for the clang and scrape of blade on blade, both men intent on inflicting bodily damage as soon as possible.

They were so intent that neither noticed Madame Hasard, not until she threw the contents of the water ewer over her son's head.

Jennifer's water bucket was empty, and Sophia had a feeling it had been that way a long time. She tossed it down in the dirt, got on her knees with Jennifer behind her, took hold of the girl's upper arms, and pulled Jennifer up onto her back. Sophia staggered to her feet. She hadn't realized Jennifer had actually grown taller than her; she had to bend almost double to bear her weight, stay balanced, and prevent the girl's bare feet from dragging.

There was no way to carry the light, so they started up the winding stairs in the darkness, Sophia's jaw clenched. It had taken time to pick the locks of Jennifer's shackles, and the need to hurry, to find Tom, was like fire in her limbs. But she could go only so fast without sending them both tumbling backward down the stairs.

"Jen," she panted, trying to rouse her once again. "Where is Tom? Can you tell me where Tom is?" She pushed her legs, one after the other, climbing by feel in the dark. For the first time Jennifer made an incoherent noise. "Where is Tom?" Sophia insisted.

"Gone," said Jennifer.

The slamming in Sophia's chest stopped and became a squeeze. "Gone where? Keep talking, Jen. It's Sophia. I need to know where Tom is."

"They . . . took him," Jennifer heaved. It almost sounded like crying. The banging in Sophia's chest started up again.

"Where, Jennifer? Where?"

But there were no more sounds from her, though she could still feel the girl's breath faint against her back. Taken. Where had LeBlanc taken him? She had no time for this. No time at all.

Sophia's legs were shaking, and she was covered in filth and sweat, muscles begging to stop, about to stubbornly do so without her permission. Then she heard the squeak of metallic hinges, the whisper and shuffle of feet. She called down an additional thousand curses on LeBlanc's head, laid Jennifer gently on the ground near the wall, and pulled out her sword from where she'd thrust it through her belt. She started slowly up the steps, legs still shaky, hugging the wall.

Light blossomed from around the bend, and then two gendarmes came down the stairs, swords out, freezing when their lantern found her. One of them was the gendarme she'd seen earlier. And so was the other.

"Wait," she said, holding out her sword but also her other hand.

She let them watch her slowly draw a black-and-red feather from her vest. The two men relaxed, though they did not put away their swords.

The first one said, "You're . . ."

". . . a girl!" finished the second.

"And I suppose you're my twins?" Everyone was stating the obvious. "Help me," she said, hurrying to Jennifer. She heard swords being sheathed, boots on the stairs behind her. One twin got Jennifer's legs and the other hooked his elbows under her arms.

Then they paused, three sets of eyes darting up to the ceiling of the passage. A faint clanging of bells was coming down the drains and into the tunnels from the prison yard, through the open metal door above them. Harsh, discordant notes that made their way straight into Sophia's stomach. Not the middlemoon bells. They were the execution bells. Someone was going to die at the next moon. At highmoon.

She looked to the twins, questioning, but they shook their heads in perfect synchronization. This meant the mob would be arriving soon—surely not all of them had gone to pillage the Upper City— and the execution team. Allemande, LeBlanc, the other ministres. One of them was going to realize the guards were gone. And all the prisoners. She gritted her teeth, held the lantern higher, and they moved on, faster, the clanging of the bells echoing in the Tombs. She had to find Tom.

The execution bells rang through the Upper City, echoing against buildings and stone, overcoming the soft hum of idle chat in the Hasard flat. LeBlanc set his wineglass unsteadily on the table. It was only half full now; Émile wished it had been empty. He saw Enzo coming down the stairs from the gallery.

LeBlanc looked at the pendant he wore, frowned, and suddenly it snapped open to show the clock inside. Renaud, who had been hovering, took a step forward, then thought better of it.

"Middle . . . moon," said LeBlanc, seeming surprised at the difficulty of saying the word. "And the bells are ringing, just as they should. And the gate . . . is opening . . . and they have their list. The leaders . . . of the mob know where to go. Renaud gave them addresses. I will have to go. Cannot miss . . . highmoon . . ."

"What happens at highmoon, Albert?" Émile asked casually.

"The Razor and Tomas . . . Bellamy. He dies at the Razor, and she will be coming . . . for him . . . too late . . ."

"I see." Émile smiled, and laid a coin carefully on the table. "Albert, I have a question I would like to ask the Goddess . . ."

While LeBlanc struggled to focus on the coin, Émile, very low, so LeBlanc could not hear, whispered, "Enzo, tell René that Tom Bellamy dies at highmoon, and tell Andre that I need him to steal LeBlanc's pendant."

The execution bells stopped ringing.

The noise of the bells faded, and Madame Hasard lowered her hand. Spear and René were staring at each other from opposing chairs, René's hair dark with wet, the powder nearly gone, hands on his head as if the noise of the bells had been physically painful. Madame Hasard crossed her legs on the edge of the bed, a sword in her hand. A semicircle of Hasards and Benoit stood in a ring that blocked escape. Benoit was deep in thought, his forehead wrinkled.

"Now, Monsieurs," said Madame Hasard. "The rules of armistice are as follows. Neither of you shall speak unless spoken to by me. That is the only rule."

"Maman, those bells were . . . Ow!"

Madame Hasard resettled the sword in her lap, having whacked René in the leg with the flat of it. "Now that we have an understanding. Monsieur Hammond, are you working for the weasel-ferret creature known as Albert LeBlanc?"

Spear eyed the sword. "No. But he thinks I am."

She turned to René, who was rubbing his leg and glaring at Spear. "And you, are you working with the weasel-ferret creature known as Albert LeBlanc?"

"No!" Madame gave René a raised brow. "He thought I was, of course, but he does not think so now."

Spear made his disbelief clear, René leaned forward, and Madame raised the sword. René threw up his hands. "Listen to me, both of you! And do not hit me with that sword, Maman! I am going to talk and you are going to listen because there is no time."

"Permission to speak is granted," said Madame.

"I will speak slowly, Hammond, so that my words may penetrate your thick skull. I have never betrayed Sophia Bellamy or her brother to LeBlanc. Someone has. But it is not me. And I am not the one who will get her killed tonight . . ."

"And you think I will!" Spear yelled, looking at the ring of uncles. "When you're the ones keeping me here, not letting me get her out of the city as we'd planned!"

"You do not have the first idea what Sophia had planned," said René. "She was not going to the Tombs only for Jennifer and Tom. She is emptying the prison. All of it. "

"What?" This had come from Andre.

René held up his hand. "LeBlanc was to put two out of three to the Razor at dawn. So she will empty every hole. Then, she is going to set the firelighter you made and use it to ignite the Bellamy fire she has been having delivered and stored in the prison. The Tombs are going to explode."

Madame sat back, her eyebrow incredulous, and there was some shuffling of feet among the uncles.

"She can do it," René said, looking at them hard.

"Yes," said Benoit. "She can." That made them go quiet.

"Oh, she can do it," Spear agreed. "Whether she was planning to or not . . ."

"She was. And she is."

"René," said Madame, her painted mouth turning upward in the same half grin as her son's. "Tell me, did I engage you to the Red Rook?"

René ignored her. "Listen carefully, Hammond. This was going to be a dangerous business. She was going to stay in the Tombs and play cat and mouse with LeBlanc until the mob dispersed and she could set the firelighter. It would have been a miracle if she was not caught. But I convinced her to let me go, to let me set the firelighter once the chase was on in the Upper City, while she was asleep in her bed and with no one aware that she had left the flat at all. But you have just told her I sent the Bonnards to their deaths. That I am the 'con man' she once accused me of being. That I have lied and taken advantage of her in every way. And now she has taken the firelighter with her, Hammond. She wants the Tombs destroyed and she wants to take down LeBlanc."

The room was silent.

"When Tom Bellamy told you to acquire that document, you thought it was going to have my signature, did you not? Or one of my family's? I took the original out of your pocket. But when it did not, you had a forgery made. You thought you were doing what Tom would want, protecting her from me. You think you still are. But now she has taken the firelighter and gone on her own. She is hurt, and reckless. I do not think she will be coming out of the prison with the others. And now the execution bells have rung, Hammond."

Spear shook his head, running his hands through hair that was usually so perfectly in place. "I don't believe you. Only that sounds so much like Sophie that I almost do."

"But that is not all. Enzo has seen LeBlanc tell his secretary that Sophia is the Red Rook. He knows she is coming . . ."

"Because you told him!" Spear yelled.

"I told LeBlanc nothing!" René's voice dropped low. "Are you certain that you did not? Because she rejected you?"

Madame Hasard's warning went unheard because Spear's chair had pushed back, René already on his feet. Then there was a knock at the door. Benoit answered and Enzo appeared.

"What is happening?" Enzo said, running an eye over René's wet shirt and the fight that was about to erupt. "You are all doing something strange every time I enter. Whatever it is, put it aside. LeBlanc is drugged, but not drugged enough. He does not seem to prefer our wine."

"Then give him one he does prefer," said Madame Hasard reasonably.

"And Émile needs you, Andre," Enzo went on. "He wants you to steal LeBlanc's pendant, I have no idea why, and he wants to tell you all that Tom Bellamy does not die at dawn. He dies at highmoon."

Claude dropped his gaze from the middlemoon, stroking his tiny mustache. The Seine Gate had opened and he was making his way up the cliff road and out of the Lower City with a seething, raucous mass of humanity, his gendarme's jacket stuffed into his bag. It did not do to wander about in uniform on your own. Especially in this crowd. But he could not get the sound of the execution bells out of his head. He stopped, letting the people roll by him.

LeBlanc always allowed the gendarmes to come to the executions, even if they were on duty, as long as a replacement could be found. But today he had been sent away. And he'd seen other guards going as well, running off to the wine and women of La Toussaint. Or the Festival of Fate, whatever they were calling it now. Then he thought of Gerard, standing behind his desk with his bandaged finger, sweating face, and that nervous tic.

Claude turned and pushed his way back down the clogged cliff road, alongside some others who had changed direction at the call of the bells. A row of landovers with the Allemande seal were coming fast through the gate, down into the Lower City. He followed them, found a clear path, and broke into a run to the Tombs.

20

The twins carried an insensible Jennifer quickly past Gerard's closed office, past the lift and to the prison yard door.

"Are the landovers arriving?" Sophia asked.

"Not yet, but they will be here soon because . . ."

". . . the Seine Gate has just been opened."

"Do you know how many?"

"No."

"The boy knows."

They meant Cartier. She had no idea who was speaking anymore. The twins seemed to share most thoughts, and divide up the duty of conveying them. She peeked out the doors into an empty prison yard that, thanks to the execution bells, would not be empty for much longer. She wondered if those bells were for Tom, or Jennifer, or for her. "How many prisoners do we have?"

"The boy has counted two hundred and fifty-eight."

She glanced at Jennifer's lolling head. Perhaps it was no wonder there were only two hundred and fifty-eight left.

"Do either of you know where Tom Bellamy is?"

"Wasn't he down there?"

"Those cells were empty. Where is Gerard?"

"Shaking like a leaf in his office. He thinks you're going to . . ."

". . . pop up out of nowhere and cut his throat."

"Right. The yard looks clear. Hurry and get her to the warehouse and see if anyone there has any medical training. I'll be coming with Tom Bellamy. Tom and Jennifer get into a landover first, or if Tom's not there . . . They must get away first, and Gerard gets on the last. The very last. And then you need to disappear, everyone gone well before highmoon. Do you understand?"

"And you?"

She wondered where Cartier had found these two, what they were doing in such a horrible place as the Tombs, and how they had ever gotten drawn into the machinations of the Red Rook. "I'll come soon."

And Cartier would know what to do if she didn't. She refused to consider what would happen if Spear did not get out of the flat with the passes. With any luck they would be out of the city and on their way to the coast by nethermoon.

Or maybe luck served only LeBlanc tonight.

LeBlanc swayed just slightly on the settee, trying to explain the workings of Luck. Émile grinned, enjoying himself while Renaud wiped the sweat from his forehead.

"But have you no faith, Cousin Albert?" Émile said, tossing a coin up and down in one hand. It landed on face every time. "Show me how your Goddess works. I want to see it with my own eyes." He watched Andre and Peter slip in, skirting around the violinists.

"Fate," said LeBlanc, his voice thick, "is not . . . a game. They began it when . . . the machines fell . . . out of the sky. The survivors . . . they knew when the satellites fell . . . that only Fate was in control. Not a game."

"I am not playing a game, Albert. I am learning about your Goddess. She is real, isn't she?"

LeBlanc stretched out a hand and took the coin. Peter was not far away, his arm around the woman with the turban, and Andre had just picked up a glass from a tray.

"The tradition of the Goddess states that when . . . when using the coin the . . . facade . . ." He turned the coin over, to show the facade of the premier's building. ". . . means . . . no. Face means . . . is . . ." LeBlanc held the coin between his palms without finishing his sentence, fingers lifted to rest just below his odd eyes. Émile leaned in, Renaud watching closely, Peter and the woman with the turban laughing as they danced. Andre had moved behind LeBlanc, bending to observe the proceedings.

"Goddess, does . . . does . . ."

"Émile," Émile supplied.

"Does Émile . . . truly . . . want to learn of you?"

LeBlanc flipped the coin into the air, and at the same time Peter and the woman with the turban bumped into Andre, knocking him into LeBlanc, then spinning into Renaud, spilling a goblet of wine between them. LeBlanc caught himself on the tabletop as the coin hit the glass and rolled, settling with a clink that was almost unheard in the aftermath.

"Oh, I am sorry, Albert, let me fetch a man to clean you up . . ."

LeBlanc looked around to see Peter brushing the red liquid from Renaud's front, and with a smooth, unseen movement, Émile flipped the coin to face. LeBlanc turned back to check the will of Fate, his face lighting up at the sight of "yes." He didn't seem to be aware that the pendant with its hidden clock was no longer around his neck.

—

Sophia slipped the sword up to Gerard's neck without him realizing she was there. He'd had his back turned, examining the window, but he went still at the chill of steel. Gerard sighed, and slowly raised his hands.

"Who will die at highmoon?" She didn't even bother with the gruff voice of the holy man. There was no time.

"Tomas . . . Bellamy. And the Bonnard girl."

Sophia tried to breathe through her anger. "And where is Tom Bellamy?"

"I do not know!" Gerard sounded frightened now. He probably thought she was about to run him through, now that his usefulness was expiring. "When I came to the Tombs . . . he was not in his cell."

"Then think, Gerard. Where would LeBlanc take a prisoner he didn't want the Red Rook to find?"

"I do not know!"

"Listen to me," Sophia said. "I do not want to hurt you. I will if I have to, but I don't want to. Your wife is waiting for you, and you're about to be gone from this place. Help me. Where does LeBlanc go when he comes to the prison? What does he do?"

The firelight was almost gone, the room smoky and dim. Sophia glanced out the window. Well past middlemoon. She poked Gerard just a tiny bit with the sword.

"There is one thing," he said. "But I do not think . . . I do not know if . . ."

"Tell me."

"The lift," Gerard whispered.

"Tell me!" Sophia prodded.

"Sometimes the lift comes down from LeBlanc's office. But then . . . there is no one on it."

She stood still for a moment, thinking. She'd set the firelighter for highmoon, and now LeBlanc had set an execution for that time. That meant there would be people gathering in the prison yard. Would René, or someone else, be coming to find the firelighter and turn it off? If she reset it for a later time, did it just give them more of an opportunity to make sure it did not go off at all? But it was a long way down to the storage hole, and she had to find Tom.

Gerard whimpered beneath her sword.

"Quiet, Gerard," she ordered. "I have to think."

"Quiet," said Benoit, and the arguing in the gold bedroom instantly ceased. Even Spear fell silent, though mostly from surprise. Benoit sat on the edge of the bed.

"You are fighting over what you should do, when you have not considered what the Red Rook is going to do. These are the things we know. We know that she is not going to follow the plan she told Hammond, because she is not going to give up freeing LeBlanc's prisoners, correct? And she is not going to follow the plan she told René, because she believes René has betrayed her and told all to LeBlanc."

René and Spear exchanged dirty looks.

"But because she thinks this, she will also know that LeBlanc knows her identity, even if her reason is false. She will not be walking into the Tombs blind."

"That is true," René said slowly.

"So," said Benoit, a mere shadow of a person next to the larger-than-life Madame, "other than emptying the Tombs, what is the one thing we know that Sophia Bellamy is going to do?"

"She is going to set that firelighter," said Madame Hasard.

"Yes," said Spear, "I think you're right."

"I told you this was a decent young man, René," said Madame, making Enzo chuckle.

"She told me to set it for dawn," said René thoughtfully, "but she will not do that now . . ." He was on his feet, pacing like a wild dog in a cage.

"So she will have set it for highmoon," said Enzo, "to keep you from unsetting it. It would have been the only safe time. Unless she heard the execution bells first."

"No," Spear said. "She'll know the prison yard will be full at highmoon. If she set it for that time, she'll turn it off."

"Unless she is already gone," said René. Spear turned to face him.

"Or maybe she never got to set it in the first place."

"Or perhaps she did, and can't turn it off because she is caught," said Madame. There was a small silence in the bedroom. If that was so, then Sophia was going to die.

René looked to Benoit. "So I will go and make certain she is away, and turn off the firelighter, if it is set at all. She will think it a betrayal again, that I am preserving LeBlanc and his prison. But she will not forgive herself if the people in the prison yard . . ."

"No," said Spear. "I built the firelighter. I should go."

René's grin was not a look of humor. "Oh, no, you should not."

"You're going to stop me?"

"I know where the Bellamy fire is."

"You will tell me where it is, then," Spear said, eyes narrowed.

"No, I will not."

"I promised Tom . . ."

"I care nothing for what you promised her brother! I will honor my promise to her."

Benoit cleared his throat. "Take Hammond with you, René."

"No!" they both yelled.

"And which of you is willing to stay behind?" asked Madame Hasard. There was no reply. "Then I have made my point."

"Maman!" René yelled at the same time that Enzo said, "Well, I'm not going . . ."

"Enough," said Benoit. "Your mother is right, René. It is foolish to go alone when you do not know what you will face. Have you forgotten that the gate has opened? The mob is coming."

"The passes," Spear said suddenly. "They won't get out of the gates . . ."

"Are we not in a flat full of smugglers, Monsieur?" Madame Hasard leaned back on one arm. "We will get the passes to the gates." Spear looked around the room, dubious.

"I do not think he trusts us," said Enzo cheerfully. "And if you want to say something, Hammond, say it aloud."

Spear opened his mouth to say something very aloud, but Benoit held up a hand.

"Hammond, set your grievances aside. There is no one in this family who would wish to see LeBlanc or Allemande win this round. We would prefer they did not live through the night. Can you believe that?"

Spear hesitated, then he nodded once.

"Then we will keep LeBlanc here as long as possible. Andre has stolen his pendant clock to set back the time, and Émile is attempting to drug him again. It was difficult to know how much of the powder in Mademoiselle Bellamy's ring was appropriate. If we would not have all of Allemande's troops come down on our heads, I would make sure it was poison."

René looked to Benoit. "What does Uncle Émile think he is doing?"

"Keeping LeBlanc busy while we get back the signet ring. There has not been time to enlighten him further. He has been busy questioning Fate. We will give you as much time as we can, but in any case, I think LeBlanc will miss his scheduled highmoon execution. Madame and I will take care of the gates. Are we agreed?"

The silence confirmed it. And then the people of the room scattered, moving quickly to their assigned tasks. Spear caught René's arm and said, very low, "One wrong move in that prison, Hasard, and I will kill you."

"Take your hand from my arm," René replied, "or I will kill you now."

LeBlanc looked at Émile's hand on his arm, at the coin he was trying to place back in his palm. His glassy stare had become wary. Like the way he was eyeing the table and the twinkling candles.

"More wine?" Émile asked.

LeBlanc shook his head.

"Oh, come, Albert," Émile said, smiling. "You are quite safe here. Ask the Goddess whether the Red Rook will live beyond the dawn."

Renaud still stood at his post, a respectful distance from the settee, feet aching and sweating profusely, not daring to interfere. The dancing had begun again; the partygoers just danced around him. Émile glimpsed Peter flitting out the front door dressed in the blue cloak of a city courier. He raised a brow, and then Andre walked by the settee and gave Renaud a little bow.

"Oh," said Émile suddenly, "that is your pendant, Albert, is it not?" He leaned down beside LeBlanc, where the cushion met the back of the settee, and held up the symbol of Fate. "Your cord has frayed, I think." Andre had done an excellent job of fraying it.

LeBlanc's pale eyes widened and he snatched the pendant, instantly flipping it open to the little clock. "Just past middlemoon," he said, stumbling on the words. "We should have time."

Renaud glanced nervously at the full moon shining from high in the sky behind him. LeBlanc tied the pendant around his neck and reached for the coin, holding it to his lips in an attitude of prayer. Émile gestured to Andre, who came to the settee and put his elbows on the back of it, as if to watch LeBlanc. Émile leaned close.

"Tell René that if he does not come out here and explain to me what is happening, I am going to slash his gold brocade coat to ribbons and perhaps also his throat."

"You had better queue up," Andre replied. "He was busy dueling with that big brute from the Commonwealth until Adèle dumped water on his head. I believe his little fiancée is in trouble." Andre's voice dropped to almost nothing. "Did you know our nephew is engaged to the Red Rook, Émile?"

"Goddess," LeBlanc was saying. "Will the Red Rook live beyond the dawn?" He flipped the coin onto the table, the clink of metal on glass adding to the music of the violins.

Sophia shoved Gerard out into the prison yard and shut the door behind him, the clink of the turning lock the only sound in the Tombs. She was eerily alone, running down the corridor toward LeBlanc's lift. Tom first, she had decided. She would get Tom into a landover, come back, and then deal with the firelighter. And if she didn't find Tom, she didn't care if the firelighter went off or not. Not for herself. Maybe the highmoon crowd would disperse if there was no execution. Maybe they wouldn't. She paused in front of the first stairwell that led down into the Tombs, pulled a small bag from her vest, and upended it. Red-tipped rook feathers floated, scattering over the stinking stones. Then she ran again, skidding to a stop before LeBlanc's private lift.

This was nothing like the lift to the Hasard flat. A plain wooden box with a simple bell pull, large enough for three or possibly four people. Gerard had said that sometimes the lift came down, but no one was in it. So if he wasn't lying, where was LeBlanc getting off the lift? On an upper floor? But if so, why would the lift come down, if LeBlanc had rung the bell to get off somewhere else? It made no sense. Unless there was another way off the lift.

She stepped inside. A lantern hung from the ceiling, still lit, though the oil was getting low. She ran her fingers over the planks of wood that formed three sides of the lift, smooth with use, the corners braced and riveted with strips of iron. Nothing seemed loose, or wished to slide. The ceiling was too far over her head to reach, but a panel in the ceiling did not seem reasonable, either. The lamp would have to be removed, and how to put it back? There was a straw matting on the floor, but she could find nothing beneath that but dirt, and something that looked suspiciously like dried blood.

She took a deep breath, willing away panic. She had to be calm if she wanted to find Tom. She started over again. There had to be something she'd missed.

Sophia ran her hand again over the wood, and then over the iron bracing and the rivets. She did notice that the two front pieces of bracing were actually one piece of iron each, bent into an L-shape to create the corners, while in the back, the bracing was made of two pieces of iron, a tiny gap in the angle. She looked at this more closely, sliding her fingers down the gap all the way to the floor, where it continued beneath the matting, running horizontally, separating the floor from the back wall, continuing again as high as she could reach on the other vertical side.

She ran a hand down the iron, quickly, this time along the rivets, stopping at about halfway down, where a rivet was missing. The missing rivet left a small, round hole. She stuck her finger in and smiled. The back of the lift was a door, and this was a keyhole. She knelt down in front of the hole in the iron and began peeling off her gloves, where she'd sewn in her picklocks.

Claude knelt in the shadows, watching Gerard scurry across the flagstones of the prison yard and bang on the locked door of the empty warehouse opposite. A building where no one should be. The door opened, shutting again as soon as Gerard had entered. Claude fingered his small mustache.

The execution team had arrived to prepare the Razor, torches sputtering to life all around a scaffold that had become a shrine. Ribbons and black and white flowers, like in the cemeteries, trailed along the bloodstained wood. There was a stone altar set up on the scaffold now, too, the sort you saw in Upper City chapels, and above it hung a gigantic flat wheel, painted half black, half white, made to be seen from the farthest reaches of the prison yard. They were going to spin it, Claude supposed, so Fate could choose the two out of three. That should be interesting. And was further proof that no gendarmes should have been dismissed from the Tombs that night. How would they get so many to the scaffold with only Gerard? It made the situation obvious. Gerard must be in league with the Red Rook.

Claude stood and stepped deeper into the dark outside the torchlight. A few dozen people had gathered since he'd arrived, sitting on cloaks and bits of blanket, saving their places for the best view of blood. He thought of Gerard's finger beneath his knife, and allowed the man a grudging bit of respect. He'd probably already let the Red Rook out of the prison, and if the Rook had Gerard, then there would be others.

He moved down an alley, circling the warehouse Gerard had entered, sidling up to the muddy lane that ran along the other side of the building. And there, lined up in a row, were Allemande's land-overs, many of them, lamps lit, taking the people of the Lower City up to La Toussaint. He watched groups of twos and threes being shuttled into one of the landovers, the window curtains drawn, another pulling up to take its place when it was full. If there was one thing Claude knew, it was the look of prison dirt when he saw it.

He turned and jogged back down the alley, then broke into a run. LeBlanc was at a party tonight, he'd seen something about it in the *Observateur.* One of his cousins, it had said, was marrying the sister of the Red Rook. A man named René Hasard. And the news-paper had given the address.

René opened the door from the back stairs of his building onto the alley just beyond the boulevard, Spear behind him. Broken glass crunched beneath their feet. The door was metal, which was good, because every window in the back alley was broken—not just the glass but the wooden panes as well, beaten and splintered inward. The stable doors had been hacked down, the horses gone, and there was shouting in the distance, not very far away. They heard Benoit drop the heavy iron bar into place behind them, the pavement spar-kling in the moonlight.

"Follow me," René said. He stole down the alley, Spear behind him, away from the clamor. But the noise increased again before the next street, more shouting and destruction, but this time with music.

They stopped short, in the dark of a door beneath an overhanging balcony.

A mass of people and torches was moving past, shouting, singing and laughing, breaking whatever was breakable, having a small parade all their own to the whistle of a flute. They sounded drunk. Some wore finery that had obviously come from a looted home or shop; all wore the masks of the Goddess. And they had a woman, also in a mask, her body held up high by many hands.

Spear made a move toward the street, but René put out an arm. The woman's masked head was on a pole, separate from her body. They stayed motionless in the shadows until the music faded and the little mob had gone by, leaving splinters and blood and a trail of black and white flower petals in their wake. René quickly tucked his hair beneath the plain black jacket he'd changed into, buttoning it to the top and flipping up the collar to hide its length. Spear did the same.

"Wait here," Spear said suddenly, turning back down the alley.

"Where are you going?"

"Masks," he hissed over his shoulder.

René waited against the alley wall, his hand on his sword hilt. "Watch him," Benoit had said. It had been good advice, though hardly needed. René glanced up again at the high-hanging moon, thinking of standing in this alley as a child, watching the jugglers and the fire-eaters go by for La Toussaint. Now all he could hear were sounds of violence, and not very far away. What had happened to the world? And what had happened to Hammond? There was no time. He nearly drew his sword as a figure came running down the alley, but it did not take long for the figure to become Hammond, two masks and one club in his hands.

René said, "Should I have the bodies removed?"

"I left them breathing." Spear thrust a mask at him. René took it, then held out his hand for the club. Spear just smiled. "You must be having a laugh."

René ran a sleeve across his forehead before sliding the mask onto his face, watching through narrow eyeholes as Spear looked left and then right, slipping down the dark street toward the gates. No, he was not laughing. And he was not allowing Hammond behind him with that club, either.

They followed the slant of the streets downward, crossing a bridge over the Seine as it rushed to its waterfall, and in only a few blocks they arrived at the fencing around the cliff edge. The tall iron gate was open, the space between thronged and loud with landovers and people traveling in both directions. A gilded chair seemed to float by over the heads of the crowd, an inlaid table following it, part of an assembly line of looted goods that were being passed hand to hand down the road into the Lower City.

Any gendarmes at the gate seemed to have long since fled, except for one, a grim young man with a determined face and a tiny mustache, pulling on his uniform jacket and running for all he was worth to the Upper City. René looked to Spear, and Spear's mask nodded. They put their heads down and melded with the uncontrollable crowd, going down into the chasm of the Lower City under the light of a rising highmoon.

Sophia pushed back the sweaty tendrils of hair that were creeping out from beneath her knitted cap. She wished she could see the moon. She was working fast, pushing the pins inside the lock one by one, already on her second attempt, having guessed wrong on which way the key would have turned. She heard the click, felt the lock give, and jumped up. The back of the lift swung silently toward her, showing another metal door behind it, and another empty rivet for a keyhole.

She bit her lip, knelt down, and started again, quelling impatience. But this time, the lock gave quickly, and the door creaked inward, pulled by a draft. She pushed it open. The lantern shone on stone steps, descending into darkness.

Sophia tucked her picklocks back into place, slid on her gloves, grabbed the lantern, and stepped through the hidden door.

"You should ask . . . the Goddess if she will find him," LeBlanc said, frowning down at the coin on his palm. "Because she will . . . not, and then . . . you will know . . ."

Renaud used a handkerchief to wipe the perspiration from his brow.

"More wine?" Émile offered.

"No!" said LeBlanc, causing a few heads to turn as his voice carried over the music. "Ask her . . . the Goddess . . . if she will find him. Before . . . highmoon."

"Of course, Albert," Émile replied. "Goddess, will she find him before highmoon?"

LeBlanc flipped the coin.

21

Sophia hurried down the stone steps, lantern held high, going lower and lower into the belly of the Sunken City. She was in some sort of tunnel roughly carved from brown stone. Mines, most likely, like all the Tombs, but whether this tunnel was new or Ancient or something in between she couldn't tell. It was absolutely silent, thick dust gathering on the sides of the steps, though the middles were relatively clear. At least she knew someone had been coming this way.

She could see an open doorway at the bottom of the stairs, not rough like the walls but carved into an arch. Intricate, intersecting lines ran in relief around the stone. She stepped through, held up the light, and her free hand jumped to her mouth, the glove stifling any noise she might have made.

She stood in a kind of curving corridor, walls soaring to heights well beyond what she could see with her light, but the walls were not made of stone or rock; they were made of bones. Stacks and stacks of them in precise, undulating patterns, diamonds of arm bones and femurs crisscrossed in rows, dotted with skulls and surrounded by delicate inlays of fingers. The pattern rose and fell in waves as the walls went on, somehow beautiful and yet so horrible it made something inside her shudder.

She walked forward in a thick brown dust that covered her boots, skirting quickly around a pyramid of skulls in the center of the walkway, trying not to think of the sheer numbers of the dead that surrounded her. There were variations in color, she noticed, the flowing patterns of straight, stacked bone ends on the lower walls more yellowed, and more fragmented. Then these must be older, with the newer stacked on top. Could she actually be looking at the remains of people who had seen the Great Death? She stared into the empty eye sockets of a passing head, wondering if that man or woman had called this city Paris. If they could have really known the kind of technology that made voices travel from the other side of the world, or pictures move. If they had died from the want of those things when they were taken away.

Sophia looked around and realized she was at a crossroads. A pillar soared upward in front of her, lines of skulls twisting round and round so that they tricked the eye. There were three paths she could take. Left, right, or straight.

"Which way, Hasard?"

They were both breathing hard, boots caked with mud, leaning against the back of a tilting wooden shanty. Spear pulled off the mask to dab at his lip, which now matched the split lip Sophia had given to René. The people of the Lower City were rioting, the trail of looted goods coming down the cliff road leaving bodies along the way. And both sets of their clothes were still too fine for anonymity. René looked up. The moon rose defiantly in the night sky, and they were only halfway to the Tombs.

"No more trying to hide," said René. "Do not use a sword if you can avoid it, but we have to go faster. There is no more time."

—

There's no more time, thought Sophia. None. She'd taken the right turn, which gently curved, came to another crossroads with an identical skull-spiraling pillar, and then, inexplicably, ended up back at the first one. The flowing patterns of the bones were disorienting, and so much alike that it was impossible to tell one place from the other.

She gave up trying to hide. If the place was full of gendarmes, they would just have to come. "Tom!" she called. "Tom?"

Her voice echoed and died in the brown dust, though it gave her a sense of the enormity of the space. A massive cavern empty with darkness and full of death. She cursed softly, drew the sword from her back, and thrust it through the forehead of a skull in the pillar, gouging a wide and gaping hole. Now there was a black, mismatching speck in the twisting pattern. Her place marked, this time she went straight.

"Go straight!" yelled Spear, as René ducked under the random swing of a fist. This was easier said than done in the Blackpot Market, where the mob seemed to have turned on itself. Throngs of people were gathered in guttering torchlight, fighting over the food and riches coming down from the Upper City. And it looked as if the beer had been flowing freely as well. René had acquired his own club, catching a patched gray square of shirt in its middle before the arms that were attached could break a chair over his head.

Spear was just ahead, forging a path, and René turned in time to see a flash of metal, a sword arm in midswing, ready to curve an arc straight into Spear's back. René caught the man's arm from below with the club, the sword flying upward with an audible crack. Spear looked over his shoulder. The man with the broken arm was crumpling to his knees.

"Go!" Spear yelled. "We're almost there!"

Claude thought he must be almost there. Then he knew it was so when he saw a troop of gendarmes beating back a crowd in front of a gray-and-white stone building that was very elegant. If those gendarmes were protecting the building, then LeBlanc must be inside it.

He whistled and got one of the gendarmes' attention, straightened his jacket, and smoothed his tiny mustache. Then he pushed his way into the crowd. In the Upper City, his uniform was respected, would guarantee him safe passage. But Claude quickly found that he was mistaken.

Sophia bent over in frustration, staring at the hole she'd carved in the skull. She'd been mistaken. It shouldn't have been a left turn. She would have to start again. Yes, that was all. Start again when she couldn't find Tom, when the prison could explode. She took off at a run down the path of bones, wondering how high the moon was.

René slowed his run, wondering how high the moon was. They were beneath a passing bank of fog, the sky lost to them. He stopped in a small space between two shacks, across the street from a dilapidated warehouse just outside the prison yard. Spear jogged up behind him, sliding the mask from his face.

"Look," René said. "Allemande's landovers."

"And there is Cartier," Spear whispered. "How many drivers did he bribe?" They watched as one landover driver slapped the reins and drove away, the next one taking its place, three bedraggled people rushing inside just as soon as it had stopped. The window curtains jerked closed from inside. Cartier turned to usher in the next group, his head swiveling right and left in the mostly deserted street. The riots in the marketplace were keeping this area quiet, at least.

"Hurry," said René.

They darted down the street when Cartier's back was turned, only for the purpose of avoiding explanations they had no time to give, skirting the buildings that formed a loose square around the prison yard. People were gathering there, joking and jeering, a peaceful crowd compared to the others they had seen that night. René swore when he saw the Razor in its new finery, and the chapel altar with its wheel.

"Walk as if you have a reason," he told Spear, striding purpose-fully across the flagstones, toward the brick building that sat over the entrance to the Tombs. There were no gendarmes in sight, so they circled to the back, where the building met the cliffs. There was a window there, not far from the ground.

Spear lifted his club, ready to smash it in, but René put out a hand and pushed upward. The window slid open. "He relies on his guards," René commented, "otherwise, there would be no win-dow here at all." René paused. "I suppose it has occurred to you, Hammond, that if we do not find the firelighter, we may die in this prison?"

"We nearly died in that marketplace."

"The prison seems more certain at the moment."

Spear tilted his head in agreement.

"You might wish, then," René said, "not to come inside."

"Maybe that's what you want, too, Hasard."

René sighed and swung a leg through. "I hope she is not in here," he said.

She shouldn't be here. She should have been with the landovers by now. And she should have reset the firelighter. Sophia knew all these things, so she ran with the lantern down the path of bones. The way was so narrow compared to the unbelievable height of the stacks that even though the cavern must be immense, Sophia felt almost claustrophobic, her need to find a way out beginning to resemble panic.

She passed the second twisting column of skulls at a crossroads, where the path branched into three. She put a hole in a skull with the sword, and this time went straight. Immediately she found a short stair going up, and then came to another pyramid of heads. But instead of a crossroads, this pyramid marked a fork, one way veering to the right, the other left.

"Tom," she called, letting her voice echo. "Tomas!"

The cavern settled back into silence. She chose left and ran down the path, wiping the grit of bone dust from her mouth.

LeBlanc wiped his mouth with a napkin, frowning down in confusion at the coin on the table. Émile frowned as well, not concerned with the prediction but by the look of lucidity that was returning to the colorless eyes of his cousin-in-law.

"More wine?" he asked.

"No, Émile, I think I have had quite enough." LeBlanc felt for the pendant at his chest, brows drawing even closer together as some memory came to him. "Renaud!"

Renaud scuttled forward, the front of his shirt damp.

"Renaud, where is the moon?"

Enzo and Andre hovered a little closer, and then the door of the flat burst open, making music fly from the violinists' stands. LeBlanc turned, and then stood, a little shaky, catching his balance on the arm of the settee. The sudden quiet stretched, every eye on Claude, who had an eye swelling and blood spattering the front of his uniform. He surveyed the clean cloth and lace, the tall hair and made-up faces.

"Do none of you know what is happening outside?" he yelled. He met with blank stares. Then he staggered straight to LeBlanc.

"The Tombs are empty!"

"They are all empty," said René. They'd found a lamp still lit in a lift, discovered a straight stairway covered in rook feathers, leading downward and leaching stink, and now they were in their first cell tunnel, the doors of the prison holes swinging in the draft, floor awash with drainage and filth. One or two red-tipped feathers floated in the scum.

"Did you ever ask her what it was like?" René said in the silence.

"No," Spear replied. He had his shirt collar over his nose. "But it changed her, the first time she came out."

"Yes," said René. "I would think it would." But he was smiling, his gaze on the rows of swinging, open doors. "She really is quite a girl. We are looking for cell 522, Hammond. And we should run."

Sophia ran. The left turn had been a dead end, only a round, chapel-shaped chamber made of bones at the end of it. She passed the pyramid of skulls and took the other branch, kicking up a cloud down a similar curving path that also ended in a round chamber. But this time there was a kind of stone pedestal in the center, a waist-high table with a surface hollowed out like a bowl. And at the base of the pedestal, someone lay chest down in the dust.

"Tom!" Sophia said. "Tom!" she screamed.

But Tom Bellamy did not lift his head.

LeBlanc did not raise his head until he was finished vomiting onto the floor of the landover. He gathered up his robes and slid to the other side of the seat, smoothing his hair as well as he could while the landover swayed. Renaud sat silent and shrinking in the opposite corner. The moon was nearing its height behind rolling clouds, and so was LeBlanc's rage.

"I will secure the prison and the Red Rook," he said aloud, "and then I will deal with the Hasard family." He'd left Claude in charge of the gendarmes around the building, not only keeping the rioters out but keeping the Hasards in, leaving the flat under siege. "I will take them to the Razor. One by one." He clutched the pendant around his neck. "One each day, and Madame and Émile shall be the last . . ."

The landover slowed, and LeBlanc looked out the window. They were passing a whole row of Allemande landovers, going fast in the opposite direction, their window curtains closed. But it was a mob of rioters in masks that were slowing his progress, blocking the way to the Seine Gate with a dead woman held high above their heads. LeBlanc leaned out the window.

"Run them down!" he said. And the landover did, causing a stampede of fleeing people. Shouts and screams overcame the music, the wheels of LeBlanc's landover bumping over a drunken man who had been sitting on his knees, obliviously playing a flute.

Sophia dropped into the dust beside her brother, chest contracting so hard she thought she might suffocate. She had failed. All this, and she had failed the one person who was counting on her the most.

And it was because she had been stupid. So, so stupid. And that had cost Tom his life.

She yanked off the knitted cap and grabbed two handfuls of her pinned hair. Grief for Tom rolled right through her, incapacitating in its strength, too much to be held inside. She let her head fall back and she screamed, a shattering noise that echoed through the stacked bones.

"Did you hear a scream?" René asked, running down the passage. Spear turned his head.

"What?" The noise of the gathering mob was falling through the drains above them. It must be nearly highmoon.

"Like a . . ." René shook his head. "Perhaps they are already killing people." He paused, holding up the lantern they'd taken from the lift, peering at a tunnel that veered upward. The numbering of the prison holes in the Tombs had no logic. "I do not think it can be this way," he said.

Spear leaned over, hands on legs to catch his breath. "And why do you think it can't be that way?"

"Because she will have had it put somewhere deep, and in the center, to bring it all down."

Spear hesitated, but only for a moment. Then he nodded, and they both began to splash and sprint down the lower corridor.

"At least we know one thing, Hammond," René said, holding up the lantern to look at the numbers on the empty prison holes. "Sophia Bellamy is not in this prison."

It was supposed to be her, Sophia thought, letting her scream fade. She should have been shackled in this prison, not Tom. She put a hand on Tom's shoulder and hair, and then leapt back as if she'd been burned, nearly screaming once more. A muscle beneath her fingers had twitched.

Tom raised his head just enough to turn it to the other side, blinking in the lantern light that was too bright for him. "Blimey, Sophie," he said, voice rasping. "Why do you have to go and wake a person up that way?"

Spear held up the lantern, trying to see the faint numbers in the light. They had hit a row of cells in the five hundreds. A few more steps, and he threw open the door to prison hole 522. This cell was a bit higher than the others, relatively dry, and there were stacks of barrels marked *pain plat* everywhere among the sacks and filth.

"Where would she have put it?" Spear panted. The moon had to be sailing almost directly overhead.

René had already dashed inside, careful to set the lantern well away from the barrels as he turned a circle, surveying the room. "Where she thinks I cannot find it," he replied.

"I didn't think you'd find me," Tom said. "And careful, Sophie. My ribs are broken on that side."

Tom was upright now, and Sophie had her arms around him. He was dirty and thin, and had a full beard, but other than that, he was Tom. He kissed her once on top of the head. "I assume you have your picklocks?"

Sophia let her brother go and nodded, coming back to herself. She wiped the wet off her cheeks and stripped off her gloves. There was no time. None at all.

"Hurry!" René said. Spear pried open a barrel that was full of Bellamy fire and nothing else, threw down the lid, and went to another one, but René said, "Wait! We should listen."

Spear went still and they stood in the prison hole. The silence beat down on their ears. "If we are about to die," said Spear, his tone matter-of-fact, "I want to tell you I was not informing LeBlanc, no matter what he told you."

"And neither was I. No matter what he told you." René was running his eyes over the cell, trying to think what he would have done in Sophia's place. He looked up to the ceiling in sudden inspiration, but there was nothing there.

"But I would forge that document again," Spear continued. "To keep her from you."

"It is good to have no regrets." René kicked the floor. Hard stone.

Spear was shaking his head. "I'd do it again."

"I will kill you for it later, then, after we . . ." René grinned suddenly. "We cannot hear. That is just so, is it not?"

"What do you mean?"

"Do you not see? We cannot hear the clock. She has buried it!" René ran a hand through his hair, then cursed a Parisian streak that made Spear's brows rise. "The barrels, Hammond! She has put it in a barrel! Where we cannot hear. No need for the fuse . . ."

Spear frowned, then raised his brows again, this time in recognition of the truth.

"Quick!" said René, spinning on his heel. "Were any of these barrels open already?"

"There was one . . ." They both looked around the room at the mass of barrels that had now been pried open.

"Which? Which!"

"Just start putting your hands in!" Spear yelled. "She wouldn't have had much time, maybe she didn't get it buried too deep . . ."

René shoved his hands into a barrel of coarse black powder, certain he was about to die. But he was still grinning. Sophia Bellamy was such a clever, clever girl.

Sophia worked frantically on Tom's ankle restraint with the pick-locks. "Have you gotten Jennifer?" he asked.

"Yes. Everyone is away except for us." She hoped it was true. If no one had found the firelighter, then this place was going to explode just like the rest of the Tombs.

"What do you mean, everyone?"

Her fingers fumbled with the picklocks. "We're the last ones left."

"LeBlanc knows you're the Red Rook, Sophie. He knew you were coming . . ."

"Yes, I know it," said Sophia, cutting him off. There was no time to feel, and she wasn't ready to spill out her misery to Tom. She thought she'd better save their lives first. His shackle gave, and she started on the next one. "Where else are you hurt?"

"Nowhere much. Do you have water?"

She shook her head. "When was the last time you ate? Or drank?"

"A while. But I don't know when now is."

"How fast can you move? Because we . . ."

Her voice trailed away at the direction of Tom's brown eyes, still darker than the skin of his dirty face. They had moved to beyond her shoulder, where the entrance to the chamber was. And she knew what it meant.

She kept working the picklocks, and the shackle around Tom's ankle clicked open just as the voice she had been anticipating said softly, "So. Fate has finally brought the Red Rook to me."

Sophia met Tom's eyes. She slid the picklock she had been using into his hand, and the ring from her forefinger. "Bury that," she whispered. Then she stood slowly, and reached over her shoulder to draw her sword.

Sophia turned with the sword in front of her while Tom stayed exactly where he was on the ground. It was only LeBlanc, she was surprised to see, with his disgusting secretary shrinking near the wall of bones, holding another lantern. No gendarmes. Maybe LeBlanc had thought they wouldn't be needed; maybe he was going to be wrong about that.

LeBlanc also drew his sword. He was not quite himself, Sophia thought. His usually sleek hair was ruffled, the cold, colorless eyes a little wild. She wondered just for a moment what could have been happening at that party after she slapped René. LeBlanc circled to her right, but she kept her feet planted in front of Tom.

"I am glad to find you here," he said, "among those that have accepted Fate."

"Accepted it or been a victim of it, Albert?" she said.

He smiled. "You realize, of course, that you have already lost."

"Have I?"

"Yes. You have. But, then again, you always were going to lose. You lost before you were born, because Fate has determined it."

LeBlanc's slow smile curled at her, and again she matched it. Reckless, that's what René would have called it. She was probably going to die here, if not from Bellamy fire, then from a knife or sword in her back from that rat Renaud. But either way, she would try to take LeBlanc with her. She felt the tiredness drain away from her bones, replaced with the tingle of hate.

"Sophie," Tom said, a soft warning. But she was spoiling for the fight. And in any case, she needed to keep LeBlanc distracted while Tom worked the picklock on his other shackle.

LeBlanc took a quick step forward and she turned her sword to defend, but he did not strike. Instead he circled left, and she went with him, staying between him and Tom.

"Tell me, Rook," LeBlanc said, "where are my gendarmes?"

Another quick step and this time his sword came at her, but she merely moved her body to the side. He backed away again as she said sweetly, "Your gendarmes? Have you lost them?"

"I have not lost them. They seem to have lost themselves. As has every criminal and traitor in the Tombs!" His last word echoed around the yellowing bones, as did the clash of steel as Sophia blocked his next attack.

"Don't be sad, Albert. You still have us," she said. Her smile wid ened. The landovers must be away, then. He hadn't arrived in time. That must have been a surprise to him. She blocked him again, then twisted her hilt over his sword and got in a quick slash to his upper arm.

LeBlanc gasped. It had been a glancing blow, but the sleeve was cut, blood already beginning to stain from underneath. LeBlanc wasn't smiling anymore. Instead he had his head tilted to the side as he again began to circle her, the ends of his robes leaving trails through the thick brown dust.

"It took much to convince me of your true identity, Miss Bellamy. And yet I was skeptical, and had to ask Fate. I was unsure whether a woman had the physical . . ."

This time she came on the attack, and LeBlanc blocked, but only just.

". . . and mental capabilities for the strategy and . . ."

She came in again, and put a scratch on his hand.

". . . swordplay." LeBlanc glanced at the small cut, an analytical appraisal. "I think you must be an aberration, Mademoiselle. Something . . . unnatural."

"Is that what you think?"

He came at her, this time across the body. She stepped out of the way and just missed cutting off his hand. They both went back on the defensive, and he watched her movements carefully, again with the look of analysis.

"I am curious," LeBlanc said, "how often a woman will choose to attack or defend."

"I think, Albert, that it could have quite a bit to do with how much a woman wants to live, and how much she wants you dead."

She came after him again, fast. He blocked her first and second, and then she caught him on the shoulder. Blood wet the robes. "Fascinating . . . ," mused LeBlanc.

Sophia bit her lip. LeBlanc was not acting like a man who thought he was about to explode, or even a man who had an execution planned at highmoon, which had to be upon them. Did he doubt her ability to blow up his prison? Or had the firelighter already been unset? She shook her head. She was dealing with a lunatic, and needed to stop requiring any of his actions to make sense. If she could kill or maim him, or get his sword to Tom, then maybe they could still get out before the blast.

She watched LeBlanc's feet and his sword arm carefully. He might be insane, but she was no better. Why did she keep hoping against all reason and every shred of her common sense that René had not unset that firelighter? That he had not betrayed her? Especially when leaving it set meant they were all about to die.

"Hammond!" René yelled. His hands were gray and stained with powder, but this time he had hit something hard inside the barrel. He felt carefully and realized it was the lid, a few inches of the black powder concealing it. Spear came running. "She has made a space beneath," René said, his fingers scrabbling at the edges of the lid, where she had left it tilted inside.

"Try not to spill it," said Spear as René lifted the lid away. The firelighter was beneath, nestled in powder, the burlap sack Sophia had carried now arranged beside it, the edges exactly where the flame would come. Spear put his hand around the machine and swiftly pushed the knob back in.

René set down the powder-covered barrel lid, sweat dripping from his face. "What time was it set for?" Spear picked up the firelighter and looked at the back.

"Highmoon," he replied.

And then, in the quiet of the empty prison, they heard, very faint, the sound of the highmoon bells falling down through the drains.

René laughed, and then Spear laughed with him.

LeBlanc felt his cheek, bleeding from a small cut, and chuckled once. "Tell me, Miss Bellamy, do you consider yourself clever? Did you do well with your schooling?"

"She seems clever enough to beat you in a sword fight, LeBlanc," said Tom from behind her. But she wasn't beating him, not quite. LeBlanc was covered in blood and sweat, but he was on his feet. She could cut him, but not incapacitate him. Or at least not yet. She was sweating as well, one small prick stinging on her forearm. And she had lost sight of the rat Renaud. She hoped he had run. She hoped Tom had gotten the lock picked on his other ankle. She grinned at LeBlanc.

"Have you happened to notice that your own Goddess is female, Albert?"

"Of course! And being female, she naturally prefers the male, which is much to my advantage."

This line of reasoning was so daft that Sophia dismissed it.

"I have noticed that more women beg beneath the Razor than men, especially when their children are climbing the scaffold next. Why do you think that is, Miss Bellamy? Will you beg, do you think?"

"And will you beg, Albert, when Allemande finds out your bloody prison is empty?"

He came after her again then, and the chamber flickered in the lantern light, loud with the clash of steel. She blocked again, and again, three times, and then LeBlanc was in close, trying to push her sword out of her hand. She knocked his arm away and kicked hard with her boot heel, catching him in the middle and knocking him into the dust. He tried to raise his sword but she got a foot on his arm, her sword tip at the base of his throat.

LeBlanc laughed against the pointed end of the blade, an eerie sound, especially in a place full of death. And then Sophia heard a yell behind her. Her head whipped around. With a glance she took in the fact that Renaud had a knife to Tom's throat, and that the picklock she'd given Tom was now sticking out of Renaud's leg. She pressed down with her boot, stopped LeBlanc's arm from squirming, and made sure the very tip of her sword was piercing his skin.

"Call him off," she said to LeBlanc.

"No," said LeBlanc, his smile curling.

"Kill him, Sophie! We'll die anyway if you don't!"

She leaned closer to LeBlanc's bloody face. "Call him off, or I will carve you up bit by bit, just the way you like to do to others."

"Whatever you do to me," LeBlanc said, "will be done to your brother. Won't it, Renaud?"

"Kill him, Sophie!" Tom yelled. "Quick!"

Sophia pressed the sword in a little harder, and then a voice from the chamber entrance said, "I would not follow that suggestion, Miss Bellamy. I really would not."

Sophia looked up to see a very small man in the doorway, neat in his spectacles and city-blue suit, surrounded by gendarmes. She wouldn't have known the face if she hadn't seen it on a coin, but she had. It was Allemande.

22

Gerard mopped his head. The Rook couldn't have been more mistaken about those tickets to Spain. He would gladly take the tickets, but as soon as Madame Gerard was safely on board, he would be trading his for one to the Commonwealth. Now that he'd thought it all over, he was more than reconciled to going. The bells of highmoon still seemed to echo in the air, the mob shouting loud and impatient in the prison yard on the other side of the empty warehouse. The last landover had arrived, and there was only himself, the twin gendarmes, and the boy they called Cartier left to get in it. They would be away to the coast with the flick of the horsewhip. But none of them would go. Or let him.

Gerard tried to speak, but one of the twins jabbed him with the hilt of a sword. They seemed to enjoy that. Gerard shut his mouth and mopped his face again while the other three put their heads together and conferred. When they were done, Cartier trotted out to the street and opened the door to the landover. Gerard sighed with relief. He hurried inside, the twins escorting him one on each side, as if he now had a wish to stay and face LeBlanc.

Cartier shut the door behind them, and when Gerard looked back he saw the boy standing in the rubbish-strewn street, watching them escape.

—

"Well," said Allemande, eyeing LeBlanc as he got himself up out of the dust. He was covered in dirt and blood. "We cannot have any escaping, can we, Albert?" Allemande turned to the soldiers who were holding Sophia. "Search her," he ordered.

And they did. Thoroughly. Sophia stared up at the shadowy darkness while they removed her vest, her gloves, her boots—she had stashed tinder, flint, and steel in the newly hollowed-out heel, and the steel could have been used as a file—the knife strapped to her thigh, the one beneath her shirt, the document from beneath her shirt, and the wire she'd threaded into her hair. They even took out the rest of her hairpins, which was a shame, because she could have picked a lock with those as well, in a pinch. There was some sort of commotion going on with Tom that she could not see, and she assumed he was being searched again as well. She hoped he'd buried the ring well enough that they would not find it. Perhaps LeBlanc did not yet know they'd been forging passes, and the landovers could get away.

"I am surprised, Albert," Allemande was saying. His voice was soft, oily-slick as he wiped his glasses on a lace-edged handkerchief. Sophia wondered if Allemande was imitating LeBlanc's voice, or if LeBlanc had been imitating Allemande's. Or maybe they were just two of the same species of evil. "You are usually so punctual. When the bells rang, I thought perhaps you had become overzealous in your devotions again."

Sophia saw LeBlanc's pale eyes widen, and he snatched up the pendant from around his neck and flipped it open. "But . . . it's not . . ."

"Oh no, Albert. Depending on technology? That is such an imperfect system. One can be executed for things like that."

Sophia closed her eyes, knowing what this must mean. It was

definitely past highmoon. The firelighter was not going to ignite anything. René had turned it off.

René finished laughing, head in hands as he leaned on a cask, Spear looking no less relieved. Then he looked at the firelighter, still in Spear's hand.

"It is an interesting thing, is it not, that we can use a machine like this to control the time?"

"I suppose," Spear replied.

"And Sophia has done an excellent job of ridding this prison of its occupants. It is quite empty, yes? And she has gotten herself away as well."

"Yes. So?"

"Do you not think that after reinventing her plans with such success, it would be a shame to leave the best of them undone?"

Spear stared down at the firelighter, his eyes narrowed.

"What I mean to say, Hammond, is that I think we should blow this hole to bits. We have the time right here, in our hands."

"Yes," Spear nodded slowly. "I think you're right. For Sophie. What time do we set it for?"

It didn't matter what time she had set it for, after all. René would have found it too soon. The ache this knowledge caused was so strong it almost made the groping hands of the still searching gendarmes go away. Why did that tiny little sliver of hope keep dying only to be reborn? Then she took note of LeBlanc. He was staring down at his clock, an expression of frantic, hysterical disbelief on his face, a complete contrast to the clinical calm when she'd been slicing him with her sword.

"It is past highmoon?" LeBlanc looked at their faces, his voice rising to a shriek. Renaud took a step back. "We have missed the execution! The time that Fate herself decreed!"

Allemande pushed up his glasses, the gendarmes paused their further explorations, and then LeBlanc picked up his sword by the blade and inexplicably struck Renaud in the head with the hilt. Renaud crumpled, the picklock gone from his leg, Sophia saw, and then LeBlanc walked toward Tom, now with the proper end in his hand, blade out.

Sophia moved before the gendarmes knew she'd left their slackened grip. She barreled into LeBlanc with a yell, knocking him sideways before they were on her again, dragging her up by the arms.

"This is unseemly," said Allemande. He waved a casual hand at the gendarmes. "Sit both the Bellamys down and use those chains. And Albert. Calm yourself and stop striking things." Renaud picked himself up from the dirt, a small wound on his head.

"I will kill her," said LeBlanc. He was shaking, a dirty, bleeding mess, and almost completely out of control. "I will kill them both!"

"Yes, yes," said Allemande, "of course you shall. Albert, you look rather worse for wear. Am I right in thinking that you have arrested the wrong man . . . person?"

Sophia watched a spasm of genuine fear flit across LeBlanc's face as she was thrown back against the stone pedestal. She glanced at the little man with the glasses. What must Allemande be if a monster like LeBlanc could fear him? LeBlanc struggled to smooth his cut and filthy robes.

"I . . . I can assure you, Premier . . ." His softness returned. ". . . that the Red Rook will soon die, and that the people will know it. And these red feathers that fight in the streets will be crushed."

"Can you promise me that? Can you really? You know I take my promises seriously."

LeBlanc nodded, eyes on the ground.

"And no more mysterious disappearances from the prisons, to keep you begging and consulting your Goddess? Can you promise me that as well?"

Sophia blinked as her shackle clicked shut. Allemande doesn't know the Tombs are empty, she realized. He must have come straight down the lift and into . . . whatever this place was. And LeBlanc, she saw, hadn't realized that Allemande didn't know it, either. His hands worked in and out, clenching and unclenching as Allemande came and stood close to his back, head barely reaching his shoulder. Allemande spoke so softly it was difficult to hear.

"How, exactly, do you expect me to put stock in any promise you make, Albert? You did not even arrest a person of the correct gender. You know I do not tolerate disorder. This mob you have created is serving its purpose, but that will soon be done with. I do not care for your revenge, or your Goddess, or which Bellamy the people think is the Red Rook. As long as they see the Rook climb the scaffold and place his or her head on the block. We must be seen to be doing this properly. That is the essential thing. But you know what I like to do when it cannot be seen, don't you, Albert? What I like to do when I am . . . disappointed in my friends."

Sophia watched LeBlanc shake. Allemande pushed up his glasses, put his hands behind his back, turned, and started across the round room of bones. Then the spectacled eyes swiveled back to Tom. "Can that one walk?"

"Yes," LeBlanc replied slowly. "But not well."

"Be certain that he can make a decent show of himself on the way to the scaffold. Both of them. Are we clear on this?"

"Yes, Premier," said LeBlanc. "But . . . we are agreed that this one limps, yes?" He indicated Tom, though his eyes slid over to Sophia.

"Yes, Albert, we are agreed on that."

Allemande gathered his gendarmes while LeBlanc moved close to Sophia. LeBlanc's voice was every bit as soft as Allemande's, his breath in her face. "Tell me where the prisoners are, and I will spare you pain until your execution."

She looked back at him and whispered, "I don't think Allemande would approve."

LeBlanc smiled. "There are many kinds of pain, Miss Bellamy." Then his hand struck like a snake and Tom gasped. The picklock that had been in Renaud's leg was now in Tom's. Tom put a hand on Sophia's arm, squeezing, not with pain but in warning. Allemande craned his neck as she leaned forward, getting even closer to LeBlanc's face.

"That was unintelligent," she hissed. "Because now I am going to tell Allemande that his prison is empty. In fact, I wrote a letter yesterday telling him so. It was my fate to rescue all the prisoners, so therefore I'd already done it, don't you see? It should have arrived with the night post. So what to do, Albert? Keep him from his desk, or get there before him?"

She watched many things flit through LeBlanc's manic eyes. Murder, loathing, the desire to hurt her, the desire not to lose his life.

"He's waiting," she whispered.

LeBlanc got to his feet, oozing blood everywhere. "One moment more, Premier," he said loudly, "and I will personally escort you to my rooms, where we can discuss all that you wish, and make you comfortable until the proper time."

Allemande watched as LeBlanc hurried around the pedestal.

Sophia tensed at LeBlanc's presence behind her, ready for a picklock or something else to pierce a part of her body she did not immediately need, but LeBlanc only ran his hands over the stone basin above her head, humming. She glanced sideways. Tom was grimacing, eyes shut, hand still squeezing her arm.

LeBlanc's humming changed to a murmur as he chanted his question to Fate. Sophia caught the words "Bellamy" and "die," followed by the clank of a casting piece on the stone bottom of the pedestal.

"Dawn," LeBlanc said.

"Dawn," said René. "The Tombs will explode at dawn."

Spear turned the wheel of the firelighter and pulled out the knob.

"They will die at dawn," said LeBlanc. "The Goddess has spoken."

"I appreciate a deity with a proper sense of my schedule," Allemande commented. "We won't even have to change the bells. Now, if you are ready, Albert? I have some questions I'd like to ask you."

Cartier slipped unobtrusively through the torchlit crowd. He'd like to have asked directions, but he was hearing sounds that sealed his mouth. Screaming, yelling, and the clash of metal. He turned the last bend in the cliff road and saw a small war at the Seine Gate. Men and women in masks of black and white against others with red paint on their cheeks, a melee of swords, bows, clubs, bricks, and broken bottles. Fate against feathers.

Cartier ducked as someone in a mask went over the cliff edge, down to where the fogs were beginning to roll off the river. He'd never heard such noise, even in the prison yard. But the best thing the red feathers could do for the Rook, Cartier thought, was let him through and show him the fastest way to the flat of René Hasard. He darted forward, fast, avoiding an ax, slid his thin body through the boundary fence, and fled into the Upper City.

"I think we will need another route," René commented. They were far below the Seine Gate, walking the zigzagged road. They couldn't see the fighting, but they could hear it. "How are you at climbing?"

Spear paused, hands in pockets, and shrugged. "Not as bad as you'd think."

René led the way back down the road, through alleys that were empty and quiet, down streets with their lights out, doors barred, until they came to a strip of no-man's-land along the edge of the Lower City, behind a row of slanting wooden shanties. Bare dirt was sprinkled with blades of grass, and an immense composting rubbish heap was piled to their right, pushed into a mound that was higher than Spear's head. The stench was unbearable even with the wind blowing in the other direction. Spear looked up at the rising cliff face, glowing in a light now on its way to nethermoon.

"It is an easy climb at first," René replied. "After that there is rope to the top."

"When was the last time you checked the rope?"

"It is tested once a week." René smiled at Spear's expression. "It is not always convenient to use the Seine Gate. Have you not found it so?"

Spear got a handhold on the rough, tumbled rock at the bottom of the cliff and started up.

"Do you not want me to show you the way?"

"No." Spear's long arms and legs had him nearly a third of the way to the rope.

"To your right!" René called. When he saw Spear grab the rope, René took another look around at the bare and empty yards, the fogs tumbling off the river. He started climbing, moving fast on a course he knew almost by feel. If the fog got too thick, he would have to know it by feel, because neither of them would be able to see the cliff face.

Sophia felt for the wound in Tom's leg that she could not see, pressing her fingers against it in the dark, trying to stop the bleeding. They were alone. The leg beneath her hand was thin, and she could hear the weakness in his voice.

"I'd hoped he was going to forget he'd done it," Tom was saying, "and leave the . . . blasted thing in my leg. A picklock would have been dead useful about now."

"I'm sorry," Sophia whispered.

"Sorry that I don't have a picklock in my leg?"

"I'm sorry about everything."

He didn't reply right away. "I don't think you have anything to be sorry for, my sister. How did you leave Father?"

He was talking like he'd just sat down to have a chat on her window seat in Bellamy House. But now it was her turn not to respond immediately. She wondered if it was for the same reason: because they were both telling lies. "He was fine."

"And you got Jennifer out? Was she all right?"

"She's out, but she was . . . very sick. I'm so sorry, Tom."

"Sophie," he said, pulling her over so she could put her head on his shoulder. "Tell me what you have to be sorry about."

And just like that, the inner mechanism that had been propelling her forward sputtered and seized, its ticking stopped, and all that had been held at bay came flooding out, spilling pain and remorse onto Tom's filthy shirt. She told him everything, unable to see his face, and she thought maybe that was best, because she wouldn't be able to see the condemnation there. When there was nothing left she said, "I was just . . . so stupid."

Tom stroked her head and said, "Sophie, do you trust Spear?"

"What do you mean?"

"Because . . ." Tom hesitated. "It's just that I know he has other motives."

"I saw the denouncement, Tom," she whispered, trying to suppress the memory of René telling her almost the very same thing on Spear's steps, his mouth and jaw so angry in the dark. She took a breath of bone-dusted air. "And I know about Spear."

"Did he tell you?"

"No, or not at first. René told me. I don't know how he knew . . ."

"Sophie, everyone knew about Spear and you. Except for you."

"Then why didn't you tell me?"

"Because it was Spear's business to, not mine. What did you say to him?"

"That I thought of him as my brother. And that I was going to marry René Hasard whether there was a marriage fee or not."

"I see. And what did he do?"

"Knocked over some furniture." She could feel Tom's breath coming shallow in his chest. She should make him stop talking. But how long did they have before they would never talk again?

"I don't know what Hasard is, Sophie, except that he's been raised to be excellent at what he does. But I do know this. Spear is a good man, but when he gets something in his head, there's . . . there's just no getting it out again. And if he thought he was doing what's right . . . Well, he could be ruthless."

"Ruthless? That doesn't sound like Spear."

"Doesn't it?"

—

This was just like Hammond, wasn't it? René felt the vibrations traveling down his rope as he climbed. A knife. And he was hanging halfway up from a smooth piece of cliff, nothing to clutch on to, nowhere to go but down. René sighed when he felt the rope slacken to nothing beneath his hands. He pushed his feet against the cliff face, spread his arms like wings, and fell backward, the cold night air whistling past his head.

A draft blew cold through the bones, a weird noise in the dark. Sophia shivered, wondering where it had come from. "Are you in pain?" she asked.

"I'm so thirsty I don't think it matters," Tom replied. "Are you in pain?"

She could feel the blood from the scratch LeBlanc had given her trickling down her arm. She shook her head.

"So who's out there, Sophie? Any chance someone will come to find us?"

"I told Cartier to get on the last landover whether I came or not. And Spear will think I'm on a landover, too. He'll be leaving the city by now."

"And what about Hasard?"

Sophia closed her watering eyes. "He's exactly where he wants to be, Tom."

René kept his eyes closed. He hated landing in the compost heap. It might not break bones like the ground would, but it did knock the wind out, which was useful only for avoiding a few moments of the stench. He supposed he should thank Uncle Émile for making him take this fall so many times. Tonight it had saved his life. But he was too angry for justice at the moment. He waited for his air to return, and when it did and his temper had settled, he opened his eyes.

The clouds had cleared and the night was glowing with the north lights. Green, hazy edges tinged with purple, but there was also a stripe of yellow. A streak of fire, he realized. Like what he had seen on the A5 from Bellamy House. And now he saw that there were dozens of them, fine, thin lines racing across the sky. What were they? Pieces of stars? Or pieces of Ancient machines still flying? He wished he could show Sophia. He wondered, impractically, if they were for the Rook. If they were for her.

He rolled himself out and slid down the stinking pile, toward the cliff face and the next set of ropes his uncles kept for climbing in and out of the Lower City. He was going to be sore from that fall. He walked slowly, thinking about Sophia, and all the different ways he might like to kill Spear Hammond.

Spear ran down a back street of the Upper City in the dark, glad he had killed René Hasard. He didn't like killing people, but if that was what it took to protect Sophia from herself, then so be it.

A woman far above on an air bridge was calling to another about the sky. He looked up and saw the north lights beginning, but there were also tiny yellow streaks, trails of sparkling fire. Like the chapel walls of his childhood. He wished he could show Sophia. Then he was approaching two wooden doors on the ground floor of a building, relieved to see they had not been broken into or torn down. He put a key to the padlock.

Aunt Francesca's landover was right where she'd left it, now with his things loaded in. If the horses he'd stolen last night were still there, and if the forged pass for the Saint-Denis Gate he'd kept back still worked, then he would be out of the Sunken City well before dawn. He would find Tom and Sophia at the coast, and Sophia was going to be so happy that he'd reset the firelighter and blown up the prison. Everything would be just as he'd said. They would start over together. And with Hasard gone, she would turn to him. He knew she would.

She would come back to him, René thought. He knew she would. He stood looking up at the tall, narrow shaft of the water lift. He was aching and tired, but he'd gotten one look at the gendarmes around his building and taken to the sewers, then to the cellar and the water lift. René used the hook hanging beside the cistern to snag the rope and pull it toward him. Up onto the edge, and then he was climbing, swinging gently over the pool of water.

He had to get to the coast, catch Sophia before she sailed. He remembered the look on her face, right before she had hit him with LeBlanc's ring. She was clever, and beautiful, and as hard as burnished bronze. Or at least she pretended to be. Beneath the shiny metal, Sophia Bellamy was very breakable indeed, something Hammond had somehow failed to notice. But more than rage or even pain, what he had seen when she hit him was betrayal. And after she had been so afraid to let herself believe in him. He would have taken a dozen falls not to have seen her looking that way at him.

René climbed the rope faster, glad there was no one at the top to cut it. Would she know she could believe when she saw the ships anchored on the coast? And if Sophia was there, Hammond would be, too, that much was certain. He would make Hammond pay for that trick at the cliffs, make him tell her the truth, at the point of a sword if necessary, and she would believe it. She had to. Because it was.

He paused his climb at the second floor. It was the Espernazos' flat, and the water-lift door was partway open. René got a toe beneath and pushed. The Espernazos had probably fled the city, anyway. He made his way out of their empty flat and took the lift to the top, the bellman looking at him rather askance, opening the door of his own flat to find chaos. Crates and boxes were all over the floor, his uncles, the staff, and some of the party guests hurriedly packing them. One of the violinists was taking down paintings from the walls. Uncle Andre left a pair of candlesticks on the settee and came hurrying over.

"Where have . . ." He wrinkled his nose. "René, did you fall off the cliffs again?"

"What is happening? Where is Benoit?"

"Our cousin knows he was drugged and we will be arrested soon, that is what," Andre said. "We are besieged from below, but LeBlanc has put the greatest idiot of all gendarmes in charge, and the man has forgotten the air bridges. We have all the plastic out and away and plan to do the same for ourselves, but Adèle does not wish to leave anything behind for your cousin to . . ."

"René!" Madame Hasard called from the window wall. "There you are. What have you done to yourself? This boy came by air bridge. He is asking . . ." The group around Madame Hasard, including Madame Gagniani—who had set aside her turban—the boy Louis, and the dark-skinned singer, parted to let Cartier push his way through.

"None of them will tell me where Mr. Hammond is," Cartier said quickly.

"I would guess that he is leaving the city," René replied.

"Leaving? Are you sure?"

"No. But should you not be gone as well?"

Cartier pressed his lips together. There was several days' worth of fuzz on his upper one. "I want to talk to you alone, then."

René looked at his mother and uncles, who did not move, so he pulled Cartier away, to the far end of the room, where the display cabinet stood empty. Though Enzo, he noted, was making sure Cartier was still in sight.

The boy leaned forward. "Swear to me that you mean Miss Bellamy no harm. Because if you do, I'll come after you myself."

René did not smile. The boy was dead serious. "I can swear it without fear of my soul, Cartier."

He took a deep breath. "Right, then. Miss Bellamy didn't come out of the prison. And neither did her brother."

"What? That cannot be so."

"She didn't come for the last landover. She told me to go if that happened, but I didn't. Plan B was the haularound with the coffins. But they're still there, and the Tombs are crawling with gendarmes. There are tunnels under the walls, but you have to get out of the Lower City first . . ."

René was shaking his head. "No. You are mistaken. I was in the prison with Hammond. We went through every hole. The Tombs are empty. We . . ."

Then he turned. There had been a sound from their front doors. Not a knock but a hit. He looked around the flat and saw weapons coming out from every side, people taking up positions on either side of the doors, behind furniture and on the gallery. There was another hit, and another. Benoit swiveled on his heel, sword in hand, and caught René's eye just before the splintering of wood.

"Down," René said, forcing Cartier to crouch on the other side of the cabinet.

"Who is coming?" the boy asked.

"I think, Cartier, that we are resisting arrest."

The doors gave way, Benoit shouted, and gendarmes poured into the room. And straight into the clanging of metal and shouts came discordant bells, harsh, from all over the Upper City. René knocked the sword from a gendarme's hand, slammed him to the ground, and got the man's arm twisted behind his back. René glanced out the window while he held the gendarme down, Cartier conveniently whacking the man on the head with a crate lid. Nethermoon. And those had been execution bells. That meant someone would die at dawn. And there were only two people from the prison who were unaccounted for.

Spear jerked the reins to a halt, half turning in the seat of the land-over to look at the moon. The clash of bells echoed all around him, striking the buildings that clustered around the Saint-Denis Gate, hurting his ears. LeBlanc was going to kill at dawn. But who? The Red Rook was out. Sophia and Tom were on their way to the coast.

"No," said Spear, "that can't be right. That can't be bloody right!"

He turned the landover around.

23

LeBlanc listened to the execution bells, more himself now, with wounds bound, new robes, and the white streak in his hair arranged just as straight as it should be. He smiled slowly. "When Claude brings in the prisoners from the Hasard flat, make certain he puts them in the first few holes, in case Allemande should look down the tunnels."

Renaud glanced through the door of the office at Allemande, who was on the hard, plain couch of LeBlanc's private rooms, feet dangling, investigating a box of sweets.

LeBlanc pulled the cork on a bottle of wine. "I will only be a moment, Premier," he called, walking to the far end of his office. Allemande's soldiers were waiting just outside, in the corridor. No need for them to hear anything untoward. Renaud followed, limping.

"And while I have him here," LeBlanc continued softly, bringing two glasses from a cabinet, "go to his office and his private rooms and be sure there is not a letter informing him of the loss of the prisoners. She may have been lying, of course, but we must be certain."

If Renaud was alarmed by an order to search the most guarded premises in the Sunken City without getting run through with a sword, he did not show it.

"After the execution," LeBlanc whispered, "I will tell the premier that the time for the other sacrifices to Fate has changed. It was improper to use his wheel in any case, and it is evident that the Goddess wanted them on another day, since they are not here. We will begin with a quiet sweep of the Upper City, to find our missing prisoners, then the Lower. They cannot get out of the gates, so there is no hurry. No reason to bother the premier. No need for him to know at all."

And if Renaud harbored any secret doubts concerning LeBlanc's ability to somehow keep an empty prison, a citywide search, and hundreds of lost executions away from the ears of the premier, he did not show that opinion, either. LeBlanc returned to Allemande with the bottle and the wineglasses.

"Well, Albert," said Allemande, "have you seen the reports? From the Seine Gate, and the Rue de Triomphe? We are bleeding rebels. And, interestingly, the mob seems to have targeted certain residences in the Upper City, addresses that we have recently spoken of. This smacks of . . . deliberation on the part of our government, and with no proper forms filled out at all. And what about the sky? It is raining fire out there, and the people say it is the sign of the saints, of the Red Rook. I have a feeling your dawn demonstration of two out of three is going to be crucial to the future of the city, Albert."

LeBlanc swallowed hard as he poured the premier's wine. Allemande meant that it was going to be crucial to the future of his Ministre of Security.

"The people are in need of a dose of terror. They must feel that they have no choice, can effect no change, or we will have more change than we currently know how to handle. And René Hasard, your cousin . . ." Allemande tsked. "To so publicly engage himself to the Red Rook—who is nothing but a little girl, I find—a little girl fomenting insurrection and threatening the stability of our city . . .

Oh, no. I do not think we can have that. We must take all their heads. Put them on sticks, I think."

LeBlanc smiled, nervous. "You will be pleased to know I have already given the order, Premier."

"Have you? And whose name did you use on the denouncements?"

"I thought it appropriate in this case to use my own name, Premier."

"Hmmm." The little man frowned, and the expression made LeBlanc cold. Allemande had no Goddess but power, and playing his games was like facing down a poisonous snake. A snake with a penchant for paperwork. He would gut his best friend if it struck his fancy—LeBlanc had seen him do so to the former premier. It was one of the nicer things he'd seen him do.

Allemande pushed up his glasses. "I am also concerned about this document that Miss Bellamy seems to have been carrying. It is the denouncement of Ministre Bonnard." He held it out. "Please, Albert, look at it."

LeBlanc took the paper, setting it on the table nearer the light, where the premier would not see his hand shaking. He only just kept his expression calm.

"Does this seem quite accurate to you?" Allemande asked. "I thought perhaps it was not." Then he said, "I am not confident your affairs are in order, Albert. Let me see the forms."

LeBlanc bowed slightly. "I will see if Renaud has completed them."

"I mean all the forms, Albert. All your files."

LeBlanc hurried into his office. Renaud had not, of course, prepared any forms for the Hasards, or been ordered to prepare any, and he was not here now. Why was Renaud never here when he was needed? LeBlanc smoothed his white streak, trying to slow his ragged breath. He would make one out himself, for show, and give Allemande the rest of the files while he forged more. He readied his pen and ink, pulled open the left-hand drawer of his desk, and stopped. The nest of velvet where his signet ring resided was empty.

He opened the drawer farther, felt all the way to the back of it. And then his smile came out, curling to the corners of his mouth. He had no prisoners in the Sunken City. Not anymore. His search would have to extend to the coast. How had any of them thought they would get away with this and live? Because they were not going to live. But his smile left him when he glanced at the door to his private rooms, where Allemande's shadow crossed the open doorway. And yet . . . Perhaps Fate had willed this night for a reason.

He hurried to the other end of the room, the bound cuts on his arms burning, and opened the plastic ritual box in the corner. There was no time for the fire and the bottles, or any of the solemn ceremony that should accompany such a question. But the Goddess would require more of him than the toss of a coin.

He selected a thick piece of paper, cut round, one side white, the other black, the swaths of color curling into each other, and laid it carefully on the center of the chalk circle he'd drawn before. Then he picked up a knife. He closed his eyes and plunged the tip of the knife into the soft pad of his forefinger. Blood welled. He opened his eyes and flicked his bleeding finger across the paper.

He leaned over and quickly counted the spatters, no matter how tiny, mouth moving, his finger dripping blood onto the floor. When he was done LeBlanc straightened, closing his pale eyes once more, this time to enjoy a moment of ecstasy. Twenty-seven drops in the black, only eleven in the white. The answer was clear, and it was death. Fate had given her permission.

"Thank you, Goddess," he whispered, going back to his desk to snatch up a clear glass vial from his drawer. The time for this was now, before the dawn. He concealed the vial in his hand and strode purposefully to the door of his private rooms.

"Premier," he said respectfully. "Renaud is finishing and needs just a few more moments while I gather the files. May I offer you more wine? Yes?"

"I die at dawn," Sophia whispered, as if trying out the idea. "Is it wrong that I don't feel terribly upset about that right now? That it almost seems easier?"

"Yes, that is most definitely wrong," Tom replied, his voice like rubbing sandpaper. "And if I thought you meant it, I'd scold you. Severely. But if it does have to be, Sophie . . . then I'm glad . . . that I got to see you again."

Sophia laid her head back down on his shoulder. She had always been so afraid of losing Bellamy House, her father, the Red Rook, of living with no reason to live at all. But for just a little while, she'd caught a glimpse of something different. It was the loss of the dream rather than the reality that was leaving her empty and aching.

"Did you really get all of them out of the prison, sister?"

"Yes. They should be away by now, Cartier and the twins with them. But there won't be any ships when they get to the coast."

"Some of them will get away, though." Tom settled his head against the stone pedestal. "I think that makes it worth it."

"Do you?"

"Yes. I do."

"Yes," said Renaud. The words came from his mouth like water dripping from a rusting pipe. "Agreed." The big blond man he'd met in the street near the Saint-Denis Gate nodded, and they completed their transaction.

It was obvious this man knew he was LeBlanc's secretary, but Renaud didn't care who the man was or what he knew. LeBlanc had finally descended all the way to madness, and Renaud had decided to be his secretary no more. He was on the run. And he had just made a glorious trade. The keys to LeBlanc's office plus certain passwords for a horse and a forged pass out of the gate. He had intended to bluff his way past the guards on LeBlanc's authority and travel on foot through The Désolation, at least until he could hire transportation. But this was much better, much less traceable.

Renaud mounted the horse, throwing his small bag of possessions across the saddle. He smiled, an expression almost as rusty as his voice, and galloped for the gate, horse hooves loud against the paving stones.

Claude's boots clattered against the stairs of the flat, knocking one by one as he was dragged down from the gallery, across the scene of battle, and into one of the interior, windowless rooms off the lower-floor corridor, where he was deposited with the rest of the gendarmes, none of which had their uniforms anymore. René was sweating, flushed, and still filthy, but the fight had made him feel the slightest bit better. There were some small wounds among them, though not many. LeBlanc's gendarmes were no match for the seasoned criminals of a Hasard family engagement party.

"Where will they bring her out?" Émile asked, tossing his breeches to the floor of the corridor, replacing them with the uniform René threw at him. The entire hallway was jammed with uncles and men and dropped articles of clothing. "Which door?"

"There is only one entrance," Benoit replied, pulling on a jacket of city blue.

"The brick building in front of the scaffold," René continued for him. "It sits over the entrance to the prison, and there is just the one door. But there is a lift through the cliff that must go up to LeBlanc's building above. There is nowhere else for it to go."

"So she must come out that door?" Émile asked.

"Yes," Benoit replied. "We can take her from there."

"And the brother," said René. "We must get them both."

"And why will the Tombs explode at dawn?" Francois asked, pulling off his shirt. It must have been a very good question, because Uncle Francois never spoke otherwise.

"Just trust me that they will," René replied. "I will try to get inside and turn off the firelighter, but . . ." He turned his head at a call from his mother. Madame was standing unaffected by the bedlam around her, a uniform in her hand. She beckoned him over.

"I suppose you must go get her?" she asked, leaving behind her usual brash tone.

"Yes, Maman."

"Then, here." She pushed the jacket and breeches into his hand. "I chose one that will fit."

"Thank you, Maman."

"And go wash or they will smell you coming."

"Yes, Maman." She patted his cheek once, and then turned to walk away. "I will see you at the coast," he added.

She smiled with both sides of her mouth, and it was a grim, hard thing. "See that you do, René."

Spear stood behind a smoldering barricade, where he'd ditched the landover, wondering if any of them would ever again see the coast.

Why hadn't he killed Hasard before he'd gotten talked into setting that firelighter? And those bells, who were they for? He was afraid he knew the answer to that. The same one who had always been scheduled to die at dawn. And now he was the one who would have to rescue them. He would have to unset that firelighter and bring them out.

This area was quieter than the neighborhoods near the cliffs, but it was still dangerous. Spear put out the lantern and jerked off his jacket, exchanging it for the blue and white of an Upper City officer, the one he carried in his suitcase. He glanced up once at the setting moon and cursed Albert LeBlanc.

Allemande cursed Albert LeBlanc as he foamed and choked on the contractions of his own throat, his glasses fallen to the floor. LeBlanc breathed in satisfaction, then opened his pendant and checked the progress of the moon, wondering what could have happened to Renaud.

He strolled into his office, shutting the unpleasant writhing and gagging away behind the door, snapped his pendant shut, and rang the bell for the lift. He'd sent Allemande's soldiers to wait at the bottom. But they weren't Allemande's anymore, were they? Because LeBlanc was premier now. The destiny Fate had ordained had been achieved. As he'd known it would be.

There was no question who the Sunken City belonged to. And it was time to make sure that everyone, especially the Red Rook, knew it.

"They'll come for us soon," Sophia whispered.

"I know," Tom replied.

"What do you wish you were doing right now?"

"Running. Or talking to Jennifer Bonnard."

"Do you really?"

"Yes. And what about you? What do you wish?"

"That I could wake up on the day of my Banns and realize that none of this had ever happened."

"Do you really wish that?"

Sophia thought for a moment. "No. I don't. I suppose what I really wish is that the real parts had never happened, and the parts that never really happened were the ones that were real."

Far away in the darkness of the cavern, they heard the creaking of a metal door. Tom took her hand. At least they would do this together.

René marched with his uncles and their friends as a troop, but they had to stop blocks away from their goal. The streets were thronged. It was the coldest, darkest part of the night as the moon sank, the north lights nearly gone, no fire in the sky. But the execution of the Red Rook was keeping the entire Lower City out of its bed.

They pushed their way through, insistent but careful not to start a fight, and when they finally reached the prison yard René felt his jaw clench tight. The Razor, its ugliness undisguised by the flowers and ribbons, towered above a mass of torchlit humanity. But the mood was not what he'd expected. More grim, and less mocking. The blue of gendarmes was everywhere, at least ten forming a pack in front of the prison door, some of them shoving and beating back the crowd.

"Get everyone into position, and I will try another way in," René whispered. "We will get nowhere if this mob turns against the gendarmes."

Spear entered LeBlanc's office building with a crisp walk and approached the guard at the desk. He brandished a piece of paper. "Long may Allemande rise above the city," he said.

"Your code?"

"One three four."

The guard nodded, tilting his head toward the stairs. Spear started to climb, and as soon as the guard was out of sight he took them two at a time, smiling at the luck of meeting Renaud in the street.

Renaud approached the Saint-Denis Gate. He saw an Allemande courier climbing back onto a horse as he handed his papers to the guard. The guard was unkempt, and a little drunk, but he looked at the pass carefully, as if he was having trouble reading it.

"Step down, Monsieur," the guard said.

They could search all they wanted, Renaud thought. His mind was on sea foam, and birds, and the clean, free air of the coast. Two more gendarmes approached, but instead of searching him, one took his arms, quickly twisting them back, and the other put a knife to his throat. Renaud's smile went away.

"Be advised," read the guard from another document, his speech slurring, "that no official . . . permissions have been given to pass . . . any gates . . . out of the City of Light. Any such pass . . . passes . . . shall be considered a forgery, and the . . . the bearer . . . subject to immediate . . . execution." The guard swayed just a little on his feet. "Sorry, friend," he said to Renaud. "You ran a little . . . late."

Renaud had only a moment to wonder why luck had abandoned him before the knife bit into his throat.

The ropes cut into Sophia's hands as she and Tom were escorted through the dusty maze and onto the lift. Two young gendarmes, who had been wide-eyed in the bizarre cavern, were half carrying, half dragging Tom. She wondered how long they would live after this. They all crammed into the lift, LeBlanc rang the bell, and then he spent the entire ride examining her face from just a few inches away, as if he could ferret out the source of her abnormalities. She just glared at him.

They stepped out of the lift, this time into the small, lantern-lit lobby of LeBlanc's office building, where the night guard sat at a desk. She caught a glimpse of a large blue-jacketed officer just disappearing up the stairs before she and Tom were taken stumbling out the door and to the back of a haularound. The bed of the haularound had a railing built like a fence around it, two posts at either end. Men were lighting short torches attached along the edges, the orange flames showing an entire troop of escorting gendarmes, swords and crossbows at the ready. A large sign on the back of the haularound read, LE CORBEAU ROUGE.

LeBlanc smiled, took one of Sophia's red-tipped feathers, and stuck it securely into her tangled hair, patting her cheek when he was done. Then she was pulled up and into the haularound, her bound hands tied tight to the post. She looked back over her shoulder, where Tom was being tied to the other post, closest to the driver. She hadn't yet seen him in such strong light. He looked terrible. Gaunt, dirty, bloody, and exhausted. But he smiled at her, even though his lips were cracked, and it made her stand straighter.

"The mob may do as they like," LeBlanc was instructing their escort, "but they may not remove the prisoners or . . ."

"Give my brother water," Sophia said. "Or he might not be able to stand."

LeBlanc went on. ". . . or we will remove them to the Tombs. Allow no one to impede your progress through the streets. Only the driver knows the route . . ."

"And what will Allemande say if he can't walk to the scaffold?" Sophia shouted.

LeBlanc turned his pale eyes on her, and then he smiled. Something about that smile made Sophia wish she'd never drawn his gaze. "There is no Allemande," LeBlanc said. He turned back to the gendarmes. "Shoot anyone who attempts to deny the will of Fate."

The haularound started forward with a jerk.

The lift jerked, and Spear paced inside it, waiting through the long, slow journey down the building and into the cliff. He'd used Renaud's keys to unlock LeBlanc's office, finding nothing but the dead, contorted body of Premier Allemande lying on a sofa, then used the same keys to open LeBlanc's private lift. He was so angry. Angry to be back here. Angry that he'd thought they were safe when they weren't. Angry that he had blood on his hands. Why had everything in his life gone wrong since he'd heard the name Hasard?

When the lift finally reached bottom, he used the smallest key on the empty rivet hole to open the false back, just the way Renaud had described, unlocked the second false door, snagged the lantern from the lift, and hurried down the dust-thick stone steps into the cavern of bones. He took one moment to stare, and then he yelled, "Sophie! Tom!"

He would unset that firelighter again if he could. But he would get Sophie and Tom first this time. And if the rest of the world exploded, then it exploded.

—

René looked up at the sagging brick structure that covered the entrance to the Tombs. He didn't really care if it exploded. He cared for nothing but getting Sophia out. The window he'd climbed through before had been boarded, guards now in front of it. And he could not get in the main door, either, no matter what story he told. No one without black robes and a white streak in his hair was coming in, not without a fight.

But it wasn't him those gendarmes needed to be worrying about, René thought. There was something moving through the mob, a subtle shift in current after the night's violence, an increasing hostility to the uniforms of the city. Perhaps his uncles had chosen the wrong disguises. Benoit had assured him again and again that when Sophia and Tom came out through that door, there would be enough gendarmes that weren't really gendarmes gathered and ready to take them. If Allemande's control was developing fault lines, would the mob help, or hinder them?

He looked up to the edge of the cliffs, where LeBlanc's office building perched, and where he knew there was a lift. The moon was gone, the sky just beginning to pale in the northeast. He wondered if he had time to climb.

Spear wondered if he should try to climb the stacks of bones and see the layout of the paths from above. Probably his light wasn't bright enough even if he could. He kicked the pyramid of skulls in front of him, putting his foot through one. He was lost, and furious, and beginning to be afraid that Sophia and Tom were not even in this godforsaken grave. He studied the hole he had made in the skull, fourth one from the corner, near the floor, and took off at a run down the next narrow path.

Sophia wondered if she would have time to climb the fencing, slip her bonds over the top of the post, and perhaps set fire to the haularound before they could catch her. But her hands would still be tied, and there would still be Tom. So she looked straight ahead, ignoring the shouts and stares, and the people standing along the streets and in the doorways of their shanties. News in the Lower City traveled much faster than a haularound, and she could see the crowds gathering farther down the road.

There had been fighting here. Smoldering wood and rubble, and doorways with something black nailed on, announcing a death. And the sign of the red feather. And now that she was listening, some of the shouts were not the mockery she had expected. "Red Rook" came at her from all sides, but they were shouts of encouragement, and there were men and women who stood in respectful silence as the haularound passed. And then she heard her name.

"Sophie!" She turned her head, scanning the crowd until she saw a young, bearded man with his hair cropped short. "Sophie!"

"Justin!" Tom called.

Sophia felt a smile break over her face. She leaned as close to the edge of her rolling wooden prison as the ropes would allow. It was Mémé Annette's son. "Justin! How is Maggie?"

"Five children!" he said as the haularound passed, his face falling as they all three remembered they were not actually having a reunion.

"Tell her we love her!" Sophia called. "And the children!"

He nodded, and Sophia watched a small crowd form around him, asking questions and listening to his response. "Justin!" she yelled suddenly. "Can you get Tom water? Do you have a flask with you? Please!"

She watched Justin patting his shirt and pants, as if he might discover water, others around him doing the same. She wondered how many would remember Sophie and Tom from Blackpot Street, the children who spent their summers selling an old woman's oatcakes and romping around in the mud and grime of a Lower City market, Tom's hair tucked up in a cap.

She heard a thump behind her and turned her head to see a leather flask at Tom's feet. He slid down the post and got his hands on it, the gendarmes around them seeming inclined to do nothing. She sighed in relief. So there was still goodness somewhere in the Lower City. It made her stand straighter as they drove the twisting streets, all the way to the turn into the prison yard.

There was a mob there the size of which she'd never seen. An ocean of bodies and faces packed into the square, the Razor rising up like an illuminated island of black and white flowers in its midst. She looked up at the sky. Surely they were early; there was only the barest lightening of the dark on the northeastern horizon. She met Tom's eyes, and he shook his head. If there was anyone in that crowd who wanted to rescue them, she didn't know how they could possibly do it. The numbers were unbelievable, overwhelming. She felt the loss of hope solidify, rock hard inside her. And then, as the people caught sight of them, one by one, the mob went silent.

Spear had gone silent, no more yelling. They weren't there. There was no one there, nothing but death. He found the steps to lead him out of the cavern, ran straight through the lift and out into the prison. There was no one there, either, no guards. No Sophia. No Tom. Dread settled on him, like the bone dust that was covering his face. He turned right and dashed down the stairs and into the stinking tunnels, feet splashing in the quiet. Surely it couldn't be dawn yet.

René turned at the strange, growing silence of the mob. Surely it couldn't be dawn yet? And then he saw a haularound, lit with torches, bright at the opposite end of the prison yard. The sight set his fear on fire. The haularound snaked a path through the mob and now he could see Sophia in the back of it, hands tied and head up, her brother too weak to stand at the other end.

He looked around, trying to control his panic. Benoit, Émile, his uncles, Cartier, and their recruits from the party guests were a short distance away, crowded around the prison door, where they'd thought Sophia was going to come out. They were cut off. René launched himself into the sea of people, swimming into the crowd, but there were many hundreds of bodies between him and the scaffold.

LeBlanc looked down on the hundreds of faces, indistinct in shadows and torchlight, and smiled beatifically. He was seated in the viewing box, his streak straight and robes perfect, all wounds discreetly covered. And he was in Allemande's chair, from where his new power would flow. The other ministres had not seemed quite confident in his story of Allemande's death by armed rebels, LeBlanc had thought. But they all knew who the gendarmes were taking their orders from. And so the ministres were around him on the scaffold, one or two yawning with the early dawn, seated in their velvet chairs, waiting to witness the death of the Red Rook.

LeBlanc opened his pendant. Its black hand pointed to dawn, and though dawn was looming, it had not precisely arrived. But the haularound had. LeBlanc sighed. This was inconvenient. And Renaud was missing, leaving him no one to blame or complain to. That was aggravating, as was the thought of training a new secretary. They could take so long to break.

And then there was this odd silence. Not the way a Lower City mob ought to behave when presented with the gift of the Red Rook's head, and her brother's. He had seem them beg for blood that was worth much less. But now they were merely standing aside, making a path for the haularound to approach the scaffold.

Sophia looked up past the torchlight to the huge, heavy blade already pulled high and hanging in the air, ready to end her life. The executioner and his team stood next to the rope, his only job now to trip the lever and let the blade fall, then pick up the head from the blood-stained basket and show it to the crowd. The Razor crept closer, and she wondered vaguely if she and Tom would go one at a time, or if they would lie down on the block and die together.

She felt curiously detached, as if this moment were happening to another Sophia Bellamy, a girl who had lived a thousand years ago and already knew the end of her story. But at the same time, little things were sharpened into importance, things that held meaning only for her. A knitted blue skullcap just like Mémé Annette's, someone who had their child sitting on their shoulders, a woman with a red-tipped feather painted on her cheek, reaching out a hand in the dim and eerie silence. And then the haularound stopped.

The gendarmes came and cut her rope from the post, pulling her down and toward the steps of the scaffold. Evidently it was to be one at a time, and she would be first. She heard a whisper of talk trickle through the mob, a current of sound running just beneath the quiet.

"Tom!" Sophia yelled suddenly. "Tomas Bellamy, do not look. When it's time, do not look! Swear it to me!"

She caught a glimpse of him over her shoulder, standing up straight now despite his injuries. He nodded once. She was satisfied.

"Let me go," she said, yanking her arms free of the gendarmes. "Let me go! I can walk on my own."

She was getting angry now. That was good. She moved just out of the guards' reach, and walked up the scaffold steps. That gendarme who cut her bonds did it a little too well, because they were loose around her wrists now. She stopped and planted her feet in front of the viewing box, bright with torches, tilted up her chin, fixed her gaze on LeBlanc, and smiled.

Somewhere far away in the crowd, someone was calling her name.

24

*Le*Blanc stood, his pale gaze on Sophia Bellamy. She looked young and small and very defiant standing down there with a bloody sleeve and a smile on her face. He could not wait to see her die. He pulled out a long roll of official-looking paper with a flourish.

"By order of the government of LeBlanc," LeBlanc shouted, voice reverberating against the surrounding buildings, "I, your most gracious premier, find Sophia Bellamy, also known as the Red Rook, guilty of crimes against the City of Light . . ."

Spear froze at the sound of Sophia's name, and looked up at the ceiling of the tunnel, where the drains of the prison yard were dark with feet.

"Sophia!" René yelled, using his elbows and body to fight a way through the crowd. The people had gone stiff, muttering. They'd been expecting Tom Bellamy to be the Red Rook, not this slim, small girl. And they'd thought their premier was Allemande. René pushed them all aside, screaming himself hoarse.

"Sophia!"

"For the removal of criminals fairly condemned of treason, and circumventing the laws that have condemned them . . ."

Sophia had stopped listening to LeBlanc. She was hearing the swelling confusion of the mob behind her, and the voice that was calling her name. She let LeBlanc keep on talking, turned from the viewing box and the solemn ministres of the Sunken City, and walked away, dropping her loose ropes onto the stolen stone altar as she passed. She approached the Razor and straddled the board, but instead of lying facedown, she chose to lay on her back, placing her neck in the stained, curved groove, chin up and facing the blade. She closed her eyes.

"Sophia!" The people in the crowd were beginning to part, to let him through, making his progress faster. "Listen to me!" René shouted. "I did not lie to you. It was not a lie! Sophia! Open your eyes!"

She opened her eyes and saw a sky of translucent blue, the kind that comes just before the dawn, and the giant wedge of metal that was the Razor, its sharpened edge glittering with the torchlight. She knew the voice. She'd known it all along. It was taking the steel from her anger and melting it into nothing. LeBlanc was still talking, but she wasn't listening. Not to him.

"Sophia!" the voice screamed. "I did not lie to you! Think! Do you believe me?"

Spear pushed against the wall, scraping his nails against the rough and filthy stone, face looking up to the drains. Sophia was on the scaffold. And someone was screaming her name.

"Sophia!"

She blinked. That time she'd heard the sound of anguish inside her name.

"I did not lie to you!"

Sophia stared up at the blade, surrounded by ribbons and flowers. LeBlanc was talking on and on. And then her gaze moved over to the executioner. He was watching her curiously, his hand out and ready to trip the lever.

"Sophia! It was real! Do you believe me?"

She leapt up from the wooden slab, knocked the executioner to one side, wrapped the hauling rope around one leg, and tripped the lever herself. The Razor came down and Sophia rose, jerked from her feet, flying fast into the air. She hung on to the rope, and the blade hit the block with its usual thump.

Spear fell to his knees in the muck of the prison tunnel at the sound of the blade.

Sophia got her knee up and over the wooden framework that formed the top of the Razor, knocking black and white flowers to the crowd below. She put her feet beneath her and stood, still with a handful of rope, legs apart for support against the breeze. Her gaze went to Tom, leaning against the rail of the haularound, his eyes riveted on her—just what she'd told him not to do—working his knots free while no one was looking.

And then she spotted the red head, swimming frantically through the humanity of the Sunken City, dressed in the blue of a gendarme. He finally gained the scaffold and came careening up the steps to stand before the Razor, chest heaving and face turned upward.

—

Spear dropped his eyes from the ceiling drains, got to his feet, and went stumbling deeper into the Tombs, looking for prison hole number 522.

Sophia swayed on the narrow framework, high above the crowded prison yard, muscles tensed to keep her balance.

"Shoot her!" LeBlanc was shouting, but she couldn't think of that now. René was staring up at her, angry and with his jaw clenched.

"I did not lie to you," he said.

She gripped the rope in her hand. She thought she could see the cut she had put on his lip.

"Do you believe me?"

"Why should I?"

"I do not know." Then René actually smiled, while she was standing on the Razor and he was on the scaffold and a dozen arrows were probably trained on the both of them. He said, "Because you choose to."

And just like that, she believed him. She chose to believe because she knew what was real. It didn't matter what name a paper said, or what role he'd been playing. He had shown her who he was. He was showing her now. And that just . . . was. She met his eyes, blue even from her height, and they understood each other. He knew that she believed, and the pull to him was like gravity, nearly toppling her from her perch, and then together they looked to the sky.

The last of the night had brightened, though not with dawn. This light was white and glaring, every face and stone in the prison yard jumping into stark clarity. The air rumbled, the white light flashed, and Sophia shielded her eyes from a sudden ball of flame, a small sun streaking so low and straight across the sky that she felt the need to duck from her high place on the Razor. Sound popped in the air, a clap of thunder that brought some screams from the mob, and a trail of fire and smoke traced a pale line across the sky.

The rumble faded as the ball of fire flew from view. Sophia watched it go, and instead of death and a mob and LeBlanc, she thought of hope, a path marked out for her in the sky. The translucent dark came down again, though not in the northeast. That part of the night was blushing pink. The mob had gone dead silent.

"Shoot her!" LeBlanc screamed. "Gendarmes, shoot her!"

René turned to the crowd and lifted his hands. "Are you the playthings of Fate, or can you make your own choice?" The slow, shouted words echoed in the silence, bouncing between the buildings and cliffs. "And if you can choose your answer, does that not answer the question already? Fate has no power when the people choose!"

"Shoot him! Now!" ordered LeBlanc. Men in city blue filtered forward to the scaffold, crossbows raised. One arrow came, but it was halfhearted and flew wide. René pointed at the viewing box.

"Did LeBlanc become premier by the will of a Goddess, or did he choose to rid himself of Allemande and seize the Sunken City?" The ministres stirred in their seats, the prison yard a mass of still bodies. Indecision hung like smog. René yelled, "What do you believe?"

LeBlanc leaned out of the box. "Look at him! Look at how the rich of the Upper City try to protect their own! If you do not leech out their blood, they will leech the life out of you! As they have always done!"

The mob stirred at this, a few murmuring agreement, and then someone shouted, "But she's Commonwealth!" The words released a small storm of noise, and Sophia heard "girl," and "Tom," and "Blackpot Street," and a woman shouted, "She wasn't leeching then!"

Sophia looked down on the restless mob, wondering when the arrows were going to knock her from her perch. LeBlanc appeared to be wondering the same. René caught her eye. The look had been a warning, but for what she didn't know. He walked to the edge of the scaffold, pointing up to LeBlanc.

"Then let him prove it to you!" René shouted. The mob settled back into an agitated listening. "He wants to rule the Sunken City. Then make him prove it. Make LeBlanc prove whether Fate is a Goddess!" He looked back at the box. "Are you willing?"

LeBlanc leaned forward until Sophia thought he might fall out of the box. "I need to prove nothing! I am the premier!" He sounded like a maniac.

Sophia's eyes darted to the base of the scaffold. Tom had gotten free of the post, but his hands were still tied, and between weakness and his bad leg, he was hobbling up the steps, unhelped, and yet unimpeded by the guards. René ran over and grabbed Tom's arms, pulling him up onto the platform. "Prove it!" Tom shouted at LeBlanc. "For your divine right to rule them!"

The mob had gone truly quiet again, such an odd silence spreading far and wide below her. René stretched his arm up as high as it could reach, something glinting in his hand. It was a coin. Sophia let out her breath. She knew what René was about to do.

"I will spin this coin, and ask the Goddess Fate to reveal herself and answer the question, 'Are you real?'"

But wasn't René's coin weighted to fall to face? Wouldn't that make the answer yes?

"If the Goddess is real," he continued, "then LeBlanc rules. He can put the Red Rook, her brother, and me to the Razor. If she is not real, then the Red Rook will destroy the Tombs."

Sophia felt her mouth open just a little. She turned her head carefully to look over her shoulder toward the prison entrance, then back to René. He hadn't disabled the firelighter; he had reset it. It was a strange time to feel that little rush of happiness, but joy did not think logically. What time had he set it for? Then she looked out at the rosy half-light spilling from the northeast. It was almost dawn. And the prison yard was packed with people.

"The Red Rook is not a spirit and she is not divine!" LeBlanc was shouting. The people were murmuring again, some looking up to the path of smoke still hanging across the sky. "She is nothing but a woman! A girl! She cannot destroy a prison!"

"She has already emptied it!" Tom shouted, but his voice was weak.

René turned again to the crowd. "The Tombs are empty! Fate was to have two out of three in the prison, but she cannot. The Rook has led them out, on La Toussaint, because their city, because he . . ." René pointed at LeBlanc. "He would put them to death! Not Fate!"

"Enough!" said LeBlanc. He spread out the black arms of his long hanging robes, the streak in his hair bright in the dim. "I am the premier of the City of Light, and the instrument Fate has used to make her will known!" His voice was authoritative and sure as it echoed. "The Goddess has decreed that the Red Rook dies. It is already done!"

"And who did Fate decree should die at highmoon?" Tom shouted.

René shouted it louder. "And who was supposed to die at highmoon? Did anyone die?"

"Gendarmes! Remove these men and let Fate's will be done . . ." The gendarmes did not move. It was as if the entire prison yard had been cursed with doubt. Except for Sophia, who had never been more certain of anything in her life. René was here, he was real, and he knew what he was doing.

"Let the Goddess speak!" she cried out. "Spin the coin. If the Goddess is real, she will tell us. But if not, then I will destroy the Tombs, and the people of the Sunken City will choose their next leader, Upper and Lower together. Do you accept the challenge, Premier?"

LeBlanc leaned out the window of his box, looking up at her on top of the scaffold like a fly he wished to swat. She could see his hands shaking. She could also see two or three of the ministres moving quietly down the steps of the viewing box and away. Like rats from a sinking ship. Then LeBlanc's face became suddenly serene, and he raised his arms again.

"I accept! But we will toss the coin, not spin. The toss of the coin is the proper way to speak to the Goddess!"

Sophia's heart banged hard in her chest. René was good at flipping that coin. But she had only ever seen him purposely catch it on face, and they needed it to say facade. He looked up at her, and smiled with half his mouth. Sophia smiled back. "Move the people away from the prison!" she yelled, looking down. "Move them away from the prison building!"

To Sophia's surprise, a group of gendarmes near the prison doors obeyed and began scooting people forward, shifting the crowd, a remarkably silent process.

René held up the coin again. "Who will witness the toss?"

The executioner and his men seemed to have slipped away as well, but a man with the arms of a metal worker or a liftman climbed the steps. He had a mask of Fate swinging by its strings around his neck. "I will witness."

The mob was still shifting, making room for those trying to move away from the prison building. Sophia looked up at the sky. The torches almost weren't needed now. She concentrated on her balance, legs aching from the strain as René went to stand behind the stone altar, the man with the mask of Fate with him. Tom had sunk down to sit on the scaffold, still trying to work his hands free.

"Are you ready, Albert?" René yelled. "Will you call the toss?"

The two ministres still left in the box sat forward. "Face is yes, and facade is no," LeBlanc shouted. "That is the proper way!"

"Face yes, and facade no," René repeated for the crowd. "Then ask her!" he said to LeBlanc, holding the coin aloft. People were still finding places to stand, some crawling up onto the scaffold itself, eager to see the truth.

"Ask her, LeBlanc!" said Tom.

Sophia held her breath.

"Goddess!" LeBlanc cried, his eyes closed. "Answer the Sunken City! Are you real?"

René flipped the coin and it went sailing into the air, glinting in the first ray of the dawn that came shooting over the cliff edge and between the buildings.

Spear stood in the stinking dark of cell 522, the firelighter in his palm, the wheel in the back pointing to the symbol of the rising sun. The soft *tick*, *tick*, *tick* and his thoughts were all he could hear. He'd pushed the knob in. There would be no explosion, and now there was nothing. He could not cry; he could not even feel. Sophia was gone, and probably Tom, too, by this time. And what was he without them? Nothing. Just like what he felt. Nothing.

Why hadn't she told him what she'd set out to do? Why had she never, ever looked to him? It didn't matter, in the end. He'd driven her down this path. It was his fault she had died, as much as if he'd thrown the lever. Had she been frightened on that scaffold, he wondered? Or had she stood her ground? Both. Sophie had done both. And she had come so close to achieving the impossible.

Suddenly, Spear smiled. And so he would do this for her now. He would give her the last thing he could. Spear set the firelighter back in its barrel and pulled out the knob. Then he sat down on the floor, still smiling, surrounded by Bellamy fire, and closed the cool blue of his eyes, letting the mechanism *tick, tick, tick* . . .

The coin turned, and turned, and turned again in the air, flashing gold in the dawn light. Sophia gripped the rope, LeBlanc leaned out of his viewing box, the man with the mask of Fate tracked the coin with his eyes. René stepped back and Tom had his head in his hands. The people of the city waited. The coin hit the stone of the altar with the tiny echo of a clink, and there came a muffled *BOOM* from somewhere deep below them.

The Razor trembled, making Sophia sway for balance on its top, four more booms in rapid succession, and then one mighty explosion that rocked the wood beneath her feet. She swung out on the rope before she fell, hearing screams and panic and a roar that made her turn her head to the prison even as she spun crazily through the air. The building that squatted over the Tombs hovered for just a moment, and then it was falling, collapsing in on itself, sinking down and inward as if the earth had opened its mouth and swallowed, exhaling a thick, rolling cloud of dust.

Sophia shinnied down the rope. The world was shaking, the hole that had eaten the prison building slowly opening wider, the surface cascading down, creating a stampede of people running in the opposite direction. Another explosion, this one with a flash of fire and wind and a noise that left her ears ringing, and then rain fell, a heavy rain, all scattered bits and pieces. The panic of the fleeing crowd intensified as they were pelted, and Sophia saw a larger piece fly past and shatter on the scaffold. One part of her brain registered that what had just sailed past her head was a skull. That it was raining bones. But the bigger part of her was intent on surviving.

Her feet hit the wood of the platform and an arm came around her, pulling her into a run. René had her, Tom on his other side, and he was dragging both of them across a scaffold that was suddenly tilting uphill. The ground was giving way. LeBlanc's viewing box fell, though whether he was in it or not she didn't know. And then they were enveloped in a choking cloud of smoke and dirt.

"Jump!" René yelled.

Sophia pushed off the edge of the scaffold as it tumbled downward into a hole, the Razor collapsing with it. They hit the paving stones hard, but just enough to stumble; the ground had not been all that far away.

"Tom!" she said, pulling him upright. "Move!"

They all three began a slow run, tripping over bricks and bones, the rumbling beneath them slowing and softening to only the occasional fall of stone somewhere deep below. The prison yard had nearly emptied, but there was a thick ring of people around the edge of it, a fence of bodies. They stopped before them, and Sophia turned to look back.

The first light shone down on air that was hazy with dust, and where the prison building and the Razor had been was a great, smoking, rubbish-heaped pit. She looked up to the cliffs and saw people there as well, pressed against the iron fences, and even higher up, black specks thronging the balconies and air bridges. Above that was the white line of smoke pointing the way across the sky. She felt Tom grab her harder, his legs giving way beneath him.

She let him slide to the ground, and then looked to the semi-circle of people, a buffer of awe making an uncrossable space between them. But when she spoke she did not sound like a spirit, or even the Red Rook.

"Can someone help my brother?" she yelled. "Please! Can you help my brother?"

"Sophie!" Justin was pushing his way to the front of the silent throng. "Here, come with me . . ." Tom's eyes were rolling into the back of his head. René came around and got beneath his shoulders while Justin picked up Tom's legs. René's face and hair were dulled by dust, mouth pressed as he lifted Tom. But he was whole. Sophia had that feeling of being another Sophia, from another time; she couldn't believe that he was here, that Tom was here. That the Tombs were gone.

"Make way!" Justin said, backing his way through the crowd. "Let us through!"

The people parted, one or two hands reaching out to touch her back as she followed René down the opening path. Something tickled her neck, and Sophia reached up and discovered the rook feather still perched in her hair.

Someone gave them a cart, and soon they were on Blackpot Street, carrying Tom into Justin and Maggie's house, a small shanty of planks and scrap boards that had at one time been Mémé Annette's. They put Tom on the bed, and Maggie went for water, dipping from the barrel in the corner, where they kept the boiled water. Where it had always been. Sophia helped her get some of it into Tom's mouth, relieved when he sputtered and choked, his eyes flying open long enough to drink half of it on his own. Tom laid his head back on the coarse sheets, breathing deeply.

"He's wasted to nothing," Maggie said, while Justin shooed sleepy children back into the bedroom they shared. "I'll heat some broth." She kissed Sophia's cheek.

Justin came back out and spoke to Maggie quietly while Sophia sponged some of the dirt and blood away from Tom, but Sophia could hear them planning. No one knew what had become of LeBlanc, or who was taking orders from whom. All the children but the baby would go to Maggie's sister. The neighbors would make sure they had warning. Just in case.

And then Sophia's head swiveled around, a little panicked, but she found René almost immediately, standing against the wall with his hands in his pockets and a great rent in his shirt, looking a little out of place. He held out an arm, and she crossed the tiny room as if she'd been pulled. He held her tight, cradling her head while Maggie cleaned Tom's face and stirred a pot, and the newest baby cried in the other room. They sank down to the dirt floor, a surface so shiny it looked polished, without ever really letting go. René leaned back against the wall, her arms around him, and held her chin so that she had to look at him.

"You believe me?" he said.

"Yes. And you won't leave me?"

"No," he whispered. He drew her head onto his chest. "My love." Sophia closed her eyes. A drowsy contentment was flowing through her, a sense of the poles of the world shifting again into their rightful place.

"René," she whispered, a little surprised. "I've gotten your shirt wet." She hadn't even realized she was crying.

"It could only be a help." He sounded exhausted.

"What did the coin say?"

"Hmm?"

"You didn't catch it; you let it fall. On the altar."

She felt him smile against her head. "What is it you say? I think it is, 'No bloody idea'? Everything blew up and I did not even see it."

She laughed once, a sound that was mostly breath, and tightened her encircling arms. "I'm glad you had it with you."

"What?" he murmured.

"Your trick coin."

"Ah. I think . . . I left that in my other pants."

Sophia frowned in the darkness behind her eyelids. "Then what did you toss?"

"A coin I found in the . . . gendarme's pocket."

Something in her mind registered that he had risked everything on that toss. She clung a little tighter, cheek against the warm skin of his chest where the cloth was ripped, listening to a heartbeat, feeling the rise and fall of his breath as it slowed.

Tom opened his eyes to slivers of sunshine peeking through the tiny holes in the roof and the smell of broth on a fire. And when he turned on his side he saw his sister sitting on the floor, her face on René Hasard's chest, the back of her head covered with his hair. They were both asleep.

25

The sun was high when Justin came again, saying he'd found a landover driver willing to take them to the coast, though the driver would not enter the Lower City. So they would borrow a trader's cart to get Tom to the Seine Gate.

"But the gates are all open," Justin said. "No gendarmes anywhere. And there's a crowd outside."

Sophia looked back to the fire. René was on his knees beside her, tending the cut LeBlanc had put on her arm, while Tom sat up in the bed, cleaner now but still with a beard, wearing René's gendarme coat to cover up some of his prison raggedness. She didn't want to think about a crowd. She was no deity, and certainly no saint. She winced as René tied the cloth tight. At least she had not needed stitches.

Justin said, "They're also saying in the market that LeBlanc has been taken."

Sophia frowned. She'd hoped LeBlanc was lying crushed beneath the rubble of his own prison. "Who has taken him?" René asked.

Justin shrugged. "The mob. The Lower City. They say they have him locked in a loo." Justin glanced at Sophia once, before he looked to Tom, shifting his feet. "Do you want to see him, before you go?"

Sophia met Maggie's quick gaze, where she sat rocking her baby. Justin was asking if Tom wanted an eye for an eye, so to speak. It was Lower City justice.

"René?" Tom said. "You have as much reason as me."

René paused his tying and looked around at Tom, and shook his head. Tom turned back to Justin.

"Who is in charge of the city?"

Justin shrugged. "No one knows. But in the market they're saying that the Rook has given them leave to choose a new leader. That we will choose a new leader."

Tom said, "Then let them keep on choosing. And let the people of the city decide what to do with him."

Sophia hugged Maggie and kissed Justin's cheek before climbing into the cart. Blackpot Street and its alleys were swarming, gathering even more bodies as they wound their way up to the Seine Gate. But it was a quiet multitude, introspective rather than raucous, and Sophia found it uncomfortable to be the center of their undivided attention. She was relieved when they switched to the landover and could close the curtains, but René leaned over and opened them again.

"I think your brother would like to see the sun," he said.

So Sophia watched the passing streets of a quiet Upper City from the shelter of René's arms, which she seemed unwilling to do without for very long. One or two people were on the streets, repairing doors and sweeping up the mess, but it was like the city was at rest after a sickness. Or maybe like a field after the battle: a needed pause, almost blissful after the chaos, but with the ramifications of all that had happened still yet to be understood. They passed a young gendarme, the first she'd seen all day, uniform covered in dirt and mud, walking down the sidewalk with a small pack over one shoulder.

"Wait," Sophia said. "Stop! That's Cartier!"

Tom leaned forward to look out the window and René banged hard on the roof, signaling for the driver to stop. The landover slowed, pulling to the side of the road, and Sophia opened the door to wave Cartier in. He trotted down the pavement.

"Thought I'd been left behind," he said, crawling in beside Tom.

"You nearly were," René replied. "Did my uncles forget you? Or was it Maman?"

"Your uncles, I think, Monsieur." Cartier seemed unfazed. "Not much blame to them, though. It was a mess down at the prison."

"And they all left for the coast? Uncle Émile, and Benoit?"

"*Oui,* sir," said Cartier, mixing his Parisian and his Commonwealth.

"Was Spear with them?" Sophia asked, settling back beneath René's arm.

Cartier looked at her, confused and a little stricken. "But . . . I thought . . ." He didn't go on. Sophia sat up again.

"What's wrong?" she said. "Cartier, what's happened?"

"It was the prison," Cartier said. "Well, it exploded, didn't it? And Mr. Hammond? Wasn't he the one that exploded it?" Cartier had switched fully into Commonwealth now, and was speaking quickly. "I was with Monsieur's uncles, all of us dressed as gendarmes, and we were ready to nab the two of you as soon as you came out the prison doors, but you came from the other way, and there was no way to get to you, not with all the people, and . . . Miss Bellamy went up the scaffold and I didn't want to look . . ."

Tom nodded. "Go on."

"So I looked down, and I was standing on a drain, and way down below me, there was Mr. Hammond, in one of the tunnels, and he was dressed like a gendarme, too."

Sophia sat back, thinking of the uniform Spear had used so often when they came to the city, but René's red brows came down. "How could you see him?"

"He had a lantern, and . . . he's just not so hard to recognize, is he? But the thing is, I was looking at him when the Razor came down. I know he thought you were dead, Miss. I did, too. Until I saw you climbing on top. And when I looked back into the tunnel again, Mr. Hammond was gone. That's why I went looking for him . . . after . . ."

Sophia sat forward, her face in her hands. She felt an ache take residence in the center of her chest, a piercing pain that was going to be difficult to bear. Had Spear gone back into the Tombs to unset the firelighter, or to set it again? She would never know. But either way, it had been for her. Right or wrong, everything he'd done had always been for her. Perhaps the guilt was going to be just as hard to live with as the pain. She looked up from her hands and met Tom's eyes, wondering if her face looked as wounded as his. "How many died at the prison today?" she asked Cartier.

"There were a fair few hurt, Miss, but I only helped bury Mr. Hammond."

She made sure the boy was looking at her before she said, "Thank you, Cartier. For everything." She stared out the window as the city passed, silent but for the tears streaming down her face.

They drove straight through the Saint-Denis Gate, no guards, not even a pause through the cemeteries, where most of the flowers and the black and white masks of the Goddess had been pulled down.

Cartier went to sleep almost instantly, leaning his peach-fuzzed cheek against the velvet-lined wall. Sophia laid her head in René's lap, soothed by the rocking motion and the wheels and René's hand in her hair. She closed her eyes. But she could not sleep. She ached too much. After a long time of stillness, she heard Tom say, very quietly, "When did you see him last?"

"Last night at the cliffs," René replied, "climbing out of the Lower City. He cut my rope when I was about halfway up. But it was my rope, placed there for a reason. I knew where to fall."

She could hear Tom rubbing the unfamiliar hair on his chin. "I take it he had the Bonnard denouncement forged."

"Yes. I saw the original. He was carrying it with him after your arrest. You requested it, am I right? Because you thought the Hasards would choose to remove the Ministre of Trade from his post? To keep their fortune?"

"I wasn't going to let my sister marry just anyone, you know."

"You were right to look. We are not all we seem, that is true." After a moment René said, "Someone hired the hotelier of the Holiday to attack me. He knew where we were hiding, knew what room I slept in. I had thought it was Hammond. But he said no, in the prison, and now I am inclined to believe him."

Sophia stayed very still beneath the safety of René's hand.

Tom said, "I told him to look. To go to LeBlanc and offer himself up, if he needed to. See if we couldn't flush someone out of the shadows. Did he find out . . ."

"I do not think he ever stopped believing it was me."

"I don't want you to think . . . ," Tom sighed. "Spear wasn't a bad man." She could hear the grief in her brother's voice. It started her tears again, leaking onto René's lap.

René said, "I think, perhaps, that he loved her too well."

The landover wheels rattled over ruts. She could almost hear Tom thinking, choosing his words. "I wouldn't have sanctioned it, you know. We never had the conversation because I knew Sophie didn't . . . and Spear was family to us." Tom took another moment. "But he would never have been happy with my sister. It was like . . . like he thought there were two Sophies: the one she is now, and the one she would be just as soon as she decided to settle down with him. And it was the Sophie to come that he loved too well, not the one she was. That she is. But Sophia isn't going to change. You know this?"

René laughed without humor. "Oh, I know this." He stroked her hair just a little. "I should tell you that the Hasard fortune is lost. I do not know what will happen in the city, but I would guess it will take some time, years perhaps, to put our finances back in order. There will be no fee. Not in time."

"And she says she will have you, anyway."

"Yes. She does."

Tom adjusted his bad leg. "A lot has changed since I crossed the Channel Sea."

"That is so."

"The Commonwealth won't recognize it."

"We could go to Spain," René suggested.

"They won't recognize it, either, not with her citizenship."

"Ah, but it is so much easier to lie about such things in Spain."

"What would you do there?"

"No bloody idea." He paused. "It is my new phrase."

"Our father might have something to say about it."

"As will Sophia, and as will my *maman*. We can all gamble on that."

"Sophie lied to me about our father, when we were in the prison. I would guess this means he's not well."

"He is grieving. And he blames his daughter for his grief."

"I see," Tom sighed. "And now he'll go to prison, grieved or not, and we are going to lose the house. Unless we find another Parisian suitor for my sister in the next . . . what is it now? Five days? I'm afraid I've lost track."

"Three, I think."

"Right you are. But I suppose everyone involved will object to that plan now." Sophia almost smiled.

"And what about you, Monsieur? Do you . . . how did you say, do you 'sanction' this?"

Sophia tried to relax her body, to not alert René to just how very awake she was. She waited for Tom's answer, René rhythmically stroking her head.

Finally her brother said, "Why don't you call me Tom?"

Sophia rocked with the movement of the landover, eyes still closed, sure she was failing at hiding a little bit of her smile. She was torn between grief for the man who wasn't there, and love for the two who were. But what were they to do now? René didn't want to go to Spain. There was nothing for him there. And what about Tom? She wouldn't be leaving him behind with no house, no inheritance, and the responsibility of their father. Neither Tom nor René would be sacrificing for her. Not if she had anything to do with it.

Then she felt René go tense beneath her. Tom hit the landover roof, and the vehicle slowed. She sat up, wiping her eyes. They were on the cliff road, nearly to the sea, and Cartier had startled awake as well, looking at them all blearily. It took a moment to see what Tom and René had, but when she did, Sophia opened the door of the landover before it had even slowed to a stop and went running toward an open green field. The trees bordering the field had been broken, a line of splintered branches showing a path from the air, and in the grass there was a burn mark, like a long, blackened rut made from a giant wheel. And at the end of this lay . . . something.

She approached it carefully, a giant chunk of gray, twisted metal, a large tank of some sort, and other parts sticking up and out that were completely unfathomable, all of it showing the warp and stress of intense heat. It was still warm, smoking or maybe even steaming in the cool air, pieces and parts scattered beneath her feet; the grass around burned in a giant ring. She touched the metal gingerly with a finger. This was a satellite, an Ancient machine fallen from the sky, and it was also, she guessed, what had flown over the prison yard when she stood on top of the Razor. What possible use could this thing have been, so high over anyone's head? And why had it returned to the earth now? She heard the others coming through the unburnt grass, and bent down to pick up a piece of metal near her feet. Just discernable were four small, stamped letters: NASA.

"How many people alive right now have ever seen such a thing?" Tom asked from behind her, sitting down carefully in the debris-strewn grass. He was breathing hard, either from excitement or exhaustion. It had taken his strength to walk that field.

"I don't know. But I've been seeing lights in the sky since the night I went to the Holiday," Sophia replied.

"There were dozens while you were in the prison," René said. "Many at once. Perhaps the satellite was much bigger, and now it is broken. Coming down in pieces."

"Cartier," said Tom. "Can you run back to the landover and see if you can find paper and a pen? See if the driver has anything . . ."

René sat beside Sophia in the grass, staring at the smoking machine while they waited for Tom to finish his frantic sketching. René said, "What happens in the past does not seem to ever go away, does it?"

"I suppose not. Or not all of it," she replied. "But we can always make sure that it doesn't happen again. Or that it does."

"Ah. But then we just cannot forget that it happened in the first place, can we?"

She thought about this, fingering her piece of scavenged, Ancient metal. "Is that the real reason you steal the plastic?" she asked. "So that we cannot forget?"

"Yes," he said. "It is."

"I will not be forgetting Spear."

"No, my love. I do not think you will."

When the landover reached the end of the cliff road, Sophia saw two ships anchored beyond the surf, in the deeper part of a natural harbor. Three masts each, their sails down, the occasional wave breaking white against a hull. They were beautiful, and they were real, and they had been here, waiting. How could she have thought otherwise?

By the time they got down the cliff path and a boat rowed out to them, the nethersun was bleak and nearing the end of its time, shining slanting rays on a full and busy deck.

"René," said Madame, lifting a painted cheek to receive his kiss as he swung his legs over the rail. "You are very late. I have nearly told Andre to sail without you."

"I am happy to see you, too, Maman," René said.

"And Miss Bellamy," Madame added, an afterthought as Sophia clambered up the rope ladder. "You appear to have been rolling in mud."

"How very pleasant to see you, Madame."

René sighed, and then helped a sailor lower a rope for Tom. Émile kissed her hand before hurrying on to his own business,

Andre gave her a small smile, but Benoit took her by the shoulders and kissed both of her cheeks. "I am happy to see you well and whole, Mademoiselle."

"And I you, Benoit. Do you know how many we have on board?"

"One hundred and twenty-three refugees between the two ships . . . ," Benoit began.

"So few?"

"There were eight lost on the way. They have been buried on the cliff side. Others chose not to board, but to make their way to family or friends in other places."

"I see." Sophia clutched the rail, still finding her sea legs. René and a sailor were hauling up Tom, his head just cresting the deck. "And is Jennifer Bonnard on this ship?"

"She is in a cabin below. Water and food have been a help, and I have had Peter inject her with penicillin . . ."

Sophia looked again at Benoit, impressed. Penicillin good enough to inject was expensive. Very expensive. Benoit gave her a self-satisfied shrug. She saw Cartier helping Tom across the deck, to the hatch that led below. Probably he'd just received the same information about Jennifer that she had. "Are we ready to sail?" she asked Benoit.

"We have waited only for you, and now we wait for the destination."

"Oh, well, Bellamy House, of course. Don't you think? If we aren't going to have it much longer, then we might as well put it to good use while we do. Straight west across the Channel, then a half mile sail up the coast."

Andre, who had been listening to this, nodded once and moved quickly to the helm while Benoit looked at her curiously. "And what will you do when you get there, Mademoiselle?"

Sophia let out a long, slow breath. She didn't quite know how to answer him. But she had been thinking.

Benoit said, "I see that you are scheming." She gave him a look of innocent surprise, and Benoit made a little Parisian *pfft* sound. "Of course you are scheming. But may I offer you advice?"

She waited. Benoit's advice was generally very good.

"Do not try to please her."

Her gaze jumped to Madame Hasard, lifting her elegant dress to go belowdecks. "And why would you say that, when I am in need of her approval?"

"Because she will not respect it. It has always been her way."

Now it was her turn to look curiously at this nondescript, enigmatic little man who spoke no Commonwealth and seemed to be in charge of the ships and, to some extent, the Hasards. "How long have you known her?"

Benoit mimicked her look of innocence. "Why, since the day she was born, Mademoiselle." He smiled. "Perhaps you did not know that Madame is my sister?"

Sophia felt her eyes widen, sure her mouth must be hanging open. "But I thought . . . you were a . . ."

Benoit tilted his head at her. "And why would you think that?" He was smiling genuinely now while Sophia's mind swept the deck, mentally counting uncles. Émile speaking quietly to René, Andre at the helm, Peter, Enzo, and Francois presumably on the other ship. What a prat she'd been. René had told her his mother had six brothers. Why had she never noticed that she'd only been introduced to five? Or even considered that their surname could not be Hasard?

"In any case, what sort of uncle would I be, Mademoiselle, to allow René to run about the Commonwealth, getting engaged on his own? He might get into trouble. Do you not agree?"

Sophia closed her mouth and returned the man's smile. "Of course I agree. And so, what exactly is your name, Benoit?"

"Benoit is our family name, Mademoiselle."

"Then what is your first . . ."

"I prefer Benoit. Just Benoit."

She wondered what given name could possibly be so bad that Benoit would prefer his own family not to use it. Surely it couldn't be worse than "Francois Benoit." Or perhaps it could.

Benoit took her hand and kissed it. "Do not try to please her, Mademoiselle. It is my best advice."

"Call me Sophia," she said, before he melted away into the shadows.

The middlesun was hidden behind thick clouds when Sophia's boots hit the shallow water of the Bellamy beach. She splashed and ran across the pebbly sand, leaving René and Benoit and Tom to get out of the boat. Orla was standing at the end of the cliff path, waiting for her. She must have spotted the ships and come running herself.

"Well, you need a wash, don't you?" she said in Orla fashion, pulling away from Sophia's hug. But Sophia had seen the tension leave her shoulders when she recognized Tom getting out of the boat. She dreaded telling her who wouldn't be getting out of the boat.

"How is Father?"

"Not well," Orla replied.

Sophia grimaced. "Has the sheriff been here?"

"Yesterday."

"Will he give us any extra time?"

"I think not."

"Right. Let's see what Tom can do, then. And, Orla . . ."

She saw Orla's eyes fix beyond her shoulder, where she was certain there must be another ship coming in. "We have the entire Hasard family, including René's mother, and one hundred and twenty-three extra people coming to stay. And some of them will be sick, and . . ." she met Orla's gaze ". . . they will have prison lice. Most of them. Or all of them."

Orla's face remained expressionless. "Well. We'll see if Nancy can bring in her husband and daughters for a few days, and if she can kill some ducks. I'll find more coal and get the oil and the combs. How long will they be here?"

Sophia smiled. She was glad to be home. Even if it was just for a little while.

By dusk Sophia had oiled her own hair, tied it in a kerchief, bunked René in with Tom, put the uncles on the ships, Jennifer in her own room, and helped Orla fill the ballroom with pallets for everyone else. By tomorrow, perhaps they could get one or two of the better bedrooms ready. Madame Hasard she had put in the more recently cleaned north wing, though the woman had not been happy about it, making her views clear as they passed in a corridor.

"I would have thought you could make your guests more comfortable, Miss Bellamy."

Having just left the bedside of a sick child with prison dirt still on his face, Sophia had found it necessary to actually bite her tongue.

"And your father has taken to his bed, I hear," she continued.

"Stop it, Maman!" René had warned from behind her. He was hauling buckets of water up the stairs. Madame ignored him.

"Isn't that considered rather . . . weak in the Commonwealth, Miss Bellamy?" Madame ventured. "I thought you were all for self-sufficiency here."

Sophia had merely walked down the hall and shut a door behind her, putting a barrier between them, just as she was shutting the door to her father's room now, attempting to block out what was on the other side. Though there were people all over the house, it was quiet outside Bellamy's room, mostly because the prisoners were exhausted and in need of rest now that they had been fed; probably that wouldn't be the case tomorrow. She sank down along the polished paneling until she was seated on the floor, St. Just immediately crawling into her lap.

Her father had been refusing food and he'd drunk very little since she'd left for the Sunken City; now he was as wasted beneath his blankets as Tom. Only Tom would heal, was already healing, while her father was determined not to. He did react to Tom's voice, however, giving him a slight squeeze of his hand. Sophia had stayed back, fearful of distressing him.

She looked up as Tom came out of Bellamy's room, still bearded and in the uniform jacket of the Upper City. He sat down beside her with a little difficulty, stretching out his bad leg. He took her hand.

"Sophie," he said. "Father's gone."

She said nothing, just frowned and petted St. Just. For a few blissful moments she felt nothing but numb shock.

"I tried to do the right thing," she said.

"I know you did."

"Do you think he ever forgave me?"

Tom put his arms around her. "Yes, Sophie. I think he did."

They both knew Tom couldn't know that, but Sophia chose to be comforted by it, anyway. First Spear, and now her father. The five of them reduced to three. Her grief for both of them was flavored with guilt the way salt flavors the sea; she could taste it in the tears.

—

It was after highmoon when Sophia stood in the Bellamy stables, watching Cartier get Tom's horse ready, Spear's horse and her own beside it. Nancy's husband had been caring for them all together in Cartier's absence. She was grieved, still dirty, and so tired she could barely stay on her feet. Jennifer Bonnard stood beside her, not much better though her fever was gone, also unwilling not to see Tom off. Sophia held her up, and had a suspicion that Jennifer might be doing the same for her. Tom mounted from his good leg, grimacing at the pain from his bad one.

"I'll see you up on the hill first thing," Sophia said. They were burying their father there at dawn, like people did in the years after the Great Death. No coffins and no fuss. "And don't start any fires!" she added.

Tom rolled his eyes once. "I'm not an idiot, Sophie." But then he smiled at her through his sadness, and smiled even more at Jennifer. He turned the horse and rode out of the stable, toward the A5 and Graysin Lane. It was going to be difficult for him to be at the Hammond farm, but there was no better place for him to hide on short notice. He might not be able to prove his ability to inherit his father's estate, but the Commonwealth saw no problem in the world with Tom inheriting his father's debt. They would have Mr. Halflife and Sheriff Burn on them. Soon.

"Will they arrest him?" Jennifer asked.

"Not if they can't find him." Her meager plans, begun in her head during the landover ride, had not changed in light of her father's death. Now, it was just Tom she was keeping out of prison, instead of her father. And she would see her brother back in a prison cell over her own dead body.

"I knew it was you," Jennifer said, looking over at Sophia. "I recognized you that night, when you shook out your hair. You always

did that when we were children. But I told them it was him. I suppose because I knew you so much better, and . . ." She ran a hand
over her head, the hair grown out only a little from its ragged cut for
the Razor. "I told Tom what I did, when we were in the Tombs, and
he said I did the right thing. Why do you think he would say that?"

Because he is Tomas Bellamy, Sophia thought, though she didn't
know quite how to express that to Jennifer.

"I think it is because he is the best man in the world," Jennifer
said. "That's why."

Sophia looked again at Jennifer. They'd been little girls the last
time they'd spent any real time together, Sophia having moved
beyond dolls and quiet games beside a fire rather quickly. She'd
never felt sorry about that, not until now. Now she was wondering
just what sort of friend she might have missed.

She gave Jennifer one slightly ferocious hug, careful of her bandaged arms, picked up the lantern, and hurried out of the stable
without another word, St. Just at her heels. The sharp air whipped
past her face, stinging her cheeks as she made her way across the
autumn dead grasses of the lawn. Someone's foxes were barking in
the distance, and St. Just barked back. She rounded the corner of
Bellamy House and found Émile waiting for her, his fading red hair
pale in the highmoon light, arms crossed as he leaned against the
house stones. He was in the fancy breeches and waistcoat of her
engagement party, evidently preferring that to the stolen uniform of
a city gendarme.

"I thought perhaps you were not coming, Miss Bellamy," he said.
"I was very sorry to hear of your father."

"Thank you, Émile." She retrieved the key and unlocked the
door to the sanctuary. "It just makes our meeting all the more urgent,
I'm afraid."

He followed her light down the winding stairs, the skitter of St. Just's claws moving ahead of them. Émile said, "I find Bellamy House fascinating, Mademoiselle. Pieces of the Time Before are everywhere. It is remarkable. And I have just discovered something else remarkable. My elder brother has confided his identity to you."

"Yes. I was a bit peeved with your nephew for not telling me that himself."

"Ah. I would never discourage you from being cross with René, Mademoiselle. It is good for him. But the fact that Benoit has told you is . . ."

He waited so long to complete his sentence that Sophia turned around on the stairs. Émile was grinning at her. Oh, dear. Daughter stealer. "I am impressed," he said, "that is all."

"And why is that?"

"Because it is a mark of particular trust. Benoit considers you one of the family."

She smiled as she continued down the stairs. "Your sister doesn't agree."

"Adèle will not give up her place easily."

"Her place?"

"I am meaning her son, Mademoiselle."

"Well. I am going to outplay her, Émile. If I can."

"And how will you do that?"

"By giving René the marriage fee, which he can then pay to me, and we can pay our debts and keep my brother from going to prison." She glanced back over her shoulder again. "She has already signed."

Émile was grinning from both sides of his mouth now. "So she has. Forgive me, Miss Bellamy, but if the fee is even more than your father's debt, how do you propose to raise such a sum on short notice, when you could not do so before?"

They entered the sanctuary, and Émile's eyes widened. "That is why I wanted to meet with you. I'm beginning to wonder what the Bellamy family has that might have been previously . . . under-valued. So, as an honorary member of your family, Uncle Émile . . ." Sophia crossed the patched floor to Tom's display shelf. "What sort of price do you think these things could fetch?"

26

Sophia sank down into the warm bath in front of her bedroom fire, aching inside and out, but incredibly grateful for the hot water she'd discovered. And the cinnamon in her soap. Orla was a heroine.

There had been very little time during the day, but she'd taken some of it to be with Orla. Orla had only ever once been moved to tears in Sophia's memory, and that had been when she was very small, when they lost her mother. And now they had lost her father. And Spear. Seeing Orla cry had made her do the same again, but when she'd tried to explain to her about René, the woman had only waved a hand. "There's no great surprise in wanting to marry your own fiancé, child," Orla said, wiping her eyes, sending her off to bed with a light smack. What had come as a surprise was who she hadn't found when she got there. Jennifer Bonnard had disappeared, and Sophia would have gambled a marriage fee that there was another horse missing from their stables, and an extra one stabled at the Hammond farm. Not that she had a fee to gamble.

Uncle Émile had given her hope for some money from Tom's collection, but not near enough to fund a marriage. She'd taken him to the ballroom gallery to see the statue of the Looking Man as well, a piece that made him say things like, "Ah, extraordinary!" and "I am amazed!" But he did not think the statue would bring actual money. Or not very quickly. Even with his connections.

"A collector wishes for small things, things he can put discreetly on a shelf and move when needed. With this . . . the transportation alone would be dangerous and difficult. A museum might risk it, but not for a tenth of its worth, Mademoiselle."

But he was taking René and Enzo and Andre up to the west fields to dig the next day, to see what could be found. Even one plastic bottle with its label on, he'd said, especially the ones with the mysterious word DIET, could bring what she needed with the right buyers, though finding one surviving in that kind of condition was rare. Very rare. It was a nebulous hope to be sure, and much less concrete than her offer from Mrs. Rathbone.

Mrs. Rathbone had come calling in what should have been their after-dinner time, though nothing was regular at Bellamy House at the moment. Sophia had just set off to find René when she spotted a flowered hat in the drawing room.

"Mrs. Rathbone?" Sophia inquired, backtracking to the door. She'd had her head wrapped up and was still in her filthy breeches, face streaked with dirt and tears. "I thought you were in the Midlands."

Mrs. Rathbone sat herself straighter in the chair before Sophia could say more. "I haven't come to chat, Miss Bellamy, though it looks to me as if we could chat all night. You seem to have been doing things I would find interesting. But as I was saying, that isn't what I came for. I have come to remind you about my offer to buy Bellamy House."

Sophia came and sat down heavily in her father's chair, and only then did she notice that Madame was also in the room, legs crossed and with a cup of something hot in her hand. Giving her what Sophia had come to think of as the Hasard eyebrow.

"I wouldn't be able to offer what it's worth, mind," Mrs. Rathbone continued. "Who could?"

Who indeed, Sophia thought. She seemed to be flush with valuable items that could do her absolutely no monetary good.

"But you could come close to the debt. I know you're two days from Bellamy's arrest . . ."

"Actually, Mrs. Rathbone . . ."

". . . and I thought this way you could at least keep the sheriff away. You might prefer it to jail and the house going to Parliament . . ."

"Mrs. Rathbone, Bellamy . . . my father has just . . . died."

"What?"

Sophia saw Madame again raise the one brow. It made her unreasonably indignant, that eyebrow. Was the woman incapable of lifting the other one? Or maybe it was just heartache that made her so irritable. Or Mrs. Rathbone.

"I'm also sorry to tell you that Spear is gone as well, Mrs. Rathbone." The woman sat still in her chair. "He was buried in the Sunken City."

"What?" Mrs. Rathbone repeated. She seemed truly taken aback. "Buried in the city? Whatever happened to him?"

Sophia stared down at the worn place her father's shoes had made in the carpet, started feeling tearful, and with that, her journey to anger was complete. She was not going to talk about what had happened to Spear. She pressed her lips together.

"Well!" said Mrs. Rathbone. "This is not what I was expecting to hear, my dear. Not at all. Then it all falls to you, doesn't it? I am so terribly sorry for you."

"If you mean the debt, Mrs. Rathbone, that falls to my brother, actually."

"Tom? But I thought . . ."

"News is a bit slow coming out of the city right now . . ." There was no telling what the papers would say when they did come. That was probably dependent on who ended up in power as much as the truth. "Tom is free. They had the wrong man."

"So they did," commented Madame Hasard.

Mrs. Rathbone shook her flowered hat. "This visit has taken me by surprise, and no mistake. Not to be crass, Miss Bellamy, but it's getting hard to keep up with which Bellamys are alive and which aren't, who's jailed and who isn't. And what about Monsieur, then? Not to get too personal, Miss Bellamy."

Sophia narrowed her eyes. Perhaps Mrs. Rathbone would also like to know the amount of money in her purse. Madame Hasard tilted her head to one side. "Mrs. . . . . ?"

"Rathbone," Sophia supplied, as if she hadn't already said the name at least ten times. "I assume you've met Monsieur's mother, Madame Hasard?"

Madame said, "I fear that things have not turned out as we had hoped in that regard, Mrs. Rathbone."

Poor woman, Sophia thought, looking at Madame. How hard she must be wishing that lie was true.

"I see." Mrs. Rathbone turned back to Sophia. She was sweating just a bit.

"So," Sophia said, turning the tables, "not that I would wish to get too personal, either, Mrs. Rathbone, but do you have that kind of money? To buy Bellamy House?"

"Oh, I've been putting it by. Your father is . . . Your father was a very dear friend, and I would be very happy to do his children a service. Think on it, Miss Bellamy."

"I'll have to speak to Tom, of course."

"Of course. Shall we say until tomorrow? That should give us time to make any arrangements before . . . well, you know."

After Mrs. Rathbone was gone, Madame Hasard had said, "Will you take the offer, Miss Bellamy? Because I would advise that you do. I would advise it strongly . . ."

Sophia slipped down lower in the tub, keeping the cut on her arm free of the water. She'd felt like giving Madame some advice of her own, but it was advice that Madame would probably rather not follow. She hadn't mentioned any of it to Tom in the end. Or at least not yet. He'd gone straight into hiding at the farm, and maybe the extra day or two that the sheriff couldn't find him would give Émile and René the time they needed to dig up a miracle.

It was when Sophia was in her dressing gown, leaning against the stone casement of her window, drying her hair with a towel, that she saw someone walking furtively across the clipped grass of the lawn. She straightened, blew out her candle, and opened the window slightly to get a better view. She knew only one person who would be tottering in heels across a lawn with a covered lantern. Madame Hasard. She watched as the woman picked her way carefully through the grass, stealing around the corner of the empty print house.

Sophia slipped on her boots, half tied them, flung on a coat, and looked out again. The bottom floor of the print house was a large, open space, and now there was a dim light passing from window to window. She unlatched her own window, swung her legs out, and stepped onto the tiles, this time going up and over her gable rather than sliding down. The air was sharp, biting on her damp head, and she knew by feel that a wintry fog would be on the ground by dawn. She also knew her route, light unneeded. A quick climb, around another gable, and to the flat place between the rooflines that gave an excellent view of the lawns. She was almost unsurprised to see another figure already sitting there.

"What are you doing?"

René looked over his shoulder. "Watching my *maman*. And you?"

"Watching your *maman*."

She saw half of his grin in the dark. She could also see that he'd come more prepared than she had. Two sets of blankets, one to sit on, the other for covering up. The top layer was now being held open for her. "Come here to me," he said.

She came, settling into her usual place between his body and arm. But as he began to wrap the blanket around her, René said, "Is your hair wet?" He muttered something in Parisian and pulled the blanket over both their heads without waiting for an answer, scooting her down until they were covered full length, and she was using his arm for a pillow. It was impenetrable blackness under the blanket, much warmer, and very full of René.

"I am discovering that you require much taking care of, my love." He ran a hand along her arm, where there was a bandage underneath, and then the curve of her side, where one end of her stitches had been. His voice was low, and very close. "Are you well?"

"Not particularly. Though better at this moment." They hadn't been completely alone since the linen closet, and he was distracting her from pain. She found the cut she'd put on his lip by feel in the darkness.

"You smell of cinnamon," he whispered.

He kissed her once, twice, and then he did not stop. She pulled him in, this time with handfuls of his hair, again pinned by his weight, this time to the blanket and the roof tiles beneath, the noise in his chest resonating in hers. He took his mouth away abruptly and put his forehead on the blanket beside her head.

"Why," he asked, voice rough, "are we always on a roof?"

"I'm thinking of climbing one every day," she breathed. She felt him smile in the dark. He lifted his head, and she began very softly kissing the fading bruises on his neck, or at least where she thought they were. The pulse at the base of his throat beat hard against her lips.

"You . . . are driving me mad," he said. "And you make me forget what I came for." He reached up and peeked over the edge of the blanket without interrupting her, then pulled it back over their heads. "The light is in the second floor now," he said. The blast of cold air had been startling. It had become very warm inside their universe beneath the blanket. She laid her head back on the blanket, stroking his hair.

"You came to get me."

She couldn't see his expression when he said, "I will always come for you. Do you believe that?"

"Yes."

"You belong with me."

"Yes."

"And you will stay with me?"

"Yes," she said. But she didn't know how to. He rolled onto his side, holding her cheek against his chest.

"What do you think she is doing?" he asked. He was referring to his mother.

"I was hoping you'd know."

"I do not know anything. She would have died before she signed that paper for LeBlanc. I know it. So why did she? And why push a marriage only to reject you now? What has changed? It makes no sense."

"Did you ask her why?"

"Oh, yes." He chose not to elaborate on the answer. "She has called a meeting of the family tomorrow, at highsun, in your dining room. I told her that Émile and Andre and I could not come, that we had a field to dig, but she insists. I would think we will be discussing what the family does next."

"René," Sophia said. "If you could be anywhere you wanted, do anything you wanted, what would it be? Where would you go?"

He propped himself up on one arm, thoughtful, holding up the blanket with his head. "I would be in the Sunken City, I think, where there was no revolution, sitting around the table in the flat with my uncles. And you would be there, seated well away from Émile, and we would be making plans for our next trip to liberate an artifact from the melters."

"Our trip? You mean you and your uncles'?"

"No. This is my fantasy, and in my fantasy you would wish to come. You would, would you not?"

"Of course. Now go on. We're about to go nick things."

"So we lay out our plans, and our plans would go almost right, but not quite, though we would acquire our item in the end, and then we would hand it over to Benoit and Émile and go . . . somewhere else. For a time."

She leaned up, trying to see the hot blue of his eyes in the darkness beneath the blanket. "Somewhere else?"

"I think so. I enjoy the game, but it would be good to know I do not have to play it, not all the time. Not if I do not want to." He ran a hand over her damp head. "Tomorrow at highsun I am going to tell Maman that I am not going back to the city. That you and I will see your forger and that we will go to Spain, where they do not look at papers with such a close eye. What do you think of that, my love?"

"That you have no interest in living in Spain, and neither do I."

"Ah, but I am very interested in living there with you. Come with me, Sophia. We will take Tom with us, so the Commonwealth will not find him."

She thought of Madame with her perfect hair and pursed lips, and it occurred to her that a woman did not often rise to the place that Madame Hasard had, and she certainly did not do it by indulging in petty dissatisfactions. The woman had some sort of private agenda, and it was not about her son. It was about Sophia, and it was personal.

She peeked over the blanket and whispered, "Look." René lifted his head.

Madame Hasard had come out of the print house and was picking her way back across the lawn with the covered lantern. If Madame dug her high heels in for a fight, which of them would come out on top? Sophia wasn't sure, but she was going to find out. Starting tomorrow.

"Will you go with me?" René whispered. "Say that you will come."

Sophia brought the blanket back over their heads. "Ask me tomorrow. But for now, I am staying right here."

It was well after middlesun when Sophia entered the kitchen of Bellamy House, her head tied again in a kerchief, face dirtied behind round spectacles, wearing a plain cotton dress that was a little frayed. Nancy and her daughters were at a near run, sweating in the heat of cooking.

"Could I bring some soup to Madame?" she asked in loud Parisian. Nancy did not speak Parisian, but she knew what "Madame" meant. She pointed to a pot on the coal cooker, wiping the tears away as she chopped more onions while one daughter frantically washed dishes and the other left with the water bucket. Sophia shook her head as she ladled soup. Nancy's family deserved a medal, or at least a lot of money. But their distraction with a house full of strangers was serving her purpose. If this went badly, it was best that none of them knew a thing about it.

She put the bowl on a tray, left the kitchen behind, walked about halfway up to the north wing, where there were no former prisoners milling, and set the tray on a small table. This was a bizarre way to behave after her father's burial rites, she knew. She should have been spending the rest of her day in quiet mourning, if not helping poor Nancy in the kitchen. But the Bellamys were a bit too desperate for that. Tom would be arrested tomorrow, if they could find him. And she'd already determined what she would risk for René. Which was everything.

She looked left, right, and then emptied the contents of a vial—what she normally kept for filling her ring—into the soup, stirring it in well. She'd really been going through the stuff lately; Tom would have to get more from the hospital in Kent, assuming he wasn't in prison. She picked up the tray, went to the north-wing door, and knocked.

"Enter," Madame called. Sophia stepped inside and Madame glanced up from the letter she was writing, eyes brushing once over the tray, but never high enough to see Sophia's face. "Set that down and you may be on your way."

Madame needed to learn that they asked, not ordered, in Bellamy House, Sophia thought. "Enjoy your soup, Madame," she couldn't help adding in husky Parisian just before she closed the door.

She waited in the dim end of the corridor, biding her time, surprised when not too long after, Madame Hasard opened the door and began a teetering progress down the hall, a black bag in hand, her unbalance having nothing to do with the height of her heels.

Sophia bit her lip. She had intended for Madame to be snoozing on her bed or on the floor. Why could no Hasard ever be drugged properly? Hopefully, anyone who encountered Madame would just think she'd been in the wine. Hopefully, she'd be able to negotiate the stairs. Hopefully, she'd never remember receiving her soup in the first place. In any case, Sophia thought, now was the opportunity. Her only opportunity. When Madame had indeed made her way safely down the stairs, Sophia dashed into her room, locked the door, went straight to the desk, and began to ransack.

It was nearly highsun before Sophia managed to find something interesting in Madame Hasard's room, and that interesting something was sewn into the bodice lining of her silk dress. And it was so interesting that Sophia had to sit down on a chair to read it a second time, a chair that she nearly missed. When she had read the documents a third time, she felt her hazy thoughts focus, sharpened against the whetstone of a hard, grinding fury. It was good to be angry. She much preferred it to being helpless.

She flung the door open, leaving it swinging on its hinges, almost running the corridor to the stairwell. Down, around the corner, down again, and then she was marching over the multicolored floor tiles of the dining room hallway.

"Miss Bellamy! Miss Bellamy!"

She heard the clack of Mrs. Rathbone's not-very-sensible shoes coming up from the front hall. She'd completely forgotten about their meeting.

"Miss Bellamy! Really! Who are all these people in your house? What . . ."

Sophia threw open the door to the waiting room and then burst into the dining room. None of the lanterns were lit behind the glass, only three sets of candles illuminating Benoit, Peter, Enzo, and Francois seated around the table, their conversation coming to a standstill at Sophia's abrupt entrance. She looked at them each in turn.

"How many of you knew?" she said, shaking the documents at them. "Who knew about this? Benoit?"

Then Mrs. Rathbone came through the door in a panting explosion of skirts. *Wesson's* page sixteen, Sophia thought automatically. "Sophia Bellamy, whatever is wrong with you? If this is the way you've been taught to conduct business, it's no wonder the family finances have gone the way of the bulb!"

Francois frowned. "What is a bulb?"

"It is a Commonwealth expression, Franc," Peter explained, "there is no such . . ."

"I want to know about this!" Sophia yelled, shaking the papers.

"Sophia! I insist that you discuss my offer . . ."

Benoit frowned just a little. The mix of Commonwealth and Parisian in the room was confusing. "Tell us what you hold in your hand, Mademoiselle, and then we shall . . ."

And then they all turned as Tom came through the door, his stick in hand.

"What are you doing here?" Sophia said. She thought he'd gone straight back to the farm with Jennifer after the burial. Tom came so quickly across the room that his limp was hardly noticeable, then not noticeable at all in the bloom of rage that erupted over his face when he saw Mrs. Rathbone. Sophia stared. Tom was never angry. Not like her. And not like that.

"Why is she here?" he asked without removing his gaze from Mrs. Rathbone.

"She made me an offer to buy Bellamy House," Sophia replied. "I haven't told you yet . . ."

"Did you accept?" Tom snapped.

"No. I . . ."

"Then ask her where she got the money."

Tom's face had been made into something hard-edged. But there was a hint of a smile from Mrs. Rathbone.

"Ask her!" Tom demanded.

Sophia glanced over at the sound of footsteps in the waiting room, and then René, Émile, and Andre filed in, mud on boots and, in René's case, streaked across his shirt.

"Ask her, Sophie!"

She turned to Mrs. Rathbone. "Where did you get the money to buy Bellamy House?"

Mrs. Rathbone looked at them all, and then she pulled out a chair and sat, her large purse perched on her knees. "Tom would like me to confess. Wouldn't you, Tom?"

27

"*I don't* mind confessing," said Mrs. Rathbone, "because it won't do me any harm or you any good. I've already called on Mr. Halflife and Sheriff Burn to let them know that Bellamy is dead and that you're both back safe and sound, and I've hinted just the tiniest bit that Tom might be taking off to parts unknown. They'll be here quite soon, I think, instead of waiting for tomorrow. But if you sell me Bellamy House . . . Well, then I imagine you can show him the money, as it were, I'll show Mr. Halflife the deed, and your troubles will be over."

Sophia stared at Mrs. Rathbone. Then Tom reached into his jacket and pulled out a piece of paper, much folded, the seal of the Sunken City showing through from the other side. He held it out to Sophia and let her read. It was the denouncement of the Bonnards, the real one. Sophia looked up again. "But . . ."

"Let me guess," René said to Mrs. Rathbone. "Your name before marriage was Jacques."

Sophia's eyes widened at the name on the paper. Mrs. Rathbone smiled. "Yes, indeed. I was born in the Sunken City. I helped Mr. Rathbone set up his trade there. Until Ministre Bonnard taxed the daylights out of imported scrap and put him out of business. I was never very fond of Ministre Bonnard after that."

"And so you sent them to their deaths. And their children! For a law you did not like," said René. Enzo was translating quickly into Benoit's ear.

"LeBlanc was going to pay someone to do it, and it was lucky for me that Bonnard didn't have the sense to take an oath when he needed to. Vengeance is sweet, young man, and money no small matter. As you should well know. Now, about Bellamy House . . ."

"You denounced them," Tom said. His expression was something Mrs. Rathbone should have been frightened of, if she'd had the sense to be frightened. "Then you took them in, pretended to help them, turned them in again, and collected. Again!" René's uncles were a row of solemn faces.

"But why?" Sophia asked.

"Because she wants the house," Tom said.

"Well, that is presumptuous, Tom Bellamy," replied Mrs. Rathbone. "Your father broke it off with me long before I met Mr. Rathbone, and while I must say I agree that it should have been my girls spending their summers in the Sunken City and betrothing themselves to handsome Parisian heirs at their Banns ball—an event they would not have failed to appreciate, I am sure—none of that is to the point. The Bellamys have mucked up the entire coast for at least a century too long now, left the whole countryside empty and the property worthless, and it's high time someone else had the power to steer the ship, young man. Now, as glad as I am that we've had this honest chat . . ."

Every head turned as the vase on its stand beside the door tumbled, smashed to the floor in a powder of porcelain. Madame Hasard stood reeling against the doorjamb, her hair half falling onto one shoulder, bag clutched in her hand. Sophia blinked. She'd nearly forgotten about Madame. The woman must have been wandering the corridors ever since she left the north wing.

"Is this the dining room?" Madame said. "Finally . . ."

"Maman, are you drunk?"

"Nope!" Madame replied.

"Excuse me!" said Mrs. Rathbone loudly. "I absolutely insist . . ."

René cut her off and put his eyes on Sophia. "She had the hotelier try to kill me."

Sophia looked sharply at Madame Hasard.

"No! Her!" René pointed at Mrs. Rathbone. "Not to keep me from the Sunken City, but to keep me from paying your family a marriage fee. She could not have the Bellamys' debt paid. She was the one informing LeBlanc, before I ever came . . ."

Sophia ran both hands through her hair. And René had thought it was Spear, and Spear had thought it was René. What a ruddy muddle all this was.

"Who tried to kill you, *cher*?" Madame was saying from the doorway. Benoit tried to coax her away from the broken shards of porcelain. And what would have happened, Sophia wondered, if she'd gone with Mrs. Rathbone on that trip to the Midlands?

Mrs. Rathbone clutched her purse. "And since our dear hotelier has not been seen since, I assume you all did away with him. Am I right? It took ages for him to realize you'd only gone down the road, and then he bungled the whole thing. I don't think his heart was in it. But really, you are all so intent on the details that you're missing the big picture. Sheriff Burn is on his way to arrest Tom. Who wants to keep Tom from going straight back to a prison when you've just taken so much trouble to get him out of one?"

"Was it this one, *cher*?" Madame slurred, passing behind Mrs. Rathbone and still on the subject of who had tried to kill her son. "Yes? Oh, well then . . ." She grabbed the back of Mrs. Rathbone's chair and gave it a violent yank. Mrs. Rathbone went over backward, crashing to the floor with her stockinged legs protruding from a confection of white underskirts.

Sophia woke up. "Émile," she said sharply, "lock the door. Tom, get that woman upright and keep her quiet." She came to the table and put a finger on the documents she'd brought to the dining room in the first place. "And one of you should explain these," she demanded in Parisian.

"What is happening?" René yelled, throwing his hands up in the air.

Benoit had just gotten Madame safely seated. "May I, Mademoiselle?" he asked Sophia. She lifted her hand and let him slide the documents toward himself. Madame watched this movement with interest, then lifted her eyes.

"Did you . . . drug me, Miss Bellamy?"

That got the attention of the room, though there was some sort of commotion going on behind her, possibly Tom restraining Mrs. Rathbone. Sophia straightened. "Yes. But not very successfully."

She sneaked a peek at René, who seemed mildly surprised, and then at the uncles, who ran the gamut from shock to amusement. But it was Madame's reaction that made her raise her brows. Madame's mouth twitched once, twice, and then she laughed, uproariously, as if she'd never heard anything so funny in her life.

"Oh," Madame said, eyeing the documents Benoit was so carefully reading while she laughed. "And I suppose you cut those out of my bodice?" Another round of astonishment from the uncles. Sophia lifted her chin.

"Of course."

Madame slapped the table and laughed more, her red hair falling all about her head. "Well, it took you . . . long enough, Miss Bellamy. But it is a good thing for you I threw the rest of that soup . . .

out the window!" She waggled a finger at her. "You do not have servants that speak Parisian."

René's jaw was beginning to clench. "Someone tell me what is happening."

"Should I tell him?" Sophia asked. Madame extended her hand in a gracious wave. Sophia turned to René. "You mother didn't sign away your fortune. Or she did, but what she signed away was worthless. She's been moving the money, and the business, to the Commonwealth for some time."

Benoit looked up from his document. "It is so, René. This is an account of deposits made to a bank in Kent, starting nearly two years ago."

"Your cousin was a maniac!" said Madame, as if this explained everything.

René sat heavily at the table, looking at the document that Benoit slid over to him. He read it without touching it, fingers tented over his nose.

"Adèle," said Émile, "why did you tell René his inheritance was lost?"

"That," she said, "was his father's fault."

René untented his fingers as Benoit slid over another document. "Your father left a stipulation that you could not inherit. Not until you were married."

"Well, that would make a mess," commented Enzo.

"Idiot," said Andre, shaking his head. He didn't look all that surprised.

"Sentimental," Madame added, "that's what he was."

Benoit scratched through his wispy hair. "Could you not have stopped him, Adèle?"

"He did not tell me! He wanted his son to have what we had, working the . . . business, together."

"Richard never was one for thinking with his head," said Peter.

"That was my job," said Madame, giggling. "We did make a wonderful team . . ."

René's voice maintained only a thin veil of calm. "Will someone please explain to me why I have never been told this? And will someone help Tom restrain that woman?"

Sophia realized they'd all been ignoring the sounds of struggle coming from beyond the table, where Mrs. Rathbone had been set upright, her hat and purse on the floor, Tom behind her chair, his walking stick braced across her middle. Francois slid out from the table, crossed the room, and suddenly Tom's stick had been replaced with a knife. Mrs. Rathbone went instantly still. And then the door latch to the dining room rattled, the lock held, and someone knocked. Silence descended.

"Sophie! Are you in there?"

"Orla," Sophia breathed. She hurried to the door and opened it.

"Sophie, the sheriff and Mr. Halflife are here, and . . ." Her angular face grew even more so at the sight of all of them hiding away in the dining room, Madame with her head on the table and Mrs. Rathbone with a knife to her side.

"Well, it's a good thing Tom is here," said Orla, calm unruffled. "They've already been to the farm looking for him. They're arresting him today instead of . . ."

"Tell them you've found a note saying we've all gone to dig on the far west downs," Sophia said. "There are holes there already. And you never saw any of this."

Orla glanced once more around the dining room before she said, "I don't even know what you're talking about," and shut the door. Sophia turned the lock.

"Maman," René was saying, causing his mother to raise her head. "I am waiting for my answer. Why did you never tell me of this?"

"Because I did not want you running off to get married just so you could inherit! Which is what you would have done. Better not to have . . . the money." Madame was starting to sound more like herself. She was also looking a bit ill. "And in any case, I had already picked out a wife for you. Years ago . . ."

"What? Who?" said Sophia and René together.

"Miss Bellamy, of course! I chose her when she was nine years old."

"But I only met you a few days ago!" Sophia protested.

Madame shook her head. "No. No. Nope. You are wrong. I met you both. Your brother was so polite, and you told me the dearest little lies about . . . circus performing."

"Sophie!" Tom said. "It's the woman . . ."

". . . from the night the rope broke!" she finished, incredulous. René lifted his head while his mother waggled a finger at them.

"And I thought," she continued, "that any little girl who could scale a cliff, fall on her brother's head, brush herself off, and lie to a stranger like a rug on a floor—even if she did get a little dramatic— and a stranger who could have had her taken up by the guard, too? Now that . . ." She pointed emphatically. ". . . was a fitting wife for my son. It was easy enough to find out who you were."

Sophia watched Benoit sit back and stretch his arms behind his head, as René did sometimes, a bit of a smile leaking onto his unremarkable face.

"But, Maman!" René said. "I agreed with your choice . . ." He paused, seeming to take in the oddity of this fact. ". . . but you are still rejecting her!"

"I had concerns."

"What concerns?" said Sophia and René together.

"For one, my son, you were very good at charming young ladies into behaving like nitwits for you. Much, much too good . . ."

Émile chuckled.

". . . and Miss Bellamy here was in need of money. Badly. This was not a good beginning. Your father may have been sentimental, René, but I did at least agree with him in wishing your future happiness rather than a lifelong misery. I had intended to be here myself, of course, to observe, but . . . alas, I went to prison."

René slammed the table. "This is nonsense. Tell the truth, Maman. Whoever I married was also going to inherit the business with me and take your place. And you could not have that, could you?"

"No. I have not given thirty years of my sweat and blood to have it ruined by your father's whim and a silly girl who has been enticed by your charms."

Sophia opened her mouth, but René's other hand came up and took hers, asking her for silence.

"However," Madame continued, her voice stronger, face and lips a little more white, "you, René, showed a rather unforeseen devotion to Miss Bellamy, one that left me pleased and quite satisfied. But Miss Bellamy, while capable of many things, had not yet proven herself capable of handling me. An essential skill when becoming a Hasard."

"Perhaps you should explain your expectations, Adèle," said Benoit. Sophia's eyes widened as he winked once at her.

"You should pay attention to my grammar, Benoit. I said 'had not yet.' I had been trying to help Miss Bellamy along by being as unpleasant and unreasonable as possible . . ."

Like mother, like son, Sophia thought, remembering the first few days she'd known René.

"But . . . drugging me and cutting official documents out of my bodice and laying it all on the table in front of the entire family? Oh, I would say that does it. I will watch my soup from now on, Mademoiselle." She giggled, though the mention of soup made her face blanch.

The door latch rattled and then someone banged. "Tom? Tomas Bellamy!"

It was Sheriff Burn, who was evidently not looking for them on the west downs. Sophia held up a hand for Tom to wait while Mrs. Rathbone made little sputtering noises. She hoped Francois wasn't cutting her throat. Or maybe she hoped he was. She leaned across the table. "Madame, is there money for the marriage fee, and will you pay it?"

"Yes. Could I trouble someone for a bucket or a bowl?" said Madame.

The door banged again. "Tom! Sophia!" called the sheriff. "Come on, now. I've got the militia with me. Open the . . ."

Sophia turned. "René, you love me, yes?"

His brow went up. "Yes."

"And I love you, too. Then will you marry me? Right now?"

He stuttered. "Well . . . yes. I . . ."

She spun on her heel. "Tom, do I have your blessing?"

Tom shrugged from behind the squirming Mrs. Rathbone; Francois did indeed have the knife at her throat. "All right, Sophie."

"Maman," said René, "is the money in Kent?"

"Not anymore, cher." Madame reached into the black bag she'd been carrying and set a box on the table. She opened it with an unsteady hand, and inside was a plastic bottle, perfect, without dents, its cap in place, a faded, scratched, but still legible plastic wrapping around its middle. Just above the lettering was the tiny word DIET.

There was a surprised silence from the room, made even louder by the banging of the sheriff. René shook his head. "Were you really not going to say something, Maman?"

Madame tossed her bedraggled hair. "She was the one who left it to the last moment." The door banged harder; it sounded as if he were ramming it with something.

"Émile, how much is that worth?" Sophia asked quickly.

He was bent over with a tiny eyescope, inspecting the bottle carefully. "The fee," he said. "Ten thousand in quidden, or probably more."

"There is a . . . valuation, signed, in the box," muttered Madame. "Could I please trouble anyone for a bowl?"

"That will do, then," said Sophia. "Can I borrow that?" She took the black bag without Madame's answer, shutting the box and shoving it inside. "Tom, come with us and be witness before the sheriff takes you . . ."

The door shuddered on its hinges.

"And, Benoit, see what you can do about her," she said, tilting her head at Mrs. Rathbone. "We have a sheriff here, the body of the hotelier buried on the cliff, and you and Orla as witnesses. And I'm sure Jennifer Bonnard would not mind backing up whatever you decide to say. It wouldn't hurt to let the sheriff know Mrs. Rathbone was trying to buy the house, too, since she ratted out Tom. He won't like that." Mrs. Rathbone struggled, then remembered the knife. "See if you can't get her tossed out of the Commonwealth at the least."

"That can be done, Mademoiselle," Benoit said, still smiling.

"I leave it in your hands."

"And Miss Bellamy," said Madame, her voice a bit weak, "when you return, I'd like to discuss the empty building on your grounds, and the empty cottages, the prisoners in your house who have nowhere to go, and the need for Hasard Glass to . . . relocate."

"Of course," Sophia replied, pausing for a moment. What an interesting thought. Perhaps she and Madame would have more in common than previously anticipated. "Have coffee with Tom and me tomorrow at middlesun," she said. "Or make that the day after tomorrow." She started toward the pantry door, and then looked back at René and Tom. The other door was beginning to splinter. "Are you coming? Either of you?"

René jumped up and they both followed, Sophia careful not to set a pace that Tom couldn't keep. She shut the pantry just before she heard the dining room door burst open, sidestepped quickly through the dusty storage room, opened a trapdoor, and slid through a short access tunnel into the closet below. René came through next.

"Now, just so I have this straight, my love," René said, turning to catch Tom's legs on the way through. "Where are we going?"

"To our wedding. Just as soon as we find the vicar. I hope he's at home."

"That is what I thought was happening. But it has been a strange day."

They got to the stables, which were not being watched—Sheriff Burn was a nice man, just not particularly good at his job—and rode at a gallop for the vicarage, Tom on his horse, René behind Sophia, setting the rookery to flight in their haste. Tom was the first to get there, startling the vicar from the loo as he came thundering into his yard. There was a sleek landover waiting out front.

"Tom!" the man said. "And Miss Bellamy . . . What?"

"We're in need of a wedding, Vicar," said Tom. "Right now, before the sheriff finds us."

Who they found waiting in the vicar's dark-paneled study was Mr. Halflife, at his ease in a leather chair.

"Miss Bellamy, my dear," he said. "How good it is to finally greet you. I had a feeling you and your charming fiancé might be coming here after the to-do that was going on in Bellamy House. I am very sorry, Monsieur, to know that your mother has such a weakness for drink."

Sophia and René glanced at each other. He must have run into Madame wandering the halls. What could she have said? There really was no telling. But it must have had something to do with a marriage. Here he was.

Tom and the vicar were at the desk, doing the paperwork, Tom with one eye on the window and the view of the A5. Mr. Halflife had no power to arrest Tom on his own, and as soon as they were married, the sheriff would have none, either. Tom would have the money, in the form of a plastic bottle, in hand.

"So I assume, Monsieur Hasard, that you are able to pay the marriage fee after all? I had heard your family was in financial difficulties."

His posh accent was jangling every one of Sophia's nerves. She answered before René could. "Why, yes, Mr. Halflife, there is a fee. So I'm sorry to tell you that the Bellamy land stays as it is, and Parliament will not have a port. Not on our coast."

Mr. Halflife smiled. "But I am afraid a port on your section of the coast is going to be paramount to the safety of the Commonwealth, Miss Bellamy. Have you never considered—but of course you haven't—what would happen if there should be war between the

Sunken City and ourselves? The Parisian shores are only a short boat ride away. Or we might wish to expand beyond our own shores one day. One never knows."

Sophia looked at Halflife with his non-Wesson jacket and slicked hair. Her father had been right, she realized, not to give the Commonwealth the Bellamy fire. The secret would go with her to her grave.

"But you also forget, Miss Bellamy," said Halflife, satisfied by her silence, "that no matter what happens today, your brother must prove his fitness for inheritance before the Bellamy land is secure." He glanced at Tom, standing beside the vicar, still prison thin and limping. "Do you think it is likely he will do so? I am not sure he will."

Sophia smiled at him. "Is that a threat, Mr. Halflife?" She knew it was. He was going to make certain Tom had no opportunity to prove his fitness at all.

"Monsieur . . . ," René said. Sophia looked at him sharply. He had taken the seat opposite Mr. Halflife, leaning back elegantly, and all at once, there was the man of the magazine. She didn't understand quite how he was pulling that off. You didn't even notice the untied hair and the mud.

"You were asking about the financial matters of my family," René went on, "which interests me, because I am wondering who could have mentioned this to you. My cousin, perhaps? The same cousin, just perhaps, who was paying you for information about what was happening on the Bellamy coast? And were you, just perhaps, using Mrs. Rathbone to find out these things that my cousin was paying you for? Letting her know of little opportunities that might come her way, like denouncing the Ministre of Trade that was opposing your plans for a Parisian port, a port Parliament says is for shipping goods, but that they will use for their own interests? Like invasion?"

He smiled at Mr. Halflife's expression. "And would I be right in thinking that Mrs. Rathbone does not want Bellamy House as much as she wants to be the wife of a Parliamentary member? That perhaps she is under the impression this will occur rather soon, when the Bellamys are removed?"

Sophia stared at René. He was right. And he looked every bit the smooth-talking, daughter-stealing smuggler that she knew he was. How she loved him.

"But please, let me advise you, Monsieur," he continued. "Mrs. Rathbone has been arrested in Bellamy House. Something to do with a dead man, and as you know, she is very much the talker. Also, Allemande is dead, and my cousin is no longer Ministre of Security. The revolution is over. When you go to Manchester, you will hear all that you wish to, I am sure. But I think it might also interest you to know that my cousin LeBlanc's paperwork will very likely become public. Soon. Of course, I am sure you have been doing nothing illegal . . ."

"Sophie! René! We're ready," Tom called. The vicar was picking up his book. Mr. Halflife sprang to his feet.

"I wish you joy, Monsieur. Miss Bellamy." And Mr. Halflife ran from the vicar's study as if St. Just had been nipping at his heels. René stood and stretched, looking very smug.

"So just how much of that was true?" Sophia asked.

"Enough to make him run, yes?" He smiled with half his mouth. "I have hesitated to ask, my love, but do you normally wear spectacles?"

"Oh!" Sophia jerked off the glasses. They were made with clear lenses, and she'd completely forgotten their presence on her face. "They were just for delivering soup."

"Ah."

She pulled the kerchief from her head as well, running a hand through wild hair. "I never thought I would marry," she whispered. "Especially in Orla's old dress and with dirt on my nose."

He took her hand, bringing her close and putting his lips on the inside of her wrist, paying no attention to Tom or the vicar. "I love you best that way," he whispered. "When you come down the stairs with your painted eyes and caramel skin and you make every man stare, I still think of you with mud in your hair and a sword strapped to your thigh and a rook feather in your hand. Are they not both one and the same?"

Yes. Just as he was the man of the magazine and the smuggler and also the man of the roof who had stood on the scaffold. She looked into the fire-blue of his eyes. "Do you think this was meant to happen?"

Was it meant to happen, or could he have chosen differently, LeBlanc wondered, his hands tied behind him. Or was the world one great, repeating pattern destined to flow in the same lines? That was the teaching of Fate, the cold mistress that had taken Luck from him, that cared nothing that he was lying here, head on a block, surrounded by the faces of the Sunken City and a new premier. A female premier! Sanchia, reading his charges . . .

He was supposed to accept the will of Fate, but this could not be right. What if he had chosen a different thread of the pattern?

"Wait," he called. "Wait!"

He had to ask. He had to know. He wanted to count the drops of blood, to toss a coin. He struggled.

"Wait! Wait!" he screamed.

The executioner raised his ax.

"I think it was meant to happen," René said, "but I also say that if we had chosen differently, it never would have. Tell me I am wrong."

She smiled. She couldn't.

Epilogue

Sophia climbed out of the water-lift shaft, shaking her arms, wondering why they had to live on the twelfth floor. She'd been up the water-lift shaft three times since the Hasards got the flat back. She pulled off her black cap and jacket, but not before she had retrieved a cloth bag from her vest and set it aside on the table. The rope in the water lift was jiggling, and by the time she had washed the grime from her hands and was back in her embroidered yellow skirts, René was swinging his legs through the opening.

"Hello," she said.

His boots hit the floor and he grinned. "Have you looked yet?"

She shook her head, the brown curls grown longer but no less wild. "I waited for you. No, let me. You're still dirty." She pulled a little hinged box from the cloth bag and opened it.

"Ah," said René. "It is in excellent condition."

They stared at a small plastic man, his colors of red and blue still unnaturally bright, strange, plastic clothes tight to show a body oddly bulged and top-heavy with muscles. Was this the way Ancient men had wanted to look, she wondered? Because surely they hadn't. But that wasn't even the part that amazed her. The man sat in a vehicle, something like a landover, only longer, elaborate, no horse attached, and with no visible way to hitch one.

René ran a finger along a yellow wheel. "Sanchia told me tonight that she thinks this little man should be destroyed because he is an Ancient idol. Do you think he is a god?"

"Sanchia thinks that she is a god," said Sophia, closing the box.

"Sanchia is half-afraid you are," René teased. "Are you aware that the Red Rook actually flew to the top of the scaffold, my love?"

"That's a new one. Where did you hear that?"

"From Sanchia. She was showing me her new tattoo."

"Was she?" Those who had fought against the revolution and in support of the Red Rook had taken to tattooing a red and black feather on their forearms. And so had some who had not fought. Like Sanchia, Sophia suspected.

René sighed. "Ah, well. She has opened the chapels and the Lower City, so we will extend her some forgiveness, even if her council is corrupt." His smile became devilish. "I wonder how soon she will miss her artifact."

"What did she think of your suggestion for a representative parliament?"

"She seems to prefer five council members to five hundred. I would have talked with her more had you not slapped me so soon." René tugged off his black trousers to show blue satin breeches underneath. "Is it necessary? To hit so hard?"

"You shouldn't have flirted so hard with Commandant Napoléon's wife. And you know those breeches are vile?"

"Of course I know my breeches are vile. And if I had not flirted so hard, you would have had no reason to hit me. It is only your enthusiasm I question."

She smiled sweetly. "But your *maman* recommends it." She waited a beat, and then they both laughed.

"Maman needs to come back to the city," René said. "Tom manages the glass factory too well and it makes her testy. She has no one to fight with."

And when Madame returned to the flat, Sophia thought, that would be just about the right time to take René back to Bellamy House. It was practically a village now, like it had been when she was a girl, only with both Parisian and Commonwealth to be heard on the lane. No ports in sight. And she would be arranging Tom and Jennifer's Banns in the autumn. The glass factory was doing well enough to pay the marriage fee, which the Bonnards would immediately give back so Tom could prove for his inheritance. The thought made her smile as she tucked the flowers into her hair. She was thinking of taking René to Finland after that, where he could be himself for a while.

"Did you hear what Napoléon was saying to me?" René was saying, buttoning his jacket. "That the premier plans to build a lattice tower, all of metal, right in the center of the Lower City? It will be taller than the cliffs."

She looked over her shoulder. "Whatever for?"

"I do not know. But Sanchia should watch Napoléon closely, I think . . ."

Sophia frowned as she finished arranging her hair. It was from Napoléon's residence that they had stolen the last three tubes of Bellamy fire, part of what Cartier had put in place for panicking the mob and never lit, there being quite enough panic as it was. The tubes had been left behind in the melee, and Sophia had often wondered how they had fallen into the commandant's hands. Mr. Halflife was no longer a member of Parliament, but she'd not forgotten his talk of war. The barrels in the sanctuary had been rolled into the sea, Tom's recipes and her father's research locked in the secret compartment of her desk in Bellamy House. But it would not be long, Sophia thought, before he, or Sanchia, or someone, discovered what her father had. The tubes they had stolen from Napoléon's safe had been opened, their contents examined.

There was a light knock and Benoit stuck his head in the door. "Is your lovers' tiff over? Because the singers are almost done." He checked the small clock strapped to his wrist. Everyone in the city was allowed to have clocks now, but the sight never failed to give Sophia a start. And they still worked terribly.

René said, "Tell Émile we have it, and that he can leave tonight for Canterbury."

"Very good." But instead of going, Benoit came inside, took out a handkerchief, and wiped a smudge of dirt from Sophia's cheek. "You might have taken care of that," he chided René, winking once before he left.

René turned to her. "Do you need taking care of, my love?"

Sophia looked up in alarm. "Oh, no," she said. "The singers are nearly done . . ." But he already had his arms around her, and she was already done protesting.

"Let's go back to the party," René whispered into her neck, "and behave so badly that everyone will go home early."

"René," she said. He pulled back just far enough to see her, but she didn't speak right away. He was beautiful, even in the gaudy jacket, which also brought out the fire of his eyes. Nothing was certain, she knew that, and the world ever circled. But she couldn't help but wonder what she would risk to keep her future exactly the same as her present.

She tilted up her chin, and knew the answer even before he kissed her. It was everything.

Polar shift really is an interesting way to end the world. The idea of what could happen if the magnetic poles of the earth reversed, as they have at least twice in geological history, is a chilling thought. Not only because of the wholesale death that would follow, but because it's a completely natural process. Humans can do nothing to cause it, nothing to stop it. But since writing about uninhabited wastelands is *not* particularly appealing, I decided to play with the idea of wandering magnetic poles, a slight shift rather than a complete reversal. Instead of destroying our magnetosphere, this would turn it into something like Swiss cheese, exposing large swaths of humanity to deadly solar radiation while sparing others, and at the same time wiping clean the digital and electronic world on which we have become so dependent. Could a shift of the poles really happen? Maybe. Or at least, no one yet has proven that it can't.

But even more interesting to me than the science of such an event is the sociology. As an amateur anthropologist and card-carrying Anglophile, I have long been fascinated by the massive cultural upheaval that the archaeological record shows took place in post-Roman Britain. Literacy, law, clean water, and heated floors gave way to the disease and anarchy of the so-called Dark Ages. This is an oversimplification of a complicated process, but the central question is: How could so much knowledge be forgotten so quickly? And would the survivors of a polar shift forget the former world? I think they would. We always have before. And if so, what would we make of the thirty-five thousand pieces of space junk that could theoretically rain from our skies for hundreds of years? How soon could we learn to survive without technology? How would we go about reforging our world? The same way we did in the Dark Ages, I concluded. And, being humans, probably by making most of the same mistakes we did the first time around.

Thinking of how far a society can regress naturally brings another personally fascinating time to my mind: the French Revolution. I find the writings of Robespierre, with their logical, well-reasoned justifications for the beheading of thousands, positively Hitler-esque. Not to mention the revolution's attempt to replace all religions with the disturbing Goddess of Reason, a cult more interested in persecution, "wild and licentious" festivals, and defacing churches and synagogues than any brand of spirituality. Robespierre guillotined the leaders of this cult and replaced it with his own Cult of the Supreme Being, with himself as high priest. He held a grand, public mass for the worship of this new cult, setting fire to effigies representing the enemies of France. Six weeks later, Robespierre had been arrested and guillotined himself.

But no matter what odd and creepy facts tickle my imagination, for me, what writing a book really comes down to is story, like the Baroness Emma Orczy's *The Scarlet Pimpernel*. I've always loved this book, the quintessential tale of love, spies, and derring-do while cheating the French guillotine of its victims. Being swept away by story can be powerful, sometimes life-changing, and I think the adventure and heroism of books like *The Scarlet Pimpernel* are the essence of what story is. But I've also always wanted to reimagine that story. To replace some of the Edwardian syrup with a savory dose of Georgian-era spice. So the novel that became *Rook* is not as much a retelling as it is an homage, conveniently coupled with all those strange and disparate ideas that I find so intriguing. *Rook* is a tribute to story, and especially to the classic drama and characters first created by the Baroness Orczy more than a century before me.

Which makes sense. History always does seem to be repeating.

Acknowledgments

Thanking everyone who needs to be thanked is always an impossible task, but since my life is full of impossibilities, I'm giving this one a go.

Undying love and gratitude to my critique group, who have read every word of every story I've ever put to paper. Amy Eytchison, Howard Shirley, Angelika Stegmann, and Ruta Sepetys. You taught me to write. You read my pages again. You told me I could be a writer and then I was.

Jessica Young, Courtney Stevens, Genetta Adair, Kristin Tubb, Rae Ann Parker, and Susan Eaddy. I don't think a day in the past 365 has gone by when one of you has failed to encourage me.

SCBWI Midsouth. You know who you are. Need I say more?

Ruta, your cabin contains magic.

Love and thanks to my beautiful, patient, kind, and oh so wise editor, Lisa Sandell. You make everything I do so much better. This is also magic.

David Levithan and my team at Scholastic: Sheila Marie Everett, Elizabeth Starr Baer, Jennifer Ung, Sharismar Rodriguez, and all those beautiful faces from Marketing, School and Library, Book Clubs, Book Fairs, and Foreign Rights. Not sure what I did to deserve you.

My intrepid agent and friend, Kelly Sonnack. I would be lost without you. Therefore I forgive your shocking lack of affinity for gingers.

Hannah Courtney, intern/blogger/writer extraordinaire. Keep those big ideas coming. You know I'll say yes.

And mostly, all of my love to Philip, Chris, Stephen, and Elizabeth. Everything is for you.

About the Author

SHARON CAMERON was awarded the Society of Children's Book Writers and Illustrators' Sue Alexander Award for Most Promising New Work for her debut novel, *The Dark Unwinding*, which was also awarded the SCBWI Crystal Kite Award and named an ALA Best Fiction for Young Adults selection. She is also the author of *A Spark Unseen*. Sharon lives with her family in Nashville, Tennessee, and you can visit her online at sharoncameronbooks.com.